DEDICATION

For everyone who needs a reason to smile this Christmas.

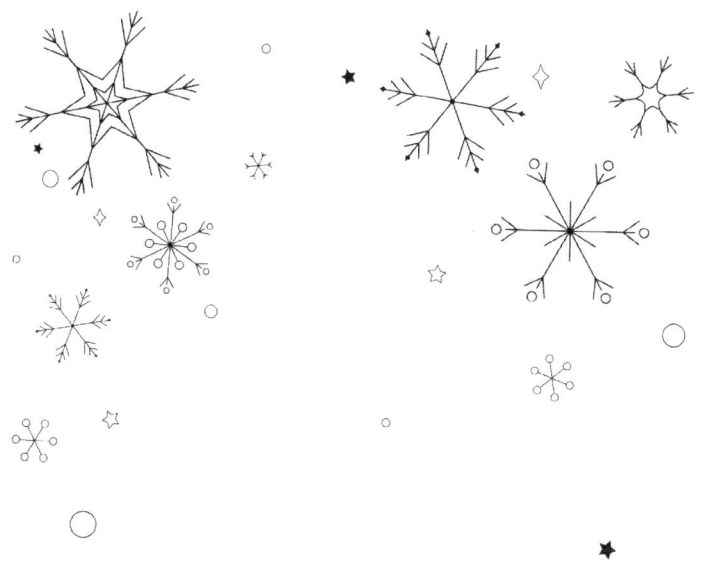

"Oh…"
PART 1

Thursday, December 8th

Ray wakes up in his cold New York apartment to the sound of his alarm blaring. Alone. As usual.

He rolls out of bed, knowing that if he doesn't get up soon he'll fall back asleep and be behind schedule for the rest of the day. Grabbing his phone, he pads to the kitchen and starts up the coffee machine.

While he waits for his first of many cups of coffee for the day, he checks his phone—his manager, Karl, has already texted him the outline for today's events; photoshoot for a magazine, promotional event for one of his shows that's currently airing, and then a night shoot for an upcoming movie. Ray just hopes he can find time for a quick bite and maybe a nap while he's being driven between locations.

It's going to be a very long day.

This was supposed to be a relatively relaxing Christmas for Ray; a couple days of filming each week, a few promotional events, nothing too bad. Then, in the middle of November, Ray had received a call from his mother.

"You know, Pumpkin, it would be nice if we could actually see you this Christmas."

"I visited you in the summer," Ray responded meekly down the phone, his excuse weak even to his own ears.

"Yes, but Christmas, Ray! *Christmas!*" His mom's love of Christmas was obvious in the way she spoke about the season, even in the passion with which she said the word.

He sighed into the phone. "I know, Ma. I'm just so busy with work these days, this season is always hectic."

"Ray Rawat Amarin! You have used that excuse six years in a row! I am not letting it go on for a seventh!"

"But Ma—"

"No, Rawat! If you don't come home, Pa and I are going to come stay with you. We want to see our son!"

He cringed. She was not going to give up.

Ray loves his parents, but he does not want them staying at his bachelor pad. He'd somehow kept them away from this place for years—excuses of "Oh, I'm going to be out of town for a shoot!" or "Ah, the elevator is broken at the moment. Can Ma and Pa make it up the nine flights of stairs?" used to postpone their visits indefinitely. He personally liked this apartment well enough, but it really wasn't the kind of place his parents would approve of; decorated in a minimalist style of stark black and white, the furniture more for aesthetics than comfort. It's not like Ray spent enough time there to really care about how it felt to live in. This was simply a place to rest his head at the end of a hard day's work. Alone. This was no place for his sweet parents—elders who spend their evenings in the cozy living room of their family home, hand-knitted blankets slung over the back of a well-loved couch.

So, he had caved, his work schedule be damned, and agreed to go home. When he brought it up with Karl, requesting a meager five days off, the man had scoffed, "Ray! I've known you—what—seven years? This is your first time requesting time off over the holidays, at least take a proper break! I'm giving you three weeks off, minimum."

Ray had barely opened his mouth to argue back when Karl silenced him.

"No complaining or I'll make it four!"

That had been enough to shut Ray up.

*

Now, Ray is cursing himself for agreeing to go home for the holidays. His late request to his manager meant that a lot of projects had to be moved earlier, keeping him busy from dawn until dusk (and often beyond that) every day. Did Karl really think he was doing him a favor, working him to the bone like this before sending him home for the holidays? To top it all off, he knew that he'd have to resume work as soon as he returned—his presence expected at an important agency New Year's Eve party. Today, however, is the last day before he goes home. And, at this point, he really does need a break.

Ray has managed to keep his energy up for most of the day—powered by caffeine and the occasional cat nap—but now he's struggling. Night shoots are the worst for Ray, the dim lighting always threatening to send him to sleep. And the fact that he's outside, sitting on a bench in a quiet park, isn't helping. The current scene requires Ray's character, a detective, to sit here and wait for his informant to approach. With the way his eyelids keep closing, blinks getting more sluggish, he'll be lucky if he's still awake by the time the crew are done checking their equipment.

"Hey!"

A slap to the back of the head jolts Ray out of his stupor, looking up to find Teddy staring down at him.

"No falling asleep on set! Can't have you all drooly and drowsy while I look hot... Actually, scratch that, please fall asleep so I can be the only hot one in this scene."

Ray chuckles at his friend's behavior.

He's known Teddy for as long as he's been in New York, the two of them scouted by the same agency at the same time. Ray had been twenty-two—finished with college but unsure whether he wanted to work in a field relevant to his business degree; Teddy had been twenty-one—a college dropout working at some corner store. They'd been paired up as roommates when they'd reached New York and become fast friends, always pulling pranks on each other and being each other's wingmen when they went out together.

"I think you will find, Teddy, that my fans consider me very attractive even when I'm asleep."

"I think you will find, Ray, that your job is to stay awake and deliver your lines." Teddy smirks at him before scurrying off to get into position for the start of the scene.

Ray shifts where he's sitting—adjusting his posture, smoothing down his jacket, clearing his throat—desperately trying to fight the threatening wall of tiredness. He knows he'll be fine once they start filming, once the adrenaline kicks in, but until then he must struggle through.

Miraculously, the shoot is done in just under three hours— Ray and Teddy dismissed for the night, and Ray not needed for filming again until after Christmas. He catches some shut eye in the back of the car, Karl driving him back to his place. Once he's there, he should be able to sleep for a few hours before he needs to start packing.

Not long now until he'll be flying home.

Ray's name has been the only thing on everybody's lips for the past few weeks. Once Mrs. Amarin had gotten off the phone with her son, she must have immediately called all of her neighbors to inform them of the news. Those neighbors surely called their neighbors, who called their neighbors... because suddenly it became the talk of the town.

THE Ray Rawat Amarin is coming back to his small hometown of Ammersfield for Christmas.

And Jamie, a worker at his parents' bookstore in said town, couldn't give less of a shit.

Well... that isn't strictly true. Jamie thinks Ray is... decent looking... good looking... Okay, fine, he finds him unbelievably attractive. But that isn't the point. He's seen what Ray is like when he isn't on camera.

*

Ray had wandered into Honeybun Bookstore this past summer, when Jamie had been working there full-time before starting his final year at college. The man had strolled in, his gait wide and arrogant in a way that had seemed rather attractive at the time. Jamie had watched in awe from behind the counter as Ray slowly sauntered through the shop, seeming to glance at various books and nod. Jamie couldn't be sure the man was actually looking at the books, though—Ray kept his shades on the whole time, even though the store was only dimly lit in order to protect the books from light damage.

Then Ray looked up. Jamie knew he was looking directly at him, he just had to be. The world around them seemed to fade away, the pair caught in each other's gaze as they stared.

The moment abruptly ended when Ray's hand, which had been merely resting on a stack of books, suddenly knocked the whole lot off the table; one sweep of his perfectly toned, muscular arm sending them flying. The action was so much like that of a naughty cat that Jamie had barely concealed the urge to scold him like he would with his pet kitty, August. But he had held his tongue—only a little gasp of shock leaving his lips as the books tumbled to the floor.

"Oh..." is all the famous actor Ray Rawat Amarin had said before turning on his heels and marching out of the store. At least he had the wherewithal to be embarrassed, if the pink tips of his ears were any indication.

Jamie scowled at the back of Ray's head through the window. "Asshole," he murmured, rageful as he stomped from his spot behind the counter to clear up the mess Ray had left behind.

So no, Jamie is not keen on the idea of seeing Ray again. Especially during what is sure to be a busy holiday season. And *especially* if that man is going anywhere near his precious books!

Friday, December 9th

Ray keeps his mask and sunglasses on for the duration of the flight, along with a cap, to hide his identity. He hadn't wanted to pay to be in first class, but he also didn't want to deal with people approaching him and asking for photos. It's not that he doesn't like or appreciate his fans, it's just that he doesn't want them to know how awkward and quiet he is. At his request, Karl, Teddy, and all of the staff at the agency have kept his social awkwardness hidden from the public for years. At the very beginning of his career, Ray had felt it was important for his success to build a cool and casual "bad boy" image. And, sure enough, that's what the majority of his fanbase now love him for. Unfortunately, that persona doesn't really allow for the bumbling, clumsy mess he becomes the second he doesn't have a script to read from. Thus, he travels incognito mode. Ray acknowledges, to some extent, that his "disguise" is an obvious one—this type of face covering combo so common in manga, K-dramas, and the like whenever a celebrity wants to hide their identity. But Ray also knows that, even if people still recognize him (which they have today, going by the whispers he's heard from a couple of rows away), few dare to approach when his appearance gives off such "don't talk to me" vibes.

    He sleeps for the majority of the flight, only waking when he needs to ensure his seatbelt is secured for landing. When passengers start to disembark, Ray notices at least a dozen people trying to subtly point their phone cameras in his direction as he waits his turn to leave. He tries not to react—fighting the urge to pose and surely make a fool of himself.

Ray spots his dad standing in front of his old, beaten-up pickup truck immediately as he leaves the airport, the distinctive scrape in the forest green paint still there from when Ray had been attempting to learn how to drive—the important word here being "attempting." Ray's father had tried desperately to teach him, but after three lessons and several, as Ray liked to call them, "oopsy moments," it had become clear that his clumsiness also applied to his abilities behind the wheel. Once Ray had started earning money as an actor, he'd offered to pay for the truck to be repainted, but his father refused, claiming the scrape "adds character."

"Pa!"

"Son!"

Ray practically falls into his dad's arms, the fatigue of travel making his limbs heavy and sluggish. His father pats his back, chuckling when Ray hugs him tighter. Ray sighs, an unexpected wave of relief crashing over him now that he's home—away from his hectic life in the big city. It's an unexpected emotion. He's used to feeling antsy when he's not working; usually craving the fast pace of his actor lifestyle. His bushy brow twitches, confused at the feeling of calm in his chest. Briefly, he finds himself wondering if this is what people are actually meant to feel when they go on vacation.

His father pulls away from the hug, one hand holding onto each of Ray's biceps to put him at an arm's length. He looks his son up and down, his cheerful smile only faltering when his gaze reaches his face. He snatches the cap from Ray's head. "What's this, huh? Think you're being so inconspicuous by wearing a hat?"

Ray gawks behind his mask.

"And take those off, too!" He points offendedly to the mask and sunglasses. "You know your ma has already told the whole town you're coming home. There's no need to go all incognito mode on us now!"

His dad laughs as he hurriedly removes the rest of his "disguise," nearly dropping his sunglasses in his haste and feeling slightly sheepish after being called out like that. Then Ray stands to attention, feeling awkward under his father's intense gaze without the designer shades to protect him.

"There's my son!" He gestures to Ray proudly, his grin so wide that the wrinkles by his eyes deepen, before going in for another hug. Ray grumbles out a "Paaa," embarrassed but endeared by his father's behavior.

They pull apart, his father putting Ray's cap on his own head. "Now come on, let's go home. Your ma is making your favorite for dinner."

Jamie notices a hush fall over the store as Mr. Amarin's truck drives past outside, clearly heading back to the Amarin residence, now with his famous son in the passenger seat. In the blink of an eye the bookstore is empty, the customers chattering excitedly as they subtly go after the vehicle, trying to catch a glimpse of Ray. Jamie huffs in agitation as he slumps against the wall, the celebrity having robbed him of what could have been some good sales.

The minutes tick by, Jamie's frustration building when no more customers enter—every passerby heading resolutely in the same direction.

Of course, he thinks, *no one cares about books now that Mr. Hotshot Actor is in town.*

He drags his feet to the front door, locking it and flipping over the "open" sign. He sees no point in staying open if no one is coming in. Besides, it isn't that far from closing time.

Jamie pouts, sulking as he turns off the lights and heads to the back of the store where a set of stairs lead to his family's apartment, cursing Ray silently with each step. He hopes his mom is cooking one of his favorites for dinner. He could definitely use the pick-me-up.

- · ★ · -

Ray arrives home to find his mom in the kitchen, busy stir-frying some pork as part of his all-time favorite food. There are various other dishes already served up, all things Ray is fond of, but her Moo Pad Kapi is what he's most excited for. He must have tried every Thai restaurant within a hundred-block radius of his apartment, but none tasted quite the same as his ma's cooking.

So caught up in what she's doing, she doesn't notice her son's presence at first. It gives Ray some time to really take in the scene; the same sunshine yellow cabinets he grew up with, the floral wallpaper more faded than he remembers, the shiny new rice cooker he'd bought his parents last Christmas steaming away on the counter. His mom is singing along to some cheesy nineties pop song playing on the radio, the sound almost entirely drowned out by the hiss of food being fried. He watches her wave a spatula to the tune of the music, her neatly-pressed skirt swishing back and forth as she sways.

Ray smiles. He's here. He's home.

His stomach grumbles.

He's starving.

"Ma!"

The woman turns on her heel, gasping when she lays eyes on her son. She's running to him within seconds, still wearing an apron and wielding the spatula as she brings him in for a hug.

"Oh, you! How long have you been standing there?" she admonishes, still hugging him tightly. "Didn't anyone ever tell you not to sneak up on an old lady, hmm? Especially one who's busy cooking!"

Ray chuckles, patting his mom on the back before letting go. "Is there anything I can do to help?"

The response is exactly what he expects; he's shooed away and told to go wash up in preparation for his welcome home feast.

The rest of his family must arrive while he's in the bathroom, because he's barely unlocked the door before he can hear his niece pounding up the stairs to him.

"Uncle Wawa!" Ray has no time to prepare for impact before Praew is barreling into him, her spindly arms wrapping tight around his torso. "Wawa, I've got so much to tell you! I made a new friend at school and— and— his name is Nick and—"

"Hey, you better not be hogging Uncle Wawa!" Malai, Ray's sister, calls up the stairs. Ray can almost *hear* her pointing her finger.

"Don't worry, Aunty Mal!" The seven-year-old shouts back, grabbing Ray's hand to pull him back downstairs while she continues to chatter away about how she's getting on at school.

He's greeted by the sight of Pim, his other sister, swatting at their dad's shoulder, her and Malai bickering with him in hushed tones: "We *told you* to text us when you picked him up from the airport, not wait until you're already home and just send the thumbs up emoji in the family group chat! I mean, I know I live close, but it would have been nice if we could have been here to greet him! And what if Malai hadn't been visiting me, hm? She wouldn't have gotten here for another—" Pim spots him.

"Little Bro! How are you?" She pulls him in for a hug that Praew worms her way into, then it's Malai's turn to hug him, and then there's Pim husband...

"Dan." Ray holds out his hand for their usual fist bump.

"Ray," Dan returns, the pair completing their friendship handshake from their college days with a hearty smack to each other's butts.

Ray hears Malai mutter something like, "So weird," making Pim snort out a laugh.

If it wasn't for Hathai, Ray's mom, calling that dinner is ready, Ray and Dan may have done their second, even more embarrassing handshake just to see if Malai would react to it with her usual eyeroll and groan. Instead, they all make their way to the dining room, excited for the feast that awaits. Ray, in particular, is *really* looking forward to it. It's been months since he's had a proper home-cooked meal.

After his sisters have left for the evening—despite Praew's whining that she wanted to have a sleepover with *Uncle Wawa* and Pim having to drag her away with the promise that they'd see him again soon—it's just Ray and his parents. And, although he'd been very happy to see his whole family, he's glad to be done socializing for today. Traveling has really taken it out of him. It's barely nine PM and he's already struggling to stay awake—eyelids threatening to close despite the loud volume on the TV show his parents are watching. He's been working nonstop lately, and his body seems to think that now is the time to catch up on some sleep.

Ray, however, has other ideas.

He clears his throat. "Ma, Pa, I've just gotta head out for a minute. I won't be long." He stands, heading for the door.

"Alright, Pumpkin. Are you going for a stroll? I might join you." His mom makes a move to get up from her armchair.

Ray grabs one of his boots, hopping on one foot as he pulls it on.

"No, Ma. I'm going to the bookstore. There's something I need to do." Ray wobbles precariously as he yanks his second boot onto his foot.

"Well, it won't be open now, Pumpkin. This isn't New York!" His mom smiles teasingly at him, tittering as she repositions herself in her chair before returning her attention to the television.

Ray's shoulders sink, one hand clutching at the jacket he's about to put on.

"Oh..." He hangs the jacket back up. "Right. Of course. Haha, silly me." His cheeks heat with embarrassment at forgetting that his small hometown doesn't function in the same way as the big city. Has he really been away so long that he could be that out of touch with this environment? He hopes he'll get back into the routine of it soon. At least enough that he doesn't feel out of place for the whole three weeks he's here.

Ray struggles to get his boots off, first trying to toe them off and then lifting his leg to pull at the stubborn footwear with both hands.

His dad, previously preoccupied by the television, pipes up, "I'll go with you tomorrow, Son. I meant to go there today—they've got a book I ordered."

Ray tugs at the boot harshly, wiggling his ankle, hoping it'll somehow help to ease the offending item off of him. One more pull and his foot is free.

"Okay, Pa-AHA!" He feels a moment of relief before the momentum of the boot-removal causes him to finally lose his balance. "WAH!" He flails as he falls, landing on his ass on the welcome mat. Ray sits there, stunned for a moment.

"Oww." Pain blooms and he rubs his lower back.

His parents merely chuckle, accustomed to their son's lack of coordination. "Maybe it's time for you to get some sleep, Pumpkin." His mom chuckles as he staggers to his feet. "You must be tired."

"Mhm." Ray hobbles over to his parents, giving them each a kiss on the cheek. "Night, Ma. Night, Pa." When he stands back up, the pain has eased considerably. He's fallen over enough times to know when and when not to be concerned. In this case, he's fairly sure he's fine.

Ray drags his feet to the stairs, finally allowing the tiredness to catch up with him as he heads to his childhood bedroom. Everything is still exactly how it was when he'd lived here; band posters, photos, and stickers littering the wall, a small desk covered in various knickknacks, a closet full of clothes he keeps only for sentimental value.

He's barely conscious enough to take off his jeans and change into a loose t-shirt before he is flopping onto the bed, eyelids drooping closed and breath evening out as he slips into a peaceful slumber.

Saturday, December 10ᵗʰ

Jamie wakes up feeling marginally less irritated than he had the day before. The knowledge that Ray is in town is still causing a constant agitation, a discomfort under his skin, but his annoyance is tamped down enough that he can at least *appear* calm. His peace, however, lasts only a matter of seconds as he quickly tunes into his mother's chattering on the phone in the hallway: "Yes! THE Ray! I think he's single, you know. You should come stay with us for a bit, see if you can run into him and…" she breaks off, giggling.

Sighing out his frustration, Jamie drags himself out of bed and heads to the bathroom to start his morning routine. His mom doesn't even look at him as he passes her, too busy squealing down the phone about *how very lucky they are* to have moved to the hometown of such a famous celebrity. Of course, they had found out about this shortly after they'd moved here a few years ago, but Jamie hadn't thought it was really that big of a deal. And he'd thought it was even less of a big deal after he'd met the guy.

Jamie and his older brother, Tommy, are running Honeybun Bookstore together today. On weekdays, the family can usually get away with just one member of staff at a time, Ammersfield being as small as it is, but they're always busier on Saturdays. On top of this, it's almost Christmas, so they're definitely expecting a few more customers than usual.

Jamie finds himself busy on the shop floor all morning with a constant stream of customers; happily advising grandparents about what books their grandchildren might enjoy, assisting people with care and efficiency in finding the titles they've come looking for, and keeping the shelves well stocked. Tommy mans the cash register, trying to greet each customer politely with a smile, despite his social skills not being quite on par with his brother's.

There is a lull as lunchtime approaches and Tommy offers to head over to the café across the street to get their usual sandwiches and some much needed caffeine. Jamie nods, taking his place behind the counter as Tommy grabs his wallet and heads out. He flops down on the stool, sighing in relief to be off his feet for a little while.

Jamie surveys the store, making a mental note to update the display near the front with something more seasonally appropriate now that they've got some new holiday-themed titles in stock. Then he must zone out, because it feels like only a moment passes before Tommy is rushing back through the door, the coffees balanced in a cup carrier in one hand, and a brown paper bag grasped in the other.

Tommy almost sprints to the back of the store, eyes wild as he hastily deposits the food and drinks on the counter as he squawks, "Ray is across the road!"

Jamie scowls.

His brother, oblivious, marches towards the stairs and shouts back over his shoulder, "I'm gonna get him to sign our copy of that romcom he was in! Watch the store for me, Jem? Thanks, love you!" He hears his brother's heavy footsteps pounding on the floor above him, no doubt running to rummage through their family's DVD collection.

Jamie eyes up the bag from the café, sighing. Well... his brother has given this food to him, surely he won't mind if he eats first. He should make the most of the fact that the store is quiet at the moment. Gingerly, he reaches into the bag, pulling out a sandwich that he unwraps and digs into.

Jamie has just taken his third bite, moaning around the mouthful, lettuce hanging out of his mouth, when he hears the bell above the door tinkle. He looks up to see Mr. Amarin walking through the door. Which, okay, it's not ideal for any customer to see Jamie when he's got this much food in his mouth, but at least Mr. Amarin is likely to laugh it off.

But when Jamie catches sight of who's walking behind him, his jaw freezes in place mid-chew.

Ray.

The actor is wearing a rather simple outfit; some dark blue jeans and a pale blue t-shirt, with a beige jacket over the top that can't possibly be warm enough for this time of year. Jamie's eyes trail upward to notice that Ray's hair is styled so not a strand is out of place, and is he... wearing makeup? Surely his eyelashes aren't naturally that perfect.

There are no sunglasses covering Ray's eyes this time, meaning that Jamie can tell the second the other sees him; his eyes widening in what appears to be panic and his step faltering.

"I-I... I—" Ray stutters out, Adam's apple bobbing.

Jamie, who still hasn't resumed chewing, quickly covers his mouth, pulling in the hanging lettuce and swallowing it down hastily.

"Ah, Jamie! Good to see you!" Mr. Amarin greets him, unaware that his son appears to be frozen to the spot behind him. Jamie takes a sip of his too-hot coffee, willing his food to go down, before he returns the greeting.

"Good to see you too, Mr. Amarin. What can I do for you today?" Jamie can't help but let his eyes flicker to Ray, finding him still stuck in the same position. *Odd.*

"I think the book I ordered is ready to collect. Your mom called yesterday morning."

"Of course! Let me grab it for you!"

Jamie hurries out from behind the counter to grab his order from the stockroom, just as Tommy is barreling down the stairs, yelling, "Okay, I couldn't find the DVD, but do you think Ray will sign my old college workbook? The girls will go crazy for it when I next see them! You know, they still haven't forgiven me for—"

Now it appears to be Tommy's turn to be rooted to the spot, stopping mid-step when he catches sight of his idol standing in their family's store. This seems to be enough for Ray to break out of his own trance, chuckling as he approaches Tommy.

"Of course I'll sign it for you!" He grabs the book and pen out of Tommy's hands. "Who should I make it out to?"

"T-T-T..." He gulps audibly, his face going red. "Tommy. Please."

Ray nods before quickly scribbling something down on the front of the book. Holding it away from himself for a moment, he admires his handiwork before he nods and passes it back. Jamie can barely suppress a scoff as he reads the inscription from over his brother's shoulder.

> Tommy,
> I hope this helps with your girl troubles
> — Ray

Jamie thinks Ray must be a special brand of asshole.

Tommy, on the other hand, seems thrilled—babbling nonsense at Ray and begging to shake his hand, claiming he will now have to frame the workbook and mount it on his bedroom wall. Jamie ignores this in favor of passing over the ordered book to Ray's father.

"Here you are, Mr. Amarin. Sorry for the wait." He hands the book over, eyes resolutely on the old gentleman in front of him and avoiding the man his brother is currently talking the ear off of.

"I've told you before, Jamie, please call me Pat! It makes me feel so old, you calling me Mr. Amarin all the time!"

"Ah, I'm sorry, Mr. A— um... Pat." Jamie forces a smile at the gentleman, who smiles back genuinely.

It isn't long before the Amarins are leaving the store, Ray trailing after his father like a lost puppy. Tommy waves at them enthusiastically as they leave, his new prized possession held tightly against his chest.

"Come back soon! See you!" Tommy chimes, continuing to wave until Ray is completely out of sight.

Jamie hopes Ray won't take Tommy's words as an invitation.

"Oh!" Pat stops after they round a corner. "You wanted something in the bookstore, didn't you?"

Ray feels his cheeks heat as his dad looks at him.

"Let's head back and you can get whatever it is you wanted." Pat turns around, heading back in the direction of Honeybun Bookstore.

"No! I, uh..." His dad faces him once more, eyebrow raising in curiosity as he eyes his suspiciously rosy-cheeked son. "I, um, I'll go back another time. It's fine."

Ray is infinitely grateful that his dad doesn't pry, shrugging and continuing to walk home instead.

"Can you believe we just met Ray?" Tommy grabs Jamie's arm, shaking him. "Ray! THE Ray!"

Jamie's eyes narrow, humming noncommittally in response as he stares through the window at where he'd caught his last glimpse of Ray.

"WE. MET. HIM." Based on the wailing note in his tone, Jamie is sure Tommy is crying now.

"Yeah. *You* met him." Jamie picks up his unfinished sandwich, digging back in with rageful bites. Still, he glares out the window, all his thoughts consumed by perfect eyelashes and faltering steps.

His brother frowns. "What do you mean? You met him, too!"

"He didn't even talk to me, Tommy," Jamie struggles around a mouthful of bread, swallowing it down quickly. "Besides, I already met him this summer."

"YOU *WHAT?!*

Sunday, December 11th

Jamie is sure he'll never hear the end of this.

It's been a whole day since he informed Tommy, as casually as possible, that he'd actually already met Ray before. Of course, Tommy had told their parents, and now they're all gushing over dinner about how Jamie and Ray are, apparently, "best friends."

Jamie scoffs at the allegation, trying to go back to eating his food in peace.

"So," His mom starts, picking up on Jamie's obvious dislike at being associated with the man—she is as perceptive as ever. "What happened when you two met? The first time, I mean."

Hi father and brother turn to look at him, the clattering of utensils stopping as they pause to listen.

Jamie gulps.

"N-nothing." He picks up another fork-full of potatoes, shoveling them into his mouth. Hoping the others will move on if he takes long enough, he chews slowly, savoring each morsel.

Unfortunately, they wait. It seems they aren't buying his response.

Jamie picks up his glass, taking a few sips of water in an attempt to get rid of the lump in his throat. He's not sure if it's from the food or how intensely his family are looking at him.

When he places the glass back down, it is with a sense of finality. "Nothing happened. He's just an asshole."

Despite the looks of confusion that pass between his dad and brother, they seem to understand that Jamie isn't going to talk about it any further, returning their attention to their plates and lighter topics of conversation. But his mother's gaze lingers on him a little longer, brow almost imperceivably furrowed, before she nods in some sort of understanding, going back to her meal.

The rest of dinner passes peacefully, Jamie disappearing off to his room once he's finished eating to study. This also has the added bonus of allowing him to avoid any further questioning about his experience meeting a certain celebrity.

He may not be able to put off talking about Ray forever, but he'll put it off for as long as he can—at least until he's figured the guy out. Something about the way Ray acts around him is... interesting.

Ray stands outside of the closed Honeybun Bookstore, looking through the window at the dark shop floor. He had meant to just go for a walk around the neighborhood, no particular destination in mind, but his feet carried him here. He knew it wouldn't be open—it's a Sunday and it's late evening now, the sun long since set. Still... he had sort of hoped he could catch him, maybe finally apologize for his behavior in the summer.

He had pictured that he would arrive and see just one light on at the back of the store, Jamie standing conveniently under it, illuminated as he cleans and tidies. He had pictured tapping on the glass of the door to alert him of his presence, Jamie opening it with a harsh "What do you want?"—the bluntness only eased somewhat by the way Jamie's gaze would catch on Ray's perfectly plump lips, somehow not chapped from the harsh winter air. He had pictured himself asking if he could come in, maybe even faking a shiver if he had to convince the man. He had pictured—

Well, it doesn't matter.

He looks up, spotting the warm glow coming from the windows of what he can presume to be Jamie's family's apartment above the shop.

Ray shoves his hands deeper into his jacket pockets, the evening air somehow feeling colder now.

He walks home without getting a chance to clear his conscience.

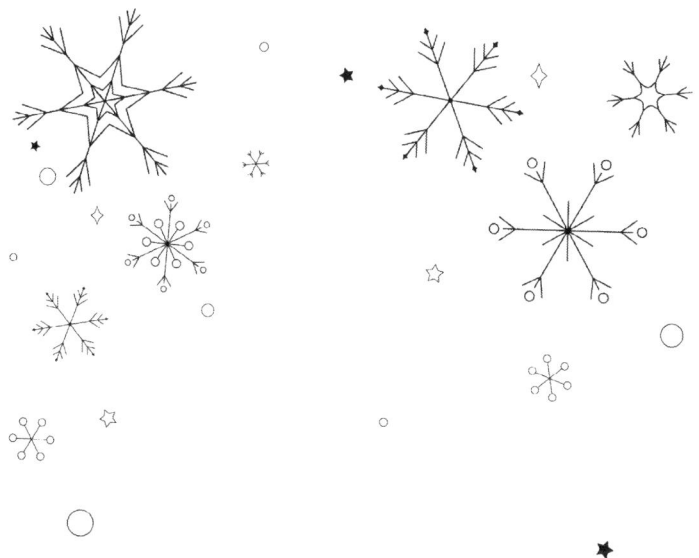

"I'm sorry."
PART 2

Monday, December 12th

Ray jumps out of bed the second his alarm goes off, heading to the bathroom and hopping into the shower. He knows it's going to take him a while to get ready today, so he can't afford to waste any time. He has to look his best when he sees—*apologizes*—to Jamie.

Jamie...

He hadn't known his name until Saturday—had spent months just referring to him in his mind as The Boy. THE Boy. It was a blessing that his dad had gone to the bookstore with him as he'd finally been able to learn his name. There was no way he would have been brave enough to just *ask*.

Ray stares at himself in the mirror as he brushes his teeth, contemplating whether he should put on some makeup like he did last time. He had been thinking he wouldn't require makeup as often while he was at home, not needing to show such a polished persona around his family, but he finds that he feels oddly naked leaving the house without anything on his face. And especially considering who he's going to be seeing today...

"Maybe just a little concealer," Ray murmurs, unzipping his makeup bag.

An hour later, Ray is in his dad's truck, the man insisting on dropping Ray off so as not to be swarmed by fans. He was embarrassed as he'd climbed into the truck, the situation feeling too much like a child being dropped off at a friend's house. He's just turned thirty, for crying out loud—what kind of thirty year old still gets driven around by their dad?

Pat parks directly outside of Honeybun Bookstore, pulling out a magazine and getting comfortable in the driver's seat.

"I'll wait for you here, alright?" Pat says, glancing up at Ray. "Anything happens and you call me, got it?"

Ray truly feels fourteen years old again; being dropped off at the birthday party of a cool girl in his class, his dad sensing his nerves and trying to soothe him. Does he really seem that on-edge today?

"O-okay."

Ray climbs out of the truck and marches up to the store door.

He stops, taking a deep breath before grabbing the handle and yanking the door open.

The store is empty apart from the person sitting by the cash register.

"Oh."

Ray is perplexed. He had been expecting to see The Boy, Jamie, behind the counter again. Instead, an older woman is perched there—hair in two long braids and reading glasses slipping down her nose as she turns the page of the book she's reading. He can only assume this must be Jamie's mother.

She glances up at him.

"AH! Umm," the woman starts. Ray feels oddly grateful that he's not the one doing the stumbling in this store for once.

"Ray— I mean, Mr. Amarin, no— I mean..." She puts down the book, waving her hands in the air and rising from her chair as she stammers at him.

Ray gives her the smile that he knows makes women fall in love with him. "Ray is fine, Ma'am."

"Alright..." Though her gaze still has that frantic edge of someone who is starstruck, she settles back in her seat a little. "Can I, um... Can I help you with anything?"

Ray looks around, debating. "No, thank you. I'm just here to browse... if that's alright?"

"Mhm!" She nods enthusiastically, gesturing vaguely to the bookshelves in a "go ahead" motion.

Ray spends twenty minutes using his best acting skills to pretend to look at books, smiling at a couple of customers when they enter and gasp at him. With his dad waiting for him outside, there is only so long he can justify staying here.

Deciding to admit defeat for the day, Ray throws what he hopes is a cheerful "Thank you!" over his shoulder as he walks out of the bookstore.

He slams the door of his dad's truck as he gets in, huffing in agitation.

Pat puts down his magazine. "Did you find what you were looking for?"

Ray makes a noncommittal noise, resting his head on his hand and pouting in the direction of the bookstore as he asks, "Can we come back tomorrow?"

Pat starts up the pickup truck.

"Sure thing, Son."

Tuesday, December 13th

When Ray gets out of his dad's truck today, he decides to get a good look through the shop window before entering. He sees the lady who he thinks is Jamie's mom in there again, along with quite a few customers, but no sign of the man he's looking for.

Ray turns back to his father, who is once again reading a magazine in the truck. He leans down and signals for his dad to open the window, placing a hand on the vehicle to steady himself, nervousness making him feel even more unbalanced than usual.

"Pa, I don't know how long this might take. If you've got anything you'd like to do for the next hour or so, please don't let me keep you."

Pat eyes him with equal parts suspicion and concern. "Are you sure?"

"Mhm."

Pat packs away his magazine.

"Okay. Text me if you want a lift home."

Ray nods and stands back up straight, watching his dad drive away.

When Ray enters the store this time, it is with a vow that he will not leave until he has achieved his goal.

*

He should have known it wouldn't be so easy.

Ray's been in the bookstore for an hour now and there's still no sign of Jamie. The lady who might be Jamie's mom has asked him if he needs anything multiple times, going so far as to offer him a glass of water and a chair to sit in when he starts to sway slightly on his feet from standing still for too long. He refuses her offers, determined to stick it out—he's an actor, for goodness' sake, and a very good one at that. He should be able to manage something as simple as standing around and looking interested.

Other customers come and go, occasionally asking him for an autograph or a selfie, but largely they just watch him from afar. It seems that being in a bookstore—a space that's supposed to be quiet—keeps people from mobbing him. Still, he can feel their expectant gaze on him as he picks up a random book about fish, deciding he should read *something* so he doesn't go mad from boredom or paranoia. He knows that some of the customers in the store are taking pictures of him, maybe even filming him. People don't hold their phones like that when they're texting. Flipping to the next page of the book, he tries not to acknowledge how observed he feels; like an animal in a zoo with the way they gasp and admire him from a distance, snapping pics as souvenirs to show to their family and friends when they get home.

The two-hour mark approaches and Ray is probably only fifteen pages into the book. He can't focus—eyes flitting up and heart rate escalating each time the bell above the door jingles. There seems to be a lull in customers at the moment, the only one other than Ray mulling about for a few more minutes before selecting a book, purchasing it, and leaving.

Now it's just Ray.

He sighs, staring blankly at the page in front of him.

"You know, I'd usually make you buy the book after holding onto it for this long."

Ray's head swivels to find the sales clerk standing next to him, her eyes sparkling up at him mischievously. It seems that she's grown used to Ray's presence, no longer in awe of him. He'd been standing there so long he's practically become part of the furniture.

"Ah! Of course!" He fumbles for his wallet. "How much is it, Ma'am? I'll—"

She chuckles, waving a hand dismissively. "I'm only joking, Ray."

Wow, she really has grown comfortable with him—talking to him so casually and comfortably in contrast to her awkward formality when they'd met the previous day. It eases Ray's nerves somewhat. He feels safe and at home with her, like she's treating him the same way she'd treat any other local who wandered in.

"I know a man waiting for something when I see one. Are you waiting for my son?"

He nods, not trusting himself to say anything without embarrassing himself.

The woman, Jamie's mom, looks at him with an expression that should feel like pity, but it doesn't. It doesn't feel as judgmental or belittling as that. Her expression feels warm and kind, if a little concerned. "He won't be in the shop today. But I can pass on a message for you, if you'd like?" She leans in intently.

Finally! An opportunity to contact him!

But... Ray doesn't know what to say—doesn't know how much he should tell Jamie's mom, or how much she already knows. As if she senses his trepidation, she runs off, grabbing some paper and a pen before returning.

"Here." She offers the items to him. "Write down your message and I'll pass it on to him. I promise I won't peek." She covers her eyes dramatically with her hands, the sleeves of her cardigan pulled over her palms.

This should make Ray feel nervous. Usually when people say things like that, in that playful of a tone, they don't really mean it. But he finds he trusts her.

He takes a moment to organize his thoughts, then pens a simple message:

I'M SORRY.
—Ray

Unlike the autograph he'd given Tommy, this one has no flourishes. No elaborately swirled signature, no perfectly angled writing like he practices before every event where he might even possibly be called upon to write. No. This is his natural handwriting; letters a messy, lopsided scrawl across the paper, his name written plainly. It's him. The real him.

He thanks Jamie's mom as she takes the folded note from him, pocketing it in the front of her denim overalls and then patting at the fabric as if confirming the note's safety.

Looking outside, Ray can see that there are quite a few people out and about. He doesn't feel like being observed any more than necessary today by walking home. "I promise I won't stay in your store much longer, Ma'am. I'm just going to text my pa and ask him to come get me. Is that okay?"

The woman smiles. "Of course, Dear, there's no rush. You're always welcome here." Ray sighs in relief, thanking her again as he texts his dad. Pat responds quickly, saying he'll be there in ten minutes.

Jamie's mom is busying herself around the store, checking that the books on display are neat and tidy while there aren't any customers to attend to. Ray feels too awkward just standing there and watching.

"Is there anything I can help you with, Ma'am?"

She seems taken aback by his offer, hands pausing where they were about to pick up a misplaced book. Her eyes blink a few times in quick succession. Ray continues, "I feel bad for being here for so long without buying anything. Please, let me help a little before I leave."

She smiles, obviously endeared, then looks around in thought.

"Hmm... The shelves are looking a little empty in places, actually. Could you help me carry through some stock from the back?"

"Of course!"

Ray brings a few armfuls of books through from the stockroom, stacking them temporarily on one of the tables as instructed, before they start placing them on shelves. They have a little conveyor belt system going—Ray handing the books to her, then her putting them in their correct places.

"So, Ray, are you enjoying being home?"

The question surprises Ray. Very few people ever ask him about non-work things. Unless it's about dating, that is. Ray is sick of people enquiring about his non-existent love life.

"I, um... I am enjoying it so far I think, Ma'am."

"That's good! Oh, and call me Apple, please—everybody does!"

"O-oh. Okay. Thank you, Apple."

She shoots him a smile over her shoulder before reaching up to place a book on one of the higher shelves.

"So, why do you only *think* you are enjoying it?"

That catches Ray off-guard again—the fact that she had picked up on his hesitation. It makes him feel a little defensive, his voice quiet as he responds, "I... I *am* having a good time."

Ray expects her to let it go at that point; either because he's been convincing enough for the conversation to be over, or he sounds timid enough to make her not want to ask further. But it seems Ray has underestimated her persistence. She turns to face him with a sad smile, crossing her arms and leaning back against the bookshelves as she asks, "Why do I sense a 'but' coming?"

It should feel intrusive to have someone push him this much. Maybe it would from anyone else. But from Apple? A sweet lady with pigtail braids and sweater paws? It only feels like the words of a caring mother.

"I am enjoying myself, I really am." Ray picks up another couple of books that he'd brought out from the back, handing them to Apple who raises an eyebrow at him to go on. He takes a breath before continuing, "But I... I'm not used to being away from my work. I feel..." He struggles to find the word, shoulders slumping as he lets out a sigh.

"Lost?" She looks at him knowingly.

Ray nods, swallowing against his suddenly too-dry mouth.

His words are slow, Ray having to take his time to try to form them. "It's like... I..." He huffs, agitated at his own inarticulateness. "I don't know—" He blinks, startled at the confession as it comes pouring out of his mouth: "I don't know... who I am... w-without the work." He wrings his hands together, trying to find some comfort in the pressure.

Apple places the books she's holding back down on the table, a sympathetic smile on her lips. Tentatively, she reaches out to grasp his hands, holding them gently in hers. Her hands are soft and warm, her delicate thumbs rubbing soothingly over the backs of his palms, encouraging him to hold her gaze.

"Your job may take up a considerable amount of your time, but it is not your entire life. You are not defined solely by your job title. You're not just an actor, Ray, but a human being. Don't forget that!" She emphasizes the final statement with a nod of her head.

Ray can only stare at her, processing her words.

The honk of Pat's truck interrupts the moment, Ray blinking back into awareness. "Ah! That will be my pa." He squeezes her hands, trying to convey his thanks, before letting them go. Another honk has him hurrying towards the door, not wanting to keep his father waiting after he was kind enough to come and get him.

As Ray is about to leave, he turns to thank the woman sincerely. "Thank you, Apple, for letting me hang out in your store. And for the advice. I... I really appreciate it."

"That's alright, Dear!"

He opens the door, already on his way out before Apple speaks again. "Oh, and Ray?"

Ray pops his head back through the door, Apple smiling at him cheekily.

"Jamie will be working tomorrow."

He blushes, nodding once before finally leaving the store.

Ray clambers into his dad's truck, cheeks still ablaze.

"Did you get what you were after?" Pat asks in lieu of a greeting.

"Sort of," Ray responds.

If Pat notices that Ray doesn't appear to have any books or shopping bags with him, he says nothing.

Wednesday, December 14th

Ray has been trying to get to Honeybun Bookstore all day, wanting to know Jamie's response to his note, but nothing's going his way.

This morning he'd been talked into hanging up some Christmas decorations around the house—neither of his parents wanted to get on a step ladder to string up the fairy lights above the windows, given their age. Ray had gulped nervously, aware that he wasn't exactly known for having good balance, but had agreed. He'd managed to get through the whole ordeal without embarrassing himself, only having one little wobble when he'd nearly—*only nearly!*—missed a step getting off the ladder for the last time.

He had hoped he could find some time to go out then, but alas, his mother had other plans; a large plate of warm food handed to him as soon as he was done with the decorations. He enjoyed every mouthful, but couldn't help eating quickly so he could finally go to the bookstore. However, when he stood up abruptly from the table and his parents asked where he was going, he'd not known what to say. Ray had frozen, not wanting to make it a *thing* that he kept going there. They might start asking questions.

So he'd silently sat back down instead, trying to pay attention as his parents chattered about things that had changed in the town since he'd moved away. Ray never really found much time to come home—only returning on a handful of occasions since he'd left for New York—so his parents always felt the need to update him whenever he came back. Usually, Ray was at least mildly interested. But this time, he had places to go and people (well, *a* person) to see.

Above the table, Ray was all perfect manners; expression intent and open. But under the table, Ray's leg bounced impatiently. Or at least it did until something his dad said caught his attention:

"The bookstore's gotten much better since the Suwans took it over, don't you think?"

Jamie Suwan, Ray thought. *Pretty.*

His mom spoke back in agreement, "Yes, though I can't help but sort of miss Jake and his hideous window displays." She and Pat chuckled, reminiscing about the old owner of the store. He'd been a kind man, but maybe not the best businessman. What kind of small town bookstore needs such a large collection of books on exercise? Was he trying to imply something about the locals?

Ray perked up. "So, uhh..."

His parents turned to him, surprised that he was suddenly showing such interest after just nodding silently through the majority of their conversation.

"How long have they, um... How long have they been here?"

Ray had felt so caught off guard when he'd gone into the store this summer—expecting to see Jake doing some bizarre exercise routine against a bookshelf like usual. Instead, when he'd looked up, he'd seen a beautiful boy with pillowy, pink lips and adorably fluffy black hair. He'd panicked, limbs moving with no control and heart thumping out of his chest. Embarrassment and attraction had colored his cheeks, and he'd not known what else to do other than abandon ship and vacate the premises immediately when he'd accidentally knocked over several books with his flailing.

"Oh, hm..." His mom thought for a moment, looking at Pat as if that would help spark her memory. "Three years? Maybe slightly longer? Something like that."

Ray nodded, biting his tongue to prevent himself from asking further questions. He'd wanted to ask about the Suwans' son, Jamie. He'd wanted to know everything his parents knew about him—how old he is, what his personality is like, ~~if he's into guys~~. Instead, he stayed silent.

Walking into town, Ray encounters a new problem. Not many people had spoken to him when his father was nearby, all five foot six of Pat Amarin discouraging fans from approaching for some reason. Knowing his father, Ray suspects he must have said something at the last town hall meeting.

Now that he is on his own, however, he can barely walk five paces without someone wanting to talk to him. Some faces he recognizes from his childhood, others he doesn't, but it's all the same—another "world's biggest fan" waiting around every corner, all wanting to congratulate him on his success. He smiles politely at each of them, thanking them for their compliments and support. All of their faces blur together after a while.

But there is one face he still needs to see.

Ray makes it to the bookstore five minutes before closing time, only one other customer browsing, who appears to remain unaware of his presence. He sighs in relief, grateful to not have to deal with yet another "fan."

Then he catches sight of Jamie.

He's sitting at the counter, just like every other time Ray has seen him. It seems he didn't hear the bell above the door when Ray entered. His expression is open and unguarded as he writes something in a notebook, with what appears to be a textbook open next to it. Ray allows himself to watch him, enamored by the simple elegance with which he holds the pen, tapping it to his lip in thought from time to time.

Jamie must sense Ray watching, his gaze suddenly flitting up to make direct eye contact. His eyes narrow, face taking on a cold edge before he returns his attention to his books.

Ray gulps, fixes his face into his best "I'm a nice guy" smile, and approaches.

"H-hEy." The crack in Ray's voice turns his smile into slightly more of a grimace.

Jamie glances up briefly, judgingly, before responding with a curt, "Hey."

Ray steals himself, knowing he just needs to rip off the bandaid and talk to the man. He leans in a little, whispering in order to not be overheard by the other customer, "Did you get my note?"

"Mhm."

Ray elaborates, "About this summer..." Jamie's pen pauses in its place. "How much to not tell the press about that?"

That is *not* how he planned for that to come out.

If Ray thought Jamie's gaze was cold before, that was nothing compared to this.

"Excuse me?" Jamie asks, glaring daggers at Ray who has broken out in a cold sweat.

Well, he's already dug himself into a hole, might as well keep going.

"To, uhh... To not tell anyone about me knocking th-the books over. And leaving. How much? You see, I'm meant to be cool. Or wait, no, what I mean to say is—"

Jamie fixes him with an expression that can only be described as disgust. "Nothing. No money. I'm not someone you can buy off whenever you're an asshole. Now, if you'll excuse me, Sir, I have a customer to attend to."

He remains fixed in place as Jamie slams his books closed, walking around the counter to go talk to the shopper who is, conveniently, all the way on the other side of the store.

Ray blinks, trying to work out where he went wrong. He'd thought he planned it all out so well—a heartfelt apology, followed by *kindly* asking Jamie not to tell anyone about his clumsiness he'd worked so hard to hide from the public. But he had intended for the apology to be the main part, and *definitely* not to just jump in offering him money. He mentally berates himself for not writing a proper script in preparation to ensure his wording was correct and came out in the right order.

He has to shuffle out of the way when the customer approaches the counter to purchase a book, Jamie moving back to the cash register to ring up the sale. He still seems angry—pressing the buttons on the register harder than strictly necessary, and his tone is slightly clipped when he thanks the patron for their purchase.

Ray hears the bell jingle above the door as the customer leaves, signaling that he and Jamie are now alone.

"Look, Jamie, I'm sor—"

"It's closing time, *Sir*." Jamie points to the clock on the back wall, displaying that it is in fact five PM. "Please leave, since you clearly aren't here to buy anything other than my silence."

Ray's mouth opens and closes repeatedly, no sound coming out.

The way Jamie had said that irritated Ray—the exaggerated "Sir," the hurtful words that make Ray sound shallow, concerned only with his image. Sure, he hadn't gone about his apology the right way, but he really has been trying! He's been doing all he can to apologize to Jamie since he got back into town, and this is how he treats him? No. Ray isn't having it. If Jamie wants to act like that, it is surely not Ray's fault if he decides to wind him up a bit.

"Well..." Ray says, taking slow steps over to one of the displays. "Who says I'm not here to buy a book?" He picks up a title at random and turns it over in his hand, pretending to read the blurb. "You wouldn't want to throw out a paying customer, would you?" He sends Jamie his signature smirk. "Especially not one with such... influence."

If steam could come out of a person's ears, that is what would currently be happening to Jamie. Ray is sure of it. The boy's hands are balled into fists by his sides, shoulders raised and tensed, lips pursed. He clearly wants nothing more than to shout at Ray, give him a piece of his mind and kick him out. But it seems that the idea Ray might say something negative about his family's business stops him.

Ray watches as Jamie forces himself to relax his shoulders, taking a shuddering breath before speaking through clenched teeth, "Of course not, Sir. It is our store policy to allow customers already in the store up to fifteen minutes after closing time to complete any purchases."

Ray smiles, pleased with himself. "Good."

He spends some time picking up various books, none of which he has any interest in, before putting them back down. His attention is solely on the boy who is grinding his teeth by the register. Ray throws him a shit-eating grin occasionally, receiving nothing more than a huff in return.

He checks the clock—thirty seconds to go. He really is trying to be as pedantic as possible right now. Ray grabs whatever book is directly in front of him and heads to the counter. When he places it down, he smirks confidently at Jamie. "See, I told you I was a paying customer. And I found *exactly* the book I was looking for, just in the nick of time. I've been looking for this title for a while now, you know. I've been told it's very good."

Jamie's glare slips down to look at the book, lips ticking up into a smirk of their own at what he sees. "I somehow don't think you were actually looking for a copy of *What To Expect When You're Expecting*, but please, do correct me if I'm wrong."

Ray glances down at the book, eyes popping out of his head when he sees that Jamie isn't joking about what he's picked up. His face is red with embarrassment by the time he meets Jamie's gaze again. "I... It's...I— uh..."

Jamie looks at him expectantly, moving his face closer to Ray's over the counter, one eyebrow raised in challenge. Ray has forgotten how to speak.

"UhhHhHHh..."

Jamie gets steadily closer, close enough that Ray could count each of his individual eyelashes if he could remember how to count. *What was counting again? Was it the one with the letters or the thing with the numbers?* He can't be sure.

And then, something magical happens: Jamie laughs.

It's light and airy, the kind of unrestrained laughter reserved for true moments of joy. It bubbles out of him, shoulders shaking as he pushes back against the counter, picking up the book.

"Come on." He pauses, catching his breath. "At least pick something good. Or relevant." Jamie returns the offending book to its place swiftly, then almost jogging to the other side of the store to peruse one of the shelves.

"Aha!" He plucks a book from the shelf before bounding back over to put the sale through the register, takes Ray's money, and hands the book to him.

Wait, what did I just buy?

Ray looks down, reading the title:

Apologies for Dummies.

"Maybe you'll find it useful." Jamie chuckles.

Ray nods, flustered after being called out like this.

"O-okay. Thank you. I think."

Jamie still has a small smile playing on his lips and Ray can't help but stare. Those *lips.*

"No problem. Now please, Sir, go home so I can lock up for the night."

That startles Ray into movement, suddenly feeling sheepish about wasting Jamie's time with his pettiness when he could have been trying to make him *laugh like that* instead.

"Of course!" He hurries to the door, narrowly avoiding knocking over a cardboard cutout of a snowman on his way. He's done enough embarrassing things in front of Jamie for one day.

Ray grabs the handle and pauses. Looking back over his shoulder, his voice is soft as he confesses, "I really am sorry, by the way. About this summer. And I didn't mean what I said earlier, it all came out wrong. I..."

He doesn't know if he should be saying this much to someone who is practically a stranger, but he *wants to.* Still, he has to glance away from Jamie when he says this—looking directly at him makes him feel too vulnerable. "I'm very clumsy and awkward. I thought Jake still ran the store, so I was alarmed when I looked up and saw someone so..." He swallows down the words that threaten to escape. Admitting his little crush would be a step too far right now. "Well... I wasn't expecting you."

When no response comes for a few seconds, Ray risks looking at Jamie. The boy looks shocked, a slight blush on his cheeks. His expression softens when their eyes meet. "It's okay. Thank you for apologizing."

He feels the need to say more, to explain how hard he's been trying despite how much he keeps messing things up. "I, um, I tried to come see you sooner. But you weren't here? I don't think?"

"Mhm. Mama told me you'd been in. I have classes a few days a week. I don't work on those days."

"Ah, I see..." Ray nods, trying to hide his excitement about Jamie sharing information about himself willingly, but still wants to know more. He plucks up the courage to ask, "And if I wanted to see you again... what days would you be here?"

The blush on Jamie's cheeks grows, crawling up to his ears as he responds, "I work here on Wednesdays, Fridays, and Saturdays."

Ray nods and finally opens the door he's been holding onto for far too long, not able to find a reasonable excuse to stay any longer.

"Good to know." The cold air hits him and he feels an odd surge of confidence, making him add, "And please, call me Ray."

He smiles once more and then leaves swiftly, feeling embarrassed at his own boldness. Despite the temperature outside and his less than adequately warm clothing, his cheeks remain heated as he walks home.

Friday can't come soon enough.

Thursday, December 15th

"Tell me everything!"

This is the first thing Win, Jamie's best friend, says while he hurries after Jamie in the college cafeteria. Win slams his tray down as he takes a seat opposite him, eyes glistening with curiosity and impatience. Jamie can feel himself blush, remembering the events of yesterday.

"Well... as you know, I saw... um..." Jamie looks around, noting that there are a few people sitting not far from them. He leans closer to Win, his voice barely above a whisper. "I saw Ray."

Win gasps as if he's only just learning this. Of course, Jamie had texted him last night and given him the full rundown of what happened, but Win prefers to hear this type of thing in person. That boy really loves to gossip.

The two had met last year, when Win was a freshman and Jamie in his junior year. They might not have crossed paths if not for the fact that they had both decided to turn up at one of the college's clubs on the same day.

Jamie had wanted to join the college's LGBTQIA+ Society the previous year—determined to live more authentically once he knew for sure that he and his family weren't going to move to a new town again any time soon. This place was going to be his home for a long time, so he wanted to really be himself here.

He'd started getting nervous on the walk to the classroom where the first club meeting of the semester was being held, and suddenly found himself turning around and sprinting back to the bus stop to go home. His mother walked to the bus stop down the road from Honeybun Bookstore to meet him after receiving his text.

> **Jem**
> Not going to club meeting.
> I don't feel well.

He'd gotten off the bus and walked directly into her arms, crying onto her shoulder in the middle of the street.

"You can always try again another time, Baby."

Of course, she'd seen through his feeble excuse of not feeling well. He had told her only that morning how both excited and scared he felt about joining that specific college club.

Jamie didn't pluck up the courage to try to attend the LGBTQIA+ Society again until the start of the next academic year. He hadn't wanted to be the only new kid turning up on some random day in the middle of the semester, so thought that this was his best opportunity to slip in among the freshmen who would also be joining.

It had started much better than his previous attempt—he'd walked with an illusion of confidence to the room where it was being held, making it to the door without bolting. But that is when it stopped going so well. He stood outside of the room for ten minutes, rooted to the spot. The sound of people chattering could be heard through the door. Jamie didn't want to interrupt them; he could already envisage how all of their eyes would turn to him if he entered the room now.

"Um... Hi."

A small voice from beside Jamie startled him out of the beginnings of his mental spiral, turning to find a guy a little shorter than him smiling nervously. His hair was a striking silvery-blond color, the strands long enough to fall around his ears and into the collar of his jacket.

"Are you here for the LGBTQIA+ Society, too?" the boy had asked, his large eyes caught somewhere between excitement and fear.

Jamie nodded. "Mhm."

The boy turned to face the door. The two of them were twin statues, staring resolutely ahead at the piece of paper with "come on in" scrawled onto it, each letter a different color.

The silver-haired boy piped up again, "I'm a bit scared. Are you scared?"

"Mhm."

Out of the corner of his eye, Jamie saw the boy turn towards him once more. He tried his best not to squirm under the gaze.

"Can you say anything other than 'mhm'?"

Jamie gulped, willing himself to think of anything to say. Unfortunately, he only seemed to have one line right now:

"...Mhm."

The boy giggled, eyes turning into shining crescents and nose scrunching up. Jamie couldn't help but find him cute.

"I'm Win, by the way." The boy, Win, held out a hand to shake. The gesture felt oddly formal considering they were both students. Okay, Jamie was likely a little older than him since he'd taken a couple of gap years, but still!

Not knowing what else to do, he reached his own hand out to clasp Win's. He hoped his palm wasn't too sweaty.

"Jamie."

"Well, Jamie, what do you say we go in together?" Win beamed up at him, dropping his hand back to his side. "Sounds like they're having a blast in there."

Sure enough, Jamie could hear people laughing on the other side of the door.

Jamie nodded. "Okay. Together."

They stood there for a moment longer, both taking a deep breath.

Win grabbed Jamie's hand that was closest to him—casual about the contact as if they'd known each other much longer than a few minutes—and placed their joined hands on top of the door handle.

"Mhm," Win confirmed, "together."

They pressed down on the handle, opening the door to a community the two of them had been too afraid to approach alone.

Needless to say, they'd been best friends ever since.

"Eeeheheeeee!" Win squeals, breaking into giggles and shaking his hands back and forth cutely to either side of his face. "He might come see you again TOMORROW?"

Jamie nods, digging into his lunch now that he's done recounting yesterday's events. Despite the fact that Ray hadn't outright *said* he would be coming back so soon, it was definitely heavily implied.

"So he must really like you then!"

Perplexed by this statement, Jamie's eyebrows furrow.

"Well, he's apologized and you've forgiven him. What reason does he have to come back now?" Win's expression turns cheeky. "He must liiiiike you!"

Jamie feels his cheeks redden. "I'm sure he just wants a book or something."

"Mhm, mhm, because he definitely couldn't have already picked up a book the last—*ohhh, I don't know*—four times he's been into your family's store in the past week," Win teases, smirking.

Jamie stops chewing so as to activate his full grumpy face; lips slightly pursed into a pout, eyelids dropping in a way that makes him look like a pissed off cat. Win just laughs at him, moving his hands in a shooing motion as if to banish Jamie's angry expression.

"I'm telling you, Jem, he *must* have a thing for you! You know I'm good at reading this sort of thing."

Swallowing his mouthful of food, Jamie speaks up, "Oh yeah? What about that guy, Luke, who you were so sure was into you? Didn't it turn out he just wanted your help on some homework?"

Win's gaze turns downward sheepishly. "I'm not as good at reading guys' feelings when they're directed at me," he whines with a pout. "Besides, you know my brain goes offline as soon as I see an older guy with muscles."

Resting a hand on top of Win's comfortingly, Jamie tries his best to nod in an empathic fashion. He knows how serious Win's problem with muscles is—the man once fell down the stairs because someone behind him merely mentioned biceps.

"That reminds me..." Win starts. The hand under Jamie's wriggles, Win sliding his fingers between Jamie's to clasp their hands together. "Jem..."

"Hm?" Jamie inquires, squeezing Win's hand in concern. He seems nervous.

Suddenly Win is leaning forward, eyes sparkly and pleading, cheeks pink as he blurts, "Can you get Ray to set me up with that muscly friend of his? Tom? Tim? Something like that, isn't it? That one, please! He's got the most *gooorgeous* pecs! What was his name..."

"WIN!" Despite how much time they spend together, Jamie can't get used to his friend's boldness when it comes to men.

"His name is Win?" Win scrunches up his nose, his next words coming out in a fast stream-of-consciousness, "Ugh, maybe not then. Could be a little weird calling out my own name in the bedroom." His expression lights up with a thought. "Oh! But I guess I could call him Dadd—"

"NO! Nope. Not having this conversation right now." Grabbing his tote bag, Jamie stands, clearing up his plate.

Win copies him, slinging his pink backpack over one shoulder and picking up his tray. "So... not having this conversation right now... but maybe later?" He bumps shoulders with Jamie, who chuckles despite himself. His friend is nothing if not determined.

"Maybe. We'll see, Winnie."

Win pumps his fist in the air, letting out a "Yes!"

"His name is Teddy, by the way."

"*Teddy!* Ah, I was so close! See, I'm getting better!"

Jamie nods in agreement and they say goodbye to each other, heading in different directions for their next classes. Win definitely has improved over the time he's known him. Back when they'd first met, it was rare for him to remember whether the name of a guy he fancied started with a consonant or a vowel, let alone what exact letter it started with. Thus, Win had typically referred to each of the guys he liked by a word that he felt described them. It didn't take a genius to work out what the defining feature of the guy he referred to as "Overcompensating" was.

As Jamie takes his seat in his class, trying not to stress about his upcoming exams, he can't help but wonder how much of what Win had said earlier was correct.

Does Ray... maybe... like him?

Friday, December 16th

Ray walks into town with a pep in his step, excited to see Jamie. He's put even more effort into his appearance today than when he'd come to apologize; some neutral-toned eyeshadow and tinted lip balm adding to his usual routine of concealer, foundation, and clear mascara. He had nearly gone so far as to put on a little eyeliner, but no—he wants to save that for a special occasion. Well, for something a little more special than dropping in to see Jamie at work. ~~Their first date, perhaps.~~

When he peeps through the window of Honeybun Bookstore, he notices how busy it is, customers lining up to get to the cash register. Tommy—Ray remembers his name—is running through the sales as fast as he can. Meanwhile, a slightly flustered-looking Jamie bags each purchase and talks to the customers with a smile, keeping them happy despite the wait. It must be the countdown to Christmas that has the store this busy.

Ray decides he must at least make himself useful. He crosses the street, heading to Sunshine Café to pick up some sustenance for the busy brothers. Only one or two people turn to gawk at him as he enters the café. It seems most of the locals have already grown far more accustomed to his presence over the last couple of days. Or perhaps they're just pretending to be used to him, since there are still a fair few not-so-subtle glances in his direction. Either way, it's an improvement on the constant attention he'd been receiving for the first few days he was in town.

He approaches the counter when one of the workers calls for the next customer.

"H-hey, um... I was wondering if, uhh..."—he points across the street to Honeybun Bookstore—"if the brothers from over there come here often?"

The worker nods. "Tommy and Jamie? Yeah, they're in here every Friday and Saturday for lunch." The worker looks at their watch. "It must be busy there today. They haven't come by yet to grab their usual."

Ray sees his opportunity to be helpful. "Ah, I was about to head over there! I can take it to them!"

"Really?" The worker looks surprised by Ray's offer—perhaps thinking celebrities don't run these kinds of errands, especially for others, or that they must have assistants to do it for them. Ray isn't the kind of famous person who looks down on doing something helpful for others, though. After all, he's just socially awkward, not an asshole.

"Yes! Their usual, please. And I'll have an Americano, the avocado and chicken sandwich, and uhhh..." He eyes the glass counter in front of him, filled to the brim with pastries and cakes. "Ooh! Two of those, please!" He points to some chocolatey-looking slices of cake, marshmallows placed on top of them to form what appear to be snowmen.

Armed with a bag full of food and a cup carrier of coffees, he heads to the bookstore, eternally grateful when a leaving customer holds the door open for him to enter. They giggle shyly when he thanks them.

Ray notices that the store is mercifully quieter than it had been earlier, the line by the cash register almost gone and only a few customers mulling about. As soon as Jamie says goodbye to the customer he and Tommy have been serving, he comes bounding over to where Ray is still standing by the door.

"Ray! Hi!"

Jamie bounces on his toes when he reaches the man, hands clasped in front of himself cutely.

It is only now, without the glass window of the store separating them, that Ray can properly take in Jamie's appearance. He looks almost the same as usual, but there are subtle differences that suggest he's spent slightly longer on his appearance today, too; hair styled neatly with a split down the middle, lips shiny with something—Ray can't be sure if it's lip balm or gloss. Something sparkling by Jamie's ear catches his attention. He hadn't noticed before that Jamie had piercings—a small, pink, heart-shaped gem now adorning each lobe.

"H-hi," Ray stammers, eyes drifting to take in Jamie's outfit.

He's wearing a baby pink t-shirt tucked into the front of some straight-leg jeans, and a pair of white sneakers that look clean enough to be brand new. Over the t-shirt is a white cable-knit cardigan, the sleeves long enough to cover his palms. That particular detail reminds him so much of Apple, Ray finds himself wondering whether sweater paws are a family trait.

Ray needs to pull himself together.

He holds up the bag and cup carrier from the café. "I, uh... I brought your usual." He tries to aim the words at both Jamie *and* Tommy, but his eyes keep shifting back to the pretty boy standing directly in front of him.

The words seem to flip a switch in Jamie, the man almost pouncing at the food. "Oh, thank god! I'm starving!" He snatches the bag from Ray before heading towards the back of the store. "Come on, Ray. Let's go eat."

It takes Ray a moment to walk after him, temporarily stunned by both the surprise of being invited to eat with him and the sight that greets him when Jamie turns around. It turns out that the jeans have back pockets. Pink pockets. Heart-shaped ones. That are *so cute*. And accentuate Jamie's perfect—

"Ahem!"

The sound of Tommy clearing his throat grabs Ray's attention. His eyes snap up guiltily. Sure enough, Tommy is glaring right at him. *Ah.* He definitely just got caught ogling Jamie's ass.

Ray chases after Jamie, even though it means getting closer to Tommy.

"What about Tommy? Isn't he joining us?" Ray tries to smile at the man in question as he says it, the expression slightly forced due to Tommy's continued scowl.

Jamie checks the coffee cups, finding Tommy's and handing it to him. "He can eat after. Someone needs to watch the store while I'm on lunch break, you know."

Tommy takes the proffered drink, taking a large gulp of the surely too-hot liquid while maintaining eye contact with Ray. It seems that even Tommy's love of Ray as an actor can't save him from the "you hurt my baby brother and I'll end you" act, if the look in Tommy's eye is anything to go by.

Ray gulps. "Ahh, I see."

Then he's led to a staircase hidden at the back of the store, the two ascending into the Suwans' home.

It appears that this floor contains the shared spaces of the apartment; an entryway full of shoes and coats leading to a surprisingly spacious living room, doors to what appear to be a kitchen and a dining room at the back. The living room is decorated in such a way that it feels homely despite its size—trinkets on every surface, and a variety of family photos and artwork hung on the walls. Ray spots a particularly sweet family portrait, with what appears to be a tiny Tommy and an even tinier Jamie giggling on the laps of their smiling parents.

Adorable.

Ray follows Jamie through to the dining room, where an open doorway connects it to the kitchen. Jamie puts the bag of food down on the dining table.

"Please, have a seat!"

Jamie gestures sweetly to the mismatched chairs set around the table, each a different size and style. It should look chaotic and messy. Instead, Ray finds it... artful...

purposeful... eclectic in a way that speaks of comfort and home. He picks one at random, sitting down while Jamie grabs some plates and napkins—the civility a stark contrast from when Ray had found Jamie shoveling a sandwich, and almost the wrapper, too, into his mouth behind the counter last weekend. He really is on his best behavior today.

Ray takes their sandwiches out of the bag, strategically leaving the cake in there as a surprise for later, and hands Jamie's to him. Jamie thanks him and they dig in.

"So, um..." Ray starts when he's a couple of bites into his sandwich. "How's your day going?"

Jamie covers his mouth, cheeks full of bread as he tries to reply, eyes not leaving his food for even a millisecond. "Mm. Ish fime!" he says around a mouthful.

Ray chuckles at the murmured response, the man obviously focused on the meal. He decides not to ask any further questions, instead appreciating the companionable silence as they eat.

Once Jamie has eaten his sandwich and downed at least half of his coffee, he seems to realize how brief his response had been earlier. "Um, sorry, yeah..." He takes another sip of the coffee. "My day is going fine. Thank you for asking earlier. And yours?"

"Better now that I'm with you." Ray mentally cringes as soon as the words leave his mouth. It appears he's not the only one, Jamie's eye twitching.

Ray grimaces, feeling like he's messing everything up again. "Ew. That was—" Ray averts his gaze from the man sitting opposite him. "That was bad. Sorry." He lets out a nervous laugh.

"It's okay." Jamie's expression is soft when Ray's gaze meets his. "And hey, you're getting better at apologizing! You didn't even offer me hush money this time!" Jamie stands from the table with a smirk, collecting their plates.

Ray gawks, needing a moment to compose himself before he whines, "Hey! I apologized for that!"

Jamie chuckles at his childish tone. "Yes, and I forgave you. It's okay."

Ray nods, unsure where to take the conversation now that he's been reminded of his own awkwardness... until he remembers the surprise he'd brought with him.

"Hey, uhh... W-would you..." Ray stutters, Jamie strolling back to the table and looking at him inquisitively. Ray clears his throat and tries again. "Would you like some cake?"

He grabs the cake box from the bag, slowly opening it to reveal the snowman slices. Jamie's eyes glisten, cheeks turning the same soft pink color as his t-shirt.

"You brought me cake?"

"Mhm. Would you like some?"

Jamie is sitting back down at the table before Ray even finishes asking the question, and grabs himself a slice from the box with his hands. He places it in his palm, poking at the marshmallows with a smile.

"Ray, this is so cute!" He lifts it, getting one last look at the design on top before he takes a large bite out of it, a hand cupped under his mouth to catch the crumbs. "Mmmm!" Jamie hums around the chocolatey, marshmallowy goodness, his eyes fluttering closed. Ray watches, amused as the man opposite him devours the cake, his own slice still sitting in the box.

Then Jamie licks the crumbs from his fingers, his cute pink tongue sticking out between his luscious lips, and Ray decides that now is probably a good time to stop watching him and eat. He picks up his cake and breaks off a third of it, offering it to Jamie. "Here."

Jamie's eyes widen, blinking a few times. "Are you sure?" Jamie asks shyly, even as his hand begins to reach for the cake.

Ray nods, moving his own hand closer to meet him halfway, placing it in his palm.

Jamie beams, eyes darting between the cake and Ray. "Thank you, Ray!"

Ray is quickly finding that food is the way to this boy's heart.

- · ✽ · -

Ray and Jamie tread back down the stairs half an hour later, Jamie coming to stand next to Tommy behind the counter. Tommy watches as Ray strolls to the door, the man turning back every few seconds to get another look at his brother. The celebrity trips on his own feet as he walks backwards out of the store, refusing to take his eyes off of Jamie until he's stumbling onto the pavement after saying goodbye.

Tommy finds it ridiculous. But also... a tiny bit endearing.

Once Ray is fully out of sight, he turns to Jamie, finding him smiling demurely. He needs to know... "What did he do that's got you so sweet?"

His brother sniffs defensively, eyes turned down in feigned indifference. "Nothing."

Tommy raises an eyebrow.

"Well... We had lunch." Jamie's eyes flitter shyly about the store, a gentle blush crawling up his cheeks.

"Yes, I am aware you had lunch. And...?" Surely a sandwich and a coffee isn't enough to win over his baby brother.

"And..." Jamie fiddles with a loose thread on the sleeve of his cardigan, quietly admitting, "he bought me cake."

Ah, that'll do it.

Tommy huffs, standing and walking around Jamie to go eat his own lunch. "Is there any cake left for me?"

Jamie's sheepish look is all the answer he needs. Tommy nods in understanding.

"I caught him checking out your ass earlier, by the way."

"TOMMY!" Jamie shrieks.

Tommy holds his hands up in surrender, heading towards the stairs to go enjoy his own lonely lunch. "Hey, I'm just letting you know that all the time you spent planning your outfit was worth it."

- • ☆ • -

That evening, Jamie lies in bed, scrolling aimlessly through social media as he thinks about his interactions with Ray—both today and over the past week.

Jamie had thought Ray was an asshole. That he was mean and rude, acting out when there weren't any cameras around just because he could get away with it. He sees now that he'd been wrong. Ray is... He's nice. He's kind.

And he's now been into the bookstore five times since arriving in town and only purchased one book—one that Jamie had pushed into his hands.

Jamie finds himself typing Ray's name into Instagram before he can stop himself. He had stopped following him online after their unfortunate meeting.

He taps the "follow" button, then takes a look at Ray's most recent post. It's a photo of a book, *Apologies for Dummies*, shot sort of artfully on a wooden table next to a piece of cake. The caption is short—"I've found that apologies go well with cake."

Jamie likes the photo, just as a notification pops up at the top of his screen.

[@rrawatamarin followed you back]

He sucks in a breath, closing the app to send Win a text.

Jem
I think you might be right.

"I like pink."
PART 3

Saturday, December 17th

Jamie has been lying in bed, staring at an empty chat box, for the best part of an hour. He's been contemplating sending Ray a message on Instagram—they are mutuals now, after all—but...

What should he say?

Should he say anything at all?

It all feels so pressured—especially with the blue check mark next to Ray's name. Jamie can't stop looking at it. It feels like proof that they are from different worlds, that it is merely coincidence that they occupy the same space right now.

He can't just drop a DM to a *celebrity*.

With a frustrated sigh, Jamie puts down his phone and gets out of bed to start the day. He's got things to do today—he doesn't have time to let himself be tormented by a tiny blue check mark!

- · ★ ·

Ray lounges on the couch, his second bowl of cereal balanced precariously next to him on a cushion. Typically he eats breakfast at the table with his parents, but he's up later than usual and they've already gone out for the morning.

Spooning some more cereal into his mouth, Ray checks his DMs for what must be the millionth time today. It's only ten thirty in the morning, but it feels like the hours are dragging by torturously slowly.

He had been so excited when he noticed @jemmmsuwan follow him last night. It was only by sheer luck that he'd even spotted it—he just so happened to refresh his notifications at the right time to catch a flash of the name. But it was the small profile picture of Jamie's face that had actually confirmed it for Ray, that this @jemmmsuwan guy was *his* Jamie, from just how strikingly beautiful he was in it. It was a black and white shot, his face at a forty-five-degree angle to the camera, the black of his outfit and background making his skin glow ethereally.

Ray wanted to see more, learn more, absorb more about the man. He had tapped onto his profile to find that, although it was public, there was very little there; a couple of pictures of the bookstore and family, and some of his cat. There were no more pretty photos of the pretty boy in the profile picture. But Ray appreciated what he could learn from the other images. They showed a boy with a strong connection to his family, who loved to play with his grumpy cat and read books in his free time.

Of course, Ray had followed Jamie back, just as Jamie liked his most recent post. He'd known that going back to the café and grabbing another piece of cake for that photo had been a good idea.

And since then, he's been waiting...

Ray's staring competition with his phone is interrupted when the house phone rings. He stumbles across the living room to answer it—knowing that if it's a neighbor and he ignores it, they're likely to turn up on the doorstep minutes later to discuss whatever they wanted to discuss. Ray would rather be awkward over the phone than face-to-face, thank you.

"Hello?"

Pim's slightly panicked voice sounds through the speaker, "Ah, Ray! Is Ma there? Or Pa? I've been called into work and I need someone to watch Praew. Dan has meetings, otherwise he could take her to the office..."

"Ah, no. They're in meeting at the town hall until twelve—Christmas Eve festivities planning. But I could watch her? Ray asks almost excitedly. He loves spending time with his niece.

"Are you sure?"

"Yes! It can be an Uncle Wawa Day! Bring her over!"

"I'll be there in ten." She hangs up before Ray has a chance to say goodbye.

He busies himself clearing up his bowl and coffee mug from the living room, washing and drying them before the doorbell rings.

Praew skips up to him in her Snow White dress as soon as the door is open, her backpack jostling with the movement, and wraps her arms around his middle. "Wawa!" The endearing nickname always turns Ray to mush. He pats her head lovingly.

"Thanks, Little Bro. You're a lifesaver," Pim says from the doorway, already turning to leave, obviously in a hurry. "I'll pick her up at six!"

Ray and Praew stand at the door and wave as Pim drives away.

"So..." Ray turns to Praew, grinning conspiratorially. "Would you like some cake?"

Cake eaten—Ray snatching one of the marshmallows from the top before Praew could eat the whole thing by herself—Praew requests that they go to the park. It seems that the park is their thing. Whenever Ray is home, that's where Praew wants to go with him. Maybe it's her way of showing off her cool *Uncle Wawa*.

Ray dutifully agrees to it, making sure she's bundled up in a coat, hat, and gloves before they set off. As soon as they're past the park gate, Praew is off—running over to climb up to the top of the tallest slide. Ray watches, keeping an eye on her as she goes down the slide and climbs back up again and again.

When she tires of that, Ray offers to push her on the swings. He swings her gently, not wanting to accidentally fling her off of it—he really can't trust his own limbs enough to push her properly. Praew grumbles, pushing her legs to try and get herself to go higher. Seeing her little legs kicking out, so uncoordinated despite her concentration, makes Ray chuckle. At least he's not the only one with uncooperative limbs in their family anymore.

Ray loses track of time and suddenly they've been playing for over two hours. He's exhausted. Praew seems as energetic as ever, still running about, jumping and climbing on everything. But Ray needs coffee. And despite Praew's currently cheery demeanor, Ray knows it's technically already past her lunchtime and she must be hungry.

They head to Sunshine Café on Main Street—Ray ordering a coffee and a salad for himself, and a sandwich and a hot chocolate for Praew. Praew's eyes widen with glee when the hot chocolate is brought to the table, piled high with whipped cream and marshmallows. Ray only manages to take a single photo to send to Pim before Praew is digging in with a spoon, taking large scoops out of the cream and marshmallows while waiting for the liquid beneath to cool.

Ray's voice is fond as he chastises, "Make sure to eat your food too, okay?"

"Yes, Uncle Wawa," she drawls.

After their late lunch, Ray drags Praew over to Honeybun Bookstore. She had refused to go at first, saying she wanted to go home and watch television instead. No matter what Ray offered—toys, more time at the park later, another hot chocolate—nothing could win her over. Eventually he'd had to let her in on his little secret; that there was a boy. A boy that he liked. A boy called Jamie. After that, she agreed immediately.

When he enters Honeybun Bookstore, he can't help but be disappointed. There is no sign of Jamie—only Tommy speaking with a customer next to a shelf of comics and an older gentleman manning the cash register.

Realizing the older man must be Jamie's father, based on both the fact that it's a family-run business and the quite frankly striking resemblance, Ray freezes. He feels like this is a big moment; meeting the father of the guy he's *mildly* infatuated with. Ray's grip on Praew's hand tightens enough for her to complain, trying to wriggle her fingers out of his grasp.

The man looks up, pushing his round glasses up his nose with one finger in the center, to get a better look at who is standing stock-still in the doorway of his store.

"Oh. Ray," he says, calmly walking out from behind the counter.

As the gentleman approaches, Ray realizes he's shorter than he initially thought—even quite a bit shorter than Jamie. Ray wishes he could shrink himself at this moment, just to feel slightly less obnoxiously tall in front of him, but Jamie's dad doesn't look at all perturbed by Ray's height.

The shorter man extends a hand. Ray shakes it, noting how smooth and delicate the man's hands are. They might even be softer than Apple's. If their hands are this soft, how soft must Jamie's hands be? Holding them must be like holding a cloud, Ray reckons.

"I'm Banlue," the man says.

"Ah! Nice to m-meet you!" Ray tries to not let his nerves get to him. "I'm Ray, as you know, and this is Praew!" Ray lets go of Banlue's hand to gesture to the little girl beside him.

Banlue's eyes look like they're going to pop out of his head, flitting between the girl and Ray. "Is she....?"

OH.

Oh god, Ray really isn't making the best first impression.

"Ah, no, she's my sister's!" he's quick to say, Praew's large, doe eyes simply watching as Ray's awkwardness unfolds.

Banlue nods. He looks neither pleased nor dissatisfied with this development, his expression completely neutral as he says, "You're here for Jamie, yes?"

Ray feels heat rise in his cheeks at Banlue's bluntness.

"Y-yes. Is he around?"

"He's out at the moment, I'm afraid. He probably won't be back until nearly closing time, I reckon, if you want to come back later."

Three o'clock now... Store closes at five... Can he keep Praew out of the house for another two hours without her getting cranky? He hopes so.

"Th-thank you, I will."

The bell above the door jingles as Ray leaves the store, pulling Praew along with him.

Ray suggests to Praew that they go to the toy store a few doors down, knowing it will at least keep her entertained for a while. She agrees—seeming keen to help out her uncle in his mission and being much more willing to hang out around town than she was earlier.

She picks up and plays with almost every toy she can get her hands on—anything from dolls to toy guns to plushies. The whole time, she won't stop asking Ray questions: "What is Jamie like?" "How did you meet him?" "Does he like you, too?"

Ray struggles to know the right way to answer—not even having a concrete answer to that last question himself. Sure, he suspects Jamie likes him a little, but he doesn't know for certain. And how to explain how they met... He knows that if he tells Praew anything juicy, she'll probably tell her mom and her aunt, and then Ray will never hear the end of it. But still, after Praew pats his hand reassuringly when he looks too nervous to answer, he tells her. He tells her how much of a fool he'd made of himself, how silly he'd felt, all because the boy behind the counter was just too pretty. Praew giggles at her uncle's antics, claiming the whole thing to be very romantic.

Somehow, they don't end up buying anything despite spending over an hour in the toy store. Ray suspects that Praew is aware that her relatives have already bought her half of the store's stock for Christmas anyway, judging by the way she smiles despite coming away empty-handed.

Knowing it's not quite time to head back to the bookstore yet, Ray and Praew stroll further down the street. The two of them marvel at the Christmas lights lining the streets as they switch on, the sun beginning to set enough for them to glow.

They busy themselves with window shopping for a while, Praew pointing to all of the things she wants to buy when she gets her allowance. She even points some things out for Ray, including a rather fetching bright pink scarf that she seems to think will suit him.

Ray can't help it—he's weak for her little, toothy smile—going into the store and buying the scarf without a second thought. He even asks the sales assistant to remove the tag so he can put it on right away, not caring at all that it doesn't match his outfit when Praew beams up at him with joy.

They walk a little more, Ray in his new, *ultra-fashionable accessory*, but he's starting to get antsy. He wants to head back. Surely it's approaching five o'clock now.

Ray gets his phone out to check the time. "We should start heading back now, Praew, so we can see Ja—"

Not looking where he's going, he collides with someone walking in the opposite direction. The two bounce off each other, both stumbling backwards a step with an "oof," but neither falling over, luckily. Ray at least has the wherewithal to check that Praew hasn't been caught in the collision, too, the little girl standing next to him completely unfazed, before he turns to the person he has bumped into.

"So sorry about that... J-JAMIE?" Ray's eyes widen, mortified to have slammed into the boy he likes.

"Ray! Ah..." Jamie blinks, regaining his composure. His eyes land on the little girl beside Ray.

"She's not mine!" Ray blurts out, still flustered.

Jamie arches an eyebrow at him before leaning down to talk to Praew, smiling when he spots the princess dress sticking out from under her coat. "Hi! My name is Jamie. What's yours, little princess?"

"I'm Praew! Wawa is my uncle." She grins as she says Ray's nickname.

Jamie glances up at Ray, mouthing the word, "*Wawa?*"

Ray goes red in embarrassment, this whole situation definitely not compatible with his cool image. But then again, Jamie has already seen plenty of his awkward, uncool side. Plus, he's currently wearing a neon pink polyester scarf over a Gucci coat—he's fairly sure he is in no position to feel embarrassed about something as simple as a cute nickname.

"Well, it's nice to meet you, Praew." Jamie smiles at the girl.

"Are you the Jemmie that Wawa keeps talking about?" She asks, as if she wasn't the one coaxing information about Jamie out of her uncle only minutes ago.

Jamie's gaze flicks up to Ray's for a second, a smile playing on his lips as if he's pleased that Ray talks about him. But maybe Ray is just reading too much into it.

Praew, it appears, isn't quite done embarrassing her uncle. "You work in the bookstore, don't you? Wawa went in there earlier looking for y—"

"HAHAHA!" Ray laughs loudly, cutting his niece off. "I think that's quite enough now, Praew." He grips her hand tighter, pulling her closer until she's behind him, as if that will somehow stop her from talking.

"Oh, did he?" Jamie practically purrs, straightening up to look at Ray as directly as he can with his shorter stature. His eyes are half-lidded, playful and teasing in a way Ray doesn't expect. Ray looks away from Jamie nervously, now blushing up to the tips of his ears under the intensity of his gaze.

Jamie clears his throat, his voice taking on a light-hearted tone as he addresses Praew again, "Well, you've found me now! How about we walk back to the bookstore together, hm? I'll even let you pick out a book if you like, since you're such a cutie."

Praew nods, beaming up at him. Jamie reaches down, looking like he intends to squish her cheeks, when he suddenly finds small, glove-clad fingers wrapping around his own. His motion falters.

She adjusts her grip on Jamie's hand, turning in the direction of Honeybun Bookstore. "I will walk with you, Jemmie."

A smile spreads on Jamie's face and Ray watches the whole exchange with conflicting emotions—betrayed by how quickly Praew had ratted him out, but so blessed when he finds out that the prettiest boy he's ever seen somehow gets even prettier when he smiles *like that*. The grin on Jamie's face as he looks at Praew is all warmth and openness; an honesty in it that is so endearing and wonderful, Ray can barely breathe. He doesn't know if he could survive if Jamie ever made that expression at him, but he wants to find out.

It takes Ray a full ten seconds to realize that they're leaving him behind, gallivanting off without him and chattering excitedly. Jamie is holding Praew's hand securely, swinging it slightly as they walk, and smiling at her like she's the most important person in the world.

Ray knows it would be weird to be jealous of his niece.

He knows that.

He is not jealous. But...

It should be *him* holding the pretty boy's hand.

He tries not to think about it too much as he races to catch up with them. "Hey! Wait for Uncle Wawa!"

"Well, I was practicing for the Christmas Eve concert!" Jamie answers Praew's query about where he'd been earlier today as they enter the bookstore, now devoid of customers and Tommy, the bell jingling above the door as it's pushed open. Jamie lets go of the door once he and Praew are safely through, leaving it to nearly smack Ray in the face as he trails after them.

"Woah! Are you in the choir?" The seven-year-old's eyes light up.

Jamie glances up to his dad at the counter, greeting him briefly and letting him know he'll close up, before turning his attention back to Praew. "Yup! And this year I'm even singing a solo!"

Praew gasps in awe. Her eyes take on an almost pleading look, eyebrows drawn together as she asks quietly, gripping one of Jamie's hands with both of her tiny ones, "Aren't you nervous? I could never sing solo like that!"

"Never?" Jamie's eyebrows raise.

Praew shakes her head. "Never! I'd be too scared!" She lowers her head, pressing her nose to Jamie's hand, clearly comfortable around him already. Her voice is so muffled against his skin when she speaks again that Ray only just makes out the words. "I have to be in the Nativity performance this year... I don't want to do it."

Jamie sighs, nodding as he crouches down to be eye-level with her, a hand on her shoulder encouraging her to stand up straighter and look at him. He smiles, his eyes sparkling. "Shall I tell you a secret?"

Praew leans in, focused solely on him.

"I get *sooo* scared before performing." He draws out the "o" in "so," lips pulled into a pout at the exaggeration. "But I just try to think about the people in the audience who are rooting for me—my mama, my papa, and my brother. They will love me no matter what happens; whether I sing the wrong note, or get the words muddled, or whatever. I know that they'll give me a big hug afterwards and everything will be okay."

Ray watches on affectionately as Jamie's lips curve upward into a reassuring expression, gaze soft on the young girl in front of him.

Praew blinks, a small smile slowly spreading across her face. "Can I root for you too, Jemmie?"

"Of course!" Jamie responds cheerfully and then Praew throws herself at him, wrapping him up in the biggest hug her small body can manage. It takes Jamie a moment to return the gesture, patting her back as she clings to him.

Ray is almost glad he'd not been involved in this conversation. Jamie had spoken so eloquently, talking at Praew's level without being condescending, and had offered such wise words of advice. Ray knows he definitely wouldn't have handled that situation so well.

"Come on." Jamie pats Praew's back a bit more firmly. "Let's see if you can find a book you'd like."

Directed by a point from Jamie, Praew bounds across to the kids section. Ray watches her go, expecting Jamie to run after her. Instead, he joins Ray, standing by his side.

"Hey... I'm sorry about stealing your niece." Jamie sounds a little shy, voice remaining mellow like how it was when he was talking to Praew. He's never spoken to Ray with quite that sweet of a tone before.

"I-i-it's okay. Praew seems to l-like you," Ray stutters out.

Jamie hums. "She's a cute kid."

Ray looks at Jamie out of the corner of his eye—finding him gazing fondly in Praew's direction. He's playing with his bangs, twirling the strands around his fingers, head tilted to one side like he's daydreaming. He's so pretty, Ray loses the power of speech, simply responding with a hum. "Mmm."

"Jemmie! What about this one?" she calls over to Jamie, holding up a colorful little book.

Jamie moves to rest his hand on Ray's back, steering them both towards Praew. Ray realizes this is the first time they've touched (if you don't count physically bumping into each other earlier, which Ray would rather forget about). His breath catches.

"Let's have a look, shall we?" Jamie smiles at Praew, his hand remaining on Ray until he moves to grab the book from the little girl's hands. There is an illustration of a princess on the front, and Jamie beams when he recognizes it. "Oooh, good choice! I liked this one!"

Praew looks up at him, surprised. "You've read this?"

"Of course! I love princesses."

Praew bounces on the spot, clearly thrilled at this discovery. "Really, Jemmie? Who's your favorite?"

"Hmm..." Jamie tilts his head in thought. "Probably Belle! She has so many books!"

"She's my favorite, too!"

Ray butts in, "Isn't your favorite Snow White, Praew? You have the doll and everything. Plus..." He gestures to the Snow White costume she's been wearing all day.

Praew rolls her eyes at him. "Well, yeah, she *was* my favorite. But now my favorite is Jemmie's favorite!"

Jamie coos at her, the young girl wrapping her arms around his waist while giving her uncle the stick eye. "Uncle Wawa is no fun—he only likes books about animals."

Ray's offended expression makes Jamie chuckle, but only for a moment. "Hey," Jamie placates, "animals can be cool!" Whether he thinks that or if he's saying it to be nice, Ray can't be sure.

Praew rests her chin on Jamie's tummy, big eyes looking up at him through long eyelashes.

"Yeah," she pouts, "but Wawa only likes dogs. I like cats!"

"I like cats, too!"

Praew's eyes sparkle up at him. "Really, Jemmie?"

"Would I have a pet cat if I didn't like cats?"

Praew gasps, a grin overtaking her features.

Ray finds himself mentally counting the number of times Praew has gasped at him in such awe—maybe three or four times ever—and begins to worry that Jamie is catching up to his score dangerously quickly.

Ten minutes later, Praew has finally decided on a book and they're ready to leave. Jamie walks her to the door, Ray once again trailing after them. She'd been torn between two books—the one about princesses and one about horses that looked very cute. Eventually Jamie had caved somewhat, saying she could take one of them now and he would give her the other for Christmas.

Ray hadn't been able to say anything to Jamie about it other than "You don't have to" and "Thank you," an odd lump forming in his throat at Jamie's sweetness.

"You'll really give me a Christmas present, Jemmie?" Praew asks as they get to the door, smiling up at Jamie who nods happily back at her. Then, finally, she separates herself from Jamie's side, going to grab Ray's hand for the first time since they'd run into him.

"Uncle Wawa," she shout-whispers, "we'll have to get something for Jemmie too, 'kay?"

Ray's cheeks must be scarlet. He feels like he's on fire with shyness and embarrassment at being put on the spot like this, his niece leaving little space for him to say no. Not that he wants to say no! But what do you buy for a guy you've only really known for a few days? Ray struggles enough buying gifts for people he's known his whole life! But for this boy? Well... he'll try.

"Mhm. Of course."

Jamie chuckles, waving at them as Ray opens the door, a small carrier bag containing Praew's book slung around his wrist.

"Bye-bye, Jemmie!" Praew waves a small hand at him.

"Bye-bye! See you soon!" Jamie sing-songs back cutely.

It will be a couple more hours before Ray looks in the bag and finds the note Jamie had slipped in there, written neatly on a piece of receipt paper:

> Here's my number.
>
> Text me next time you're bringing Praew to the bookstore so I can have her gift ready ☺
>
> -J.

Sunday, December 18th

Jamie wakes groggily from a night of tossing and turning. He'd kept himself up worrying about whether giving Ray his number was the right thing to do. Perhaps Ray would find it silly—they already had each other's Instagrams, surely that was enough for them to contact each other if needed. He didn't *have* to give Ray his phone number.

But that blue tick next to his name...

The contact information for his manager in his bio...

Ray's Instagram account was clearly for business, not... whatever this is.

Phone numbers are neutral ground; no follower counts or verification ticks, just a string of innocuous numbers forming a direct connection between the two of them.

Now he just has to wait.

At least Jamie makes it one step out of his room before the questioning begins, Tommy leaning against the wall by his bedroom door. "So... Ray was here again yesterday..." He raises one eyebrow suggestively.

Jamie tries his best to maintain his composure, fighting off the smile that threatens to appear at the mention of Ray's name.

"Yes. He was." He walks past his brother, heading for the bathroom.

Tommy presses, "And....?"

Standing in the bathroom doorway, Jamie contemplates his options. He could:
1) Gush about Ray and tell his brother every detail.
2) Give him a brief response—something short, but enough to stop him from asking again.
3) Just slam the door shut and avoid the question.

He takes a deep breath, settling on what he wants to say. "And... it was nice."

Tommy nods. Jamie closes the bathroom door.

The questioning resumes once he's out of the bathroom, dressed in some sweatpants and a comfy hoodie, as he makes his way to the kitchen.

"Morning, Sweetie," Apple greets him, busy pouring more pancake batter into a pan. There's a decent stack of them already piled on a plate next to the stove.

"Morning, Mama." Jamie presses a kiss to her cheek as he passes her, going to the fridge for some juice.

"Did you have a nice time with Ray yesterday?"

It is no surprise that she knows he had been with Ray yesterday—his parents tell each other everything.

Jamie always feels better opening up to his mom or dad than his brother—not that he doesn't get along with Tommy, they just... Their relationship isn't like that. There's an unspoken agreement between them not to get involved in each other's business. Sure, they sometimes tease each other about crushes or potential partners, but they never speak about that kind of thing seriously.

"I did, Mama. And I got to meet his niece! I'm sure she's been into the store before with her parents, but it was nice to get to know her a bit more through Ray, you know?"

Apple fixes him with a knowing smile.

Jamie eyes her curiously. "What?"

"Nothing, Dear. You just seem very comfortable with him, is all."

Trying to work out where she's going with this, Jamie just stares at her, blinking repeatedly.

"You didn't seem so fond of him when he first got into town." She returns her attention to the pancake, flipping it. "A lot has changed in a week, hasn't it?"

Jamie opens the carton of orange juice he's been holding onto, pouring himself a glass while he mulls over her words. "I... I may have been wrong about him—about what he's like."

Apple smiles. "Don't I always tell you that people deserve a second chance? 'Don't judge a book by its cover' and all that?"

Sipping the juice, he hums in agreement.

"Do you think you'll be seeing him again?" Her expression seems soft and hopeful as she asks.

Jamie considers her question, lips pouting against the edge of his glass. He has been enjoying hanging out with Ray lately...

His phone vibrates in his pocket with a new message. He checks it, finding a text from a number he isn't familiar with.

???

Hey Jamie, it's Ray. This is my number :D Thank you for yesterday x I hope you have a wonderful day today <3

Jamie feels himself blushing. He locks his phone and shoves it back into his pocket.

"Yes. I think so."

Apple nods, and then the two of them make their way to the table for breakfast.

- · ★ · -

It's mid-afternoon and Ray is watching television with his parents.

Well, his parents are watching television. Ray is watching his phone—glaring at its black screen where it sits silent on the coffee table. He can't stop his leg from bouncing, a mixture of anxiety and impatience running through his veins.

Ever since he sent that text this morning, he's been waiting for a response. He even switched his phone onto "Do Not Disturb," setting only two contacts as the exceptions: his manager and Jamie. Ray wants to be able to reply immediately when his phone dings.

If it ever dings.

Ray brings his feet up onto the couch, pulling his knees tight to his chest. He sighs.

Why won't it ding?

- • ☆ • -

After a long day of studying for his final exams of the semester, Jamie is relaxing on the couch with his dad. Jamie takes up most of the seat; lounging sideways with his legs dangling over the armrest, his back resting against his father. August, Jamie's cat, is curled up in his lap, trying to sleep despite Jamie bothering him constantly. There's some reality show on the television with some people singing—Jamie isn't quite sure what it is, he isn't watching. He's too busy staring at the text message from Ray that he still hasn't answered.

Ray
Hey Jamie, it's Ray. This is my number :D Thank you for yesterday x I hope you have a wonderful day today <3

Does it really need a response? It's not like Ray had asked a question.

So he could just leave it.

He could...

Jem [draft]
I

Jamie starts typing out a message.

Jem [draft]
Hey :D no worries!
My day was good, how
was yours?

Nope, too eager.

Jem [draft]
np. yeah it was fine.

No, too rude.
...Aha! He snaps a quick photo of August.

Jem
[Jem sent a photo]

Jem
I've got a cat in my lap.
I'd say that makes today a wonderful
day.

His dad shifts behind him. "So, this, uhh... This Ray guy..."

Jamie locks his phone on instinct, despite knowing that his dad respects his privacy too much to snoop—it's just coincidence that he's asking this now.

"You like him?"

He loves his dad. He's not always the best with words, but he always means well and finds a way to get his point across. It puts Jamie at ease.

"Mhm. Yes. I do." Jamie shuffles around a bit, turning so he can actually watch the television now that he's done looking at his phone, careful not to disturb August.

"Like him? Or... *like* like him?" His dad's eyes are wide when he asks, as if he's surprised at the words coming out of his own mouth.

"Hmm... Like like, I think."

"Okay. Cool," his dad says, nodding before he returns his attention to the television.

Jamie's phone buzzes, the screen lighting up with an incoming message.

Ray
meow ฅ^•ᴥ•^ฅ

How Ray could ever call himself cool is completely beyond Jamie's comprehension.

Monday, December 19th

Jamie wakes up to a new message on his phone.

> **Ray**
> Good morning :D

He types a quick "good morning" back before he gets up to get ready for college.

Jamie knows it's rude to get his phone out at the table, but all of his manners fly out the window when his phone buzzes with an incoming text halfway through breakfast.

> **Ray**
> I hope class is good today x

Ray remembers that he has college today?

> **Jem**
> Thank you! It's all exams and revision now though :(
> What are you up to today?

Ray
Ohh good luck!
And I'm not sure yet!
Maybe some shopping.

Jem
Have fun for me.

Ray
Will do <3

After his first exam of the day, now in the middle of a revision class, the next message arrives.

Ray
What's your favorite color?

Jamie ignores it for the time being, sliding his phone into his bag so he can stop staring at it and instead pay attention to his professor. He's pretty sure he needs to know this information for his exam this afternoon.

When Jamie sits down in the cafeteria alone, with no sign of Win yet, he decides to check his phone. He finds there are a few new messages.

Ray
My favorite color is black.

Ray
Or white

Ray
They're both nice!

At this point, Jamie knows for sure that Ray isn't afraid of being a double-texter. Or a quadruple-texter, in this case.

Jamie tries to think about the best way to answer Ray's messages...

He could be honest. He *wants* to be honest. But he feels vulnerable. People mocked him as a child whenever he answered that question truthfully.

He doesn't want to lie—pretend his favorite color is something safe like blue or brown—or just say something like "Me too!" to avoid properly answering.

So lost in thought, he doesn't notice Win approaching until the man speaks, head plopping down onto Jamie's shoulder.

"Ray!? No way! You scored his number already?"

"Actually, I gave him my number so we could organize a time for me to give his niece a Christmas present."

One of Win's eyebrows raises incredulously. "Can you even hear yourself right now?" Win moves to sit in the chair next to Jamie, haphazardly dropping his backpack onto the table.

"You've met the man, what, five times? And now you're getting his niece a Christmas present?" He sits back in his chair, looking awed. "Man, you guys are moving fast."

Jamie groans. He definitely needs to fill Win in on the events of the weekend. His lunch will have to wait.

"So, yeah, I gave him my number."

"And he's just been, like... texting you? About non-Praew related things? Since when?"

"Since yesterday," Jamie replies before finally being able to take a bite of his now cold pasta since he's caught Win up on the Ray situation.

"That's amazing! I told you that he likes you!" Win is radiating joy for Jamie, eyes sparkling and grin wide. The grin on Jamie's face, however, is fading fast.

"But... I don't know how long he's in town for. What happens when he goes back to New York?"

Win, probably sensing Jamie's unease, tamps down his own smile. He rests a hand on Jamie's shoulder, rubbing in soothing circles. His expression has taken on that edge of seriousness he very rarely shows.

"Don't think about that, Jem. Just enjoy it. Either that or..." Win's gaze breaks from his for a second, the boy sighing. "Or maybe break things off before it gets too serious. I don't want to see you get hurt, okay?"

Swallowing down both his food and the lump in his throat, all Jamie can do is nod.

It takes Jamie until he's on the bus home, looking out of the window at the dark sky, to come to a decision. He opens his text chat with Ray, the same messages as earlier still looking back at him.

Ray
What's your favorite color?

Ray
My favorite color is black.

Ray
Or white

Ray
They're both nice!

Jamie types out his response.

Jem
I like pink.

Pink has been Jamie's favorite color for as long as he can remember. To him, the color feels like a hug; soft and warm and comforting. It's the blush rising on someone's cheeks when the right person says something sweet. It's the petals of a flower, plucking "he loves me, he loves me not" and ending in a positive. It both calms him and sets his heart racing. That is what pink has always been to him.

But now, a new image pops into his head, joining the rest. What is pink?

Pink is an ugly scarf wrapped around the neck of the boy he's falling for.

Ray
Pink is pretty.

Ray
It suits you.

Jamie's heart has been set ablaze.

Tuesday, December 20th

The texting continues much the same—exchanging "good morning"s and "what are you up to"s—until a rather curious message from Ray around midday.

Ray
What time do you get back today?

Jem
My last exam finishes at 3 (woohoo!) and the bus gets me back into town just before 4.

Jem
Why?

Ray
...no reason.

Jamie is suspicious.

His suspicions are proved correct when the bus pulls up to his stop and there is a well-styled Ray leaning against a nearby wall, looking weirdly attractive considering he's wearing that hideous pink scarf again and an ugly Christmas sweater. This ugly sweater doesn't just have a simple pattern worked in with the yarn, but also 3D accessories—pom-poms sticking out from it to make comically large snowflakes in a wintery image. It looks odd to see a designer coat over the top of such a kitsch item.

Jamie thanks the bus driver before walking over to Ray. He knows Ray has seen him—he'd seen the man catch his eye through the bus window, posture then shifting into an illusion of casualness. Ray is clearly trying to act cool, eyes smoldering into the middle distance in the opposite direction to Jamie.

"Hey," Jamie greets. He tries to not let himself feel self-conscious; dressed as he is in a rather bland outfit of jeans and a hoodie, since he hadn't been expecting to see Ray today and had wanted to be comfortable for his exams. It's ridiculous that he feels concerned about his appearance at all, really. (Again, Ray is in a *very* ugly Christmas sweater.)

"H-hey!" Ray jumps up from his pose, taking a few steps towards Jamie. The way Ray's hands shift in his coat pockets, almost like he's reaching out before he stops himself...

Was he going in for a hug?

"How did your last exam go?"

Jamie allows himself a small smile as he breathes out a sigh of relief. "I think it went okay, thank you for asking."

Ray nods. "Good, good..."

Then Ray looks nervous, speaking up again, "Do you, uhh... maybe wanna grab a drink from the café?" He points a thumb back over his shoulder in the direction of Sunshine Café, as if Jamie isn't as familiar with the area as he is.

Jamie doesn't fight it when his smile widens.

"Sure."

- · ★ · -

After Ray pays for their drinks—insisting he owes Jamie after how kind he'd been to his niece—they make their way to an empty table by the window.

The way Jamie strolls to this particular table at the front of the café with such surety, not really looking where he's going yet somehow avoiding bumping into anything, suggests that this is a spot he frequents. Jamie even checks to see whether a folded-up menu is still under one of the legs, clearly there to stop it from wobbling, before taking a seat. Ray sits down opposite him, the two men now just looking at each other.

Ray's hands begin to sweat where they rest against his thighs, mouth gone dry. He'd been the one to orchestrate this whole meeting, but now he feels nervous. He had intended for it to be a date, but he hadn't actually *said* the word "date." For all he knows, Jamie could think that this is just two friends hanging out. And that's fine, it really is. But Ray *really* wants this to be a date.

Why do I keep going about everything the wrong way?

"...Ray?"

Snapping his gaze to Jamie's, he notices the boy is eyeing him with a concerned expression.

"Hm?" Ray inquires.

"I was asking if you're alright. You're looking a bit pale."

"Ah! No, I'm good. I was just thinking. Nothing serious, don't worry." He flashes his signature smile, hoping that will be enough to ease Jamie's mind.

Jamie's eyes narrow. "Hm, okay. If you say so."

Ray nods, shifting in his seat to try and escape the butterflies fluttering in his stomach. "And how are you?"

"I'm good," the younger man replies, an awkward silence hanging between them.

It's a relief when their drinks arrive, the pair now at least having something to focus on.

Jamie's hot chocolate looks even more impressive than the one Praew had gotten. There's a candy cane looped onto the edge of the mug, and along with the customary marshmallows atop the whipped cream, it also has a sprinkling of chocolate shavings. Jamie's eyes light up at the sight.

Ray looks up to the server delivering the drinks to say thanks, just to see them winking back at him with a smirk. It seems that even the server is aware that they're on a date. Ray can only hope Jamie knows, too.

The way Jamie is wriggling in his seat, eyes fixed on the drink in front of him, shows how keen he is to start drinking it. He touches his finger to the outside of the mug, trying to ascertain the temperature, before he pulls the digit away sharply.

Jamie plucks the candy cane from the mug with a sigh, slipping it into his mouth as he gazes out at the street.

Ray should probably try to talk to him instead of just staring.

"So, um..." Ray starts. Jamie's eyes meet his, his lips still wrapped around the mint candy cane. It's so cute that it takes Ray a moment to continue, "You moved into Ammersfield a couple of years ago, right? What brought you here, if you don't mind me asking? It's rare to see new faces in a town like this."

"Mm." Jamie removes the candy from his mouth. "Before coming here, we had to move a lot because of my father's work. Usually a new city every couple of years. Sometimes it was smaller towns, but more often than not it was wherever the big business was."

He stops for a moment, sucking on the candy cane as if in thought. "Papa's job paid well. It had meant that Mama didn't have to work while we were growing up—that she could focus on raising us. That had been her dream."

Ray nods in acknowledgement. He remembers his own childhood; walking home with his sisters after school, the house always being empty when they arrived. His parents had owned a hardware store on the other side of town and were rarely home before six PM. He thinks it must have been nice to come home to a parent's affections.

"But with Papa getting older... Well, something had to give." Jamie takes a sip of his hot chocolate, though it's probably still not cool enough for him to drink comfortably if the way he winces is any indication.

"Papa was getting sick a lot from the stress. So he and Mama agreed, the next time we moved would be the last time—no more bouncing from town to town. Mama started looking for some sort of business we could take over as a family, something with an apartment nearby, and found that." Pointing with the candy cane, he gestures to Honeybun Bookstore across the street before smiling at Ray. "We moved in three months later."

"You really like it here, huh?" Ray can't help but ask, given how sincere and happy Jamie seems. It's not that he doesn't like his hometown—he loves it, in fact—but he knows how different it is from city life.

Jamie smiles into his mug, one finger rubbing at the porcelain. "Mhm. This is the first place that has truly felt like home."

Ray watches his smile falter.

"But it was so lonely, Ray. All those years... Every time Tommy and I finally began to get comfortable, it felt like it was time to move again." Jamie's eyebrows furrow. Ray wishes he could reach across the table and smooth them out with his thumb, the boy's eyes glazing over forlornly. "I don't know how to make myself believe that this is real. That I get to actually... *stay* here."

A laughing child on the other side of the café snaps Jamie out of his trance, the man blinking a couple of times as he clears his throat. "Ah! Sorry, Ray, I don't know what came over me there. Please, ignore me."

Ray doesn't really know what to say about that, blurting out a stuttered, "N-no, no need t-t-to apologize. It's, umm..." He takes a deep breath. "It's nice. To learn so much about you. And I hope you're less lonely now, Jamie."

Jamie nods, lip quirking upward despite the sadness still lingering in his eyes.

"What about you, Ray? Has your family always lived in Ammersfield?"

Ray gives Jamie the rundown: his family have always lived here, their house once belonging to his great grandparents. He's got two older sisters—Pim is the eldest, and Malai is the middle child.

He tells Jamie about what the town was like twenty years ago, back when he was a well-behaved ten-year-old who liked to spend his allowance at the candy store at the top of Main Street. The store closed years ago now, replaced by a phone repair shop, but sometimes Ray still finds himself wandering in that direction out of habit, hoping to pick up some strawberry bonbons whenever he's in town.

Ray lets Jamie in on the legend of the ice-skating rink that is installed in the town square every winter; that the relationship of any couple who goes there is doomed to fail unless they both fall over on the ice. The legend had led to so many accidents—couples purposefully tripping over each other's feet in the search for luck—that the rink had actively tried to stop the myth from spreading. Of course, this had only made people talk about it more.

He tells him the story of his sister, Pim, and her now husband, Dan, going to the ice rink for their first date. They really hadn't fallen over on purpose. In fact, they had done everything in their power to avoid it. But they'd ended up flat on their faces after Pim had lost her balance, one flailing arm accidentally punching Dan in the chest and taking him down with her. Malai and Ray had thought it was hilarious when Pim returned home battered and bruised but smiling from ear to ear.

Ray had been the one to introduce Pim and Dan—him being an upperclassman in a basketball club Ray joined at college purely to try to attract a girlfriend. That hadn't worked out for a variety of reasons (namely, his clumsiness and not-quite heterosexuality) but he ended up gaining a cool guy for a brother-in-law, so it wasn't all bad!

The mention of college steers the conversation into more relatable territory—Jamie opening up about his college life so far. Ray learns that he's in his final year, having taken a couple of gap years before his family moved here to think about what he wanted to study. He's now studying Chinese, and has a best friend called Win who is, supposedly, cuter than Jamie. Ray doesn't see how that is physically possible, but keeps that thought to himself, not quite sure how to say it out loud without it sounding like a cringy pick-up line.

Their mugs empty, hot chocolate long since gone, Jamie's energy begins to wane. Despite trying to listen intently, his blinks have started to take on that sluggish drag of tiredness, and his head is resting on his hands a little too heavily. He looks adorable with the way his cheeks push out above his hands, forcing his lips into a cute pout, but it's clear that he's going to fall asleep if they stay here any longer.

"Do you want to head home, Jamie? You must be tired after your exams. I'm sorry, I didn't think about that when I came to meet you. I just—" Ray gulps. He's come too far to stop talking now. "I just wanted to see you."

He watches as Jamie's sleepy expression somehow becomes softer, cheeks turning pink as a smile spreads across his features. "I wanted to see you, too."

The words are so quiet amongst the chatter of the café that Ray almost doesn't hear them. And he's still not sure he heard them right—maybe his mind is just playing tricks on him. What else could Jamie have said that Ray may have misinterpreted? Ray can't think of any sentences that sound similar enough for him to have heard it wrong.

"Oh..." is Ray's very articulate response.

Jamie just beams at him, hopefully endeared by how red Ray's face has gone at even the *idea* that his feelings might be reciprocated.

Despite Jamie literally living on the other side of the street, Ray offers to walk him home. He holds his arm out for the sleepy boy to hold onto when Jamie staggers to his feet. Jamie's hand wraps around his bicep a second later and they make their way to the door.

Ray walks him not just to the front of Honeybun Bookstore, but into the shop. He leads him all the way to the bottom of the staircase at the back—delaying the moment they have to say goodbye for as long as possible.

Jamie squeezes his arm once before slowly removing himself from Ray's side, his touch lingering like he doesn't really want to let go. He turns to face Ray, looking up at him through pretty eyelashes. "Thank you for today, Ray. This was nice."

Before Ray can think of a decent response, his arms are suddenly full of Jamie, the man throwing his own arms around Ray's neck for a hug. Hesitantly at first, Ray hugs him back. When this elicits a pleased hum from the boy against his chest, he hugs him tighter, pulling Jamie against him. It's everything Ray has been longing for, everything he's been craving. It's warm and strong and soft and perfect.

Eventually, Jamie pulls away, stuttering for possibly the first time in front of Ray. "W-well, I, um... I better g-get going." He points up the staircase awkwardly as cute giggles escape his lips, cheeks rosy.

Something about seeing Jamie so flustered soothes Ray—like it's proof that Jamie is falling as hard for him as he is for Jamie. "Have a lovely evening, Jamie."

"You too, Ray."

Jamie's eyes linger on his for a few extra moments before he makes his way up the stairs, leaving Ray gazing longingly up at his retreating form. He sighs once the boy is out of sight.

Ray turns to leave and comes face to face with Apple. She's clearly been there a while judging by the way she's leaning against the doorframe leading to the shop floor, arms crossed casually and an all-too-knowing smile on her lips.

"You really like him, don't you?"

He wants to tell her. He wants to tell everyone.

Ray gulps. Once he's said those words, he won't be able to take them back, but...

"Y-yes. I like him. A lot."

Apple nods. "Good." Then she raises a finger, pointing it at Ray in warning. "You better not hurt my baby!"

With that, Apple follows her son up into the apartment, leaving Ray stunned at the foot of the staircase. He walks out of the store in a daze, not even acknowledging Banlue where he sits behind the counter.

Was he just given permission to pursue Jamie romantically?

Wednesday, December 21st

"Have you seen Jemmie again?" Praew asks the second Ray opens the door. He'd agreed to look after her today, on the first day of her winter break, since his sister has an important work meeting out of town. Although Praew is very polite and well-behaved, Pim hadn't wanted to make her sit in a boring meeting room all day. So, Uncle Wawa to the rescue!

"Can we go see him today? Please, Uncle Wawa! I wanna see Jemmie!"

Ray guffaws and stutters through some excuses, trying to put off answering her questions entirely for now. Pim is still here, standing next to Praew, smirking at Ray in a way that he knows means she's already going to tease him about this later. The less fuel he gives her, the better.

It's only once Pim has left that Praew finally gets some of the answers she's been waiting for. Ray tells her about their little sort-of date yesterday, and about walking him home all the way to the staircase of his apartment. She just keeps letting out little "aww" sounds, her eyes big and sparkly with each piece of information Ray shares. She seems so in awe of Jamie, the boy obviously having left an impression on her, in how attentively she listens to Ray. Of course, Ray leaves out some details—his niece doesn't need to know about how his heart had sped up when they'd hugged, or about Jamie's childhood and moving frequently. That last one in particular is not his story to tell.

Once she's sufficiently caught up, they come up with a plan for the day—Praew still determined to get a gift for Jamie. They decide they'll stay home this morning to brainstorm gift ideas, eat some lunch, then head into town to buy Jamie's present. If all goes well, they should be done in time to surprise Jamie at work at the end of his shift.

The brainstorming session has Ray feeling like he doesn't know Jamie as well as he wishes he did. Despite his best efforts, the list of things he knows Jamie has an interest in is relatively short: cats, Chinese (he is studying it, after all), and the color pink. He also presumes Jamie must like singing, given the fact he's in the choir, and Praew adds that Jamie likes princesses. She retrieves a set of markers from her bag and writes the list down on the page of her notebook, Ray helping her with spellings when she gets stuck.

Jamie
- cats
- Chinese
- pink
- Singing
- princesses

What on earth could we buy him based on this?

After staring at the list for far too long, Ray sighs and turns on the television, needing a break from all of this thinking. He finds some cartoons and decides to leave those on, Praew shifting next to him on the couch to get comfortable and watch the show.

When lunchtime rolls around, no progress made, Ray goes to the kitchen to make some sandwiches. He passes one to Praew, coming back to sit with her in front of the television while they eat. They should sit at the table, really, especially with Praew being at such an impressionable age. But... Ray wants to sulk about how little he knows about the boy he likes. And it's much more pleasing to do that when you're staring unseeingly at a screen. Plus, it's the first day of Winter Break for Praew, so she should be able to do whatever she wishes. If that means watching cartoons over lunch, then that is perfectly fine with Uncle Wawa.

Ray keeps checking his phone, hoping to see an incoming text from Jamie. He knows there won't be any message—Jamie is working today and the store is sure to be busy with Christmas a matter of days—but still... he should check at least one more time.

Still nothing.

He places his phone on the arm of the couch with a huff, taking an angry bite out of his sandwich. When he goes to take another bite, his phone screen lights up with a message. It's not from Jamie, but it could give him the opportunity to talk about him, which is almost as exciting.

Teddy
How are things going with bookstore boy?

Ray had told Teddy a little about Jamie. Nothing particularly juicy (not that anything like that has even happened between them... yet, but still!), only enough for him to know about Ray's crush. After all, he'd needed to retell the story of their first meeting to *someone* when he'd returned to New York, the ex-roommates getting drunk while Ray whined about the cute bookstore boy.

Would it be weird for Ray to call Teddy and gush about his little café date with Jamie? Because that's what he wants to do right now. He wants to run to his room and throw himself down on the bed, tummy first, and tell Teddy all about Jamie while kicking his feet in the air like a besotted teenager. Maybe he'd even ring Teddy using the old-fashioned phone that is still installed in his bedroom, just so he can twirl the cable around his fingers while he talks. But Teddy is not good with mushy, emotional stuff. So...

Ray
Good.

Teddy
Good.

And that concludes that conversation.

Ray sets his phone back down, only for it to immediately start ringing—his manager's caller ID appearing on the screen. It seems like everyone apart from Jamie wants to contact him today.

"Ray! Thank goodness you picked up!"

Ray's eyebrows knit together. That sentence never means anything good. Especially from Karl.

"Remember that talk show you were meant to appear on this winter to promote your new movie?"

Ray hums down the phone, vaguely recalling it.

"When I told you to call them and cancel it, because you wouldn't be in town when it was scheduled to happen, did you?" Panic rises in Ray's chest immediately, while Karl starts to ramble, "You know I would have canceled it for you if I could, Ray, but that asshole presenter's manager won't listen to me. I did keep reminding you to do it—I sent you texts about it and brought it up with you in person. It's happening today and I just received a phone call asking why you haven't arrived yet. Please tell me you remembered to let them know you wouldn't be there and this is just a mix-up on their part. Please, Ray—"

Ray is pretty sure his soul has left his body. He feels sick, his voice wobbling as he admits, "N-no. I didn't."

This has never happened before. Ray is a professional, after all. He knows the importance of following through with plans and not making enemies within the industry. But now, maybe all of that work to build a good reputation is about to go down the drain. This is a lot worse than him knocking over a few books in a bookstore...

"Wha— What do we do?" Ray is sweating, rubbing his face with his free hand as he practically whimpers down the phone.

"Don't panic!" is Karl's very useful reply. "I-I have an idea," he continues. "Give me ten minutes."

Suddenly the line goes dead, leaving Ray with his spiraling thoughts.

"Wawa?" Praew shuffles across the couch towards him, placing her tiny hands on his shoulder. "What's the matter?" Praew's large eyes gazing at him with such concern are nearly enough to make him cry, emotions running high.

"It's okay, Praew. Just some work Wawa forgot to sort out. It'll be okay." He isn't really sure whether he's saying that more for Praew or himself. "It'll be okay..."

Karl calls back eight and a half minutes later. Thank god it hadn't been the full ten minutes. Ray isn't sure he could have held himself together that long, biting his nails anxiously.

"So?" he asks, in lieu of greeting.

"We have a plan." Karl's words are slightly reassuring, but Ray knows better than to relax just yet. "I managed to get through to that asshole's assistant instead—nice guy actually, Matty, met him once and we got on super well, maybe I should ask him out for—"

Ray clears his throat loudly. He's happy Karl has maybe found a love interest, but this is not the time.

"Ah! Yes, well, I talked to Matty."

"And?"

"And you can do the interview virtually instead! It turns out that one of the other guests will be doing that anyway, so Matty says it's no trouble for you to do that, too. You took your laptop with you, right?"

Ray nods before remembering that Karl can't see him. "M... Mhm. Yes."

"That'll work fine! So just put on whatever nice clothes you brought with you, find a blank wall to sit by—don't wanna accidentally have anything in the background that needs blurring out for copyright reasons—and we'll be fine! Show is in an hour. I'll email you the relevant info!"

The line goes dead again. Ray only feels marginally less panicked than the last time, springing up from his seat to go rummage through his closet. He turns back as he's about to leave the living room, addressing the little girl who is staring at him from her spot on the couch, "Praew, can you be good for Uncle Wawa and stay here for a bit?"

Once she nods, Ray pounds up the stairs to his room, throwing open his closet doors to search for something adequate. This show has a notoriously strict dress code. He can't show up in the old gray t-shirt and off-brand jeans he's currently wearing, even if he's only attending via video call.

And what is he going to do about Praew?

The whole talk show process—getting ready for it, reading over whatever information or notes he needs, and filming the show itself—could easily take three hours, maybe longer. He can't leave Praew alone that long, but he can't bring her on camera either. Ray has always avoided his family being in the media, knowing from conversations with them that they don't want to deal with the secondary fame. He definitely can't let the seven-year-old, whom he isn't even the legal guardian of, wander in on the interview. Her life might never be quite the same.

Ray pauses in his outfit-locating mission to scroll through his contacts.

He can't call Pim or Dan to come and get her—Pim at that important meeting and Dan on the other side of the country for a couple of days to close a deal with a client, that being the whole reason Ray had the opportunity to look after her in the first place. There's no point calling his other sister, Malai, either—she lives too far away to get here in time. And Ray's parents are out visiting Malai today. *Great.*

Who can he trust to keep an eye on Praew?

Ah!

He presses the call button, then puts it on speaker, resuming his rooting around in his closet.

The call connects.

"Hello?" Jamie's confused voice is tinny through the speakers of Ray's phone.

"Hi hi hi! Jamie, it's me, Ray. Wait, you know that already, you have my number saved. Well, I presume you do, otherwise this must be— ah, sorry, I—" Ray knows he's rambling but he's panicking here! Not helped by the fact that he still hasn't found a suitable outfit.

"Y-yes...?" The boy on the other end of the phone doesn't sound any less perplexed yet. This probably isn't how he imagined their first ever phone call going, if he's ever imagined it. (Ray certainly has.)

"I've, um, I've got a favor to ask. Aha!" Ray spots the suit he'd worn to Pim's wedding tucked away in the back of the closet. It's not ideal, but it's formal enough that he can get away with it.

Beginning to remove his comfy clothing, he explains, "See, um— WAH!" Ray stumbles out of his jeans, banging into his dresser. That's gonna bruise, for sure. "Uh, basically, there's a talk show I'm meant to be on in an hour. It could take a while, and I-I'm looking after Praew today. But... Mhhh—" His voice is momentarily muffled as he pulls his t-shirt over his head, getting stuck for a second before he frees himself of the fabric.

"But it means I'll be on camera today. Praew can't be on camera. And my family are all out of town. So I was wondering..." Ray begins to realize that this could be considered quite a big ask. He doesn't even know if Jamie is used to being around children—let alone if he'd be comfortable looking after Praew, but... "I didn't know who else to call."

Ray stands in the middle of his room wearing nothing but boxers and socks, staring at his phone pleadingly, willing Jamie to say something.

"You, um... You'd like me to... look after Praew?" Jamie asks hesitantly.

Ray takes a moment to respond. "If it wouldn't be too much trouble."

Jamie says something to someone on his end, the words muted and unclear for a moment, probably covering the mic for some privacy, before he replies, "You're at your parents' place, right? The one on Emmaly Street? I'll be there in fifteen. Do you need anything?"

Ray lets out a breath he hadn't been aware he was holding.

"Thank you. Thank you so much, Jamie. No, I don't need anything." Ray takes the suit pants off of their hanger, stepping into them. He probably doesn't need to wear these them for a video call, but it'll be just his luck that he'll have to stand up at some point and everyone will see he isn't in the proper attire if he doesn't put them on. "Well, actually, I need to find somewhere suitable to set up my laptop for the call—my room has too much stuff on the walls, I can't get it camera-ready in time. Oh god, am I going to have to do this from my parents' bathroom? That's literally the only room here with a neutral background. Ugh. Sorry, I'm rambling, this isn't your problem, I—"

"Use my room," Jamie blurts.

"I... I'm sorry?"

"My bedroom walls are off-white and there's nothing on them. That's a neutral enough background for your call, right?"

Ray starts pulling on the shirt that had been stored with the suit, finding it to be a bit tighter around his arms and chest than the last time he'd worn it. His haphazard workout routine must be paying off. "Well, yes, that is neutral. But I'm sure it would be a bother to get ready..."

"My room is clean and tidy, thank you very much." Ray hears some tapping noises. "See."

Buttoning up the shirt, Ray walks over to look at his phone screen, opening the incoming text—a photo attached. Sure enough, Jamie's room is the very definition of neutral; plain walls, plain bedding, a nondescript desk and chair set up by the window. If Ray didn't know any better, he'd think it was a spare room. It doesn't look like anyone actually lives there.

"My room is at the back of the building, so you don't hear much noise from the street below. And Tommy made sure we had the best WiFi possible in this town—he enjoys playing online games too much to accept anything less."

This boy is far too giving. But right now, eyeing the layers of photos and posters piled upon his own bedroom walls, Ray is immensely grateful. "Are you sure you don't mind?"

"Ray, it's fine. Just head over and do what you gotta do, I'll keep Praew entertained."

That does sound like a very good offer...

"Are you *sure* you're sure? I don't want to—"

"Get here soon or I swear to god I will come get you and drag you over here myself!" It seems Jamie isn't taking no for an answer. "Now, go finish getting ready. Don't forget to bring your laptop."

Jamie hangs up on him, leaving no room for argument.

Five minutes later, Ray and Praew are speedily exiting the house, Ray in his suit with a coat over the top and a backpack slung over one shoulder. He's thrown everything he thinks he might need into it; laptop, charger, phone, hairbrush and styling products. He had squeezed his makeup bag in at the last moment, in case he finds the time to at least put on some light concealer.

Ray tries to maintain some semblance of a calm persona as they speed-walk into town, though his sweaty and strong grip on Praew's hand gives away his true feelings. The last twenty minutes have been a whirlwind he could have done without.

Everyone who has ever told Ray that holidays are relaxing can stuff it.

Jamie is waiting outside the door for them, waving as Ray and Praew round the corner and come into view. Ray feels an odd compulsion to run—the man in front of him like his personal oasis, a beautiful spark of hope. Somehow he restrains himself from sprinting, instead just walking a touch quicker.

"Hey! Come in, come in!" Jamie ushers them into the store, obviously sensing Ray's urgency from their phone call and his probably quite frazzled appearance. He takes Praew's hand from Ray, greeting her as he leads them to the back of the store and up the staircase. Ray greets Apple and Banlue briefly as he passes them at the counter, throwing a "hello" and an awkward nod in their direction. Once up the first flight of stairs, Jamie directs Praew to sit in the living room, while he and Ray continue up to the next floor.

"Here," Jamie says when he opens a door on the third floor. The room is the same as it was in the photo, apart from the fact that the few items that had been on the desk earlier have been removed, the desk now as bare as the walls.

"You'll be okay sitting here, right?" Jamie pulls out the chair and sits in it, checking what will be seen in the video by framing the imaginary shot with his hands. "People should only see this wall and maybe my closet. It's pretty plain looking, so it shouldn't be a problem, I don't think."

When Ray stands next to him to check, he finds that this is true. The wall that will be seen in the webcam is magnolia in color, and the closet next to it is the same. No posters, no photos, not even any distinctive handles on the closet doors. There's nothing.

"Y-yes. This is perfect, Jamie. Are you sure this is oka—"

"Good." Jamie cuts him off. "Do you need anything? Water, coffee, a snack...?"

He is in no position to ask for any more kindness, despite how dry his mouth feels from stress and nerves. "No, thank you. This is perfect."

"I'll bring you some water." It seems Jamie can see right through him at every turn.

"Oh, and here's the WiFi details." Jamie hands him a slip of paper before turning to leave, presumably going to grab that glass of water for Ray. The piece of paper is... Well, it's a post-it note, one of those very cute ones. It's pink and shaped to look like cat ears at the top. It's absolutely adorable.

Jamie returns before Ray has moved an inch, still making puppy eyes at the cute piece of paper.

"Ray? Here..." The boy passes him the water, and Ray is stunned. Not by the water, but by just how generous Jamie has been—with his time, with his space, everything. What has Ray done to deserve such care?

He clears his throat, forcing his emotions down so he can focus. "T-thank you."

He has work to do.

- • ☆ • -

Once Ray is settled in his bedroom, laptop set up, the glass of water a decent distance away from it(knowing Ray is too clumsy for the glass to be near any sort of electrical item), Jamie makes his way back down to Praew.

Since Ray first called, Jamie has been thinking about the best ways to entertain Praew. He wants her to have fun, and to have fun *with him*, not be left sitting somewhere reading or watching television alone. Therefore, Jamie had asked his parents to keep an eye on the store for the rest of the day.

"So..." he says as he enters the living room. "How would you feel about baking some chocolate chip cookies?"

The way Praew's eyes light up is priceless.

They have to keep their volume down while they bake, not wanting to disturb Ray. Sure, he's on the next floor and not directly above them, but it's better to be cautious, Jamie thinks. It's clear Ray cares about his family's privacy, and Jamie wants to do his best to respect that. But also... Praew is very cute when she laughs.

The little girl is currently helping him mix some ingredients in a bowl, her small hands over the top of Jamie's on the handle of a wooden spoon. Jamie keeps making little noises as he mixes—sounds he makes subconsciously—and they keep making Praew laugh. Little giggles bubble out of her with each "wahhh!" or "oooommm" that falls from Jamie's mouth. Jamie is smitten.

He helps Praew spoon the mixture onto the baking trays, first showing her how much dough she needs for each one, and then allowing her to try. She sticks her tongue out in concentration as she copies Jamie's demonstration, dumping a lump of cookie dough down onto the tray.

While the cookies are in the oven, the two sit on the couch and watch cartoons. Jamie had recently discovered a new kids cartoon about a cat that he likes to watch before bed, and just has to show it to Praew. The second she lays eyes on the adorable main character, she's hooked.

When the timer goes off, signaling that the cookies are done, Jamie and Praew bound into the kitchen, excited to see (and eat) the fruits of their labor. They find that the cookies are all slightly different sizes; all weird shapes, and some of them are stuck together. They're perfect.

The pair make their way back to the living room, Jamie carrying a tray with two glasses of milk and a few cookies on a plate. Praew follows closely behind, excitedly giggling.

Jamie presses play on the television once they sit back down, and Praew picks up a warm cookie. He tries to snap a sneaky picture of Praew to send to Ray later—just to confirm to him that they did in fact have a good time and he hadn't left her alone. Praew hears the shutter noise and immediately turns to look at him, temporarily forgetting about the cat on the screen.

"If you're taking pictures, I want a picture with you, Jemmie."

Before Jamie can really comprehend what's happening, Praew is crawling into his lap, still holding the large cookie in one hand. She flops herself down and gets comfortable while Jamie is frozen.

"Jemmie, come on!" She taps at his phone screen with a greasy finger, getting his attention. Flipping his phone camera to selfie mode, their slightly grainy faces appear on the screen.

"Smile, Jemmiiiie." The way Praew says his name is enough to get him grinning, the smile spreading naturally. Praew holds up her cookie so it's visible in the shot, and Jamie takes the photo.

He presumes that just one photo is enough, but it seems Praew has other ideas.

"Like this!" she directs, mouth open in a gasp while looking wide-eyed at the cookie. Jamie mirrors her pose, snapping another picture. "And one like this!" She holds up two fingers in a cute peace sign. Jamie does it, too, and then Praew is leaning closer, pressing her cheek to his for the cutest picture ever. She's so adorable, Jamie almost forgets to take the photo.

They dig into the cookies after that, Praew breaking off half of the one she's holding in order to share it with Jamie. She makes no move to get off of his lap as they munch away and drink their milk. Eventually, Jamie decides to ask, "So, Princess, I was thinking about getting something for Uncle Wawa for Christmas... Can you help me? I remember you said he liked dogs?"

Praew turns around to face him and grins. "Mhm! He loves Balto the most!"

"Balto?" Jamie queries. "Like the book?"

Praew nods. "It's his favorite."

Jamie can work with that. Maybe.

"Do you know *why* he likes Balto?"

"It's kinda a long story..." the seven-year-old replies. Jamie encourages her to go on and opens the notes app on his phone, ready to pay attention to every word Praew says. She may be young, but she knows more about Ray as a human being than any article on the internet could possibly tell him.

- · ★ · -

The talk show went fine—much better than Ray had expected, given the circumstances. Almost all of the questions he'd been asked had been about work, which he was grateful for, only having to dodge one or two questions regarding his personal life. At one point, the host had asked where he was. It had thrown him for a second, because how could he possibly explain? He couldn't just say, "Oh yeah, I'm in the bedroom of some guy I've been hanging out with, who I have a massive crush on, while he looks after my niece." No, that wouldn't have gone down well at all. So, Ray had claimed it was a hotel room. And given how plain the room was, there was no reason for anyone to question it.

Now that his work is done, Ray has the time to take in his surroundings a little better. He closes the lid of his laptop, packing it and the charger back into his backpack, and then turns to look at the room.

There really is nothing to see. Off-white walls, a bed with beige bedding in the center of the room, the same hardwood flooring as in the rest of the apartment. There's a small rug by one side of the bed, and Ray guesses that this must be the side of the bed Jamie gets out of, not wanting his feet to touch the cold floor first thing in the mornings. The items on the bedside tables feel like the only hint of Jamie's personality in the entire room; a pink bedside lamp in the shape of a sphere on one, and a small stack of books on the other—most appearing to be in Chinese.

The blankness of the room bothers Ray. Everything feels too tidy, too well put together, too clean. It feels like Jamie could pack up his stuff and leave in under an hour, not a trace left behind. Ray understands now what Jamie had said about not believing he could stay. Clearly, the boy still lives like he's on the move.

He sighs before pulling himself up from the chair and tucking it in neatly. As he makes his way down to the second floor, he can hear the muffled sounds of a television.

The sight that greets him when he gets to the living room melts his heart. Jamie is fast asleep, slouched back against the couch, with Praew asleep in his lap. She's not even facing the direction of the television—instead turned towards Jamie, attempting to burrow into his chest while her hands loosely hold onto the wool of his sweater.

Ray, obviously, takes a photo. Then another one. Then one more for good measure.

He contemplates what to do now. It's not polite to just watch people sleep. But they look so peaceful and cute...

Ray's clumsiness makes the decision for him, as he somehow drops his phone, which clatters loudly when it hits the wooden floor.

"Mm... Hia?" Jamie murmurs, sleepily opening an eye in Ray's direction.

...*Hia?* Ray blushes. He's vaguely familiar with the Thai term, a friendly way to address someone a little older—usually of Chinese descent—but he's never been called it before. It reminds him of that part of his heritage in a way few things do in this old-fashioned little town.

"I... It's just me." Ray keeps his voice soft, watching Jamie's eyes flutter open and then shut again. One of Jamie's hands, previously wrapped about Praew, moves to pat at the empty couch cushion beside him—an invitation.

Ray sits down gingerly, intending to keep some space between himself and Jamie. This flies out of the window when Jamie shifts closer, leaning to let his head rest against Ray's shoulder. A soft hand finds Ray's, the fingers intertwining with his. Ray was right with his earlier assumption—holding his hand really is like holding a cloud.

"This okay?" Jamie whispers.

There is no stutter, no stumble, when Ray responds: "Yes."

Jamie hums before drifting back to sleep.

- · ✱ · -

If Apple is being honest, this is pretty much exactly what she'd been expecting to see when she and Banlue make their way up to the apartment at the end of the workday. The two boys are leaning on each other, hands intertwined, Praew in Jamie's lap, all three of them asleep. Banlue seems slightly caught off-guard, a little "oh" falling past his lips. To an outsider, maybe his tone would be seen as rude. But Apple knows what that particular "oh" means. It means he's pleased.

- · ★ · -

Ray wakes up to the sound of people talking lowly and the smell of food, the unmistakable scent of Thai green curry filling his nose as he inhales deeply. It's nice. Wherever he's sitting is nice, too. It's soft and warm, wherever he is. Very warm. Especially on one side.

The warm object pressed against him makes a noise, nuzzling closer, and Ray suddenly remembers where he is.

He's at Jamie's house.

In Jamie's living room.

And he'd fallen asleep on the couch with...

He opens one eye cautiously, needing visual confirmation. Sure enough, Jamie's head is still resting against his shoulder. Ray feels his ears heat up. Now that he's not running on adrenaline or too exhausted to think, he feels shy at being so close to the boy he likes. It's when he goes to tense his hands into fists in an attempt to contain his shyness that he remembers another detail; the fingers that are linked with his. He stares at their joined hands resting on Jamie's lap. It feels like some sort of destiny, the way they fit together so perfectly.

Wait... Ray scans the area as best as he can from his position—not ready to move and disturb the man leaning against him just yet. It's fairly dark in the room, the only light coming from the Christmas tree in the corner. There's no movement around them. *Where is Praew?*

He's about to jump up and frantically start calling for her when he gets his answer in the form of a child's laugh coming from the direction of the kitchen. The sound is followed by Apple's voice, muffled through the kitchen door. Praew must be with Apple. Although it seems she's having fun based on the laugh, Ray should probably check on her—he's meant to be watching her, after all.

It takes Ray a couple of minutes to wriggle out from Jamie's grasp, coaxing the sleeping boy to lean against the residual warm patch on the couch once he's up.

"Ah, Ray! Nice of you to join us!" Apple chuckles as he enters the kitchen.

It turns out it isn't really Apple keeping Praew occupied, the woman merely stirring a pot on the stove. Ray's first impression of Banlue may have been entirely wrong, judging by what he sees when he turns around. One of the chairs in the adjoining dining room has been turned to face the kitchen, Banlue sitting in it with Praew in his lap. He bounces her as he cheerfully sings a silly song:

> I sat next to the duchess at tea,
> It was just how I feared it would be,
> Her rumblings abdominal
> Were simply phenomenal
> And everyone thought it was me!

He marks the end of the ditty by blowing a raspberry at her, Praew erupting into fits of giggles and throwing herself backwards, nearly off of his lap. Banlue's arms catch her and he chuckles, wrinkles forming by his eyes with the sweetness of his expression.

"Again, again!" Praew beams at Banlue as she pleads, slapping her tiny hands against his shirt to emphasize the request.

Ray watches until Apple gets his attention. "Dinner will be ready soon."

"Mmm, it smells good." It really does smell good. And Ray is starving! How long has it been since lunchtime? He pulls out his phone and blanches—he should have been home with Praew twenty minutes ago for Pim to pick her up.

"Oh shoot, I've got to go. I'm so sorry. Praew was meant to be home—"

"Relax, Ray. I've already spoken with your parents," Apple interrupts.

What is it with people making him feel like a teenager again? She's spoken to his parents? What next—they've organized for him to have a sleepover? Though he can't say he'd mind...

But how does Apple have his parents' number?

As if reading his mind, Apple clarifies, "No one lives in this town more than a few months without knowing the Amarins, Dear. Your family is very important to this town." She opens a cabinet and grabs some plates. "Now, could you please wake up my youngest son while I set the table?"

Slightly dazed, Ray agrees.

Returning to the living room, he sees that Jamie has moved from where he left him—the boy now lying curled up on the couch, hands tucked under his head. Soft breaths puff out from gorgeous, pink lips, his eyelashes resting prettily upon his cheeks. And Ray can't help but think that, despite his beauty, he looks lonely in the way his limbs are pulled in tight towards his torso, making himself smaller and isolating himself in sleep.

Ray kneels down next to him, letting his hand ghost over Jamie's hair. "Jamie..." His voice is a low hum, an edge of emotion making his throat tight towards the end of the word. The sleeping man barely stirs.

He lets his hand fully rest on Jamie's hair, slipping his fingers gently over the silky strands. "Jamie," Ray tries again, slightly louder but still soft, "it's time to wake up."

Jamie's face scrunches up slightly, lips pulled into a pout and cheeks puffed. Ray is helplessly enamored, gazing upon his features and chuckling. His eyes slowly blink open. "...Hia?"

That name again.

Opening his eyes wider after a few more blinks, Jamie's lips curve up into a beautiful, soft smile. "Hia is still here?"

Okay, that name is definitely aimed at Ray.

Suddenly aware that he's still got his hand in Jamie's hair, Ray begins to pull his fingers away, not sure whether the touch is welcome. Jamie's fingers curl around Ray's in an instant, applying gentle pressure until Ray's entire hand is resting on his head, confirming that this is okay. Once settled, Jamie moves his own hand away, allowing Ray to make the choice.

"Mhm, yes. Hia is still here, J..." There's a Thai term Ray could use in return. It feels intimate—maybe too intimate—but he wants to try. "I'm still here, N... Nhu."

Still half asleep, Jamie's eyes sparkle, lips curling up more at the term. Ray dares to run his fingertips through Jamie's hair as his own smile spreads. He'll call Jamie that a million times if it means he'll look at him like that.

Jamie hums contentedly, eyelids fluttering closed against Ray's ministrations, looking like he might just fall asleep again. "Your mom says dinner's almost ready," Ray tells him, trying to encourage him to stay awake but not having the heart to actually make him get up.

Seeming just as reluctant for the moment to end, Jamie doesn't move. Neither of them do; the pair lost in their own little world of a hand caressing through dark locks, of familiar terms and soft breaths as they merely enjoy each other's company.

"Boys," Apple calls, suddenly throwing open the dining room door. "Dinner is ready."

Ray and Jamie dart away from each other in an instant, reeling back as if caught doing something much more scandalous, and the moment is over. But still, as they spring to their feet, a trace of *something* remains—both boys left with cheeks painted red, Ray with a phantom sensation of how Jamie's hair had felt as it slipped through his fingers.

Entering the dining room, Ray faces a new conundrum: where to sit. He *wants* to sit next to Jamie, but the look Tommy gives him when he enters the room... He's not sure. Did Tommy see them both asleep in the living room earlier and not approve?

It's Praew that ends up making the decision for him, claiming that she has to sit between "Uncle Wawa" and "Uncle Jemmie." Ray doesn't miss Jamie's blush at the endearing title, the boy stumbling over his agreement like he's not sure whether it's okay for Praew to think of him so fondly despite how pleased it clearly makes him.

The seat Praew chooses for Ray happens to put him next to Tommy. Which is great. Just great. Well, at least he won't receive death glares across the table this way. But still, this feels big. It's Ray's first meal with Jamie's family.

Once Ray's initial nerves wear off, dinner is a cheerful affair; full of laughter and smiles as they fill their bellies with Apple's famous Kaeng Khiao Wan. Sure, dinner with his own family is nice, but Ray thinks that something about this might be even nicer. Everyone seems so carefree, so open with each other—even Tommy and Banlue smiling from ear to ear each time Praew speaks. It's not that Ray's family are particularly guarded people, but something about this... It feels comfortable in a way that Ray has never known.

Eventually, the evening must come to an end. Ray bundles Praew back into her coat and hat after double-checking that they've not left anything behind. Her own small backpack is bulging now—a large tupperware of cookies stuffed into it. She insists on hugging each member of Jamie's family before leaving, even Tommy, who returns the unexpected embrace with an awkward pat on the back.

Jamie walks them down the stairs before taking one of Praew's hands in his. Praew's other hand is held by Ray, the two of them swinging her arms back and forth as they walk to the front door. The little girl practically koalas herself to Jamie when they reach it, small arms squeezing tight around him.

"Thank you, Jemmie. I had fun today."

"I had fun too, Praew."

The little girl beams. Ray wants in. He wraps his arms around two of his favorite people, Jamie letting out a noise of surprise at the action.

"Really, Nhu, thank you so much. You truly saved me this afternoon."

Jamie chuckles, a gentle blush on his cheeks. "It's okay, Ray."

"Oh, back to calling me 'Ray' now, are we?" Ray can't help but tease fondly, watching Jamie's cheeks go scarlet as he whines something unintelligible about hoping Ray wouldn't bring it up.

Ray laughs, pulling him closer to tuck Jamie's head under his chin. "It's okay, Nhu. You're very cute when you're sleepy."

A yawn from Praew means it really is time for them to leave, Jamie holding the door open for them as they walk out into the chilled night air. Ray turns back to Jamie.

"Goodnight, Nhu."

"Goodnight, Praew, Goodnight, H..." Jamie hesitates, averting his eyes for a moment. "Goodnight, Ray."

Ray has never felt a twinge of sadness at being called his own name before.

*

"Uncle Wawa..." Praew starts quietly from where she's tottering along sleepily next to Ray.

He hums inquisitively, looking down at Praew but unable to see much other than the hat on her head. She looks up at him, a concerned expression contorting her face. "We still haven't gotten Uncle Jemmie anything for Christmas. What are we going to do?"

"Well, um, we just need to think of a gift he might like. I'm sure we can work something out. Uh—" Ray knows he doesn't sound convincing, but the little girl next to him looks so upset at the idea of Jamie not having a present that he needs to come up with *something*. And quick, given that Christmas is in four days. "Let's think..."

Taking a deep breath, he gives the words time to form, listing out the things Jamie likes in the hope it might spark an idea. "He likes cats..." Praew nods up at him, the pom-pom on the top of her hat bouncing back and forth. "And he likes pink..." Ray continues, Praew once again nodding and Ray watching the pom-pom on her hat bob cutely again.

Oh! Maybe...

"I have an idea!" He pulls his phone from his pocket, hastily typing out a message to his sister.

Ray
You can knit, right?

The response is almost instant.

Mal
its called crochet u idiot but yes

Ray
How long would it take you
to make a hat?
I'll pay you, of course.

Mal
what? did my little bro run out
of designer hats to wear?

Ray
It's not for me.

Mal
???

Ray
You know that guy I mentioned
who works at the bookstore?

Mal
shut UP

Mal
I'LL DO IT FOR FREE

Mal
TELL ME WHAT KIND OF HAT
UR THINKING AND I CAN FINISH
IT WITHIN A DAY!!!

"Praew, what about designing a hat for Jamie?"

Her awed gasp is enough for Ray to feel sure that this will be a hit.

When Ray gets into bed that night, he notices some messages from Jamie. And... *photos?*

He opens them, finding Jamie and Praew's faces filling his screen. There's a couple of pictures—mostly of Jamie and Praew together or of Praew holding a cookie. Ray has no idea how to handle this level of cuteness. What does he say in response to this without coming on too strong, or sounding ingenuine?

Ray decides to send Jamie the best photo he took of him and Praew asleep on the couch, since they seem to be sharing photos from the day. He accompanies this with a message—the boldest he can muster.

> **Ray**
> I think she likes you almost as much as I do.

He sees when Jamie has read the message. A text bubble appears and disappears over and over for a few minutes, before he finally gets a response.

> **Jem**
> Perhaps. Goodnight, Hia x

> **Ray**
> Goodnight Nhu x

"Beautiful."
PART 4

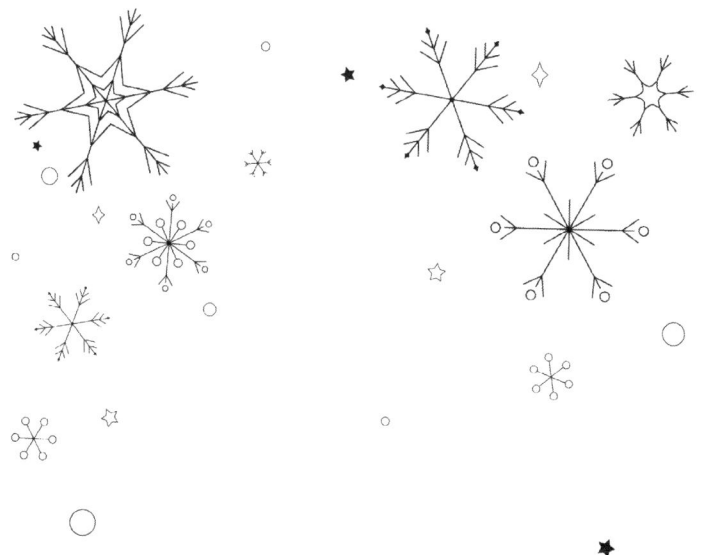

Thursday, December 22ⁿᵈ

"Win, I don't know about this..." Jamie twirls slowly in front of his phone camera, giving his friend a 360 view of the latest in a series of outfits he's tried on. This one is entirely Win's choice; white slacks and a white mesh vest with diamantes down the front. Even with the longline jacket over the top, he feels very exposed. Honestly, he's not sure why he even owns this mesh top. It must have been something Win persuaded him to buy on one of their shopping trips.

"But Jemmmm~" Win whines and pouts, his scrunched up face filling the screen of Jamie's phone. "You look so hot!"

"Yeah, well, if I wear this I'll freeze. And I don't want to freeze my nips off on our first date!" He throws off the jacket before unbuttoning the neck of the vest, pulling it over his head. There's no way he can wear this—it's the middle of winter!

When Jamie had woken up this morning he had thought it would just be an ordinary day; get up, have breakfast, stroll over to the town hall to rehearse with the choir for Christmas Eve... But then he'd gotten a text from Ray.

He'd come back to his room from the bathroom, freshly showered and wrapped in a plush towel, when his phone had vibrated with an incoming message.

Ray
Let me treat you to a meal today to
say thank you for your help yesterday!
Do you want to grab lunch?

Jamie had grinned. Ray wanted to see him! But...

Jem
I can't, sorry! I've got choir
rehearsal until 3 :/

A few choir members always brought food to share when they had long rehearsal sessions like today's. Jamie would feel like he was being rude if he just snuck out. He could have invited Ray to come watch the rehearsal and join everyone for lunch, maybe...

No, no, no.

Logically, Jamie knew that Ray might hear him sing soon—if he and his family chose to attend the Christmas Eve concert. But the idea that he could listen to him sing for the first time today, during rehearsal, when he'd not had time to mentally prepare himself...

He'd gulped.

Ray
Dinner then?

That sounded much less stressful. And had the added bonus of ensuring that some of the older ladies in the choir wouldn't tease him any more than usual, like they surely would if THE Ray Rawat Amarin just turned up. People would talk!

Jem
Dinner works.

Ray
It's a date!

...a date?

Jamie had started to panic—he needed to find something to wear! Immediately!

While Win is busy pouting about the fact that his best friend doesn't want to catch hypothermia, Jamie checks the time.

"Ah! Winnie!" he gasps. "I've got choir rehearsal in fifteen minutes!"

He turns to rummage through the pile of clothing on his bed, trying to pull together something half decent for rehearsal. Grabbing the first pair of jeans he finds, he pulls them on, then scrambles through a small stack of button ups. He finds one with a cute cartoon sun on the front and shrugs it on. "I'll come back later and change."

"Hey, that's cute, actually! Is my pink sweater still at your place? Wear that over it!"

After retrieving Win's sweater from a bag at the bottom of his closet—Win always keeps some of his belongings here for when he stays over—he picks up his phone from where he had propped it up on his desk. "Gotta go, Winnie! Love you!" Jamie blows a kiss to Win through the screen before ending the call, already running for the stairs.

- • ★ • -

"We really must stop meeting like this." Jamie chuckles as he approaches Ray. Despite Ray trying to play it cool now with his own huff of a laugh, he has been waiting outside the town hall for the past half hour—ear pressed to the door more often than not to listen in on the rehearsal.

Ray opens his arms for a hug, hopeful that this is okay after their cuddle yesterday. Jamie walks into his embrace easily, humming happily. If Ray then buries his nose in Jamie's hair, breathing in his scent of his perfume... Well, no one has to know except them.

"How come you're here?" Jamie murmurs against him.

Jamie steps back, taking hold of Ray's hand and looking up at him expectantly.

Ray is internally screaming. Jamie. Is. Holding. His. Hand. Not just reaching for him sleepily on the couch, but *holding* his hand, purposefully, in public, and smiling at him *like that.*

"I, um... I thought I could come meet you after rehearsal. Maybe wander around town before dinner or something? I'm not sure, really..."

I just want to spend time with you, he wants to say.

"O-oh. Okay," Jamie stammers, averting his gaze. It doesn't stop Ray from noticing how he's blushed, Ray's own cheeks surely a matching shade of pink.

They take off in a random direction, strolling down the street hand in hand and chatting about nothing in particular. Jamie pulls Ray into a couple of stores as they walk, and Ray goes willingly. He'd gladly be dragged anywhere by this boy.

"Hia!" Eyes wide and sparkling, Jamie gasps at something in the window of the jewelry store they're walking past. A second later, Ray is being yanked through the shop door, Jamie bounding up to a sales assistant to ask about whatever has caught his eye.

Jamie can't seem to stop bouncing on his toes while he waits for the sales assistant to return, little squeals of joy escaping his lips as he sees them making their way back to him with the item.

Ray hasn't seen what it is yet, but for Jamie to be this excited... It must be something special. Ray is intrigued and desperate to see what has caught his attention so completely. But he also isn't sure if he'll be able to take his eyes off of the beautiful boy beside him long enough to see what all the fuss is about. Especially with Jamie now lifting his hands, shaking them excitedly. Ray's right hand shakes, too, their fingers still intertwined.

When Jamie speaks again, his voice takes on a dreamy quality. "Aren't they pretty, Hia?"

Well, now Ray definitely needs to see. His eyes trail down the line of Jamie's arm, down to his hand, to where slim fingers are gently caressing the... earrings? Earrings. Two beautiful North Stars—golden in color, with some sort of clear gemstones in the middle. Ray thinks they look like the kind of stars you see in kids' movies, like following them would lead you to some place magical.

Are they pretty? Yes. They're lovely. They're delicate and shiny and sparkly. But Ray's eyes keep shifting back to Jamie. He's *gorgeous.*

"Mhm. Beautiful."

Jamie's gaze lifts to his, catching Ray's unabashed staring, but Ray has no intention of breaking eye contact now—of breaking this connection. Not when Jamie's breath is ghosting over his lips, his large eyes close enough that Ray wants to drown in their depth.

"Um—" Returning his attention to the sales assistant, Jamie turns away from Ray. "How much are they?"

"A hundred and twenty dollars, Sir."

Jamie winces, inhaling sharply through his teeth. "They are very beautiful but, I'm sorry, I can't buy them today."

The sales assistant merely nods, smiling politely as they take the earrings to put them back in the window. Jamie watches the process forlornly before sighing. "Let's get going, Hia." Despite his words, he doesn't move, eyes fixed to the display where the small stars are once again placed.

Ray hums, giving his hand a squeeze. He decides that it's his time to lead the way—gently pulling Jamie out of the store, hoping that his sadness will dissipate once those earrings are no longer within his line of sight. Ray glances once more in the direction of the star-shaped jewelry as they leave, committing the details of them to memory for... reasons.

Once they've strolled past a couple more stores, Jamie seems to cheer up a little, playfully bumping his shoulder with Ray's as they walk. Then he catches sight of something in the distance, suddenly tugging Ray in the direction of the town square. His eyes sparkle as he speeds up his steps, forcing Ray to do the same. Ray can't wait to find out where Jamie is taking him.

"Nhu..."

"Hmm?" Jamie queries from where he's knelt down in front of Ray, fastening a pair of rental skates onto Ray's feet.

"I really don't think this is a good idea."

Looking up at him through long eyelashes, Jamie asks, "Hia, do you trust me?"

Ray nods.

"Then it will all be fine."

The way Jamie beams at him as he says it is enough for Ray's worries to melt away, at least for now.

It will *not* all be fine.

Ray stands at the entrance to the rink, legs shaking and knees bumping together. He can barely stand on the skates on normal ground—how on earth is he going to stay upright on ice?

Jamie, on the other hand, steps out into the rink with ease. And Ray realizes that he's not had a proper look at Jamie's outfit from this angle, suddenly hit with a sense of déjà vu. They'd been so plastered to each other's side since meeting up, of course he hadn't realized his date is wearing *those jeans* again. The ones with the heart pockets.

Oh, sweet Jesus. How is Ray meant to focus on putting one foot in front of the other when there are hearts drawing attention to Jamie's gorgeous—

"Hiaaa!" Jamie admonishes, turning back to face Ray, the man still unmoving at the gate. "Come on! I'll hold your hand the whole time, okay?"

Now that sounds like a very lovely offer. Ray could get behind that idea if he wasn't so sure he'll fall and pull Jamie down with him. He's not sure his pride could handle that.

Perhaps seeing Ray's lack of cooperation, Jamie goes for a different tactic, leaning in as close as he did at the jewelry store—clearly on purpose this time. Ray feels a hand ghost over his shoulder and down his arm. Jamie's voice comes out a soft purr: "Come on, Mr. Famous Actor. Don't tell me you're afraid of a little ice, hm?"

Ray gulps, gaze flitting down to where Jamie's gloved hand now rests over his on the barricade, then up to the pretty lips mere inches from his, then back to the hand, then back to the lips... *Those lips.*

He can't do this.

"You know, Jamie, suddenly I don't feel so well. I better get home and—"

"Nah-ah-ah!" Suddenly both of his hands are held by Jamie's, the boy tugging him onto the ice with surprising force. It's all Ray can do to not faceplant immediately, legs locking in fear once his blades touch the ice, as he tries to achieve some semblance of balance.

Jamie chuckles, skating backwards to pull Ray around the rink. Ray barely moves his feet, just letting himself be dragged about like an inanimate object. His knees might give way if he tries to unlock them, anyway. At least the rink isn't too busy—the likelihood of him injuring a stranger reasonably low—but there are still quite a few people skating past them, lapping them over and over. He tries not to feel self-conscious about how silly the two of them must look.

"Come on, Hia! You can do it!" Jamie encourages Ray to stand up straighter once he's pulled him to a quieter section of the rink, stopping by the wall so he has something to lean against other than him if he wants. Ray hesitantly straightens his back a little, feet sliding back and forth on the ice as his center of gravity shifts. His grip on Jamie's hands tightens. There's no way he's confident enough to let go of Jamie and grab the wall.

"That's it. Doing so good," Jamie murmurs under his breath, like he isn't even aware he's saying it. "So good, Hia." And okay, Ray now feels a little like a toddler being praised for doing something as simple as standing. But also... It's nice. It makes him feel cared for. No one ever talks to him with that soft of a tone—usually seeing him as in control and mature, even if clumsy. But maybe he could get used to this.

Once Ray's stance looks similar to Jamie's, no longer in some odd half-crouch, more praise and encouragement spills from Jamie's mouth. "There you go! Look at you!"

Jamie lets go of one of his hands, much to Ray's chagrin, to pull his phone from his pocket and snap a picture of him merely standing on the ice. Or maybe it's a video... "Come on, Hia. Come to Nhu!" Jamie pulls on the one hand still holding Ray's, encouraging him to totter forward. Ray thinks he must look like a baby deer the way his legs keep buckling out from under him, his balance precarious at best. But with Jamie smiling softly at him, Ray can't bring himself to care about his appearance too much.

One rather spectacular wobble and indignant screech from Ray is enough for Jamie to finally pocket his phone, returning his other hand to Ray's. Jamie glides backwards, eyes on Ray, giving him pointers as they slowly make their way around the rink. At least Ray is actually able to propel himself forward a bit this time.

After making it a couple of times around the rink without any major incidents, Jamie claims Ray is stable enough to need only one hand for support. Ray can't help but clench his date's remaining hand, as if gripping that bit tighter will somehow make all the difference. Jamie skates next to him now, no longer facing Ray, instead admiring their surroundings and greeting passing skaters. It makes Ray feel vulnerable—no longer able to pour all of his attention into admiring the gorgeous man in front of him, a sort of bubble forming around as they'd held each other's gaze. He worries that things could feel a little awkward now, Jamie no longer praising him each time he glides without wobbling. What are they meant to talk about? Ray definitely needs to come up with something to say—needs to keep the boy whose hand he's squeezing entertained.

"So, um, do you come here often?"

Really? That's the best line Ray can come up with? "I-I mean like, um... Do you skate here often? It wasn't a pick up line. Well, it kind of was since I do want to, *y'know*, but—"

Jamie's laughter cuts him off. "You really do trip over your words, don't you? It seems your tongue is as clumsy as the rest of you."

"I think you'll find my tongue is not clumsy at all, thank you very much!" Ray can't help but sass back, voice maybe a tad too loud given the rather public setting and potentially suggestive words. Some nearby skaters definitely hear, a few of them turning to glance over their shoulders at Ray with confused and alarmed expressions. It seems Jamie picks up on the unintended euphemism, too, pulling his lip into his mouth in mock seriousness and struggling to hold in a laugh until the other skaters are further away. The snorting laugh inevitably worms its way out anyway when Ray snootily lifts his nose in the air and says a haughty, "What?"

Jamie actually stops skating, asking Ray to hold on to the barricade before he starts to cackle relentlessly, holding onto his stomach and leaning forward with a hand on his knee as the sound bubbles out of him. Ray hopes that the blush of embarrassment on his cheeks looks like it's just from the cold, or perhaps from the exertion of skating. But it also seems that Jamie's laughter is contagious, Ray unable to stop himself giggling moments later when he realizes the absurdity of his defensiveness.

The whole "clumsy tongue" moment dissipates any nerves or tension lingering between the two men—Jamie seeming more relaxed than before when he offers Ray his hand once more. "Come on, Ray. Let's see if we can get those wobbly legs to be a bit more confident on the ice."

Perhaps Ray is more relaxed, too—reaching his hand out to Jamie with unfounded confidence. "Unfounded" because a moment later he's falling, feet slipping out from under him and tumbling forwards.

"WAH!"

His landing is softer than he expects, knees hitting ice but head falling on something cushiony.

"Hia! Are you okay?" Jamie's hands are on either side of his face, guiding Ray to look up at him from where he's lying on Jamie's stomach. *Oh. That's what was so soft.* And Jamie is now looking down at him with so much care and concern, eyebrows furrowed as he turns Ray's head from side to side to look for damage that isn't there.

"Cute," Ray blurts.

Jamie must think he has a concussion, judging by the slightly panicked look in his eyes, despite how his cheeks go pink.

"I— Yes. Yes, I'm okay. Sorry," Ray soothes, watching as Jamie breathes a sigh of relief. Still, Jamie's hands are holding his face, and Ray thinks he'd like Jamie to hold his face like this to kiss him—to draw him in with soft palms and press a gentle kiss to his lips. He lets his gaze slip to Jamie's mouth, watching a hitched breath leave it. Ray licks his lips subconsciously, longing to give the plump lips in front of him the same treatment.

He could...

He could lean forwards. He could whisper, "Can I kiss you?" into the infinitesimal space between them, breath pausing as he waits for a sign of approval. He could—

He should move.

Ray shuffles backwards off of Jamie, clearing his throat, while Jamie remains frozen.

"Are you okay, Nhu?" Realizing that he basically tackled the man onto the ice, he now feels bad about not asking sooner.

"Did I hurt you when I fell?" Ray's eyes dart over Jamie's body—not to appreciate his appearance, for once, but to check for anything worrying.

Jamie blinks a couple of times before responding, "Oh. No, I'm okay, Hia."

He gets up, attempting to brush off the ice stuck to the back of his legs, no sign of injury. Then he holds a hand out to Ray, his other hand on the barricade for support as he says with a bright smile, "Shall we try again?"

An hour later, they're sitting in a local restaurant having just ordered their food, Ray grinning from ear to ear despite the ache in his legs from the unfamiliar strain of skating.

"So, you never answered me earlier,"—*because I made a fool of myself and ruined the moment*—"do you skate often?"

Jamie takes a sip of his drink and nods. "Yes. I'd never skated before we moved here. But with a rink now so close by in the winter and so cheap, well, what was there to lose? I tried it one day and found I loved it!"

The way his finger rubs back and forth on the glass, swiping through condensation, makes Ray think Jamie is considering saying something else. He waits patiently, giving him space to do so if he wishes.

"I..." Jamie starts, "I don't like all the nonsense that comes with playing sports—guys always say I'm too feminine-looking and therefore *can't possibly* be good at sports, and girls are only interested in having me as a gay best friend."

Oh? So he is gay. Good to know.

Not that Ray hadn't already been pretty sure Jamie was into guys—he did agree to this date after all. But still, it's nice to know for certain. Anyway, Jamie is still speaking. "But skating... It's so freeing!" His eyes are wide and sparkly when they meet Ray's. "Don't you think?"

Ray's personal experience with skating, having only tried twice in his life—once today and once as a small child, when his sisters had forced him—does not make him think of the word "freeing." Perhaps "freezing" would be a better way to describe his first skating experience; memories of the cold seeping into his bones through wet garments, making him shiver after falling multiple times on the ice. But Ray had seen Jamie skate today. He'd managed to convince Jamie to go around the rink a few times without him, his own muscles aching and in need of a break. He had seen the way Jamie had glided—no, flown—he had *flown* around the rink, hair ruffling up from his impressive speed, arms extended gracefully as he rounded a corner with ease. Ray was sure Jamie's eyes had fallen closed at one point, as if reveling in a moment of complete peace.

He wishes he had pulled his phone out at the rink and captured Jamie's expression when he'd skated alone, the ethereal calm of his features. He hopes he'll get to see that expression again someday. This boy sitting across from him deserves to feel like that every day.

"Yes, Nhu. I can see how it could be freeing."

Once the food arrives, Ray expects their chattering to peter out, for Jamie to be too interested in his meal to continue the conversation. But after Jamie takes a good look at his dish, he meets Ray's eye. "Thank you, Hia. For inviting me out."

"You're very welcome, Nhu."

It seems Jamie is waiting for Ray to take a bite first, wriggling impatiently in his seat and eyeing the food with an expression not dissimilar from a cat before pouncing on its prey. So Ray digs in, trying not to feel self-conscious with the way Jamie's gaze focuses on his mouth as he raises his fork. Then Jamie follows his lead, picking up his own fork and composing the perfect mouthful, humming delightedly at the flavor.

"Mm! This is good!" Jamie covers his mouth as he talks, eyes sparkling and bright. Ray hums in agreement. He also can't help but notice how small Jamie's bites are as he continues to eat, obviously trying for politeness and taking his time to chew each morsel and make it last.

"So, um..." Jamie takes a pause to swallow. "How come you're back in town for Christmas this year? Your mom's been telling everyone that it's been years." He looks up at Ray shyly from under his eyelashes, this being an official date seeming to make him more reserved.

"Ah, well, uh... My work. There's always so much to do around the holiday season, so I don't typically find the time to come home."

"That must be difficult."

"Mm. I miss my family a lot, especially around the holidays, but I've always had to put my career first." Ray takes a sip of his drink. "And then Ma basically said I had to come home this year or else. And I know better than to disagree with my ma when she says something like that. So here I am." He huffs out a small laugh, wanting to keep things lighthearted.

Going back to pushing his food around with his fork, Ray continues, "But maybe... Maybe taking some time off isn't so bad. Especially when it means I can spend time with those I love and, um... get to know some of the town's other residents better." He lifts his gaze to Jamie's, lips ticking up into something between a smirk and a smile. Now is the time to be brave. "There's this boy who's kinda new in town—his family now owns the bookstore—that I've grown rather fond of."

Ray can't be sure in the low lighting of the restaurant, but it definitely looks like Jamie is blushing, the apples of his cheeks round and rosy with a hopeful smile. He seems unsure—a little doubtful. Like he wants to ask, wants to make sure that Ray is talking about him. Of course, the answer would be yes.

"I'm glad you got to come home this year," Jamie responds.

Feeling emboldened by Jamie's reaction, Ray adds, "Maybe I should come home more often."

Jamie's eyes widen slightly before dipping into something confident and perhaps a little sultry. "Maybe you should."

It seems that good food makes them both bold.

"That *wasn't* planned?" Jamie squawks, gawking at the man walking beside him.

"Nope. Everyone assumes it was written in the script but no, I just tripped over my own feet halfway through the line and the director decided it added depth to my character." Ray adjusts his hold on Jamie's hand, grasping at gloved fingers for no reason other than because he can. "It was a little odd though—then having to fall over again and again at the same point for each take."

"I didn't think about that... Gosh, your poor knees!" Jamie gasps.

"It's okay, Nhu. I fall over a lot anyway."

"Mm," Jamie agrees with a hum. "You are ridiculously clumsy."

"Hey!" Ray lightly protests, bumping shoulders with him. The two giggle and slow to a halt, their faces illuminated by the streetlamp outside Honeybun Bookstore.

"Well..." Jamie motions to the shop. "This is me."

Ray won't let go of Jamie's hand just yet—not until Jamie lets go of his. "So it is."

A tug on Ray's arm has him tipping forwards, falling into Jamie's waiting embrace. "Thank you for today, Hia."

Ray wraps his arms around Jamie, bending their bodies closer together. "Thank you for letting me take you out on a date." As Ray pulls back, he dares to press a quick peck to Jamie's cheek.

It takes Jamie a moment to recover, eyes flitting between Ray's features with a dazed expression. Ray worries for a second that he's misread the situation, that he's made Jamie uncomfortable... But then Jamie is raising a hand to his cheek, brushing his fingers over the spot Ray had kissed, and his lips pull up into a cautious smile.

Jamie turns away, clearing his throat as he finds his key and opens the door. "I..." Jamie gulps. "I would invite you in but, um... I've not checked whether that's okay with my parents this evening. But... I'll see you tomorrow?"

"Yeah," Ray replies, oddly breathless. Over dinner, they had discussed the best time to meet up so Jamie could give Praew her present and agreed that tomorrow afternoon would work. "Tomorrow."

Jamie nods, stepping through the door.

"Goodnight, Nhu."

"Goodnight, Hia."

- · ☆ · -

Jamie isn't surprised to find his mom sitting in the living room, turning off the television when he makes it to the top of the stairs.

"How did it go, Baby?" She asks him expectantly.

"It went well," Jamie tells her. He's been smiling so much that his cheeks ache. "Really well."

- · ★ · -

"How was it, Pumpkin?" Ray's Ma calls from the living room when she hears the front door slam shut. Pat sits nearby, eagerly awaiting his son's response, smiling at Ray's obvious happiness when he bounds into the room.

"Amazing, Ma! He's amazing!" He'd practically skipped home from town, unable to suppress his glee. "And I'm seeing him tomorrow with Praew to exchange Christmas gifts. I already spoke to Pim and she said it's fine. We'll go towards the end of Jamie's shift."

"My boy, why don't you invite him for dinner?" Pat asks.

Jamie? Here? Meeting his parents? Sure, Jamie has met his parents before at the store but...

Sensing Ray's trepidation, his mom adds, "The whole family are staying for dinner anyway—what's one extra guest? And that way you won't be disrupting his work."

Hm... He can't argue with that logic.

"O-okay. I'll ask him."

Friday, December 23rd

Jamie makes it to the Amarin residence fifteen minutes before he's expected, having been too nervous to wait at home any longer. Now he paces on the doorstep, worrying about how early is *too* early—what if they're not ready for him yet? Or Ray's parents can't stand it when people are early? Surely it's better than being late, but still...

A muffled squeal and the sound of something tapping on a window grab Jamie's attention. He turns towards the noise to find Praew's face squished up against one of the house windows, her small hand raising from the glass to give an excited wave.

Jamie waves back nervously, then spots Ray behind her and throws a shy smile in his direction, too. Ray lets go of the he'd been holding aside for Praew to peek through as the little girl turns away from the window, taking off in the direction of the front door.

Seconds later the door is being pulled open by an out-of-breath Ray, Praew bouncing at his feet before she flings herself at Jamie.

"Uncle Jemmie!" Her arms wrap around him, burying her head in Jamie's coat-clad tummy.

Jamie giggles, endeared. "Hey, Princess." The pet name once again slips off his tongue without a thought, his gloved fingers raising to pat her head gently.

He lifts his eyes from Praew, letting his gaze travel up to Ray, the man standing dumbly in the middle of the doorway. Jamie takes in his ridiculous socks covered in dogs, followed by a pair of nondescript black jeans, and that same ugly Christmas sweater he'd seen Ray wearing earlier in the week. Well, at least Jamie now knows he probably picked the right outfit to wear this evening, his own Christmas sweater currently hidden beneath a thick winter coat.

It seems Ray has done something a little different with his hair and makeup tonight, maybe since he's home with his family. His bangs hang loosely on his forehead, not styled into the usual almost-quiff, and Jamie can see a couple of small beauty marks by his jaw that he's never noticed before. *Does he usually cover them with makeup?*

Jamie's breath leaves him in a giddy rush when he finally opens his mouth. "Hi."

"H-hi, Nhu." Ray gestures into the house with an arm, eyes flitting to and from Jamie in shyness. "P-please, c-come in."

Jamie nods in response before entering, Praew still clinging to his side as he opens his arms for a hug from Ray once he's closed the door. Ray wraps his arms around Jamie (and Praew, by extension), leaning in enough to plant a sneaky kiss on Jamie's cheek before burying his face in his neck. Jamie's shoulders tense for a moment, surprised, before he relaxes into the embrace, enjoying the way Ray's large hands hold him close.

The sound of slippers tapping across the floor towards them has Jamie pulling back, Praew deciding to cling onto Ray now instead. Tension once again rises in Jamie's frame as Ray's mom comes into view.

"Jamie!" she greets him warmly as she approaches for a hug, a festive red and green apron covering her outfit. "So good to see you!" She squeezes him tightly, while he can only manage a weak hold in return, not sure of the proper etiquette for meeting your *requited crush's* mom.

"Good to see you too, Mrs. Amarin. I hope I'm not intruding this evening?"

She holds him at an arm's length for a moment, delicate fingers curled into the coat he's still not taken off. "Nonsense, Sweetie! And call me Hathai—no need to be so formal!" Hathai comes back in for another hug, swaying Jamie from side to side with a cooing noise like she's trying to soothe him. Perhaps she can sense his nerves.

A timer going off in the kitchen gets her attention. "Ah! I better deal with that. Please, make yourself at home." Hathai scurries off in the direction of—presumably—the kitchen, Praew skipping after her with a sing-songed, "Grannyyy~ how long until dinner?"

- · ★ · -

Ray can't help but stare after his mom as she walks away, silently pleading for her to turn around and come back. He's nervous. *So very nervous* to be left alone with Jamie. What if he makes a fool of himself again?

He clears his throat, collecting himself as much as he can. "Ah! Um... Let me, uhh... Let me t-take your coat?" He doesn't intend for it to be a question, but his nerves bring an embarrassing amount of squeakiness to his voice. Gesturing to the shoe rack, he continues, praying his voice won't break again, "And y-you can put your shoes down there. We've got spare slippers if you want to borrow some."

"Okay. Thank you." Jamie toes off his shoes and shrugs off the coat to reveal his Christmas sweater; pale pink and slightly fluffy, with the visage of a smiling polar bear in the center, its pom-pom nose and ears protruding from the fabric enough that they bounce with Jamie's movements. Why is that so hypnotizing? Ray can't stop watching them as they jiggle.

"Are you okay, Hia?" he asks, passing Ray his coat.

Ray swiftly meets Jamie's eyes, feeling a little sheepish. Sure, he hadn't been staring at his ass this time, so it could have been worse, but it's still not polite to stare at any part of a person. "Y-yes. You? How, uh... How are you?" His eyes wander back down Jamie's figure of their own accord, though he averts his gaze a little when Jamie turns away and leans down to put his shoes on the rack.

"I'm good," he says quietly once he rights himself, the tremble in his voice betraying how on-edge he is, too. Ray reaches out to take Jamie's hand, hoping the touch might ground them both. He gives the smaller hand a reassuring squeeze, smiling when he receives a similar squeeze back.

"You ready to meet the rest of my family?" He smiles earnestly, trying to cover his own nerves.

Jamie nods a little too enthusiastically. "Yeah. I'm ready."

- • ☆ • -

Jamie is immensely grateful that Ray's family don't even look their way when they enter the living room at first, too caught up in a cheery discussion to pay them much mind. It gives him a moment to familiarize himself with the location—doing a little "your exits are here, here, and here" in his head as he takes note of possible escape routes in case this all goes wrong.

"Guys," Ray says, "this is, uh..." Jamie gulps as the eyes of Ray's loved ones all turn to him. "This is Jamie."

It takes all of his willpower to not hide behind Ray, to not draw his shoulders in to make himself smaller. Instead, he tries to stand proud beside him, though his grip on Ray's hand definitely tightens.

Ray gestures to the person closest to them, a man with short brown hair styled back off his forehead. "This is Dan." Dan lifts a hand in greeting, lips pressed into a tight smile.

Next, he introduces his sisters—Pim smiling softly, everything about her having an air of elegance; Malai sending a cheeky smirk in Ray's direction, looking up at him from under her bright purple bangs, before she greets Jamie. He tries not to analyze what that smirk was about.

"And of course, you've met Pa."

Jamie nods to the older man where he is sitting in what is clearly *his* armchair, the book he'd recently picked up from the bookstore perched on a side table next to it. "Yes, great to see you, Mr. Am—"

Pat raises an eyebrow at Jamie.

"I mean, great to see you, *Pat*. How's the reading coming along?"

Pat perks up. "Oh, fabulously! It's been an amazing book so far! Be sure to thank your mother for me—she's the one who recommended it." He picks up the book to show it off, squinting at the small text of the blurb as if he's going to read it aloud, before ultimately deciding not to. Instead, he reiterates, "It's been good. Really good."

"I'm glad to hear that." Jamie takes a seat close to Pat to talk with him a little longer, comforted by the presence of someone he knows and the fact that they can talk about books as if he's talking to a customer in the store. But then Pat gets up.

"I better go help the wife with dinner, but it's been nice chatting with you, Jamie."

Jamie tries not to let his panic show as Pat walks off, but his rising anxiety is quickly dispelled by Malai's sassing. "He's just trying to eat all the good stuff before it gets to the table," she says from where she's curled up at the end of the couch, Pim, Dan, and Ray all tittering in agreement when Pat sends an offended "Hey!" in their direction.

Pim extends a hand to Jamie, resting it on his knee. "It really is so nice to properly meet you, Jamie. I've heard so much about you—both from Ray and my daughter." If it wasn't for her cheerful expression, Jamie wouldn't be so sure if that's a good thing; whether Pim was already fed up of hearing about him before they'd even met. But her kind eyes and warm smile make him think that isn't the case. Or so he hopes.

"It's nice to meet you, too. Oh, and I hope you don't mind that I brought some presents for Praew this evening."

He retrieves the gift bag from inside his tote. "Hia—" *Maybe not in front of his family. I've only just met them.* He clears his throat. "*Ray* seemed to think that was okay, but I didn't have a chance to check with you until now, sorry."

Pim waves her hand, telling him that it's fine but probably best to hide the gifts until after dinner so the family will be able to eat in peace. According to her, Praew always gets a little overexcited when she opens presents.

The whole family piles into the dining room when Hathai calls them, Jamie offering to help when he sees both Pat and Hathai struggling to carry plates and bowls through from the kitchen. Pat refuses assistance—claiming that, as a guest, Jamie should just sit back and relax—saying that Ray can help instead. Ray is out of the dining room for longer than it should really take to walk between the two rooms, but Jamie is so caught up with Praew calling for "Uncle Jamie" to sit next to her that he decides to pay it no mind.

Jamie feels shy taking a seat by Praew with the way Pim and Dan watch on fondly, the couple opting to sit on the complete opposite side of the table. It seems Praew has once again asked to sit between Jamie and Ray, the seat on the other side of her remaining empty until Ray comes in carrying one last platter of food.

Once Hathai tells them to dig in, Jamie finds himself not putting food onto his plate to begin with, instead offering to help Praew pick out dishes. He spoons various items onto her plate before serving himself. Only afterwards does he see that Ray had been prepared to do the same thing, now holding a spoonful of food without a particular destination after he'd grabbed it for Praew, not considering someone else might do it first. Ray ends up placing it on his own plate, smiling as Jamie continues to dote on his niece.

"So, Jamie, Praew says you work in Honeybun Bookstore?" Pim addresses him across the table once they're all tucking in.

Jamie nods. "Mhm, yes. It's my parents' store. I help out there a few days a week."

"You work that much *plus* study full-time? Gosh, you must be so good at time management!" It seems Pim wasn't kidding when she said she'd heard a lot about him—he's sure he hadn't told her himself about his studies yet. "What are you studying, by the way?"

They chat easily about college and how his Chinese studies are coming along, with Dan offering to help. The man quickly retracts his offer when Jamie says something to him in flawless Mandarin, sounding much more natural than his own fumbled, out-of-practice attempts.

Praew tries to copy the unfamiliar words, eyebrows knitted together in concentration. "Is that right, Jemmie?"

"Hm... Not quite." Jamie repeats the phrase—slowing down his speech so she can hear the sounds—until Praew is able to say it back to him with moderate success, a round of applause breaking out around the table.

"Have you given much thought to what you'll do after college?" Pat asks once Praew goes back to eating.

"Mhm. I want to find some remote work as a translator— ideally for literature, but I'd settle for translating websites or something like that. Other than that, I just want to keep living in this town and working in the bookstore. I'd like to take it over someday. My brother, Tommy, isn't really that interested in books, so I don't think he'd mind if I wanted to run the business."

Jamie raises his fork to his mouth, chewing slowly. "Maybe it sounds silly to stay here, working in a bookstore, after studying Chinese for so long. But I've fallen in love with this town. I like living here, so I want to stick around."

When Jamie looks up from his plate, he finds Pat smiling at him fondly. He's not sure why, but he finds himself adding, "If that's... okay with you?"

Pat laughs. "Of course, Jamie! You won't hear any complaints from me!"

Jamie can't help but laugh, too. He can feel his ears burning, surely bright red from embarrassment, and he breathes a sigh of relief Hathai changes the subject.

- · ★ · -

"I like living here, so I want to stick around."

Ray stops chewing. He'd known Jamie liked it here, but the fact that he wants to stay here indefinitely, keep the family business going here for... Maybe the rest of his life? Any far away fantasy Ray had let himself have about someday asking Jamie to come live with him in New York is immediately dashed. There's no way he could ever ask that of Jamie, not now that he knows how sure he is on wanting to remain in this town. He tries not to show how defeated he feels at that moment, a half-formed image of their possible future crumbling like sand.

Ray lets his gaze linger on Jamie, his meal forgotten as he tries to catalog everything about him; how fluffy and soft his hair looks no matter how he styles it, how his breath hitches when shyness colors his cheeks, how his lips look when they curl up into a smile—eyes shining as bright as all the stars in the sky combined. It's not just about his physical appearance, though. This boy's personality is just as perfect. He's kind and caring and sweet, always looking out for others and treating everyone he meets with respect. He can also hold a grudge when he needs to (which Ray experienced first-hand after being an absolute ass the first time they'd met) and can be grouchy when something isn't going his way. When he has that pouty, grumpy expression, Ray wants nothing more than to scoop him up into his arms and pepper his face with kisses until he smiles, until there is only joy and laughter between them. This is just a small selection of the things Ray wants to remember. These are the memories he wants to store away for when his life isn't as perfect as it is right now.

He might not be able to keep this man by his side for long... but he's going to make every second count.

- ‧ ☆ ‧ -

"Present time!" Praew skips into the living room after dinner, almost tripping over her own feet in her eagerness. "Mommy, I can give Jemmie his present now, right?" The puppy eyes she makes at her mom make her agree instantly.

Praew bounds over to the Christmas tree, grabbing a small present from the top of the pile, but then turns shy. She approaches Jamie nervously, eyes downcast as she holds the gift out in front of her as far as she can. "For you."

"Thank you," Jamie says quietly, gently easing the gift from her hands. It's wrapped in slightly crumpled brown paper with a large pink bow tied lopsidedly around it. Jamie guesses Praew must have wrapped it herself.

He moves to open it but is quickly stopped by Hathai's call of, "Wait, wait, wait, let me take a picture!"

A chorus of "Maaaa!" sounds out around the room, all of her children clearly accustomed to such interruptions.

Jamie waits dutifully for Hathai to return with a digital camera, feeling a little awkward when she starts snapping photos of him holding the gift. The saving grace is Ray standing behind his mom, close enough that Jamie can sneak some glances at him instead of the camera to soothe himself.

Once he has permission, he delicately unties the bow, the room quiet enough for him to hear the sound of the ribbon slipping from around the gift. He takes his time in removing the paper, pulling it out of its scrunched up form to reveal something pink and woolen underneath.

"Aw, Praew, did you get me a hat?" He unfurls it and notices the two points on the top of it. *Huh?*

"No, I *designed* a hat and Aunty Mal made it!" Praew takes it from his hands before he's done inspecting it, going up onto her tiptoes to pull it onto his head. "A special hat! Just for Jemmie!"

Jamie can hear the camera shutter going off over and over as he pulls Praew in for a hug, genuinely touched by the thought that must have gone into this. When he lifts his eyes up, intending to look into Hathai's camera, he notices Ray's phone is pointed at him, too. Not only that, but Ray is covering part of his face with his free hand, trying and failing to hide the blush crawling up his cheeks and a cute bunny-toothed smile. Seeing such a fond expression on the face of the boy he likes has Jamie smiling brighter, too, eyes softening at the man behind the phone.

He keeps fiddling with the hat as Hathai and Ray take pictures, feeling shy at the attention. And how can he even be sure that it's on the right way around and in a flattering position? He's still not sure what the points are at the top or how they're meant to sit...

"Stop fiddling, Nhu, it looks good," Ray chastises, making his way towards him. "See."

When Ray perches on the arm of his chair to show him his phone, Jamie expects to see one of the photos Ray has just taken. Instead, it's open on the camera app, now in selfie mode. Surprised, his eyes widen, and Ray snaps a couple of photos of the two of them before Jamie really takes in his appearance.

Jamie's eyes light up at the two triangular ears on top of the hat, a cute face with whiskers stitched neatly into the front. "It's a cat?"

Praew beams up at him, nodding enthusiastically.

"I love it, Princess!" He bundles the little girl up into his arms again, making her giggle as he jostles her. "And thank you, Malai. It's wonderful." Jamie smiles warmly at Malai where she's sitting on the arm of her mother's chair.

"You're very welcome, Jamie." Malai grins back, obviously pleased with her handiwork.

"Okay, now it's your turn, Praew." Jamie shifts Praew to sit up on his lap so he can lean to the side and grab his tote bag, pulling out the pink and purple sparkly gift bag from inside it. Praew's eyes go large, the lights from the family's Christmas tree reflecting in them as she claps her hands excitedly, reaching into the bag.

Her tongue sticks out the side of her mouth in concentration as she rummages through tissue paper before pulling out a rectangular gift, clearly a book, and tears off the silver wrapping paper gleefully.

Praew grins at her mom. "It's the book, Mommy! The book Uncle Jemmie said I could have!" She seems incredibly excited about it considering she'd picked it out herself and knew she was going to receive it. Wrapping her arms around Jamie's neck, she giggles out a "Thank you, Jemmie~"

"That's okay, Princess." Jamie pats her back. "But, hmm..." he squeezes the bag, directing a cheeky smile at her. "I think there might be something else in here, too."

Praew squeals, both of her arms diving into the depths of the bag while Jamie holds it for her. She pulls out a sort of circular-shaped gift—something disk-like but taller on one side. Immediately she rips into the gift, pieces of wrapping paper flying about the room until she unveils the silver object inside.

"A crown!" She holds it aloft, staring at it in awe.

"A *tiara*, Praew. Perfect for a princess." Jamie boops her nose with a finger as laughter bubbles out of her at his words, distracting her momentarily from gazing at the object that has a large heart-shaped plastic gem set in the middle. He takes it from her and places it on her head gently, careful not to let the small combs at either end scratch her scalp as he positions it. "There we go," Jamie mumbles once he's satisfied with the placement of the tiara.

Of course, many more photos have to be taken now—by Hathai, by Ray, and by every other person in the room. This level of cuteness simply must be documented.

Praew won't separate herself from Jamie, even when everyone is rising from their seats an hour later because Pim and Dan need to take Praew home, her bedtime fast approaching. Jamie is all too happy to let her cling to him as they walk to the door, the tiara still perched on her head and Jamie's hat still firmly on his. Then, as she looks up into

Jamie's eyes to plead for him to come over to her house sometime for a tea party, she spots something above his head in the entryway.

"Look, Jemmie!" She points up, and Jamie follows her finger to see... "Mistletoe!" Happy squeals fall from her lips as she says it. Jamie doesn't remember *that* being there when he arrived. If it had been there earlier, it would have been suggested that he kiss...

He can feel his cheeks heat up at even the thought of kissing the boy he likes. Shaking his head, he tries to stop thinking about it. Now is not the time to daydream.

"Would you like a kiss, Praew?" His eyes dart to Pim and Dan for a second, not really sure how affectionate is too affectionate for their family, and both parents give a nod of approval.

Praew beams up at him, nodding as well, before turning her head to one side. She pokes at her cheek. "Right here." She pushes her cheek out in readiness.

"Okay~" Jamie crouches down and she leans towards him expectantly until he finally presses a kiss to her cheek, right where she'd pointed. Praew giggles at the exaggerated lip-smacking sound Jamie makes as he does it.

"Now it's my turn!" Praew says. Already, Jamie is turning his cheek towards her, ready for the sloppy "Mmmmwah!" she places there.

When Praew, Pim, and Dan finally make it out of the door, it is with a promise that they will see Jamie tomorrow; that Ray's family will sit with Jamie's family right near the front at the concert tomorrow night so they can cheer Jamie on together. Praew will also be involved in an earlier performance at the town hall—the Nativity play being put on by the local school—and Jamie confirms that he will make sure to come sit in the audience with everyone from both families to support her, too.

- · ★ · -

Ray and Jamie keep talking in the living room long after everyone else has either gone to bed or gone home, the two of them sitting at either end of the couch. Jamie's legs are curled up under himself cutely, sitting sideways and leaning his head on the backrest as he converses with Ray. Earlier, their conversation had been energetic—a buzz of excitement and nerves surrounding them. Now, it has a sleepier tone, voices quiet and slightly husky from so much use while they exchange anecdotes.

"You know, um... Nhu," the older of the two says awkwardly, Jamie humming for him to go on. "I actually got you a present, myself. One that isn't from Praew."

He watches as a pleasant blush rises on Jamie's cheeks, visible despite the low light from a lamp, lips slightly parted in an excited gasp. Ray takes that as approval and gets up from the couch to grab it from where he'd hidden it deep under the tree, not having told anyone about his little shopping trip earlier in the day.

"Ah, Hia! Hold onto it a little longer, please, actually!"

Ray's eyebrows furrow. Has he made Jamie uncomfortable by offering him a present? He turns back to face him.

"I'm getting you something too, Hia. It's just not here yet."

Oh.

"It wouldn't feel right—taking a gift from you before I have anything to give in return."

Ray thinks about arguing back. He'd give this boy anything he wanted and ask for nothing in return if only he'd let him.

"Okay, Nhu." He starts walking back towards the couch, trying not to let himself feel disheartened. Really, he knows Jamie's response means Ray can give him his gift eventually. He just... He'd been ready to give it to him tonight.

Jamie slowly rises from his seat to meet Ray halfway, until they're chest to chest. The shorter man buries his face in

Ray's neck. Being alone in the living room, Jamie seems more comfortable being affectionate than earlier. Ray wraps his arms around him, trying to pour all of his emotions into the embrace through its sincerity.

"I'd better get going," Jamie murmurs against him. Ray wants to ask him to stay longer, to stay the night, to stay as long as possible. But Jamie has a big day tomorrow with the concert... Ray should let him go home to his own bed to rest.

"Mm." Ray removes one arm from Jamie so they can walk side by side, his other arm still wrapped around Jamie's waist to keep him close as they stroll to the door. He leans against the wall and watches fondly as Jamie pulls on his shoes, then darts forward to grab his coat from the stand before Jamie can do it himself. Ray holds the coat out for him to slip on, sliding it up Jamie's arms with the utmost care as the man mutters a shy "Thank you."

"I had a nice time tonight, Hia." Jamie smiles, looking up at Ray with tired but happy eyes.

"I'm glad," Ray replies, expression soft. Then he smirks. "You know..." His eyes flick upwards once before returning his gaze to Jamie. "People usually kiss under mistletoe."

The younger man chuckles, looking away from Ray as he shakes his head. "I'm not going to kiss you, Ray."

Ray is disappointed, thinking about how he'd had to sneak off from the table at the start of dinner specifically to hang up that mistletoe in the hope it would make it easier for him to ask Jamie for a kiss. He'd meant to do it earlier in the day, but with all his family at home it was difficult to find an opportune moment. The plan wasn't to force Jamie into kissing him, of course, he just thought it would be a good way to start the conversation—*"Oh, look at what just so happens to be above us! How would you feel about... hmm, I don't know... maybe... a kiss?"* Something like that.

As their eyes meet again, there is a spark of something exciting and playful in Jamie's gaze. Maybe not all hope is lost. Jamie continues, "When we kiss, I want it to be because you want a kiss from me, not because a piece of mistletoe tells you to do it."

"When"?

The surety of Jamie saying "when we kiss"—*WHEN*—is enough to have Ray's brain stuttering to a halt, unable to string together any kind of response.

They're going to kiss.

Not now, but it's going to happen.

Because apparently it's a "when," not an "if."

"But, I guess..." Jamie goes up onto his tiptoes and presses a quick kiss to Ray's cheek. The touch of his lips is featherlight, a barely-there pressure that is there one second and gone the next, but the tingly feeling it leaves in its wake might last forever. "This much is fine."

Ray is still in shock, watching in a daze as Jamie starts to move away from him and open the front door. He wants to grab him—pull him back in for a hug or... Or something. Instead, he stands there uselessly, mouth opening and closing in what probably looks like a rather convincing impression of a goldfish.

"Goodnight, Hia."

The nickname he's already far too fond of seems to snap him back to the present enough to respond.

"Y-yes." He gulps, moving forward to hold onto the edge of the doorframe. Whether it's to keep him balanced and not actually swoon, or if it's just to be closer to the boy he likes for one more second, who can tell? "Goodnight to you too, Nhu."

Jamie smiles at him once more before turning and walking away.

"And text me when you get home!" Ray calls after him. He'd offered to walk Jamie home earlier but had flat out been refused—*"This isn't some big city, Ray, it's not like I'm gonna get mugged. Besides, it's surely even more dangerous for a celebrity like you to be out alone at night."*

A "Will do!" floats through the air in response.

Jem
I'm home.
Zero mugger encounters x

                                                       Ray
                                   Glad to hear it xx

Jem
Anyways, big day tomorrow
so I'm off to bed. Night, Hia x

                                                       Ray
                          Of course. Sweet dreams Nhu x

Saturday, December 24th

As the hours tick by until Jamie's performance, his nerves begin to build. It's not that he hasn't felt nervous up until this point, but now that his final rehearsal is over, it's all starting to feel a bit... real. He's going to sing. This evening. In front of the boy he likes. Who likes him, too.

Jamie is sitting on the couch with his mom, trying and failing to pay attention to the sitcom they're watching, when he gets a text from Ray.

> **Ray**
> I got you four seats near
> the front, right next to us.

Since Praew's Nativity play is before Jamie's concert, Ray's family have headed to the town hall already for the kids' final run-through of their performance, along with a pep-talk from their teachers. Ray had offered to reserve some seats for Jamie and his family when they got there — after all, Jamie did promise he'd be there to support Praew.

Jamie replies to Ray's text with a thumbs up emoji. Typing actual words feels too difficult with his brain in such a muddle.

*

He's broken out in a cold sweat by the time he and his family are getting ready to make their way to the town hall, almost forgoing putting on his coat because he suddenly feels too hot. The neckline of the woolen sweater against his skin, which he's worn many times without issue, feels itchy where it rubs against him now. His jeans feel too tight, his shoes too loose, his hair too long and prickly against his forehead. But his mom gives him a reassuring hug before they leave the apartment, telling him everything will be alright.

"Regardless of how tonight goes, you know we love you," she whispers in his ear, patting the back of his head.

Jamie knows that, he really does. But Ray is going to see him perform tonight. Will Ray love—?

Jamie squeezes his mom tightly in his arms. "Thank you, Mama."

Logically, Jamie knows that his family has met most, if not all, of Ray's family; all of the Amarins except for Malai live in town and frequent the bookstore. But as Ray waves him over to their seats now, it feels different. The knowing chuckle from his mom and the glint in Pat's eye remind Jamie that both of their families are aware of their fondness for each other. This evening isn't them meeting up as acquaintances. This is about their families getting to know each other better, learning more about each other in case, *for some reason*, their families start spending more time together in the near future.

Jamie waves to all of the Amarin family before taking his seat next to Ray, the rest of Jamie's family following suit.

"H-hey," Ray greets him, cheeks pink—probably feeling equally as nervous about their families spending time together. In the confined space of their seats, neither boy tries to go in for a hug, instead just settling next to each other awkwardly.

"Hi," is all Jamie can manage in response, distracting himself by removing his coat and resting it on the back of his seat. He glances around the room as he does so, noticing how the hall is really filling up now in preparation for the children's Nativity play. A pleasant chatter fills the space, the air sweetened by the scent of the hot chocolate being served just outside the door.

And then the lights are lowering, a hush falling over the crowd as heads turn to the stage.

Praew's part isn't until near the end, and Ray lifts his phone in readiness to capture her performance before she's even on the stage, the man clearly having paid attention during the run-through.

Jamie's heart melts as Praew waddles onto the stage, legs bulky in her sheep costume. She is definitely the cutest sheep on the stage. Malai clearly made the outfit for her, judging by how the woman is now lifting her own phone to take pictures, punching her brother's arm with hissed whispers of "Look at it!" The costume is a onesie in soft cream-colored fleece, with cute floppy ears on the hood and a pom-pom tail on the back. She looks especially well-put-together compared to her fellow herd members; the two other "sheep" in simple tights, with vests covered in what appear to be cotton wool balls. Not that the outfits really matter—it should be about the performance, after all. But... Praew is just so cute. And she gets even cuter when she raises her thumbs in a double thumbs up to Win as she takes her position on stage, Win taking that as his cue to press play on the recording of "Away in a Manger."

Jamie is surprised he hadn't put two and two together before now—knowing Praew must attend the local elementary school, where Win happens to be a student teacher. Win had always wanted to work with kids and, seeing him now, Jamie can see how perfectly it suits him.

Win mimes the words of the song exaggeratedly from where he's kneeling in the central aisle, leading the children. He performs the rudimentary choreography he had personally prepared for this number, too, some of the kids watching him closely as they fumble along, the bells on his reindeer antler headband jingling as he wiggles and gestures. Praew seems to be one of the more confident singers and dancers now that she's up there, still looking at Win but with a smile pulling at her lips.

Never did Jamie think he'd have a Christmas Eve quite like this. Sure, he'd come along with his family to see the Nativity performance every year since they moved into this town, but he didn't think he'd ever know one of the kids in the performance like this. He didn't think he'd ever feel this pride in his chest over something as simple as a little girl in a sheep costume. The knowledge that all of the people who he considers dearest to him are right here, in the room with him, being joyful with him, does nothing to ease how overcome he feels by his emotions.

It's surreal to Jamie how much his life has changed in the past two weeks—the list of his "dearest" people has grown more in the last ten days than he could have ever imagined. Ray coming back to town has turned his life upside down in the best way possible.

He never thought he'd even speak to Ray again after this past summer. There's no way he could have predicted how close they would become. Everything feels different now; he's still in the same town, living in the same house with his family, but now he has *this*. He has Ray in his life, and Ray's family, and they all seem to like him as much as he likes them. His world is opening up, possibilities blooming before his very eyes.

Jamie gently places his hand on Ray's thigh, craving something to ground him. He needs to convey how he's feeling, to press his fondness into his skin. He'd hold Ray's hand if he could right now, but doesn't want to bother the man—still busy holding his phone steady with two hands, capturing his niece's performance so he can watch it back for years to come.

I could get used to this. Going to see his favorite little princess in school plays with this man by his side, both their families surrounding them... He wants this forever.

No. Jamie shifts his gaze away from Ray, though he can't quite bring himself to let go of his leg just yet. It's far too soon for thoughts so gooey and sentimental. He's not even sure what will happen at the end of the holidays—when Ray might be leaving or how long he'll be gone this time. But, no matter what comes next, it won't be the end for them. It can't be.

He realizes his grip on Ray's thigh has tightened, fingertips digging into the denim of his pant leg in a way that would surely be uncomfortable if Ray wasn't so focused on Praew. Jamie forces himself to relax. The last thing he wants is to worry Ray.

They'll work something out.

Won't they?

After the school's Nativity play, there is a break in the performances scheduled for the evening, enough time for people to make their way out to the food trucks and drinks stands set up outside for some sustenance.

The families of the children who had been in the play linger, taking photos of the kids as they pose on stage. A couple of the school teachers get up onto the stage with them, and it doesn't take long before the children are pleading for Win to join in, too. With a dissonant chorus of "WinWin!" from the kids, Win makes his way onto the stage, his headband jingling with a fond shake of his head. Every member of Ray's family, including Ray, is on picture-taking duty, snapping a frankly alarming amount of photos of Praew with her classmates and teachers.

Once everyone is done taking photos, one of the teachers leads the kids backstage to collect anything they'd left there earlier and get changed out of their costumes if they wish—the kid who had been playing Mary looking very uncomfortable in a too-long dress. Jamie's family excuses themselves, saying they'll go line up to get food for everyone, while the rest of the group waits for Praew. Jamie isn't sure who he should stay with right now. He thinks Praew might want to see him when she comes back, but he doesn't want to intrude if her family would rather greet her first. So maybe he should go with his parents for now—he can always congratulate Praew later.

It's Win that makes the choice for him, leaping recklessly from the stage now that there aren't any little kids to see his naughtiness.

"Jem!"

Win envelopes him in a warm hug, jumping up and down in the embrace to make Jamie do the same. The ridiculousness of their actions makes Jamie giggle, the sound tinged with embarrassment because his crush is literally *right there*, probably watching this happen. But he quickly pushes the shyness away—nothing is going to stop him from hugging his best friend.

"You did such a good job with the Nativity, Winnie!" Jamie says once they're finally done jumping.

"Thanks! It was fun!" When Win pulls away from the embrace, a cheeky smile has formed on his face, eyes flitting over to Ray. "And when are you going to introduce me to your celebrity boyfriend, hm?"

Suddenly pink-cheeked, both Ray and Jamie splutter out some variation of, "He's not— I'm not— I mean, we're—"

Win just laughs, walking over to Ray casually and extending a hand. "I'm Win, Jamie's best friend."

"Hi! I-I'm Ray," he stutters as he belatedly grabs the man's hand, Jamie observing Ray's awkwardness with a smile.

"Yeah, I gathered that much," Win sasses back, that cheekiness still present in his expression. "So, what are your intentions with—"

"I did it!" Praew comes bounding up to her family, saving Ray from having to bumble through an answer to that question. The little girl jumps into her father's arms, squealing as Dan spins her around in the air. He brings her into his chest, Pim wrapping her arms around her husband and daughter to coo at Praew and praise her.

Praew only stays in their arms for a handful of seconds before she's wriggling, making grabby hands at Jamie. The man in question is frozen. Sure, he's held her on his lap before, but he's never outright carried her. Or any child. Not sensing Jamie's nerves (or perhaps just choosing to ignore them), Dan passes the little girl over to him, her small arms wrapping around his neck in an instant. She's seven— probably too old to still be doing this, or she will be soon—so this might be the only time Jamie gets to carry her.

"I did it, Jemmie."

Her part in the Nativity performance may have only been small, but Jamie knows first-hand that getting up on stage at all can take a lot of guts. He nuzzles his nose against the fleecy fabric still covering her head, speaking softly enough that no one else can hear. "I'm so proud of you, Princess."

All of Praew's limbs squeeze tighter around him and he makes sure to squeeze right back, to wrap her up in whatever safety and comfort he can possibly offer her.

Eventually, he has to put her down—she's still got other people to hug and greet. Jamie watches on fondly as she approaches each member of her family for a cuddle, until she spots that Win is still lingering near them.

- · ✻ · -

Win knows he probably should have walked away and helped with packing up the Nativity props. And he is doing that... sort of. He's *very busy* checking out the condition of the one hay bale that just happens to be near where Jamie and Ray's families are standing. Definitely not eavesdropping. Much. Hey, this is the first time he's seen Jamie interact with Ray or any of Ray's family, so who can blame him for being a little curious?

"WinWin..." Praew approaches, a small hand lifting to grab the sleeve of his sweater. Win crouches down to be at her level, smiling at her encouragingly. "Thank you. For checking on me."

Before the performance had begun, Win sensed the little girl's nerves. He'd taken it upon himself to call her over to a quieter space backstage to make sure she was okay. Praew had immediately burst into tears, sobbing over how scared she was about messing up. She hiccupped through telling Win about something her uncle had supposedly said to her, about focusing on the people who were there to support you. Win comforted her as best he could, telling her that her uncle sounded very smart while he patted her back. Honestly, it sounded like good advice—the kind of thing he could imagine Jamie saying, that boy wise beyond his years. Not that there was any chance he was the "uncle" she spoke of. Surely they weren't that close already. *Right?* And either way, it was not the time to think about such things; there was a kid crying, for goodness' sake! She was still sniffling, nose running and tears staining her face. There couldn't be long now until the show would start, so Win had to find a solution quickly. Since Praew seemed particularly nervous about her first song, Win decided to make her a promise—he wouldn't start the music for the number until she'd given him a thumbs up. Praew had given him a watery smile in response, extending a pinky to him to seal the deal.

"That's alright, Praew! You did great up there!" Win pats her head, the little girl's smile much brighter now than it had been an hour ago.

- · ★ · -

After speaking to Win, Praew totters back to her family who greet her with another (although much shorter) round of hugs. Then, as she's unwrapping her arms from Ray's middle, she seems to realize who's missing.

"Where are Apple and Tommy?" she asks, eyebrows furrowed as she scans the room. "And BanBan. I need to hug BanBan." Her eyes are large and tear-filled as she pouts up at Ray, bottom lip quivering like she might start crying or throwing a tantrum if she can't hug Banlue—"*BanBan*"—right this instant.

"Uhh..." Ray feels kind of panicked. He'd heard Apple say that they were going outside, but he'd been too excited to chat with Praew to really pay attention to where they were going.

"They're just outside, Princess, standing in line for hotdogs!" Jamie to the rescue.

Praew jumps up and down, clearly excited—by the idea of hotdogs, learning where Jamie's family is, or maybe both of those things. Whatever the reason for her joy, they're all making their way to the exit a moment later, led by the most adorable little sheep any of them have ever seen.

All of Ray's family are surprised by the unusual friendship between Praew and Banlue, the girl running right to him for a hug once she spots him in line for food, and a wide smile forming on the man's face. None of the Amarins (other than Ray and Praew) have seen Banlue smile before, the gentleman who they had all seen as indifferent and cold now seeming soft and caring as he congratulates Praew sincerely.

Once Praew has had a cuddle with Apple and a very awkward one-armed hug from Tommy, she insists on holding Banlue's hand. She doesn't let go until he has to grab his wallet to pay for the food, and even then she grumbles about it.

Jamie goes quiet when he's nearly done eating his hotdog, his anxiety clearly starting to get to him. He might still be smiling, nodding along to the conversation going on around him, but Ray can tell he's not really paying attention.

Ray takes a risk, he places his hand on Jamie's back. When the contact is met with no visible discomfort, he slowly starts to rub circles into the man's shoulders. He feels when Jamie starts to lean into it, seeking the comforting pressure. He keeps it up until Jamie has managed his last bite of food, until he is turning towards Ray, pressing his face into Ray's neck. Jamie's arms remain limp at his sides, even when the older man draws him in as close as he can.

When Jamie pulls away, his gaze meets Ray's. He looks at Ray like he is the only thing keeping him tethered; glazed eyes boring into him, their unfathomable depth drawing Ray in. All he can do is keep his own gaze steady on Jamie until the man is burying himself against his chest, shoulders shuddering on a shaky exhale.

If the pair had shown this level of physical affection at any time other than this, Malai might have teased them. She still looks like she's tempted to do so—come on, she's only human—but a glare from Ray tells her not to start anything right now. He knows she'll probably tease him about it later. After all, she's only got a few more days to embarrass Ray before he heads back to the big city.

- • ☆ • -

"Dear, isn't it time for you to head inside and get ready?" Jamie hears his mom's voice over the static sound filling his head. He nods in response when he sees a couple of other choir members making their way back into the hall.

Like a much more somber version of Praew's earlier cuddles, Jamie hugs each person from both families before he leaves. Most of the embraces feel hollow as he makes his way from person to person, everyone trying to squeeze some of his usual bubbliness back into him but to no avail. If it wasn't for the look of concern he sees from Praew, Jamie wouldn't even try to put on a brave face, forcing a smile when he turns to her.

She dives at him, wrapping her arms around his tummy. "I believe in you, Jemmie."

"Thank you, Princess."

He hugs Ray once more before turning to head back into the hall, making it all of five paces before Ray is catching up to him, grabbing his wrist.

"Nhu..."

Jamie looks at him with a combination of surprise and curiosity.

"Can I kiss you?"

One of the younger man's eyebrows lifts incredulously.

"On the cheek. You know, for luck," Ray quickly clarifies.

Jamie glances around them before making a decision.

"Okay, Hia. You may."

- · ★ · -

Ray can feel his hands sweating. Now that he knows he can do it, he feels shy. He leans in slowly, not wanting to spook Jamie. Though maybe he should have just done it quickly—what if his glacial pace makes Jamie think he doesn't want to kiss him? He can't have that! He swiftly closes the last few inches. Unlike the last time he'd kissed Jamie's cheek, when it had been the briefest contact of soft skin against his lips, he lets himself linger this time. In reality, his lips are probably on Jamie's cheek for no more than two seconds, but it feels like a lifetime with how they both hold their breath. It's charged with something, too—a need to soothe that wasn't there before, like he's trying to pull the worry out from under Jamie's skin through the kiss.

He remains close as he reluctantly removes his lips from Jamie's soft cheek, whispering into Jamie's ear in a way that he can only hope is reassuring, "You can do it, Nhu. I know you can. And you know it, too."

- · ☆ · -

"I know you can. And you know it, too."

Somehow, despite being the most clumsy-tongued person Jamie has ever met, Ray had actually said the right thing.

Jamie keeps thinking about his words as he and the rest of the choir warm up and go over their setlist one more time. They might not be professional singers, but this concert is important to the town—a tradition that has been upheld for as long as anyone can remember. The local choir has always performed on Christmas Eve, and is always the last act of the night; their voices spreading festive cheer for the days ahead.

He's nervous. More so than usual. He's sung with the choir the past two Christmases, but this is the first time he's had a solo. The other choir members had been trying to get him to take the solo since he first joined, but Jamie had always refused. He didn't want to be in the spotlight; he was content to stand at the back, blend in, let his voice just be one of many that filled the air. But after years of persuasion (well, nagging), Jamie had caved and agreed to do it. He's regretting that decision now, feeling unbearably lightheaded and nauseous at the sight of people making their way back to their seats, showtime looming near. But...

"You can do it, Nhu. I know you can. And you know it, too."

Jamie gulps.

He can do this.

Besides, his solo is near the end, he's got plenty of time to ~~freak out~~ *get used to* being on the stage before then.

- · ★ · -

As the choir's performance goes on, Ray finds himself getting more and more curious about what Jamie's solo might be. Such a mixture of traditional and modern tunes have been sung already that it really feels like it could be anything at all. Ray pictures Jamie singing a classic carol—perhaps something like "O Holy Night." Sure, Ray hasn't really gotten to hear what Jamie's voice sounds like on its own yet, his attempts to listen in on choir practice having been rather fruitless, but from what he has heard of it, he already knows the boy could deliver that song. Or perhaps Jamie will choose to sing something more pop-y—not "All I Want for Christmas Is You," come on, this isn't *Love Actually*. But maybe something like...

A vision of him dressed in a short red dress with white trim and shiny black buttons pops into his head, Jamie swaying his hips with a false coyness on his face as he croons out the lyrics of "Santa Baby." Jamie holds onto a microphone stand, fingers grazing up and down it in a way that feels increasingly lewd, a heated gaze directed at Ray, a smirk on his lips as he lifts a delicate hand to undo the buttons of the dress, revealing—

Now is not the time for such thoughts.

Ray shifts in his seat, cheeks as red as Jamie's imaginary dress as he tries to rid himself of the mental image enough to concentrate on the performance. He only manages to really focus on the choir again when Jamie is being introduced, stepping forward to take center stage. Praew is sitting next to Ray, reaching for his hand as she also spots Jamie making his way to the front.

Ray waits with bated breath, watching as Jamie takes in one last shaky inhale before he begins to sing "Have Yourself a Merry Little Christmas." *Of course.* Ray leans forward in his seat, readying himself.

Nothing could have prepared him for this. One verse in and Ray has already stopped breathing, emotions lumped together in his throat. This man... his voice...

Ray can feel where goosebumps have broken out all over his skin. It feels like even the hairs on his scalp are standing on end. He grasps Praew's hand tighter in his. He'll drift away on this melody if he doesn't have something to hold him down.

- · ☆ · -

Halfway through the song, Jamie risks a glance in Ray's direction to find that the man's reaction is better than anything he could have hoped for. Ray's lips are slightly parted and it seems like he keeps forgetting to breathe; alternating between holding completely still and then gasping in breaths like he's inhaling the words right out of Jamie's mouth. His eyes are full to the brim with tears, even with how many are rolling down his cheeks. It seems like he's so intent on watching every moment of Jamie's performance that he can't even blink, eyelids merely fluttering half-shut each time they become too watery to see.

He looks in awe, completely starstruck, but not in the way of an obsessed fan. This is a look that says, "I am so blessed to know you." It says, "You mean the world to me."

He looks at Jamie like he loves him.

Perhaps he does.

Jamie closes his eyes as he holds a high note, finding the vision of Ray imprinted onto the inside of his eyelids. It's everything he needs. But for how long will he—

He can't look at Ray again.

He won't be able to sing if he lets his emotions get the better of him. He just needs to get through the last line, hoping the wobble of his voice is covered by his vibrato.

The song ends and the whole hall is silent, suspended in awe, until the applause erupts. Jamie finally relaxes, relief flooding over him.

- · ★ · -

Ray can't be sure if he's the one who starts the standing ovation—can't see anyone but Jamie as he rises from his seat to clap as hard as he can. He wants to holler and shout, but his chest is so tight, his lungs and heart constricted from the sheer amount of adoration he feels for that man. All he can do is keep clapping and hope that no one hears his sniffled sobs.

He waits impatiently for Jamie to come down from the stage after the performance, practically vibrating where he's standing. He pulls Jamie into a bear hug as soon as he's within arm's reach.

"You were incredible!" Ray leans back and grabs at Jamie with both hands, shaking him to accentuate his words. "Incredible!" he reiterates as he yanks the man back and forth once more. Jamie's body bends with the action, his face ending up closer to Ray's as he wobbles forwards. They're a hair's breadth away from each other now, close enough to hear and feel when their breaths hitch—both of them, in sync. Jamie's eyelids keep fluttering as his gaze flicks between Ray's lips and eyes. Their faces are so close. So close, Ray can almost taste—

"Thank you, Hia." A rosy-cheeked Jamie pats Ray's shoulders, removing himself from the embrace. All the intensity sparking between them dissipates, Ray overcome now with worry. Jamie said they'd kiss—Ray won't forget that it's a "when," not an "if"—so why...?

Jamie leans down to allow Praew to fling herself into his arms, her hands grasping at the back of his sweater. "I'm proud of you, Uncle Jemmie." It's clear that her words have Jamie choking back tears, holding onto her until she lets go of him first. When Jamie rights himself, he clears his throat, willing his lip to stop quivering with a smile.

Ray watches as Jamie is hugged and greeted by everyone else; his parents, his brother, Ray's family. After that, Ray hopes he'll get a chance to talk to Jamie, but then more people are coming over to congratulate him—people from the choir and other locals approaching to tell him how well he did. Jamie keeps sneaking glances over at Ray, the smile on his face wide and genuine, his eyes soft and sparkling.

He seems happy and at ease. Especially when he looks at Ray.

So... why won't he kiss me?

Everyone makes their way outside for the last event of the evening—a visit from Santa himself! Ray pulls his jacket back on as he steps out into the night air, while Jamie beside him already has his coat on, now busy positioning the pink cat hat onto his head just right. The tinny sound of a recording of jingling bells alerts the children that Santa is almost here; on the back of a small float covered in fairy lights, fake snow, and oversized candy canes.

Ray glances at Praew as Santa's float comes to a stop in front of the hall, wishing he had his phone out to capture the look of wonder in her eyes. Two "elves" clamber down from the float, asking children to start lining up to meet Santa, and Praew is off—dragging her dad to join the back of the line. Jamie chuckles, sliding his hand into Ray's as they watch on fondly.

"We're gonna head home now, Dearies." Apple informs Ray and Jamie, pulling a rather tired looking Banlue behind her, Tommy trailing after them. "Be sure to give Praew a big hug from all of us and wish her a Merry Christmas!"

As Apple tries to walk off, Banlue stops directly in front of Jamie. "Don't be home too late." One side of his lip quirks up infinitesimally as he says it, chuckling lowly when Jamie gasps out a scandalized "Papa!"

Praew bounds up to the pair not long after Jamie's family have left, waving a lollipop above her head. "Look what Santa gave me!" She wiggles the lolly. "He said I'll also get *loooads* of presents tomorrow since I've been so good." Her chest puffs out, clearly proud to be on Santa's "nice" list.

- · ☆ · -

"But I want to watch it with *both* of my uncles!" Praew whines, her small hands fisted angrily in her dad's coat as she frowns up at Dan. Earlier, Pim had told Jamie that their family has developed a tradition of watching *The Muppet Christmas Carol* on Christmas Eve over the past few years. When Dan had said it was time to go home, Praew had been super excited—babbling about this being the first year she'd get to watch the movie with Uncle Wawa. But now that she knows Jamie isn't joining them...

Pim rests her hand on her daughter's head. "Praew, Sweetie, Jamie should spend time with his own family this evening, too," she reasons. The quiver of Praew's lip suggests she's going to protest.

"Mhm." Jamie nods in agreement with Pim, despite the urge to give in to the little girl's angry sniffles. "My family will be expecting me home soon."

He crouches down, a soft smile on his lips. "Hugs?"

Praew half-stomps over to him and shoves her face into his neck, allowing him to cuddle her. Accepting that Jamie won't be coming over tonight, she relaxes into the embrace after a moment, her arms coming up to clutch around his back tightly.

"Maybe we can invite Jamie over some other time to watch a movie. What do you think?" Dan asks. Praew is immediately springing up out of Jamie's arms, all signs of her earlier frustration gone and replaced with pure joy.

"Really, Daddy? We can invite Jemmie over?" She bounces between Dan and Jamie, cheeks made round from her wide smile.

Dan nods, holding out a hand to her, which she makes to grab. "Come on, now. Let's head back and get ready for the movie with Granny and Grandpa. Wawa will join us in a bit."

Praew pauses at her dad's words, a pout forming that Dan is quick to soothe before it can escalate into a tantrum. "He has to walk Jamie home first, then he'll come over, right?" Dan's gaze flicks to Ray, waiting until Ray nods.

"Yes. I'll be there soon." Reassured, Praew takes her dad's hand and they head home.

- · ★ · -

Jamie and Ray spend a while longer enjoying the ambiance outside the town hall, Ray buying them both hot chocolate to drink as they find a place to sit and watch the world go by. They talk about inconsequential things; their favorite movies, what food they like, the best toppings to have on hot chocolate. But eventually, when Ray's cup is almost empty and he knows his time to ask is running out, he finally spits out what's been on his mind.

"I— um..." Ray's stuttering has Jamie turning to eye him quizzically. "Um... Earlier. I thought..." He knows his cheeks are red, unable to look directly at Jamie lest he evaporate from shyness. "I thought you were going to kiss me."

Jamie hums thoughtfully, bumping his shoulder with Ray's. "I wanted to."

The admission has Ray's gaze snapping to Jamie's, eyes flitting about his face to take in how widely he is smiling, the glint in his eyes.

"Why didn't you?"

The long answering sigh is concerning, Jamie clearly having to take some time to organize his thoughts. "We can't, Ray. Not in public. People will talk."

"Let them talk," Ray responds quickly. He lets himself lean in towards Jamie, aching to close the gap between their lips at last.

"Ray..." It seems Jamie only calls him "Ray" when it's something serious. It makes him nervous. "I'm not ready for that."

Ray tries not to show how his heart drops. Really, he gets it. It's a lot—to be with someone who has celebrity status. But surely, in this small town, no one would photograph them or tip off a gossip magazine, would they?

He thinks back to when he'd first got into town; how crowds of people had tried to subtly follow him whenever he was out of the house, taking pictures of him when they thought he wasn't looking. Considering this and just how much time he's spent with Jamie lately, it's a miracle that no rumors about the two of them have popped up online yet. But Ray has never dated a man in the public eye before, has only ever had rumored relationships with his female co-stars, and has always carefully sidestepped any questions about his sexuality. Maybe his presumed heterosexuality is enough of a veil for them to get away with being as affectionate as they have been. But if someone sees them kissing? Well... Ray sees Jamie's point. It would take an idiot not to realize that they're something more than friends.

"But I do want to be with you." Jamie rests a hand on his leg. "Can we just keep things private for now, please?"

A part of Ray knows he should probably point out that "for now" might be all they have. But a larger part just wants to enjoy the time they have together.

"Of course, Nhu."

Ray's phone vibrates incessantly in his pocket, and he pulls it out to find quite a few messages from Pim.

> **Pim**
> Hey
>
> **Pim**
> I know you're having fun but maybe start heading home
>
> **Pim**
> I've told Praew to go put her PJs on but we both know she's gonna start asking for you soon
>
> **Pim**
> I can only distract her with popcorn for so long

It's Jamie who speaks first, probably able to tell from Ray's crestfallen expression that he needs to go. "It's getting late, isn't it? Shall we head back?" Jamie has at least agreed to let Ray walk him home today, so they won't have to say goodbye just yet.

"Mm. But first, um... Could I take a picture with you?" Ray sees Jamie pulling back at his words and rushes to say, "I won't post it anywhere, I promise. I just... I would like to take a picture of you. Of us."

The gentlest smile forms on Jamie's lips. "Okay, Hia."

They pose in front of one of the many Christmas trees wrapped in strings of lights, taking a simple selfie standing side by side, cheek to cheek. There is no need for filters or gimmicky poses—their rosy complexions say it all, shyness and happiness rolled into one.

Jamie stays close when they look over the picture together on Ray's phone. "Thank you, Nhu." He pockets his phone after he sends the photo to Jamie, holding a hand out to the younger man. He figures that if someone wanted a picture of them holding hands, they'd have taken one already. "Are you ready to go?"

The man seems to take one last look at his surroundings, making Ray do the same. The lights strung up above their heads, the faces of joyful locals, the sparkle in Jamie's eye... Ray never wants to forget this.

Jamie takes Ray's hand.

The stroll back to Jamie's place is slow, neither man wanting the night to come to an end quite yet. They can still hear the music being played near the town hall, quieter at this distance but still loud enough to provide a soundtrack to their walk. Jamie hums along to the song currently playing, while Ray just listens. He can't get enough of this man's voice, even now, as it breaks from overuse when he tries to hit one of the high notes.

Ray lets go of Jamie's hand to wrap an arm around his waist instead, encouraging him closer now that they're on an empty street. Jamie nuzzles into his side, eyes half closed as he hums his approval into Ray's neck. He must be tired, Ray realizes; he's had a long day of stress, though hopefully he's able to relax now that the concert is over.

They turn a corner and Honeybun bookstore comes into sight, not far from them, and all Ray wants is to take this boy home and cuddle him. He wants to show him how much he adores him and how much he means to him. If he was better with words, he'd write a poem. But, for now, he'll have to settle for whatever words he can gather.

When he opens his mouth to speak, his voice is a low rumble—quiet, soft, yet carrying everything he needs to convey. "I'm so proud of you, Nhu." He presses a kiss to the top of Jamie's head—well, to the cat hat on Jamie's head.

"And your voice... it's..." Ray has no idea how to finish that sentence. It's... wonderful? Calming? Full of passion? Everything he's ever needed and never known?

They're standing outside Honeybun Bookstore now, their figures illuminated by the streetlamps and a light that's been left on inside the store. Ray gazes into Jamie's eyes. There's anticipation in them, an excitement swirling in their depths, but a hint of self-doubt creeps in the longer Ray goes without finishing his sentence.

"Your voice is beautiful," he concludes.

Or maybe he shouldn't stop there. Maybe there's still more for him to say. He steels himself, drawing in a deep breath. "Everything about you is beautiful."

Ray watches Jamie's mouth open in a gasp, the cloud of his exhale visible in the cold air.

Jamie's eyes are darting around Ray's features as if looking for something, some sort of sign, while Ray is unsure what he should do after confessing how enamored he is.

"You know, Hia..." Jamie's gaze sets into something more confident. "There's no one around now..." He takes a step closer. "And there's no mistletoe pressuring us."

When Ray tries to hum in response, not sure what words might fly out of his mouth if he tries to speak, he finds that even that noise comes out broken.

Jamie raises his head up, his nose almost brushing Ray's. "Would you like to kiss me, Ray?"

All of the air in Ray's lungs leaves him in a rush. "Yes."

And then they're leaning forwards, eyes fluttering closed, hands coming up to touch, to caress, as their lips—

The door of the bookstore swings open, the shrill ringing of the bell startling the boys apart. Of course, it's Tommy standing in the doorway. He doesn't offer them any greeting. Instead, he stares resolutely at Ray with a look of "I'm planning the easiest way to dispose of your body if you mess things up with my brother." When he speaks, the message is clearly aimed at Jamie, despite how his eyes are still glued calculatingly to Ray. "Mama said Ray is invited to her birthday party on the twenty-sixth."

Ray blinks a few times, trying to calm his heaving breaths from just... everything that's happened in the last thirty seconds.

He clears his throat and does his best to keep his voice steady, not wanting to be seen cracking under Tommy's scrutiny. "Please, tell her I'd love to attend. Just let me know if I should bring anything and what time, and I'll be there."

Tommy nods, then turns to Jamie and tips his head back, gesturing for Jamie to come inside. Jamie, face beet red, lowers his gaze sheepishly, taking small steps towards the door. Just before he passes his brother, he turns back around to face Ray. Before Ray can prepare himself, his face is being held in Jamie's hands, the man pressing a kiss to Ray's cheek much like he'd done the previous night. He mumbles a quiet, "Goodnight, Hia. Merry Christmas," before he pulls away.

Ray is marginally more collected than when he'd received a cheek kiss yesterday, able to respond after a moment. "Thank you, Nhu. H-have a good Christmas. And..."—it's like now they've started kissing each other on the cheek, they just can't stop, Ray planting one on Jamie's cheek before finishing—"sweet dreams, Nhu."

The sound of Tommy faking a cough has Jamie's posture going stiff, turning quickly to his brother and scurrying through the door. Tommy remains in place for a few extra moments after Jamie is gone, like he might say something to Ray—maybe verbally warn him to not hurt his brother. However, it seems Tommy is a man of few words; choosing instead to stare at Ray in a way that has him shifting uncomfortably. Tommy doesn't even blink until Jamie is calling him to go back inside.

The door to the store closes and Ray exhales. He takes a moment to breathe before he heads to Pim and Dan's house, walking quicker each time his phone vibrates with another message from Pim.

He spends the next hour and a half watching the movie at his sister's house; Praew in his lap on a large beanbag, while his parents, Pim, and Dan are squashed together on the couch.

It's cozy, he finds, to be surrounded by people he loves like this. But he can't help but wish Jamie was here with him.

The thought remains as he drags himself to the guest room after saying goodnight to Praew, changing into a loose t-shirt and climbing into cold bed sheets. He shouldn't feel so alone; under his sister's roof, with his niece fast asleep in the room next door. Perhaps it's the absence of his favorite book on the bedside table that makes his loneliness so acute. Perhaps he's still not used to being without it. That book could always bring him comfort. Or perhaps he just misses Jamie alread—

Ray's phone buzzes and he rushes to answer it, hoping it might be Jamie. It isn't.

Teddy
Did Praew's thing go okay?

Despite how uncomfortable Teddy is with emotions, he's always had a soft spot for Praew. Ray had told him how nervous Praew had been to perform, so it's no surprise that he's texting Ray to check on her.

Ray
It went well! One sec,
I'll send a pic

Ray scrolls through the hundreds of photos he's taken this evening, trying to pick out the best one to show Teddy. Initially, he intends to send just one of Praew, but then he realizes... this could be his opportunity to show him Jamie.

He could send one of the pictures he's taken of him today. But he wants to be a little discreet about it.

He selects a few photos; one of Praew on her own in her costume, one of her on stage with all her classmates and teachers, and one that he'd secretly taken of Jamie hugging Praew after her performance.

Teddy
WOAH who's the hottie?

Ray
The guy in the last pic is Jamie.

Ray
You know—bookstore boy

Ray is ready to start waxing poetic about Jamie, about their evening, about their almost kiss, but...

Teddy
No, not him. He's okay but

Teddy
Who's the one on stage with Praew? Center left, with the reindeer antlers

He has to take a moment to look at the picture, pinching the screen to zoom in enough to check who he's talking about.

Oh.

Ray
That's Win. He's a student teacher at Praew's school, I think.

Teddy
Win... I like it

Teddy
Is he single? Maybe I could
WIN over his heart?

                    Ray
          He's Jamie's best friend.
          I could ask him for you?

Teddy
Thanks bud. You're the best.
Gtg, talk soon!

Well... that's an unexpected development.

Sunday, December 25th

"It's Christmas!"

Ray wakes up with a start as the door of the spare room bangs open, Praew running in, dragging an overflowing stocking behind her. He barely has his eyes open before Praew is jumping on top of him. "Wawa! Did you hear me? It's Christmas!"

Freeing his arms from under the comforter, he wraps the squirming little girl in a hug. "Mhm. Happy Christmas, Princess."

Praew giggles, worming her way out of his arms. "Hey, only Uncle Jemmie calls me Princess!"

"Well, is it okay if I call you that, too?"

She sits back on her heels, a tiny finger tapping at her chin in thought. "Hm... Okay!"

Ray wrestles her into another hug. "My Princess~" he sing-songs, swaying her from side to side until she's whining to be let go of.

"Look what I got!" Praew pulls each item out of her stocking to show him, Ray sitting up against the headboard and smiling fondly at his precious niece. Once she hears Pim calling that breakfast is ready, she scampers off, leaving Ray to chuckle as she toddles away with her gifts.

Judging by the pale strip of light coming through the edge of the bedroom curtains, it must be early. He reaches for his phone.

It's seven AM. Jamie probably isn't awake yet. But... *Just so that it's there for him when he wakes up...*

Ray
Merry Christmas Nhu x

- • ☆ • -

Jamie wakes up to the smell of pancakes. But not just any old pancakes; these are *gingerbread pancakes*, the ones his dad always makes on Christmas Day.

He hums, stretching out his sleep-stiff limbs like a lounging cat, before pulling himself out of bed.

When he grabs his phone, he finds that amongst the texts from his friends and classmates wishing him a happy Christmas, there's also one from Ray.

Ray
Merry Christmas Nhu x
[sent 2 hours ago]

He chuckles. Praew must have woken Ray up early.

Jem
Have a lovely Christmas, Hia xx

Jamie might not be meeting up with Ray today, far too shy to even suggest it given how significant that might seem since it's *Christmas Day*, but that doesn't mean they can't text. Every moment where it wouldn't be seen as rude to do so, Jamie has his phone out, exchanging small messages with Ray about how the day is going and the occasional photo. Like the one Jamie has just received...

Ray
Does it suit me?

Jamie snorts at the image of Ray in a brand new ugly Christmas sweater. It's somehow even more visually offensive than the one he's been wearing lately, the front largely taken up with an approximation of Santa's face, the festive figure's expression unsettling with its wide eyes and Cheshire cat grin. The rest of the sweater is no less eye-watering; made up of thin red and green stripes that have Jamie's eyes crossing with the effort it takes to look at them.

It's hideous. Absolutely atrocious. Should be burned immediately.

But... it's on Ray... and Jamie can see his cute bunny-toothed smile at the top of the photo...

Jem
You look very handsome.

Ray
(ᴜ ω ᴜ)

This guy is such a dork.

Jamie doesn't realize that he's zoned out, smiling at his phone screen, until Tommy playfully punches his arm. "Hey! Stop texting your boyfriend and help me set the table." And with that, Tommy takes off for the dining room, leaving no room for argument.

Jamie stomps after him, embarrassment coloring his cheeks.

- · ★ · -

Eventually, Ray has to stop looking at his phone so he can get ready to head to his parents' place for Christmas dinner with the whole family. He barely pulls on his shoes and coat before Pim is handing him several bags full of gifts to carry over, Dan already carrying far too many. It takes Praew some coaxing to put her hat on—wanting instead to wear the tiara Jamie gave her. The compromise they come to is that she can wear the tiara *on top of* the beanie.

The tiara crisis sorted, the four of them stumble out of the door, noses quickly tinted pink by the cold winter air as they walk the short distance to the Amarin residence.

Ray doesn't have an opportunity to talk to Jamie again for several hours; too busy with Praew and the rest of his family to really notice time passing, until he's finally settling into his childhood bed. Once he's comfortable, he decides it's time to check in on Jamie.

Ray
Hey

While he waits for a response, he checks Instagram. Plus, he knows he should probably post something—he has a public persona to maintain, after all. He scrolls through the pictures he's taken today to look for something that will satisfy fans without showing too much of his family or their home. After a few moments, he settles for a picture he'd taken of the mountain of wrapping paper Praew had left in her wake, the little girl very determined to open all of her presents in the shortest time possible. He captions it, "The aftermath of Christmas," and posts it.

It's barely ten seconds later that he sees Jamie like the post, despite the boy not replying to his text yet. Well, that just won't do. And it has been almost twenty-four hours since he last heard Jamie's voice—far too long, if you ask Ray.

He presses the "call" button before he can talk himself out of it.

"Hia?" Jamie answers after only one ring.

"Mhm," is all Ray says, at first. It seems Ray isn't so good at this whole "phone call" thing. Maybe this wasn't his best idea... And the only other time they've spoken on the phone was when Ray asked him to look after his niece, so it's really no wonder Jamie isn't speaking either—likely unsure why Ray is calling. Ray pulls himself together. "I wanted to ask how your Christmas has been."

"Oh..." He doesn't need to see Jamie to know that man is blushing, his voice taking on the tone it only has when his cheeks are rosy. "It's been good. And yours?"

Ray sinks down more against his pillow, lying flatter now to stare up at the blank ceiling as he considers how to respond. "It has been a wonderful day," he confirms, eyes tracing the shape of his faded light fixture, "but I miss you."

Jamie giggles down the phone. Or maybe it's not a giggle—the sound is a little breathy, a little more mature than that, suggesting a sense of satisfaction in what Ray has confessed.

"Hia! You'll see me tomorrow!"

"Mm. But I miss you *today*."

Jamie sighs, but there's a fondness to it.

"Do you miss me, too?" Ray wants to ask. *"Are you feeling as lonely as I am, on your own in your room?"* But instead, "Tell me about what you got for Christmas," Ray asks, though it comes out more of an instruction than a question.

"Well, I got some slippers from Mama—she buys all of us new slippers every year. Usually, she gives me ones that match Tommy's and Papa's but, um..." Jamie pauses. "Today she gave me ones that match hers."

Sensing Jamie's self-consciousness at the admission, Ray is quick to respond, humming his approval and asking, "Do you like them?"

That seems to be enough to soothe any of Jamie's lingering worries, as Ray barely has the words out before Jamie is squealing down the phone, "Yes! They're so cute! They're pink and fluffy and, *ahh!* I just love them!"

Ray chuckles, closing his eyes and allowing himself to picture said slippers. Maybe Jamie is wearing them now, looking down at them and smiling warmly, turning his feet to admire them from different angles. "They sound lovely, Nhu. What else?"

"Tommy got me this really soft cardigan I saw in a store a couple of months back. You have to feel it next time you come over, Hia, it's like a cloud! Oh, and Win booked a spa day for him and me to go on. How exciting is that? We're going to get massages!"

Ray tries to put out the spark of jealousy that lights in his gut at that, knowing it's ridiculous to be jealous of the pair's friendship. But also... he wishes he were the one taking him for a spa day. He wishes he could take him on a trip, just the two of them, somewhere relaxing and romantic.

"What about you, Hia?" The question knocks Ray out of his spiraling thoughts.

"Ah! Uhh... I got that new Christmas sweater from my parents, and Praew got me a little cuddly toy dog. Us siblings don't really get each other anything anymore, we'd rather get things for Praew, so that's kind of it."

Jamie hums down the phone, and his voice has started to take on a softer, sleepier tone. "So, what did Praew get? And tell me more about your day! What is Christmas with the Amarins like?"

Ray keeps his own voice quiet and smooth as he answers the question—telling him about all the gifts Praew had received, what they'd had for Christmas dinner, the boardgames they'd played after.

At first, Jamie responds with hums and occasional comments, but by the time Ray is done, the only sound remaining is steady breaths. Ray knows that sound—couldn't possibly forget it after he'd first heard it from Jamie on the Suwan's couch when they had fallen asleep against each other, Praew in Jamie's lap.

"Nhu?" He asks it so softly, not wanting to disturb the other boy if he really is asleep. When no response comes, Ray knows it's probably time for him to hang up. He doesn't think it's a particularly good idea to fall asleep on the phone with him, as much as he wants to, as he's aware that he snores. Jamie doesn't need to know that just yet (if he isn't already aware).

"Goodnight, Nhu. I love—"

Ray freezes.

The words had nearly slipped from his mouth so easily.

He waits, wanting to make sure Jamie didn't hear that or give him time to respond if he did.

A minute passes and still, all Ray can hear is soft, even breathing. Ray presses the "end call" button and blinks up at his ceiling, heart hammering in his chest.

He loves—?

- • ☆ • -

Jamie is in that dreamy, half-asleep state. He can hear Ray talking, telling him a story or something. Honestly, he can't even remember if he asked Ray a question. All he knows right now is that Ray's voice is pouring through his phone, somehow still pure velvet despite the quality of the speaker. Jamie is listening as much as he can, but all the words feel foreign now that he's so close to unconsciousness.

"Goodnight, Nhu. I love—"

...Huh?

Jamie must be dreaming. That's the only explanation for what he's just heard come out of his phone.

Waiting, Jamie uses any remaining brain power he has to focus on if Ray says anything else. He'd hold his breath to listen in better if he was awake enough to do so.

He tries to keep listening, but with no more sound coming from the phone, he finds himself being pulled under, the lure of sleep too strong. Jamie gives into it and drifts off.

It must have been a dream.

There's no way Ray would just...

Surely it was just a dream.

Monday, December 26th

Ray texts Jamie once he's outside Honeybun Bookstore, bouncing nervously on his toes and clutching at the bouquet of flowers he'd bought for Apple's birthday. He had been hoping to arrive early, to impress the Suwans with his impeccable time management, but he'd been too busy obsessing over his hair to notice the time passing. It's not his fault he's anxious; he knows that a lot of Jamie's relatives will be here today.

He's so caught up in his own thoughts that he doesn't notice Jamie approaching until he hears the store's bell tinkling, the shorter man yanking the door open.

"Hey," Ray breathes, Jamie opening his arms and bringing him in for a hug. Ray pushes his nose against the side of Jamie's head, inhaling the sweet scent of his shampoo to calm himself.

"Hi." Jamie's response is muffled against the shoulder of Ray's coat.

When Jamie pulls back, he takes Ray's free hand and begins to pull him towards the stairs. Ray keeps his fingers intertwined with Jamie's even once they reach the living room, the contact soothing him.

Apple spots them and makes her way over, beaming when she sees the flowers. "Oh, Ray, these are beautiful! Thank you!" She takes them from Ray, inspecting each bud.

"Happy birthday, Apple. Are you having a nice day so far?"

Ray tries to concentrate on her as she tells him about all of her relatives and friends arriving, focusing on her happiness instead of the dozen or so pairs of eyes that turned to him when he'd entered the room. It had become rather quiet then, but the hum of conversation starts to pick up while Apple chats with him. Still, he feels on edge. What if someone were to take pictures of him here today, at a party almost exclusively for family?

Apple admires the flowers once more. "These really are lovely, Ray."

A squeeze to Ray's hand has him turning his gaze to Jamie, seeing the pleased expression aimed at him that he thinks means he did good.

"Jamie, could you be a dear and put these in a vase for me, please?"

Jamie nods, taking the proffered bouquet from his mom and heading to the kitchen. Ray thinks about following after him, maybe getting one more reassuring hug from him in the secluded kitchen area, but Apple's hand on his arm stops him.

"Relax, Ray." Of course she can sense his nerves. "I've already spoken to everyone here; they won't say a word about you being here today. Not until you're both ready, at least."

Ray nods, eyes darting about the room with some lingering sense of unease. Sure, not many people are looking at him now, most going back to their own conversations, but still... These people are strangers to Ray. He doesn't know if he should trust them. Especially with how many of them have their phones out, snapping shots of their loved ones together.

Subconsciously, Ray rounds his shoulders and takes a step towards the back of the room, wishing to make himself small and short enough to blend into the background of these people's photos.

"The same goes for photography," Apple continues, coaxing him to the back wall and standing with him, reassuring him. "Everyone knows not to upload photos from today online or publicly share anything that has you in it." This statement has Ray ready to interject, to tell her that it's okay, that he doesn't want to be a bother and could just leave, but— "None of us are big social media users anyway, Ray. It's no trouble."

It seems Apple can read his mind just like Jamie can. Ray nods.

"Besides..." She shuffles closer, nudging her elbow against Ray's and nodding to direct his attention to something on the other side of the room. Ray follows her gaze to where Jamie is holding a vase full of the flowers Ray had brought, talking to an elderly couple. He looks beautiful, effortlessly so, as he laughs and smiles with them. But that's probably not why Apple had drawn Ray's attention to him. It's that Jamie isn't looking at the people he's speaking with. He keeps glancing over at Ray instead. And whenever he does, his expression becomes so warm and bright that it lights up the room. Apple chuckles—whether at Jamie's doe-eyed gaze or Ray's equally besotted one, who can tell? "I'd do anything to keep that smile on my baby boy's face."

"So would I," Ray responds, the words honest as they spill from his lips.

"I know, Ray. I know." Apple pats his back. "Don't break his heart, okay?"

He nods, forcing out a tight "Mhm" against the overwhelming emotions in his chest. "I won't," he says, still unable to pull his eyes away from the pretty boy holding the pretty flowers.

Jamie comes back over a few minutes later, excusing Ray and himself from Apple so he can drag Ray over to meet the couple he'd been talking to on the other side of the room. Ray had known there would be a lot of introductions to do today, so many of Jamie's relatives in attendance, but he still feels his heart rate spike from nerves.

Meeting people is one of Ray's least favorite parts about his celebrity lifestyle—the pressure to present himself appropriately at all times, especially around important colleagues and contacts. But at least at a family party such as this, it's unlikely that a poor introduction will cost him a job. Well, unless someone posts about it online, but Apple has already assured him that that won't be an issue. Here, the only real risk is of him making a fool of himself in front of people he really, *really* wants to impress.

"This is my great aunt, Suzie, and her husband, Kei," Jamie introduces, and Ray bows his head to the elders, trying to keep his cool. They chat with them for a little while, just small-talk about the weather and the couple's journey to get here today, before Ray is being pulled along to greet the next group of people. This cycle repeats itself as Ray makes his way around the room—greeting someone, finding out a bit about their relation to Apple, followed by a little small-talk— until Jamie says he's sure Ray has met everyone. The experience makes Ray extremely grateful for the memorization skills he's honed from years of learning scripts, remembering everyone's names with relative ease. Or so he hopes. Only time will tell, really.

He'd half been expecting for it to feel like a meet and greet—having to smile through person after person going, "Oh, I loved that movie you were in," or "What's such-and-such like to work with?" in the way people tend to do upon meeting him. However, it seems Apple has briefed them well. Or perhaps Jamie's family are all naturally this understanding and polite. Not a single person he'd been introduced to mentions his career, instead opting for questions like, "Are you having a nice Christmas?" or "Jamie said he took you ice skating—how did that go?" It's... nice. Refreshing. To just be *Ray*.

Win arrives fashionably late, somehow timing his arrival to coincide with when Tommy, Jamie, and Ray have just finished placing the last platter of food on the dining table. Jamie had told Ray he didn't need to help out, but Ray wasn't keen on the idea of being left alone with so many of Jamie's relatives, so had ended up following him to the kitchen like a lost puppy and trying to make himself useful.

"Winnie!" Jamie calls, jogging over to wrap his friend up in a hug.

Luckily, Ray has met Win before, so there's no need for a formal introduction; instead he just nods and says hello before they're all making for the buffet table.

Once the guests fill their plates with food, they all start looking for a place to sit and eat—guests soon resorting to perching on the arms of chairs when there's no space left on the seats themselves.

Ray trails after Win and Jamie as they manage to snag a few cushions from the back of the couch before making their way over to a quiet corner of the room, sitting themselves down on the floor as they talk idly about their Christmas gifts. Each of them has a cushion to sit on, Jamie patting the third, placed between him and Win, for Ray.

The three of them are mostly silent as they begin to eat, focusing on their food and absorbing the pleasant atmosphere around them. But then Ray realizes that now is probably the best time to ask Win a question...

"Hey, so, um— I... I wanted to ask," Ray stumbles over his words. He's not sure the right way to ask this. "Are you single?"

Win, who had previously been munching away at his plateful of food, stops chewing. He swallows, puts down his plate on the floor, and turns to face Ray with a perplexed expression. "Excuse me?"

Jamie is still eating, not easily deterred from stuffing his face, but his eyebrows are knitted together as he looks to Ray, definitely curious about what's going on.

Meanwhile, Ray is extremely confused as to why they're looking at him quite so weirdly. They look almost offended. Is it offensive to ask if someone is single? Ray has no idea.

"I was wondering if you're single." He says it with a smile, hoping to ease whatever distress the friends seem to be in.

The smile is short lived however when his question is met a rather synchronized and scandalized "What the fuck?" from both Win and Jamie.

Ray's eyes flit between the pair, not sure why he's being met with such hostility. He's just trying to help out a friend— Teddy wants to know if Win is single, so Ray is finding out. In the past, he's acted as Teddy's wingman in nightclubs and such, but he's never had to play wingman without the man he's wingmanning actually present. It's new territory for him; he can't just say, "Hey, here's my friend Teddy, he thinks you're cute," when the man isn't actually *here*. And he can't pull out his phone and show Win a picture of Teddy, like he's a matchmaker presenting a suitor for an arranged marriage. That would feel very weird. So what else is he supposed to do? And why do they look so mad about it? It's not like...

Oh.

OH.

Ray now sees how his question must have sounded.

"Not for me! I mean— uh— for my friend!" He tries to clarify, tripping over his words. "My friend, you see, he's interested. I sent him pictures of Praew from the Nativity performance and he saw you in one of them and... And..."

Jamie and Win are just staring at him, mouths hanging open, clearly processing Ray's words as Ray keeps whipping his head back and forth to look at them both.

"You— um... Do either of you know of Teddy Supasawat? The actor?" Ray waits until Jamie nods his head slightly, still seeming a bit hesitant and dazed, before continuing, "It's him. He..."

Jamie gasps, leaning forward to make eye contact with Win. "It's *Teddy*," he whisper-shouts.

A few moments pass, Win staring blankly back at Jamie, occasionally blinking. And then something seems to click, his eyes going wide, mouth twisting into an open smile. Ray truly has no idea what is happening. All he knows is that the pair's previously horrified expressions have been replaced with ones of excitement and delight as they turn to look at him expectantly.

"He thinks you're hot," Ray finishes lamely.

Win leans over Ray's plate to grab Jamie's hands, shaking them vigorously as he squeals, Jamie giggling back at him with just as much glee. Is Ray caught in the middle of some bizarre business deal?

When Win finally calms down, huffing in exhaustion as he sits back, he grabs his plate to resume eating. He picks up a carrot stick, and for a moment Ray thinks Win won't answer his earlier question, that maybe he needs to ask again.

As Ray is opening his mouth to ask, Win speaks up, grinning widely, "Well, you can tell your handsome friend that I am indeed single." Win bites down on the vegetable with an audible crunch.

Taking a mental note to message Teddy later, Ray nods before going back to picking at his food. He's not going to try and understand what just happened—he's gotten the answer he was after.

Jamie is just finishing off his second plate of food when Banlue pops his head out from the kitchen doorway, signaling something to Jamie with hand gestures that Ray simply can't comprehend. But he trusts that if he needs to know, Jamie will fill him in. And sure enough, as Jamie makes to stand, he pipes up, "Papa says the birthday cake is ready. You better warm up your vocal cords, Hia."

Ray's eyes nearly pop out of his head. Caught up in the joy of being invited to a Suwan family party, Ray had forgotten that people typically sing "Happy Birthday" at birthday parties. Ray is *not* known for his singing abilities.

Win coaxes Ray to his feet as Jamie disappears into the kitchen and he swallows down his nerves. This is a family party. It doesn't matter if he's offkey. In fact, there's so many people here, it's likely no one will even be able to hear him. It's all fine.

199

Then Banlue is dodging around the edge of the living room to switch off the lights, a hush descending over the guests as Jamie and Tommy reappear carrying a birthday cake adorned with candles. Despite Jamie's focus being on the cake, staring at it like he can stop the candles going out if he looks at it hard enough, his voice is tuneful as he sings "Happy Birthday." Everyone else joins in after a moment, but Ray can still hear Jamie's voice above the rest; a sweet melody breaking through the dissonant chorus.

"Make a wish, Mama," Jamie says once he and Tommy are standing in front of their mom, still holding the cake between them. Ray doesn't miss the way Apple's eyes dart between her boys; from Tommy, to Jamie... and then to him. Ray startles but Apple just smiles at him warmly, face illuminated by candlelight, before she closes her eyes and makes a wish.

People cheer when Apple blows out the candles, and she looks like she can't stop smiling, grinning from ear to ear as she thanks her guests. Ray feels grateful to be one of them, to get to be a part of this experience, to be here with Jamie.

Cake eaten and the party winding down, the guests gradually begin to head out. Many of them come up to Ray and Jamie as they leave—Ray even receiving hugs from several people as they say goodbye. It makes him feel like he's really part of the family, completely accepted and integrated into the event as if he's known them for years. And he loves it. He wishes he could have this forever.

When even Win has left, sleepily trudging out of the door after hugging Jamie for a full three minutes, Ray knows he should probably leave or risk overstaying his welcome. But also... he could make himself useful as an excuse to stay a little longer. Surely, none of the Suwans would object to him helping clear up.

He starts gathering up all the plates and glasses littering the room, carrying them through to the kitchen and filling the sink to do the dishes. It's calming; the sound of the water splashing lightly as he scrubs at the plates, the activity perfectly monotonous and mindless after hours of socializing.

Ray doesn't hear anyone enter the kitchen, not noticing Jamie's presence until a pair of arms wrap around his stomach. Jamie rests his chin against Ray's shoulder, and Ray melts when Jamie turns his head to press a kiss to his neck.

Forgetting his task, Ray wraps a hand around Jamie's wrist where it sits against his stomach, soap suds still clinging to his fingers. He pulls Jamie's arm tighter around him, not caring about the water from his hand saturating the fabric of Jamie's sleeve. He needs this—has been craving it all day—a moment of closeness, of calm, of *them*. Perhaps, judging by the way Jamie hums contentedly, he's been needing it, too.

It's a while before either of them speak, Jamie eventually murmuring against his back, "Would you like to meet August?"

Ray had asked where August was earlier, hoping to meet the cat after somehow not seeing him upon his last visit to the Suwans' apartment. Jamie had informed him that August was quite antisocial, making it unlikely that the cat would come down from the quiet top floor today until everyone had left. So, of course, given the opportunity to meet this reclusive cat, Ray agrees. "Yeah, just let me finish the dishes first."

"Hia~" From how close Jamie is pressed against his back, he can both hear and feel as Jamie stomps his feet in discontent. "You're our guest—you shouldn't be doing this anyway! Come on."

If Ray wasn't such a pushover for Jamie, he'd definitely argue back. Instead, he lets himself be led away from the sink and up the stairs.

The last time Ray had been in Jamie's room, he hadn't the wherewithal to feel shy or embarrassed; too busy panicking about the work he had forgotten to cancel, suddenly having to appear on a talk show. But now... Now it feels so intimate to be in this space with Jamie, to be sitting on Jamie's bed. Especially when Jamie closes the door behind him, just the two of them existing in this space together. Oh, and the cat.

Jamie coos at the gray tabby as he approaches it and Ray swears he sees the cat roll his eyes. Undeterred by the cat's apparent disdain, Jamie picks August up, jostling him in his arms much like one might with a crying baby. To be fair, August looks like he would cry if he could. Or maybe scream for help.

Ray is handed the quietly furious furball and worries for a second that August will freak out, scratch him anywhere his paws can reach, since he's apparently so antisocial. Instead, August buries his head against Ray's chest, snuggling up against him after sniffing him a few times. And, okay, Ray is typically a dog person, but this cat might have just won over his heart. Or, *would have* won over his heart, if that didn't already belong to Jamie.

As Jamie cuddles up against Ray's side, bothering August where he's peacefully purring in Ray's arms, Ray can kind of see the similarities between owner and pet; they're both a little reserved, cuddly, and unbearably cute.

Ray can't resist. He ducks his head forward quickly and presses a kiss to Jamie's cheek. But when Jamie looks up at him in a combination of surprise and joy, big doe eyes sparkling, Ray feels shy. He looks away, choosing to focus on the cat instead, hoping that will settle the butterflies in his stomach.

It's only a matter of seconds before Jamie is getting even—planting a kiss on Ray's cheek. Ray makes eye contact with him, a mischievous grin forming, and the game is on: Ray kissing Jamie's nose, only for Jamie to then kiss Ray's chin; one to Jamie's forehead, and one to Ray's eyelid. Both are giggling and so wrapped up in their own little bubble that Ray barely registers August wriggling out of his arms, no doubt disappearing off to some corner of the room where he doesn't have to be caught in the middle of such gross displays of affection.

The game comes to a rather abrupt halt when they both go to kiss each other's noses and suddenly their lips are millimeters apart.

Jamie gasps at the closeness, pulls back a touch, but doesn't move away completely. Ray remains still. Even his breathing stops.

He takes note of their current position; sitting side by side on Jamie's bed, legs tangled together, Jamie's hand on his thigh while his own hand rests upon Jamie's cheek. They're so *close*.

"Hia..." Jamie's voice comes out a near whimper, so soft and small, ghosting over Ray's lips.

"Nhu... May I kiss you?"

Jamie's eyes flicker down to Ray's lips, then back up to his pleading eyes. He nods.

Ray isn't going to miss this opportunity, is not going to allow anyone or anything to interrupt them. His hand cradles the back of Jamie's head gently as he leans forwards, the space between them getting smaller and smaller, Jamie inhaling one last sharp breath and then—

Their lips touch.

Sparks fly behind Ray's eyelids, a warmth spreading out from his lips and filling his entire being like nothing he's ever experienced. It's like Jamie is the Sun, Ray basking in his glow as he tilts his head just slightly, wanting him closer. What he wouldn't give to have this for a lifetime...

- · ☆ · -

Jamie is overwhelmed with the rush of elation and relief and *home* that he feels run through him as Ray's lips meet his. His heart is thumping, beating hard enough to jump out of his chest, at how perfect the kiss is. He wants Ray to take his heart, to keep it safe for him. He—

Ray pulls away, wet lashes fluttering open to reveal eyes filled with an emotion so soft; something so warm and open and vulnerable and... Jamie is helpless to do anything other than lean back in, capturing Ray's lips once more. It's no less breathtaking the second time, Jamie drowning in the pure emotions coursing through him. He loves—

He loves Ray.

"Goodnight, Nhu. I love—"

Maybe Ray loves him, too.

Maybe it's too soon to be speaking of such things as love. For now, he'll just keep kissing Ray. They have all the time in the world to work out the rest.

Don't they?

Jamie stumbles back to his bedroom, love-drunk, after sending Ray off with a goodnight kiss. Though if it can even be called that when they'd kissed several times just getting down the stairs to the door before the official "goodnight" kiss... Well, that's something to think about another time. Right now, Jamie needs to not think about Ray's kisses so he can actually calm down enough to get ready for bed.

Pajamas on and teeth brushed, he snuggles down under his blanket, his room illuminated softly by his pink bedside lamp as he checks his phone to see whether Ray has made it back home yet. What he finds instead are several message notifications from his own family and guests from today's party. Curious, Jamie decides to open the family group chat first, and it becomes extremely obvious what all the fuss is about. It seems that, since everyone was told not to post any photos featuring Ray on the internet, Jamie's family has taken to sharing the photos with each other in the family group chat instead.

Mama
Doesn't Ray look particularly handsome here?

Tom
Mother!

Jamie snorts with laughter when he sees what his dad has written, and his brother's response...

Papa
Yes. Very handsome.

Tom
FATHER!?!?

Scrolling up, Jamie finds the picture they're talking about—a candid shot of Ray and Jamie talking to each other, standing close and looking into each other's eyes like they're the only people in the room. Ray is smiling his cute bunny-toothed smile at whatever Jamie is saying, listening intently. It's almost like Ray is trying to wrap the younger man up in his embrace without even touching him, the way his body is curved around him, hands hovering over Jamie's hips and head dipped forwards to bring himself closer. And as for Jamie, he is looking at Ray like that man hung the stars in the sky, leaning towards him like there is some magnetic force between them.

It takes Jamie's breath away, seeing how they look from an outsider's perspective, how obviously infatuated they are with one another.

Jamie saves it, sends it to Ray, then scrolls through his camera roll until he finds the picture Ray had taken of the two of them on Christmas Eve. Just to look at it. Both pictures are so full of... Of something, of an emotion that Jamie wants to put a name to.

Before he can stop himself, Jamie is digging out the polaroid-style photo printer his mom bought him a couple of years ago. She'd thought he might like to take photos of things he likes and decorate his room with them. He's never really seen the point before.

He starts with their Christmas Eve selfie, taking time to fiddle with the settings first to make sure it'll print perfectly. It's cute. He doesn't want to ever stop looking at it.

Carefully carrying the freshly-printed photo, Jamie goes over to his desk, rooting through one of the drawers for something to stick it to his wall with. He's just finished putting it up when his phone rings.

"Hia?" He answers the call, padding back over to his bed.

"Mhm," comes Ray's response, "I'm just calling to let you know I'm home. And that I like the photo you sent. You look gorgeous."

Jamie blushes at the compliment. "You look gorgeous, too."

Ray seems genuinely surprised, responding with a questioning, "Yeah?"

"Yes." There is no room for misinterpretation in Jamie's answer, "You're always so handsome."

Jamie had thought Ray would be used to receiving such compliments, the man's Instagram comments full of people telling him how attractive he is, but it seems he's not used to receiving such words from *Jamie*. Ray's nervous giggle sounds through the speaker of Jamie's phone—a bout of shy laughter brought on by his elation at being called handsome by him—and it's quite possible that it is Jamie's new favorite sound.

He looks over to his desk—to the small photo stuck to the wall above it, the first thing he's ever put on his wall. It looks small, surrounded as it is by empty space, but Jamie hopes that this is just the beginning. He hopes that he'll soon have many more photos to put on his wall. And he hopes that they'll all be of *them*.

- · ★ · -

They end up talking on the phone for another twenty minutes or so, somehow finding things to talk about despite spending so much of the day together, until Ray says goodnight. He doesn't tell Jamie the other reason he'd called; to check on him. Given how their relationship had progressed today, Ray was worried Jamie might be feeling overwhelmed, or would maybe even regret kissing him. But with how fondly Jamie had talked to him over the phone, Ray knows that he's okay—that *they* are okay.

Ray lies down on his back, staring up at the ceiling in the dark. He must have left his curtains open a fraction because the light from a streetlamp outside cuts across his ceiling. His eyes follow the beam of light, tracing the shape of it back and forth.

Things are good between them. Ray is happy, Jamie is happy, and it's all so... *nice*.

But Ray still needs to tell Jamie that he's meant to leave town in four days.

"I..."
PART 5

Tuesday, December 27th

Ray huffs in agitation at the sunlight seeping through his bedroom curtains. He's not sure how much he's slept, if he's slept at all; too busy trying to work out how and when to tell Jamie that he'll be leaving town soon. Things are just so good between them right now, and Ray doesn't want the precious time they have left together to be shrouded in sadness or desperation. He doesn't want to see Jamie sad about him leaving—no more so than necessary, at least.

Perhaps... Perhaps he can put off telling him for a little longer.

He sighs as he rolls to lie flat on his back and stares at the ceiling again.

He should tell him today, shouldn't he?

Ray groans, scrunching his eyes shut as if pretending to be asleep will help him avoid the inevitable.

When Ray approaches the bookstore, it is with a clear goal in mind—to tell Jamie when he's leaving. It feels much like when he'd visited the store a couple of weeks ago to apologize; his hands are sweating and his heart is racing just the same as he peers through the windows. He spots Jamie's family inside, surrounded by cardboard boxes and carts full of books. *How unusual.*

When he gets to the door, he realizes that the sign reads "Closed." *Ah.* Ray probably should have texted Jamie beforehand to ask if he could come over. Especially since, although he can see Apple, Tommy and Banlue, he can't see Jamie... Maybe he's out today. Maybe Ray should come back later.

As he's contemplating what to do, Apple looks up and spots him. She waves at Ray through the window and beckons for him to come in.

Ray pushes the door open.

"Come in! Come in!" Apple greets. "We could do with a big strong man like you!"

Ray laughs at both Apple's words and Tommy's answering scowl, the man clearly offended to not be considered "a big strong man" by his own mother.

"So, uhh... What's, uhh...?" Ray gestures at the boxes and general disarray of the shop floor.

Cheerful as ever, Apple replies with a smile, "Ah! We're moving some of the displays, so I thought we should give the place a good clean and reorganize while we're at it!"

Apple groans as she picks up a large cardboard box full of books she's just finished filling. Instead of carrying it to join the pile of boxes in the middle of the room, she offers it to Ray. "Can you carry this to the stockroom for me, please?"

Slightly bewildered at being given a task so suddenly, Ray just nods and complies, taking the box from her. As he walks to the back of the store, he realizes he can hear someone humming in the stockroom. Or, well, not just someone, but Jamie.

Ray enters the room quietly, wanting to take the opportunity to listen to Jamie a little first. He finds Jamie standing with his back to the door, picking up books from a stack on one side of the desk and putting them in a box on the other side once he's made a note of something on a sheet of paper. He hums as he does so, muttered lyrics falling from his lips from time to time amongst a formless melody.

And at this point, Ray really should say hello instead of just staring at him. And these books are really heavy...

"Hey," Ray says softly as he makes his way towards a low stack of boxes, putting the box he'd been carrying on top.

Jamie gasps, head whipping around to Ray. "H-Hia?"

"Mm." Ray opens his arms for a hug. "Good morning, Nhu."

Humming in approval, Jamie steps into Ray's embrace, wrapping his arms around Ray's shoulders. He smushes his face into Ray's neck, inhaling deeply. Ray can't judge though; already nosing at Jamie's hair and cheek. They only saw each other yesterday, and they're already like this. How are they going to cope when Ray has to—

Jamie wriggles out of Ray's tight hold just enough to be able to look up at him. His eyes search Ray's. And then he's darting forward, pressing a quick, chaste kiss to Ray's lips before shyly whispering, "Hi."

By the time Ray realizes the kiss is happening, it's over, Jamie's face once again buried in his neck. If it weren't for the fact that he can see Jamie's ears and neck are now glowing pink, the younger man embarrassed after his own forwardness, Ray almost would have thought the kiss hadn't actually happened.

Squeezing Jamie tight, he chuckles. "'Hi' to you too, Nhu." Ray kisses Jamie's hair, his cheek, his ear, whatever he can reach given their current position until Jamie is squirming out of his arms.

"How come you're here, Hia? Did I miss a text from you? I don't remember seeing anything about you coming over..."

Ray should tell him, he really should.

"No, no. I just thought I'd come see what you were up to today. And I was wondering if maybe we could, uh..."—*talk*—"go on a date."

Close enough. People do tend to talk on dates, so it could work.

Jamie's blush deepens as a small giggle bubbles out of him.

"Hia, I'd really like that." Then the man pouts. "But I'm needed here today."

"Then I'll stay and help." The sooner Jamie's done with work, the sooner they can hopefully talk.

"You don't have to."

"I want to." Jamie's pouting is too cute to resist. Ray nudges his head forwards to peck Jamie's lips, effectively stopping him from arguing back, and then heads for the front of the store.

"Apple, Banlue, do you have any other jobs for me?"

The next couple of hours consist of Jamie and Ray moving countless books off of display tables and shelves, Ray carrying them out of the way, and Jamie cleaning the now empty surfaces. Meanwhile, Banlue, Tommy, and Apple are busy planning out the new layout. Well, *Apple* is busy with the new layout; holding up a clipboard and pointing to various parts of the room while she explains her ideas. Banlue and Tommy nod along and follow her instruction when she asks them to move the tables and display racks.

It should be boring, completing such mundane tasks, but somehow it isn't. Something about having this kind of company, this family around him, keeps Ray smiling. Even when Apple asks him to help move a particularly heavy bookcase, he feels content. He's happy to be spending time with such lovely people, and happy that he's being helpful. Working as an actor, he's often treated like a fragile, helpless thing—a security detail surrounding him when traveling to and from events, not being allowed to do his own stunts when there's a risk of anything greater than a papercut. This—moving heavy furniture in a bookstore—is a far cry from his regular life. It should make him feel nervous and uncomfortable, doing something he hasn't done before. But instead it feels like freedom.

So caught up in his tasks, Ray forgets to check his phone until he hears it ding on the desk as he's grabbing a box from the stockroom. He finds a few messages from his eldest sister, the first one from half an hour ago.

Pim
I just took Praew to ma and pa's
to see you but you're not here?

Pim
Where r u??

Ray probably should have told someone where he was going before he left the house today, but he'd been so lost in his thoughts that he'd completely forgotten.

Pim
U at Honeybuns?

How did she guess? Has Ray really spent so much time here lately that it's become that obvious?

There's a gap in the messages, and then the text that just arrived:

Pim
???

Ray should definitely text her back if Pim's become irritated enough to communicate solely using punctuation.

He's halfway through composing a response saying he'll stop by later when he hears Apple greeting someone, the bell above the store door jingling. Ray would bet money on that being his sister. And, based on the childlike giggles he can hear, also Praew.

Ray jogs back to the shop floor to greet them. "Hey, Sis. Hey, Princess."

Praew comes up to him, nuzzling into his side. Ray chuckles, looking down at her fondly and patting her head. Busy with Praew, Ray almost misses the way Jamie smiles at hearing *his* nickname for Praew fall from Ray's lips.

Once Praew has tottered off to Jamie for a hug, Ray explains to his sister, "Sorry I didn't reply to your texts. I've been a bit busy." He smiles, gesturing to the state of the store.

- · * · -

Pim has never seen her brother look so relaxed, throwing a genuine smile in her direction. It reminds her of when they were kids—before they'd been weighed down by responsibilities, before *he'd* been weighed down by fame. She's glad. He deserves to be able to feel at ease.

"I can see that!" She turns, looking around the room. And then she catches a bit of Jamie's conversation with Praew...

"Can we do a movie night tonight, Jemmie?" Praew pleads.

"Aw, I'm sorry, Princess, but I've still got lots of work to do here. I'm gonna be busy all day today. What about you come over next week, okay? Uncle Wawa can bring you over and we'll watch a movie together, whatever you like."

"But Uncle Wawa is—"

"UH!" Pim exclaims, to stop Praew from finishing her sentence. *If Ray hasn't told him yet...* Jamie deserves to hear it from the man himself, not from Praew.

Everyone in the room turns to look at Pim—Apple, Banlue, and Tommy pausing in the work they've only just returned to since her arrival.

"What do you say I go grab us all some lunch, yeah?" Spotting the clock on the back wall, Pim is able to confirm, "It is lunchtime after all. HAha... ha..." She breaks off into nervous giggles, sidestepping in the direction of her idiot brother.

"Oh, I couldn't ask you to do that, Dear!" Apple speaks up, waving a hand dismissively.

"Ray's treat!" Grabbing the sleeve of Ray's sweater roughly, she yanks him towards the door despite his stuttering protests. "God knows he's rich enough, am I right?" Pim fakes a cackled laugh, the sound largely backed by the building hysteria within her as it threatens to give way to anger.

"We'll be right back." The bell tinkling above the door when she pulls it open irritates her in her already frazzled state, but she maintains a fake smile to address her daughter. "Praew, Sweetie, be good for Mommy and stay here with Jamie and his family, okay? I love you."

- · ★ · -

By the time Pim turns her back to the store, her face is stoney. She says nothing as she continues to grip Ray's arm, dragging him across the street and into Sunshine Café. Ray has a feeling he might be in trouble.

She only lets go of him when it's time for them to order, arms crossed as she asks Ray to order for the Suwans since he knows them better than she does. The way she says it, the tone she uses, is usually reserved for when Praew is being particularly naughty. And as Ray takes in Pim's side profile, the woman refusing to look at him, he can see how clenched her jaw is. He knows she's pissed. And he knows why.

Pim doesn't say anything else to Ray until a few minutes later, when they're waiting at the end of the counter for their order.

"You haven't told him yet."

It's not a question, but Ray knows he's supposed to answer.

Trying to combat some of the anger radiating from his sister, Ray pretends to focus on his phone, scrolling through some random article that he has no real interest in. He decides to play dumb: "I have no idea what you're referring to."

"Ray Rawat Amarin!" Pim chastises, voice now taking on a disappointed note that makes Ray think of their mother's scolding.

"What? I'm gonna tell him today! I just..." Ray can feel the heat of embarrassment and shame coloring his cheeks when he makes eye contact with his sister, who is staring at him in a combination of rage and disbelief. "I haven't found the right time yet."

"You don't have *time* to wait for the right time, Rawat." Pim stops talking as one of the café's workers approaches to pass them their food and drinks. Thanking the worker with a smile, Ray takes the bags, trying to act as if nothing is wrong to minimize any possible rumors.

Ray wishes he'd let his sister grab their order, just to keep her hands busy. As it is, there's nothing to stop her from gesturing wildly as they leave the café, occasionally slapping Ray's arm while she screeches about how much of an idiot he is. It's catching the attention of a few passersby, a couple of people slowing down to listen.

He clears his throat, getting his sister's attention. Ray looks at her as she pauses in her rant, makes sure she's looking at him, and then darts his eyes to where people have stopped to watch them. She seems to understand quickly, lowering her arms and reinstating a neutral expression.

Pim walking silently next to him definitely feels worse than when she was flailing; a tension building as they come to a halt in front of the bookshop.

"We go back in there, you say you need to talk to him somewhere private, and you tell him. You hear me?" She turns to him, eyeing him expectantly.

Ray nods, head tilted down sheepishly.

"Speak up, Ray. Tell me you'll tell him today."

"I..." He really doesn't want to. Everything has been so nice lately, and this will surely ruin it. He gulps. "I'll tell him today."

Pim nods once before pushing the door open.

They reenter the store to the sound of Praew's laughter; finding the little girl sitting on Jamie's lap in the mostly emptied kids section. She's clapping and laughing as Banlue reads aloud from a book, giving each character a distinct voice as he does so. Praew is probably a little too old for the basic picture book, but Banlue makes it entertaining; flapping a cleaning rag about like a cloth handkerchief as he mimics the posh Victorian lady on the page.

It's not just Praew who has become enthralled by Banlue's dramatics, Tommy and Apple leaning over one of the empty display racks to watch, chuckling at each of his exaggerated expressions.

When Ray and his sister approach, Banlue greets them without breaking character, voice high and wobbly, "Ah! Duke Ray and Lady Pim, I see you have returned from your treacherous travels."

Pim chuckles, though the sound is odd and tight to Ray's ears. Ray smiles but doesn't attempt a laugh. As much as the sight in front of him amuses him, he knows he can't let himself get swept away in the merriment. He needs to talk to Jamie. But he doesn't know how to bring it up. Not with everyone so close by...

Luckily, no one seems to notice Ray's unease, all continuing to laugh along as Banlue finishes reading the book. Ray just stares resolutely at Jamie, trying to work out what to do. Maybe, if he looks at him long enough, Jamie will just *know* Ray needs to talk to him and Ray won't have to go through the awkwardness of asking him.

Book finished, Apple remembers the bags of food Ray is still carrying. "How about we all sit and eat down here, hm?" she suggests, gesturing to where Jamie and Praew are already sitting on the floor. "Jamie, Ray, maybe you could fetch some blankets from upstairs? We could turn it into a picnic!"

Praew's eyes light up at the word "picnic," turning to her mom with a wide smile.

Tommy pipes up as Praew starts to shuffle off of Jamie's lap, "I could just go grab stuff, Mama, it's okay—"

"You can help me move this rack so we've got more space to sit down, Tom. Leave the blankets to Ray and Jamie." By the time she's finished speaking, Apple is already in position to pick up the display rack. The reassuring smile Apple throws Ray's way suggests that at least one person has picked up on his change in mood.

When they make it up the stairs, Jamie turns to Ray, eyes full of concern.

"Are you alright, Hia?" He reaches out a hand, caressing Ray's cheek softly. Ray leans into the touch, allowing his eyelids to flutter shut so he can focus on the feeling, on the warmth.

He has to tell him.

"I..." *I leave town in three days.*

He needs to say it.

"I..." *I don't want to go.*

He opens his eyes, letting the sight of Jamie ground him.

"I..." *I love you.*

Which should he say? How should he end that sentence? He knows what he's supposed to do, knows he needs to be honest with him about how soon he'll be leaving. But...

I can't.

"It's nothing." Ray turns his head, pressing a kiss to Jamie's wrist. Jamie looks like he wants to push for a better answer, but Ray won't let him, turning away to search around the living room. "Where are the blankets?"

Pim sidles up to Ray when he and Jamie come back downstairs with armfuls of blankets and cushions. She hovers near him until Jamie is busy chatting with Praew, the two of them setting up the blankets on the floor, before nudging Ray.

"Don't, Pim." Ray's voice comes out harsher than he intends, frustrated at his own inaction. "Just don't."

Pim huffs. Then Praew is calling for *Uncle Wawa* and he takes the opportunity to escape from his sister before she can berate him further. Despite being an actor, Ray finds that it takes all of his effort to muster up a cheerful smile as he joins the others.

*

Praew is almost falling asleep by the time she finishes her lunch, apparently worn out from all of that laughing she was doing with Banlue. She snuggles herself up in Jamie's lap with a blanket, clearly intending to take a nap there. Jamie chuckles, moving the little girl's hair out of her face as she settles.

Ray is equally tired, though not from something as pleasant as laughter. So little sleep and then doing so much physical labor would have left him feeling drained anyway, but adding his current emotional turmoil into the mix? It's fair to say he's exhausted. And the way Jamie is leaning against him isn't helping—Ray finding it difficult to keep his eyes open with how warm and cozy he is, Praew's blanket draped over their laps and a couple of cushions behind his back. He would be content to stay here for... For as long as he could.

"Praew and I should probably head out before she actually falls asleep," Ray hears his sister say. He doesn't remember his eyes falling shut, but they must have. He drags them open.

"Come on, Little Missy," Pim addresses Praew, placing a hand on her shoulder. "Let's head off and leave these people to their tidying." Grumbling, Praew pulls herself up out of Jamie's lap before plastering herself to her mother's side. She waves to everyone as she's led out of the store, apparently too tired to even hug Ray before leaving.

Ray feels a hand rest on top of his. "Hia... Are you sure you're okay?"

He can't bring himself to meet Jamie's eye. "Mhm. Just tired, Nhu."

"Why don't you head out now—catch up with your sister? You could go home and take a nap," Jamie suggests.

"No." Ray wraps his arms around Jamie, pulling him so close that he's practically in Ray's lap. "Want to stay here with you."

Forever, Ray wants to say. *Let me stay here forever.*

*

It's a while before Ray lets Jamie move, but eventually he knows he has to—they've got work to do, after all. The younger man starts to fold up the blankets they used for their "picnic" and Ray follows suit, a companionable silence falling over them. Once the blankets are stacked and the cushions have been gathered up, they make their way upstairs to return the items to their rightful places.

Ray is about to head back down the stairs when Jamie grabs his wrist. He pauses in his step. Is Jamie going to ask him if there's something wrong again?

The seconds tick by and still Jamie hasn't spoken.

Ray turns to look at him, expecting to be met with a face of concern.

Instead, Jamie's lips are suddenly on his.

Much like the kiss they shared earlier today, it's a quick peck; a pressure that's there one second and gone the next. Only this time, it's followed by another. And another. And another. Each one has a slightly different angle to it, like Jamie is testing which he likes best. He seems to like all of them once Ray starts kissing back, deepening each kiss.

Jamie pushes gently at Ray's chest after a moment, easing the man away from him. Ray complies, worried Jamie is upset until he sees his smile.

"As nice as this is, Hia, we should head back downstairs."

"You started it," is Ray's very mature response.

Jamie laughs, taking Ray's hand and starting to descend the stairs. They only stop once or twice to steal a couple more kisses from each other before rejoining Jamie's family in the store.

Ray is so swept up in *Jamie* that, for a while, he forgets how little time he has left here.

Maybe, if Jamie just keeps kissing him, he can forget for a lifetime.

- · ☆ · -

Jamie doesn't know what's up with Ray, but something is definitely wrong. It was cute this morning, seeing him so enthusiastic to help out, like an overeager kid trying to earn his allowance, but... something's not right. He's been a little clingier than usual, a little quieter in the moments he thinks no one is looking, and there is a sadness in his eyes even when he smiles. Jamie has tried to ask, but Ray keeps saying everything is fine.

He'd been hesitant to kiss Ray when they'd gone back upstairs, given the man's obvious distress. But Jamie decided to go for it when he realized that a kiss was at least unlikely to make Ray's mood any worse. He had pressed innocent kisses to his lips, refusing to stop until he felt the tension slip from Ray's shoulders.

For a while after that, Ray had seemed fine.

But now he looks all mopey again as he starts putting the crime novels in their new location, sighing to himself over and over.

Jamie doesn't know what to do...

Maybe, for now, he should just trust Ray.

If it's something important, surely he will tell him.

He can give Ray some time.

- · ★ · -

Ray groans in annoyance as he flops down on his bed at the end of the day. He'd gotten so close to telling Jamie he was leaving, so many times, but just couldn't do it.

How will he ever work up the courage?

He's ready to let himself sink into the pit of despair that is his spiraling thoughts when his phone rings. Ray answers the call without even looking at the caller ID. He knows who it is. There's only one person who calls at this hour. "Nhu?"

"Hi, Hia."

It seems this is a thing they do now, these goodnight phone calls. Even when they've spent the entire day together, they find things to talk about. Ray loves it. He loves hearing Jamie's voice. He loves Jami—

"Have you had a nice evening?" Ray asks, dragging himself up the bed to rest his head on a pillow.

"Mm, yes." Ray hears the rustling of Jamie getting comfortable, perhaps shifting against his own pillow. "We got a bit further with the YA section after you left, but then we decided to call it a day. We think we can finish things up tomorrow, though."

"Can I come help out again?"

Maybe Ray will tell him tomorrow.

"Of course, Hia!"

Maybe.

Wednesday, December 28ᵗʰ

Ray is awakened from a restless sleep by his phone buzzing with an incoming message. He groans as he blindly reaches out an arm to grab it from the bedside table, eventually locating it and sleepily forcing his eyes open a fraction to look at the screen.

> **Jem**
> Good morning!
>
> **Jem**
> Maybe don't come to the bookstore today, Hia.
>
> **Jem**
> Mama has some paperwork to take care of and Papa and I are heading out of town for something. Not sure what time we'll be back.

These texts pique Ray's curiosity for a couple of reasons. Firstly, Ray has never known Jamie to be awake before him, that boy seeming to be more of a night-owl than an early-riser. And secondly... "heading out of town for something"? Just last night, Jamie had said he could come over today. What could have possibly changed in such a short time?

Ray ponders the subject for a while before responding:

Ray
Morning x

Ray
What are you out of town for?

When a couple of minutes go by without a response, Ray thinks it's probably best for him to get up and start making alternative plans for the day; perhaps see if he can hang out with Praew, Pim and Dan. Maybe he'll watch a movie with them, or take them out for lunch if they don't have anything planned. After all, it's not long now before he's meant to head back to New York.

He drags himself out of bed with a heavy sigh, scrubbing a hand over his face.

When am I gonna tell Jamie...

Ray needs to do something to clear his head, especially if he's going to visit his sister's place in a bit. She's definitely going to give him an earful when she realizes he still hasn't told Jamie that he's leaving. He needs to make sure he's calm and collected for that.

Time to go for a nice, long walk.

The cold air does Ray some good, he thinks. It's freezing out, and he really doesn't have enough layers on, but he needs this. He needs that icy, prickly coldness to hit him, to slap him across the face and tell him to pull himself together. If the breeze won't do it, it'll be his sister doing it later, and that is bound to hurt a hell of a lot more. So... *Please*, Ray wishes into the wind, *tell me what to do.*

He comes to a stop on an empty street corner, turning his eyes to the sky in the hope that someone or up there can hear him.

Tell me how to not break his heart.

His tears feel hot against his skin as they roll down his cheeks.

- · ☆ · -

Jamie is fast asleep, his face pressed against the car window, for most of the drive. It's not until they pull up outside their destination that Banlue is gently shaking him awake.

"Jem..."

Jamie grumbles, trying to shift away from his father's grasp.

"We're here."

Any tiredness is suddenly forgotten when Jamie processes his dad's words. He's wide awake now; in such a rush to get out of the car that, at first, he tries to climb out with his seatbelt still on. After a nervous giggle, he manages to free himself from the offending item and exit the car.

- · ✳ · -

Banlue watches Jamie approach the door of the house. He takes a second to fiddle with his hair before knocking, then flexing his fingers by his side, clearly trying to work the nervousness out of his system. The door opens and Jamie bows politely, greeting the person inside the house. They pass an item to Jamie, and he bows once more in thanks before the door is being shut, Jamie bounding back to the car with the biggest smile on his face.

Jamie lets out giddy giggle when he's back in his seat, clutching the package to his chest.

"Let's get a bite to eat somewhere before we head back," Banlue suggests and Jamie nods. After all, they should celebrate this little mission of theirs being a success—it's taken them since last Wednesday to sort this out!

- ˙ ☆ ˙ -

While his dad drives, Jamie checks his phone, finding messages Ray must have sent him while he was sleeping.

Ray
Morning x

Ray
What are you out of town for?

He's tempted to reply with something like "it's a secret"—keep the man guessing. But he's too excited for that!

Jem
I had to pick up your present!

Jem
Are you free tomorrow? Maybe you can come over and we can finally exchange gifts?

The drive continues as Jamie anxiously waits for a response. It doesn't arrive until he and his father are at a diner, ordering milkshakes and burgers to celebrate the morning's achievements. And when Jamie opens Ray's message, he beams, butterflies filling his stomach.

Ray
That would be lovely Nhu :)

Jamie taps his feet excitedly under the table.
He's going to give Ray is gift *tomorrow.*

- · ★ · -

"Are you still planning to give him those earrings?" Pim asks as she sets down two steaming mugs of coffee on the table. She'd ushered her husband and daughter out the door ten minutes ago to deliver thank you cards to all of the neighbors who bought Praew Christmas gifts, and Ray had gulped, knowing what was coming. Sure enough, she'd started grilling him the second Dan and Praew were out of earshot. But Ray still hadn't been expecting *that question* in particular, wide eyes now meeting his sister's.

"How did you..." he trails off, eyebrows furrowing. "How did you know about the earrings?"

"People talk, Ray. I know someone, who knows someone, who's friends with the girl who served you."

Ray nods, taking in the information. It seems he hadn't been able to keep that purchase quite as under-the-radar as he was hoping.

"I don't think people know who they're for, though. Not really," Pim adds, like that clause is somehow a way out, like he could give the earrings to her or Malai instead.

There's not much else Ray can do other than nod again, watching the steam rise from the mug that's been placed in front of him.

- · ✳ · -

"So..." Pim shifts closer, a look of concern in her eye. She knows they don't have long before Dan and Praew will be back, so she asks again, "You're *really* still going to give them to him? Even though..."

"Yes," Ray says, the word delivered as he meets his sister's gaze with a surety she's not used to seeing from her bumbling little brother. There's a fire behind those eyes that she rarely sees, though it's quick to fizzle out as he stammers, speech turning shaky, "I-it's... It's the r-right thing to do."

Pim nods.

She's not sure whether he's still talking about the earrings really. But, whatever he's talking about, she hopes he's right.

- · ☆ · -

When Jamie is back home and wrapping Ray's present, he calls Win, eager to fill him in on recent developments.

"Jem!" Win greets as the call connects, his face filling the screen of Jamie's phone where it's balanced against the wall by his desk.

Jamie greets him back with a hello and an enthusiastic wave before getting back to the task at hand; smoothing out the wrapping paper he bought specifically for this.

"Is that Ray's gift?" Jamie glances up to see Win raising his head, as if he were in the room, trying to get a better look.

Jamie nods, lifting the book to show it to his friend. "Praew helped me pick it."

"Ooooh!" Win's lips curl up into a pleased smile. "Did she, now? Well then, Ray is sure to love it."

He tries not to blush at his friend's teasing tone, focusing instead on making sure the corners of the floral wrapping paper are folded just right, and that when he ties the bow on the top, it sits at a perfect, artful angle. It's ready. But... is he?

"Speaking of love..." Jamie dares to start, glancing up at the screen in time to be rewarded with the sight of Win's mouth falling open. "I'm going to tell him..."

"Jem!" The other man squeaks back. "Don't tell me you—you..." He points at Jamie through the screen, giggly and giddy. "You're going to confess? You love him? Like... you really love him?"

Jamie giggles, hair bouncing as he nods repeatedly. He can barely believe how happy he is to finally admit it to someone. Sure, he hasn't said the actual words out loud yet, but now Win *knows*. And Ray will know, too, once he opens his gift.

- · ✶ · -

"I'm going to tell him tomorrow," Jamie confirms. "After all," Win watches Jamie's smile fade a little, "I don't know how much longer he's staying in town. I don't want to miss my chance."

Win hums. He could tell Jamie that he warned him about this, about the possibility of getting his heart broken if he pursued Ray, but it would do little good to say that now.

"What if..." Jamie's voice is so quiet, Win has to bring his phone closer to his face. "What if he's not leaving?" Big doe eyes look at Win's through the screen, wide with both hope and fear. And Win really doesn't know what to say. Does he allow Jamie's hope to build, or does he try to be realistic?

Then Jamie adds, "That's silly, sorry," a cold laugh following the words. Win watches as his friend closes himself off, shoulders hunching as he looks away from the screen. He can't bear to see him like this.

"Hey," Win calls to him, trying to get Jamie to look at him. "You won't know unless you ask him, Jem." Jamie lifts his head once in a nod. "So talk to him, okay?"

There's a knock on Jamie's door, his mom informing him dinner is ready, and they have to end their call, both blowing kisses at each other before Jamie hangs up.

Win doesn't move for a while.

He just sits and thinks—processes the situation.

Jamie is in love with Ray. Ray, Win thinks, is in love with Jamie, too.

And Ray is likely leaving. Soon.

Shit.

Win sighs.

What had he said to Jamie back then?

"Don't think about that, Jem. Just enjoy it. Either that or... Or maybe break things off before it gets too serious. I don't want to see you get hurt, okay?"

Jamie's going to get hurt, isn't he?

- · ★ · -

"So, what are you going to do about New York?" Pat asks Ray over dinner. It's just the three of them tonight; Ray, Pat, and Hathai.

Ray continues eating. "What do you mean?"

His mom is the one who responds, "Well, are you still going to go back?" It seems his parents have planned this ambush—a dual attack over one of his favorite meals so he can't escape without answering a few questions, at least.

"Of course."

Pat's turn to speak: "Why?"

"My work is there."

"But... it doesn't have to be, does it?" Hathai's voice has taken on that soothing, motherly tone, likely sensing how tense Ray is getting. Not that it's hard to spot; his knuckles white with how hard he grips his fork. "You could always do something else."

"They need me back in New York, Ma. You know how it is with my work." Ray stabs a piece of asparagus with his fork, using a bit more force than necessary. "My schedule is already packed. I probably won't have more than a couple of days off until September at the earliest. So, I've got to go back. They're expecting me."

"And that's why you're doing it? Because it's what you're *expected*"—Pat makes air quotes around the word—"to do?"

Ray nods, gesturing with his fork as if to say, "Obviously."

"Ray, my darling." Hathai's hand finds Ray's. It's awkward with him still holding the fork, but she wraps her hand around his regardless. "When have you ever done what was expected of you?"

Ray finally stops chewing to simply stare at his mom, urging her to go on.

"Grandpa bought you toy cars, you played with your sisters' Barbie dolls; we had you join your school's sports teams, you just sat on the bench drawing animals in your notebook; you went to college to study business, you ended up an actor." She chuckles, pride and fondness gleaming in her eyes. "You've never done the expected, Ray."

"Well, I'm doing it now."

"Why?" Hathai hits back.

"Because..."

Because the idea of giving up my career is terrifying.

Because, if I stay, I'll want him by my side forever.

"Because it's the right thing to do." Appetite gone, Ray puts down his fork. He stands and tries not to wince at the sound of the chair scraping against the floor. "I'm not feeling well. I'm going to get some sleep."

He trudges up the stairs to his childhood bedroom knowing he won't sleep for hours, if he sleeps at all. He'll be awake worrying about his decision. But he knows he's doing the right thing. It *has* to be the right thing.

Because, of all the ways to break his heart, a clean break is surely the kindest.

-·✻·-

Hathai looks at the empty chair that had been occupied by their son until moments ago, shocked. She's never known Ray to act like this. "Do I dare say our son has become *too* responsible?"

Pat hums in agreement, sad eyes turning in the direction of the staircase Ray has just stumbled up.

They both hope their son will prove them wrong; throw caution to the wind, do something so reckless that his life will never be the same again. They want to tell him as much, shout it clearly enough for him to understand.

But no.

Ray needs to do this on his own.

They can only hope he works it out before it's too late.

- · ★ · -

Ray is in the middle of a staring contest with his ceiling when his phone rings.

"Hello?"

"Hia?"

Of course it's Jamie.

"Mm." Ray doesn't want to speak. It feels like a lie to speak and not *tell him*. And it would be wrong to deliver news like this over the phone. So, for now, he'll just hold his tongue. All he needs to do is say just enough to keep Jamie talking. He knows it's selfish to hold back while also trying to get so much from Jamie, but he needs to savor every last moment of them being *them*. "How's your day been?"

He listens as Jamie goes on, telling him how early he and Banlue had set off in order to pick up Ray's gift, and about the diner they'd stopped in before coming back. Jamie tells Ray all about what he's been up to since he got home, and how he'd played with August after dinner. Ray just listens. He wants to keep listening to Jamie. His voice is so beautiful, Ray can't help but think how nice it would be to fall asleep to it; to be lulled to sleep by the sound, not because of boredom, but because it feels safe, and warm, and like home.

Ray lets his eyelids slip shut.

If only Jamie were here...

He allows himself to imagine it; Jamie by his side, telling him about his day, his tone even more comforting when not distorted through the phone's speaker. Ray would rest his head against his chest, letting the vibrations of Jamie's voice thrum through him. Perhaps it would feel like a purr, a gentle rumbling, soothing away the worries of the day. Perhaps Jamie's fingers would run through his hair or stroke his cheek—that boy always seems to be fiddling with something, after all.

Ray wants... He wants nothing more than what his imagination has conjured. He wants Jamie next to him. Tonight, tomorrow night, and every night after that. It already feels painful to be away from him, and he just saw him yesterday. How is he going to cope when he can't even call h—

"—ia? Hia?"

"Hmm?"

Ray loves him.

"Are you alright, Hia?"

"Mhm."

He loves him so much.

"I thought— I thought maybe..." It's unlike Jamie to sound so nervous, and it makes Ray tense, holding his breath in anticipation for the end of that sentence. "I thought that maybe something was wrong? You seem... distracted."

He can't tell him over the phone.

"Nothing is wrong, Nhu. I'm listening," he reassures. "I'm all yours."

"I'm all yours."

Ray has never spoken truer words.

Thursday, December 29th

Jamie wakes up earlier than usual, butterflies in his stomach from a of nerves and excitement. A smile forms on his face as he bounds out of bed, heading to the bathroom to get ready for the day ahead. After a long shower, he takes extra care in drying and styling his hair just right, and makes sure to put on an outfit that is both comfortable and stylish. It's important he looks good today, even if he needs to help out at the store. After all, it's not every day that you first tell someone you love them.

- · ★ · -

Ray's stomach is in knots. Yet again, he's barely slept a wink. He aches all over, like his emotions have taken physical form within his body, their weight pushing down on his ribcage and pulling at his limbs. Once he drags himself out of bed, he takes a while to get ready, accidentally shampooing his hair twice when he loses his focus—too busy trying to plan out exactly what to say to Jamie.

No matter how hard he thinks about it, he can't find the words. Or maybe he just doesn't *want* to find the words. Like if he never speaks them aloud they won't be real, and he won't have to leave.

It's a nice thought.

Unfortunately, it's not reality.

He skips the breakfast his mom offers him, unsure if he can keep anything down in the state he's in, opting instead to head over to the bookstore early. Before he leaves, he makes sure to grab the small jewelry box that's been sitting on his bedside table for days. It's time he gives him this gift. And it's time he tells him he's leaving. There's no putting it off any longer.

Today's the day.

Ray tries to stay calm as he walks into town, forcing himself to take strong strides despite how his knees threaten to give out. He feels weak, worn out from stress and worry. Of all the ways he expected to feel at the end of a three-week vacation, he never thought he'd feel like this.

Honeybun Bookstore comes into sight and Ray's stomach flips uncomfortably. These past couple of weeks, the bookstore has become a place of great joy for him; a place full of love and acceptance, where he can truly be himself. As he approaches the door, he wanders how much longer it will feel that way. An hour? Maybe less?

Movement towards the back of the store catches Ray's eye, looking through the window to find Jamie waving at him. Jamie's lips part in an excited gasp before forming into a beautiful smile, his eyes glistening like stars as he gestures for Ray to come in. He's absolutely breathtaking.

Ray almost wishes he weren't. He wishes that boy would make it easy for him; be rude and mean and... the complete opposite of how he is. Anything to make Ray feel slightly less awful about what he needs to do.

With a sweaty palm, Ray pushes the door open.

"Hia!"

Jamie closes the distance between them, throwing himself into Ray's arms before the door has even closed. Has Jamie missed him this much after only one day apart? Ray has missed him, too—would have run to him just as quickly if it weren't for his shaking legs. If they're both like this after only a day apart, how are they going to get by when—

"Good morning, Hia," Jamie mumbles against Ray's chest, tightening his grasp on the back of Ray's jacket to bring him closer. Then Jamie lifts his head and goes up on his tiptoes, lips pouted. It's clear what he's asking for, and Ray complies once he's swallowed down his nerves, allowing their lips to meet.

It's just as perfect as the first time, and every time after that. In fact, it might be even better now, with a familiarity that wasn't there before. And Ray wants to savor this. After all, this might be the last time they—

"Good to see you again, Ray!" Apple chimes as she comes out of the storeroom, a large box of books in her arms.

Ray pulls away from Jamie enough to greet Apple back, feeling a little sheepish at getting caught kissing her son. Apple doesn't seem to mind, going about her business like it's nothing out of the ordinary. Perhaps, in another life, this could be their normal; Ray always at Jamie's side, in this bookstore, in this small town.

No.

Ray needs to stay focused.

He turns to Jamie, the younger man blinking up at him sweetly. "Nhu, should we, um..." Ray trails off, taking the wrapped jewelry box out of his pocket and waving it in the air. "Presents?" That's the best he can do. He has no idea how to get out full sentences right now, his throat tight and chest heavy with the knowledge of what's to come.

Jamie's grin is wide and full of excitement as he draws in a shaky breath. "Yes, Hia. Let's go upstairs." He takes hold of Ray's hand, either not noticing or choosing to ignore how sweaty it is, Ray's heart beating a mile a minute. He thinks he hears Apple chuckle, the woman perhaps seeing Ray's nerves and mistaking them for excitement. *If only she knew...*

Ray can't take his eyes off of Jamie as he's led up to his room. He wants to remember every detail of how he looks right now, down to the last strand of hair. Sure, he's spent a considerable amount of time over the past couple of weeks trying to commit this boy to memory, but today is *the last day* he'll see him.

Jamie takes a seat on his bed, pulling Ray down with him. "Nhu..." Ray starts, but then Jamie is looking at him, really gazing at him, and he's so beautiful. He's all gorgeous dark hair and pretty eyes and kissable lips, with a heart of gold and the voice of an angel and—

"I..." Ray can't get the words out. Or any words at all, for that matter, his throat closing up uncomfortably. He tries again, opens his mouth, but the words die on his tongue.

He hands over the small gift, allowing himself a few extra moments to think of what to say. As he presses it into Jamie's hands, he can't help but let his fingertips linger against Jamie's skin, a feather-light touch to his palm before he pulls away.

Jamie smiles down at the box, then at Ray. "Hia, let me grab your present, too!" Jamie turns to pick up Ray's gift from the bedside table, but Ray stops him, a hand grabbing his elbow.

"Nhu... Will you open yours first, please?"

Jamie blinks a few times, seeming to mull over the request before agreeing. He readjusts to sit facing Ray, legs crossed beneath him on the comforter. He eyes the small gift curiously, lips slightly pouted as he turns it this way and that as if trying to ascertain its contents from the outside. As he starts to tear at the outer wrapping paper, revealing the black jewelry box beneath, a small smile plays on Jamie's lips. Then he looks at Ray, waiting.

"Go on," Ray encourages, smiling a little despite himself. How could he not, when Jamie looks this adorable? "Open it, Nhu."

Jamie's eyes go back to the small box in his palm as he wiggles back and forth happily, getting comfortable before he slowly lifts the lid.

"Hia..." Jamie gasps, eyes going wide. "Hia, these..."

Ray clears his throat before speaking, willing his voice to stay steady. "I hope you can wear them and, um..." He can't hold Jamie's gaze, instead looking at those two golden North Star earrings, the embedded crystals twinkling. "...think of me... and our time together fondly."

"Mhm! Of course, Hia. I'll wear them next time we go on a da—"

Now is as good a time as any, right?

"I go back to New York tomorrow."

There. He's said it.

"I just wanted to give you these before I... Before I go." This gift was Ray's one exception to his "clean break" rule. He couldn't stand the idea of not giving these earrings to Jamie. They belonged to him, just as much as Ray's heart does.

Ray glances at him.

Jamie looks... surprised. But he seems to be alright. He's not crying. So maybe he doesn't like Ray as much as Ray thought, or maybe he'd been expecting it, or...

"But you'll be back soon, won't you?" Jamie asks, voice even, not a hint of anything other than happiness.

Ray's answer is one simple word: "No."

Jamie's cheerful expression dulls for only a moment before it's back in full force. "Then I'll come visit you in New York! I'll graduate in a few months, so I could come visit you in the summer!"

Ray needs to be firm. "No." He looks away.

Jamie is silent for a long moment. He reaches his hand to Ray's. "Then I'll wait for you, Hia."

"It could be a year until I come back."

He squeezes Ray's hand. "I don't care."

"Well, I do." Ray's eyes meet Jamie's for a moment—the younger's full of confusion—and he has to look away again. He can't bear to watch, can't bear to be seen.

"I won't come to the bookstore again." Ray gulps against that persistent lump in his throat, wishing he could also gulp away the tears that are threatening to fall. "I can't promise you'll never see me around town, but I'll do my best to stay out of your way."

Jamie lets out a nervous, perhaps hysterical, chuckle. "Ray, I— I don't understand. What...?"

"Your life is here, Nhu. Mine is in New York. Surely you know that." The grip Jamie has on Ray's hand now is so tight it hurts. Ray wishes it hurt more. He deserves it.

"Well yes, but—"

"It's better this way." Ray wishes he could believe his own words.

"I thought you loved—" Jamie's voice breaks and Ray feels his heart shatter with it. "I love y—"

He needs to end this.

"It was never going to work." Is that true? Ray isn't sure. Maybe if he was braver, he'd have come up with something. But, alas...

It takes every bit of strength Ray has to not grab Jamie's hand as the younger man pulls away, to just watch out of the corner of his eye as Jamie wraps his arms around himself. The younger man digs his fingers into the flesh of his upper arm, pressure turning the flesh white.

Jamie's voice is a broken whisper the next time he speaks.

"Get out."

It's startling enough to get Ray's head to snap around to look at Jamie properly.

Ray opens his mouth to say... something. He needs to say something.

"I..." What could he possibly say to Jamie now? *"I care about you"*? *"I love you"*? No. Although those words are true, he mustn't speak them. Not now. Not ever.

"I'm sorry, Nhu."

"Get. Out." Jamie snarls.

Ray can't move. Can't do anything other than watch the boy in front of him shake, fat tears tumbling down his cheeks.

"I said GET OUT!" Jamie pounces forward, grabbing harshly at Ray's shirt to drag him to his feet, yanking him towards the door. Ray doesn't resist, doesn't have the strength to.

Jamie turns to grab Ray's still-wrapped gift, shoving it against Ray's chest to push him backwards. "Merry fucking Christmas, Ray." His eyes are fire—they speak of anguish, destruction, and pain—as they meet Ray's for the last time.

"And a happy New Year," Jamie spits out in anger.

The door slams shut not an inch from Ray's nose.

The sound seems to echo before being followed by a wounded cry, the noise barely muffled through the door, and Ray is frozen in place. Jamie's sobs surround him, hold him there. He doesn't want to leave him like that. He wants to turn the doorknob and go in, gather Jamie up into his arms and hold him until he stops crying, hold him even beyond that. He wants to promise him that he'll stay, that they'll be together, that everything will be alright. But he can't.

Ray lets his head fall forward onto the wood of the door.

Never again, Ray pledges. *Never again will I love someone as much as I love you.*

Belatedly, he realizes he's crying, droplets pouring down his face and stomach muscles convulsing with uneven breaths. He forces himself to stand up straight, regardless of how much he wants to crumble onto the floor. He pulls his lip between his teeth to quiet some of the noises that threaten to spill out and heads for the staircase. Jamie told him to get out, so that's what he's going to do.

When Ray makes it down to the store, he finds the rest of the Suwans waiting for him, all having paused in their work. They're silent, looking at him with worry and disappointment. They must have heard Jamie's shouting despite being two floors away.

"Ray, Dear, what happened?" Apple asks tentatively, slowly approaching Ray. "Is everything alright?"

Her hands come up to hold the top of Ray's arms. It's like she's holding him steady, as if afraid he might fall over at any moment. Had Ray been swaying on his feet? Maybe. He's not sure. He's not sure what he's doing anymore.

"I..." Ray draws in a shaky breath. "I told him—" a sob cuts through his words "—I'm leaving tomorrow."

Apple's shoulders fall, a sigh passing her lips. "I see." She squeezes his arms once, then lets go. Sure enough, Ray almost topples forwards. Apple makes no move to catch him, instead dodging past him towards the staircase. She stops on the second step, though she doesn't turn around as she speaks.

"When I told you not to break my baby boy's heart, I meant it."

Ray doesn't know what to say other than, "I'm sorry," the words coming out hoarse, distorted by tears both shed and unshed.

Apple walks up the stairs without another word, and Ray watches her go, bottom lip trembling.

He turns to Banlue and Tommy, unable to quite meet their eyes, and bows low. "I'm so sor— sorry." His hands are clenched into fists, as if, if he squeezes tight enough, he can hold himself together. But he can already feel himself falling apart at the seams, ripped to shreds by a situation of his own making. He needs to get out of here before he becomes any more pitiful.

Ray makes for the door, the jingle of the bell loud and grating, and stumbles out onto the street, into the cold, frigid air. He makes it a few paces before he hears the bookstore door being pulled open again, someone following him out. For a second, he thinks it might be Jamie, but—

"Ray!" Tommy calls.

Ray doesn't want to turn around, but he does, forcing himself to make eye contact with him as he waits for Tommy to speak.

"You're in love with him." It's not a question, but Ray nods in reply.

"So why do this?"

Now that... That is a question. And not one Ray really wants to answer. But he does, forcing the words out, "I didn't have any other choice."

Two paces and Tommy is in his face, sucking in a harsh breath, an argument surely on the tip of his tongue. Then the man deflates, shoulders slumping. He begins to turn, as if he's going to head back into the store, when suddenly he whips back around to Ray at full force, hand raised.

Slap.

A searing heat spreads from Ray's cheek.

"There is always another choice, Ray," Tommy spits before heading back inside.

Ray bites his lip, willing himself not to let more tears fall in such a public setting. The last thing Jamie's family needs right now is to be connected to a scandal involving Ray. Some locals may have *seen* the slap, but it's unlikely they'd have had their phones out in time to catch it. He needs to leave before anyone starts filming. So, he makes himself move, dragging his feet across the pavement in the direction of his parents' house.

It's funny, in a way, how backwards it all feels. If he keeps moving forwards, he'll arrive at his past—his childhood home, a supersized time capsule of his family history. His life will go back to how it was before, with late-night film shoots and early mornings spent in makeup. It will be like the last three weeks never happened.

But if he turns around... If he dares to head back...

No.

There's nothing there for him now.

He keeps walking home.

- · ✳ · -

"Jem, Baby, can I come in?" Apple asks, listening to Jamie's cries through the door. She hears him scrambling to his feet, opening the door to dive into her arms as a fresh round of sobs break free from his throat.

"Mam—" he hiccups in a breath, "Mama."

"I know, Baby, I know." Apple pats his back, squeezing him as tight as she dares. He feels fragile in her arms, so small. It doesn't matter whether he's five years old or twenty-five, Jamie will always be her little boy. And right now, with the way he's trembling, she almost wishes he was still that tiny child he once was; that his sorrow was from failing a level in a video game, or not scoring first place on a test. But this? Ray? This is going to take more than a bowl of ice cream and a hug to get over.

His crying subsides into pained sniffles, temporarily out of tears to shed. Apple knows there will be more later. But for now...

"Get some rest, okay?" She coaxes Jamie towards his bed and he goes willingly. Apple makes to pull back the covers for him when she spots the little box, lid open and earrings on full display. Apple gasps. She'd heard rumors that Ray had bought some earrings from a local jeweler recently, but she hadn't known quite how pretty they would be. Or that they were destined for Jamie.

She reaches for the earrings, to move them off the bed, maybe take them with her out of the room so her son won't have to look at them, but he stops her.

"Leave them," Jamie says. The sharp tone is enough to have Apple pausing in her movements. Then Jamie is rounding his bed, getting in on the other side to his usual preference. He turns to face... either his mom or the earrings, Apple isn't sure, curling his body around the small box.

"Can you pat my hair, Mama?" He sounds so broken.

"Of course, Baby." Careful to avoid jostling the jewelry box, she takes a seat on Jamie's bed and starts to stroke her son's hair. She's even more gentle with her touch than she would usually be, but Jamie doesn't seem to notice, eyes glazed over as he stares at the two shining stars in the little black box.

He starts to cry again, barely any sound or tears coming out, and buries his head in his pillow.

Apple stays until Jamie cries himself to sleep, then heads to the kitchen to grab a glass of water for him to drink when he wakes up. After placing it on his bedside table, she creeps back out of the room, leaving the door ajar—a signal that all he needs to do is shout and she'll come running.

She takes one last glance through the crack in the door, heart breaking at the sight of her heartbroken son.

"My poor baby boy..."

Ray better make this right. Sooner rather than later.

Friday, December 30th

Ray knew it was going to hurt.

Before he'd even done it, he knew it was going to feel like a piece of his soul was being ripped out.

And he was right.

He feels hollow, like an empty shell of the man he was only twenty-four hours ago—a Ray Rawat Amarin who was in love with—

Ray can't bear thinking about him. But he can't *not* think about him, either. Jamie was, is, and always will be everything Ray could have ever asked for in a partner, and so much more that he would have never dared wish for.

He deserves someone better, Ray tells himself as he shoves the last of his clothing into a suitcase, zipping it up to take downstairs with the rest of his things. He's not even sure he's actually packed up everything—he quite likely forgot some charging cables or socks, or maybe picked up some of his dad's things by accident—too lost in his own melancholy thoughts to really pay attention to what he's throwing into his suitcases. All he knows for sure is that he's leaving. Today. And won't allow himself to come back to this town again until he can't possibly avoid it any longer. He owes Jamie that much after the stunt he's pulled—announcing he's leaving just as they were settling into something that felt warm and hopeful and right, *so very right.*

*

His family have come to see him off—Malai, Dan, Pim, and Praew all gathering around him by Pat's loaded pickup truck for goodbye hugs, Hathai and Pat hanging back for the moment. None of the adults ask why a certain someone isn't also here to say goodbye. From how Ray is struggling to muster even half a smile, they know how yesterday must have ended. But Praew...

"Are you gonna stop at the bookstore to say bye-bye to Uncle Jemmie?" Wide, pleading eyes look up at him. It's like she can tell something is wrong, that Jamie not being here means *something* even if her seven-year-old brain can't fully it piece together.

"No, we, um..." How does he explain this to her? And what will this mean for her? Will it be awkward if Dan or Pim take her into the bookshop? And what about that movie night they were meant to have?

Ray looks to Pim for... support? Guidance? He's not sure. But the gaze that meets his is equal parts anger and pity, sympathy and rage fighting for dominance in her eyes. Ray deserves nothing less.

"We said goodbye yesterday." He delivers a half-truth; an answer that is technically correct while allowing for interpretation—that perhaps he means, "He wished me a safe trip and to come back soon," and not, "It's over." It would probably be better for him to be clearer with Praew, but he can't. He can't bring himself to say it just yet.

Praew nods as Pim huffs out an exasperated sigh.

A flash of disappointment crosses Hathai's face as she pulls her son in for one last hug, holding him tightly in her arms, and it throws Ray. Surely, she should be happy—he'd come to visit like she asked, helped out with chores and cooking whenever she let him, and is now returning to his well-paid job in a big city. Fine, his career isn't the most typical, but he's a hard worker and is incredibly successful. So why is she looking at Ray like he's let her down?

*

Pat is silent as the drive begins. Ray isn't sure if he's grateful to not be questioned about what happened with Jamie, or if he wishes he would ask. At least that way he'd get one last chance to talk about him. There is no one Ray can tell once he gets to New York—too much of a risk of rumors spreading if people hear how fond he is of a boy back home. Jamie hadn't wanted to go public with Ray straight away even when they were seeing each other, so Ray owes it to him to keep him out of the spotlight now. Perhaps he could tell Teddy about what happened—maybe over a drink back at his place the next time they're in the mood to pity themselves—but other than that, Ray needs to keep his lips shut once he's back to being famous actor *Ray Rawat Amarin.*

So caught up in his own thoughts, Ray doesn't realize the truck has stopped until his dad taps his knee. Ray looks at him, then looks out the window... at the sign for Honeybun Bookstore.

"Son," Pat tries, nodding his head towards the bookshop, "are you sure you don't want to...?"

Ray keeps trying to pull his eyes back to his father, but he can't stop looking into the shop, trying to catch one last glimpse of the man he loves. But he can't see him—can't see any of the Suwans, for that matter, the store empty and dark.

"Pa, I—" Tears catch in his throat, the small amount of composure he has quickly dwindling. "I can't. I left hi-im," Ray hiccups, bottom lip already trembling. "I-I told him that I'd never— never go into the bookstore a-again."

He crumbles forwards, burying his head in his own lap, his hands grasping at his hair. The position makes it harder to breathe but he doesn't care—he can't keep holding himself up with all of these emotions weighing him down. He wants to drown in it all, let his sadness and shame swallow him whole.

A hand comes to rub his back, his dad's voice full of sympathy. "Oh, you silly boy."

Pat says nothing else, just starts up the truck again and the drive continues, the pop music on the radio doing nothing to cover the sound of Ray's choked sobs all the way to the airport.

- ⋅ ☆ ⋅ -

Jamie isn't sure how much time has passed. All he knows is that every member of his immediate family has been into his room multiple times to check on him and bring him food and water. Tommy even wrangled August into the room at some point, cursing as he carried the hissing furball over to Jamie's bed. August had been unusually compliant and allowed Jamie to cuddle him for a full minute before he wriggled away, hightailing it out of the room. Jamie can't find it in himself to care all that much.

He feels lonely in a way he thought he'd never feel again once his family had settled down in Ammersfield, giving him roots and a community that he hoped would keep him going for a lifetime. Now it feels like the ground has been ripped out from beneath his feet and he's in freefall, eyes closed, with no idea where he'll land or if there's even anything for him to land on. Logically, he knows the future he always thought he'd have is still waiting for him—finishing college, continuing to work at the bookstore, maybe finding some work that would use his language skills—but it all feels empty now. He doesn't want any of it anymore. He'd give it all up to stop feeling like this, to stop this unbearable ache in his chest.

If he'd been given the choice, he'd have gone with Ray. Even if only to extend their time together by a week, or even just a day. He could have been packed and ready to go within the hour, purchasing a plane ticket with his savings.

Instead, he's here, his body quaking as he sobs, yet again. He's exhausted, thoroughly rung out, but knows he won't be able to sleep. It feels wrong to go to sleep without Ray's voice lulling him through the phone. He'd gotten too used to that too quickly. But, in time, he could surely learn to live without that man by his side. He could go back to who he was before Ray, if he wanted to.

He pulls his blanket tighter around himself, trying in vain to find some comfort in the warmth. It does nothing to soothe his aching heart. He won't ever find that comfort he's looking for. Not without Ray.

- · ★ · -

Ray's apartment feels unbearably empty as he drags his suitcase through the front door, every step seeming to echo off the cold, stone floors. There is no one waiting for him—no excitable niece calling for Uncle Wawa, no relatives cooking dinner, no pretty boy bounding up to him with the sweetest smile and the prettiest eyes. There's nothing. Just objects. Things Ray doesn't really need and never really wanted. None of it feels like *him*.

He trudges to his bedroom in a daze, perching on the edge of his bed. Although his apartment is the same as it always has been, it feels wrong now, different in a way that he can't describe. Now, sitting here, he feels—

"Lost?" Apple had asked him, almost three weeks ago. It feels much longer ago than that.

Ray had nodded, feeling exposed in how easily she had read him. If only he'd known how quickly he would get used to her ability to always know what he was thinking.

"It's like... I... I don't know—" He had been surprised at how the words had formed in his mouth, almost against his will, *"I don't know... who I am... w-without the work."*

That's why he's back in New York now, isn't it? For the work?

Yes. He has contracts to uphold and deals that he shouldn't back out of. And without Jamie here, that boy won't have to go through the horrors of being picked apart by every gossipy news outlet there is.

Ray's done the right thing.

Hasn't he?

"Happy New Year."
PART 6

Saturday, December 31st
AMMERSFIELD

— 1:00 PM —

Win
Jemmmm

Win
How'd it go?

As Win sits in Sunshine Café, sipping at a ridiculously sugary iced drink that he really has no business consuming in December, he stares at the messages he'd sent Jamie two days ago.

They're still only marked as "Delivered."

That, in itself, isn't overly unusual. Jamie isn't the biggest fan of social media or technology in general, unlike the majority of people his age, so sometimes Win has to wait weeks to get a simple heart reaction to a meme. It's the timing of Jamie's digital disappearance that makes Win nervous; the fact that Jamie hasn't checked his messages since he was meant to exchange presents with Ray, confess his love to him, and maybe talk to him about when he's leaving town...

According to the gossip Win had *just so happened* to overhear when he was getting his hair done this morning, Ray might have already left—apparently spotted on his way to the airport in his dad's pickup truck yesterday.

If that's true... what does it mean for Jamie?

Has he gone with Ray? Is he going to drop out of college to go to New York? Do his parents know? What about Tommy? Or... did Jamie's confession not go well? Did Ray really leave? Did he leave *because* of Jamie's confession?

Staring blankly ahead, Win's brain runs through several possibilities, each more bleak than the last. He doesn't notice the person approaching him until they speak.

"Win?"

He blinks, forcing his eyes to uncross and focus on the man standing across from him.

"Tommy!" he greets with a smile. Win forgot it was Saturday—one of the days Jamie and Tommy always get lunch from here. Those boys really are so predictable, such creatures of habit that—

Peering around the café, Win can't see Jamie. Did Tommy come here on his own? Well, that's not necessarily a bad sign. Often, just one of the brothers will come and pick up lunch to go if they're having a busy day at the bookstore. But... the store is closed today.

"Where's Jamie?"

Tommy winces and Win feels his stomach sink. Taking a closer look, Tommy does look a little off—dark circles under his eyes, lips tight, hair disheveled as if he's run his hands through it over and over. And now, Tommy won't meet Win's eye properly, looking at him for a fraction of a second before glancing away. Something isn't right.

Win doesn't want to ask, but, "Did Ray...?" His eyes are wide as he slowly inclines his head, trying to convey the rest of the question without speaking it.

Tommy just sighs, rubbing at his neck. "You better come over."

That's all the answer Win needs.

— 1:15 PM —

If Tommy's attitude hadn't already made Win uneasy, the pitying smiles Apple and Banlue send his way when he enters the bookshop would. As it is, they simply solidify Win's theory: Ray is gone.

Tommy pauses when he gets to the bottom of the stairs, voice soft and low as he says, "You, um... You go up first. I'll give you guys a minute."

Win silently nods before ascending the staircase.

One thing Jamie rarely is is silent, usually singing or humming when immersed in a mundane task, which is why the sight of Jamie silently washing the dishes is so unnerving to Win. He's almost slumped over the sink, the only sound the dull clunk of dishes sloshing about in the water as Jamie scrubs at a plate.

"Jem..." Win approaches cautiously, like one might with a scared animal.

The smile on Jamie's face when he turns around is so fake it makes Win cringe. "Winnie! Just let me finish doing the dishes, okay?" Jamie's voice comes out distorted, forced as it is to form itself into something cheerful against its will.

Win gently places a hand on Jamie's elbow as the boy tries to turn and resume washing dishes, halting his movements. He doesn't give Jamie any time for excuses before he's pulling him in for the biggest hug ever, squeezing him tight. Win says the only words he can think of: "I'm sorry."

With those words, Jamie's cheerful facade breaks, falling into his friend's embrace.

"He—" Jamie gasps out a breath. "He left." Tears begin to wet the shoulder of Win's sweater as soon as Jamie buries his head there. Hands grip at Win's back, twisting fistfuls of fabric, grasping desperately. Not once has Win ever encountered such all-consuming despair as he can feel radiating off of his best friend when Jamie collapses against him, knees buckling under the weight of his grief as he sobs, "He left m-me."

The cry that is ripped out of Jamie's throat shakes Win to his core.

— 1:50 PM —

It takes a while for Win to convince Jamie to move, the boy not loosening his hold on him even as Win walks him to the living room to sit down. Win had intended to go back to the kitchen once getting him seated—to make him a hot chocolate or something equally as sweet and warm—but Jamie still refuses to let him go. He pulls Win down onto the couch with him, sniffling turning into sobbing once more as he curls into Win's side. There is nothing Win can do other than pat his back, run his fingers through his hair, and hope that this will pass.

Despite the soothing aura Win tries to exude, anger runs hot through his veins. He wants to get on a plane, fly to New York, and give Ray a piece of his mind—maybe even force him to come back here and grovel at Jamie's feet. He feels like he's vibrating with the urge to fight, to scream, to shout until he has nothing left. But Win has a best friend to comfort, and that is far more important than any ill feelings he might have about a certain actor right now.

Tommy tiptoes up the stairs at some point, dropping off Jamie's lunch. Those brothers could be as thick as thieves at times, but with this situation... it's clear that Tommy has no idea what to do. He tells Win as much, whispering quietly to him while Jamie appears to be asleep; that all of his attempts at comforting his brother seem to end with the boy in tears. "I can't bear to see him like this... I'm hoping that you, and some good food, can help."

Win hopes he's right.

— 7:45 PM —

"Are you sure you're gonna be okay, Baby?" Apple asks, perched on the arm of the couch as she pats Jamie's hair, pushing it back out of his eyes. Jamie doesn't seem to even notice for a moment, gaze glazed over, staring in the direction of the television. The rest of the family have gotten dressed up in their thick winter coats, ready to go out for the evening. Each year, the whole town gathers in the town square for New Year's Eve—eating, dancing, merriment continuing past the midnight fireworks. Jamie's entire family usually goes to it together, but it seems this year might be a little different.

"Yeah. You guys go." Jamie's voice comes out raspy, hours if not days of crying turning it hoarse. "I'll be fine."

Apple looks to Win, a silent plea of, "Look after him," before she nods with tight lips, making her way to the door with Banlue and Tommy in tow. They each sending a worried look in Jamie's direction before they head out. Win knows they wouldn't dare go if it wasn't for him being here. They still look hesitant about spending an evening without him, but Jamie had insisted all day long, probably not wanting them to miss out because of him.

— 10:30 PM —

After eating a rather sad frozen pizza and exhausting themselves with channel surfing—Win speedily flicking past any channel showing romance movies or anything that looks sad—Win has to check something.

"It's getting late..." he starts. If Jamie has changed his mind, maybe wants to go out, this would be a good time to start thinking about it. There's still an hour and a half until midnight, so there would be plenty of time for dancing and food. Win is about to continue, to say all of this to Jamie, but—

"Stay!" Jamie's panicked eyes meet his before he throws himself into Win's lap. "P-please, don't l-leave me." He clings to Win as his body is racked with sobs once again.

"I'm not leaving, Jem," Win soothes, running a hand up and down Jamie's back. "I was going to ask"—it's pointless asking if Jamie wants to go out, really, that boy is too distraught—"if you're ready to go to bed yet." It's probably best if Jamie can get to sleep soonish, not be awake when it's officially the new year and Jamie has no one to kiss. Well, Win could kiss him at midnight, it wouldn't be the first time they'd shared a small smooch, but Win has a feeling that it would only serve to make Jamie's grief more acute.

Jamie nods, and Win leads him up the staircase to his bedroom. They stay side by side even as they brush their teeth, Jamie barely letting Win out of his sight as they change into their pajamas. When they climb into bed, he immediately wraps himself around Win, grasping at him like he'd disappear. Win can't blame him for this level of insecurity after what he's been put through. But Win isn't leaving. Not now, not ever.

"Do you want to sleep?"

Jamie shakes his head. "Talk to me, Win. Tell me something nice."

So Win talks. He talks about his Christmas, about his week, about his new kitten, Buttercup. He talks about anything that isn't Ray or love or loss. He talks until he's losing his voice, until Jamie is slumped, asleep, against his shoulder. Even in his sleep, Jamie is plagued by grief, whimpering as he clings to Win.

Carefully, he pulls the comforter up further, trying to wrap Jamie in it as much as he can in the hope that the warmth is soothing. Although Jamie doesn't fully stir at Win's movements, his grip tightens on Win's t-shirt with a whine.

"Jem..." Win sighs.

Then there's a knock on the door. Not the shop door downstairs, but Jamie's bedroom door.

— 11:47 PM —

The first thing Jamie notices when he wakes up is that he can hear Win talking. He vaguely remembers falling asleep listening to Win, but Win's voice sounds further away now, muffled slightly. Forcing his sore eyes open, Jamie confirms his suspicions; Win has gotten out of bed and must be talking to someone outside the bedroom door. Perhaps he's on the phone, checking in with his parents or—

"It's too fucking late for that!" Win shouts.

Who the hell is Win talking to? Did an ex call him or something?

Win's voice is quieter now, so much so that Jamie can't make out the words, but he can tell he's still angry; talking quickly, breathing harsh, surely spitting venom at—

When Win stops talking, there is someone else's voice.

Jamie's breath hitches.

That voice... He'd know it anywhere. It's the same one that's been haunting him for the past two days.

Jamie rises from the bed in a trance, eyes fixed to the door as he approaches it. He moves slowly, as if the voice will suddenly stop if he goes any quicker.

As he turns the doorknob, inching the door open one fraction at a time, he still can't tear his eyes away.

He knows who's on the other side of the door, he's sure of it, no matter how impossible.

There, beside Win, is—

"Hia?"

Saturday, December 31st
NEW YORK

— 2:00 PM —

Ray stays in bed past noon for the first time in his adult life. He has maybe stayed in bed this long a few times ever—only whenever he got really sick as a kid. If only he were ill right now. If only the events of the last two days were nothing more than a hallucination, a nightmarish fever dream brought on by sickness, that could be over any minute.

He knows that he's the one to blame for this mess. He shouldn't have tried to get close to Jamie, shouldn't have led him on when he couldn't guarantee a future for them, shouldn't have hidden how soon he would be leaving. These past three weeks were meant to be time he could spend with his family, celebrating the holiday season. The only interaction he should have ever had with Jamie was to briefly apologize for his clumsiness, that's all.

But he had to go and fall in love with him, didn't he?

Being with Jamie had been a dream come true. Or, no, it was something even more beautiful and wonderful than that, something so unfathomably perfect that Ray would never have dared to even dream of. And now it's over. Having to end things with Jamie and leave town was just the wake-up call, forcing him back into this dull existence.

Maybe, if he stays hidden under his blanket long enough, he'll fall into another fitful sleep. Maybe he'll dream of Jamie, of being beside him, both of them in ugly Christmas sweaters and discount jeans, dozing on a well-worn couch.

However, the real world seems to think Ray should get out of bed. He groans, listening to his phone ring with an incoming video call for what must be the seventh time, and finally gives in, answering it with a "What?"

"You're doing that good, huh?" Pim greets as her face fills the screen. Ray catches a glimpse of himself in the corner, though he tries not to, and has to fight to stop his expression from souring. He looks rough; eyes puffy, hair a mess, lying among wrinkled bed sheets.

Ray huffs. "I'm really not in the mood, Pim. If you just called to be sarcastic then—"

"Is that Uncle Wawa?" Ray hears faintly, followed by the stomp of small feet. Praew comes into view at the bottom of the screen, worming her way into her mom's arms.

"Princess!" The name falls off Ray's tongue before he can stop himself and it doubles the pain in his chest. That had been *Uncle Jemmie's* nickname for her. And Ray had found it to be the sweetest, most lovely thing in the world. Now, the name makes fresh tears form in his eyes. He wills them away—he doesn't want this evening's makeup artist to have to deal with his eyes being any puffier than they already are.

"Actually, we just wanted to call and wish you luck for tonight's event!" Pim's voice sounds through the phone, the video taking a second to catch up. It's unusual for her to call over something like this. The event he'll be going to is his agency's New Year's Eve party—a networking event disguised as fun. Sure, it's important, but he's been to many such parties before; even if forced socializing makes him nervous, he knows he can handle it. Ray suspects that Pim is only worried about this event because this is the first one after... After everything.

"Yeah! Good luck, Uncle Wawa!" Praew makes a thumbs up to the screen, and even that reminds Ray of his time with

Jamie; of when Praew had done that on stage to Win, while Jamie was sitting next to him, his hand resting on Ray's thigh. Ray forces out a chuckle, knowing he usually would feel cheerful enough to do so when seeing Praew act this cute. It comes out hollow. He hopes they can't pick up on it through the tinny speakers of the phone.

They talk a minute longer, and Ray is about to hang up, knowing he should probably get out of bed to get ready. But then Praew brings up the one person the whole Amarin family have avoided mentioning since he left: "Wawa... Have you opened Uncle Jemmie's present yet?"

Pim shushes her instantly, harshly whispering to her that now isn't the time, though she just keeps asking, "Why?" in the way children tend to do.

Well... Ray will need to tell her at some point. He wishes he had done it yesterday, when he could have explained it to her in person and offered her a hug if she was upset. Like this, through the phone, what is he supposed to do?

"Prin— Praew." He catches himself this time, and Praew stops pouting at her mom to look at Ray through the phone. "Jamie and I... Things didn't work out."

"But you have the present he gave you, right?"

Ray blinks at Praew's question. *Does* he still have it? No, no, he shouldn't even be asking himself that. It doesn't matter.

"I might, but, Praew, I don't think I should—" Ray exhales harshly, annoyed he can't find the right words. Jamie would have been better at explaining this.

"Open it, Wawa." The tone of Praew's voice is serious enough to silence Ray. Any hint of the little girl's usual playfulness has vanished, replaced with something tight and pleading. Even Pim is silent, confused at her child's behavior.

So what else can Ray do but finally crawl out of bed to rifle through his still mostly packed suitcase? "It should be in here somewhere..."

Where Ray has set his phone down on the floor, propped up against a set of drawers, he can only just hear his sister talking. "Praew, Sweetie, maybe we shouldn't make Wawa open that. He's trying not to think about— About h-him, okay? So let's forget about it, yes? You hear that, Ray? You don't need to—"

"No. I'm opening it." Ray had forgotten he even had the gift, and now that he has been reminded of that fact, he needs it; needs any piece of Jamie he can get, anything that might take away this empty feeling in his chest.

He moves a couple of scrunched up t-shirts out of the way and there it is, still wrapped in the same dainty, floral paper it was two days ago. It somehow feels faded now, like the golden swirls on it have lost some of their shine, no matter how silly that sounds.

"Got it."

Praew lets out a relieved sigh when Ray brandishes the gift in front of the phone.

He settles on the floor, crossing his legs and getting comfortable. If this is the only thing he has of Jamie, he's not going to rush unwrapping it. Even the wrapping paper deserves to be cherished, so Ray takes his time to painstakingly untie the bow, to peel the tape from the paper, trying his damnedest not to rip any of it.

The anticipation has his hands sweating, nerves skyrocketing when he knows all he needs to do now is push the paper aside. Just one move, that's all it will take. His fingers rest on the paper, toying with the edge of it. Then, finally, he opens his gift.

It's a book. With a pink, cat-shaped post-it note stuck to the front, with Jamie's neat handwriting on it.

> I know it cant possibly replace your copy,
> but I thought this might bring you some comfort.
>   - your Nhu x

Ray runs his fingers under the note, pushing it out of the way to reveal the title beneath.

He stills.

He only realizes he's crying when a fat tear lands on the cover, and he rushes to swipe it away.

"—ay? Ray?" His sister is calling to him, sounding increasingly panicked by Ray's tears.

"He got me"—Ray has to pause to hiccup in a breath—"a copy of *Balto*."

He turns it over in his hands, admiring the front and back cover through watery eyes. It looks just like the one he'd had since he was a small child, though with significantly fewer dog-eared pages. He'd taken that book everywhere; on every school trip and every family vacation, then to every audition and on every flight when he had to travel to film on location. It was during one such trip a couple of years ago that he'd lost it—left it in a hotel room after checking out, and when he'd called them to enquire, the hotel staff said it couldn't be found. Ray had half suspected they sold it, maybe thinking they could make a quick buck selling a book that had belonged to a celebrity. He'd even set a notification on his phone for if any copies owned by "Ray Rawat Amarin" were being sold online, but none had ever turned up. Up until he'd lost it, Ray had always read it to Praew each time he was in town, telling her how it brought him luck and made him feel brave.

"How did he know...?" Ray mumbles absentmindedly. He doesn't expect a response, but one comes anyway.

"Jemmie asked me all sorts of questions about things you like while you were doing that TV thingy." Praew pulls a funny face as she says it, clearly not impressed with her uncle's fame. "And I told him about *Balto*! Did I get the picture on the front right, Wawa?"

Ray nods, overwhelmed. Not only had Jamie bought him a copy of *Balto*, but he'd gone so far as to get one with the same cover as the one he'd had growing up.

He opens the front cover. And he knows, he really does know, that it isn't his copy. But he still finds himself thinking he'll see the same "RAY" written in block capitals on the inside when he opens it.

Of course, six-year-old Ray's scrawled handwriting isn't there. But... his name *is* there. It's further down the page, in someone else's handwriting, handwriting he doesn't recognize, but it's there, along with...

"It's signed," he states, somewhat dumbly. "I-it's actually signed... by the author... to me."

Ray finally looks to his phone, makes eye contact with his sister and Praew as best he can through the pixelated screen. "*How* is it signed to me?"

Praew shrugs. "Dunno. He said he had a friend who could help."

He notices something sticking out from the book, a white corner poking out between the cream-colored pages of the novel. Flipping the page, the item falls into his lap.

It's the photo—*the* photo—of them on Christmas Eve. Jamie is grinning at the camera, his pink cat hat firmly on his head. Ray is smiling just as wide, a bright pink scarf wrapped around his neck.

More tears well up in his eyes and he has to wipe them away with his hand, he has to keep his vision clear so he can keep looking at the photo. It feels like it was taken a lifetime ago. He can barely recognize the beaming man next to Jamie as himself.

He doesn't know what compels him to do so, but he turns the picture over. And there, in the same small, tidy handwriting he's come to know:

I love you

A sob escapes him and he has to cover his eyes. He has to stop looking at the words in front of him, ashamed of what he's done. He doesn't deserve those words.

"Ray, what is it? What's wrong?" Pim asks, sounding even more worried than before. "Ray?"

"It's... He—" he breaks off, unable to catch his breath through his tears. He can't talk. He can't say anything. What is there to say?

"Ray?" Pim tries again. She keeps talking, keeps asking him what's going on, but Ray isn't listening—can't hear anything anymore other than the shouting in his own head of *Why, why, WHY?* Why did he come back to New York? Why did he leave Jamie? Why didn't he try to make it work? He's been such a coward. Such an absolute fool. And Jamie *loved him.*

"There's always another choice, Ray." Tommy's words ring in his ears.

Was there?

If he had been brave... If he had really, truly tried... Could this situation have turned out differently?

Yes, a voice in his head tells him. It sounds suspiciously like Jamie's.

Is it too late to...?

There's only one way to find out.

"I've got to go." Ray is rising to his feet in an instant, the book left on the floor as he scrambles for some clean clothes, photo still in hand.

"Ray, what are you doing?" He hears Pim ask, and he retrieves his phone from the floor.

He looks at the words on the back of the photo again and it's like he can feel the sincerity of them, the honesty, the emotion. "Doing what I should have done two days ago."

Ray hangs up, already pulling a clean t-shirt over his head. He should probably shower, but he doesn't have time. He needs to go. *Now.*

As he's pulling on a pair of shoes—Are they a pair? He hasn't actually checked. Doesn't matter, he's got places to be, who cares about matching shoes?—there's a knock on his door.

Could it... Could it maybe be—? Has he followed me to New York, tracked me down? Is it....?

Ray stumbles to the door, yanking it open to reveal—

He groans.

"Teddy." Of course. He's meant to be picking Ray up to head to the office and prepare for tonight's event.

"Hey." Teddy's eyes take in Ray's appearance, drifting downwards and back up again judgingly. "Where are you going in such a hurry?"

"I've gotta go see Jamie." Ray tries to barge past Teddy but the man stops him.

"Wait! Ray, hang on, just—"

"No, Teddy, you don't understand! I have to go!" Tears fill his eyes as he tries to break free of his friend's grasp on his elbow. "I love h—"

"Chill, Dude, I'm not stopping you. Just put on some pants first, okay?"

Ah. Yes. That would be smart.

— 2:35 PM —

Fully dressed, Ray hurries to the elevator, Teddy rushing after him only for the two of them to then stand awkwardly while they wait for it to arrive.

"Are you really not gonna stop me?" Ray asks.

"Not only am I not going to stop you, my friend..." The elevator arrives and they step in. Teddy presses the button for the first floor. "I'm coming with you."

Ray's too busy thinking about what he wants to say to Jamie to hear Teddy's muttered, "I gotta meet that hottie from the picture," which follows his heartwarming statement.

— 3:40 PM —

Ray stops in his tracks as they approach the airport entrance, and Teddy knows this can't be good. Ray's had a couple of minor breakdowns during their journey here and, based on the way he's staring blankly at the floor, he's about to have another.

"Oh god, Teddy. There's no way we'll make it there," Ray wails, sinking to his knees, and Teddy doesn't know what to do. He isn't good with *feelings*. So he just stands there while Ray falls apart over... *What is he crying about this time?*

"What do you mean?"

"It's *New Year's Eve*, Teddy," Ray exclaims around a sob. "There's no w-way there are any t-tickets left for flights. What do we do? I... I need to see him, Teddy." And now Ray is grasping at Teddy's legs, pleading. Teddy hopes that no one nearby recognizes them, Ray is close to causing a scene at this point. "Teddy, I *need* to see him."

"Bro... You really got all the way here and didn't even think to google for some tickets?" Ray doesn't respond, watery eyes staring up at Teddy. "Luckily, I knew you'd be this forgetful."

Hope and confusion fill Ray's features as he grips at Teddy's calves tighter.

"I texted Karl while you were finding some pants and explained the whole sitch. You know Karl is a hopeless romantic. He bought the tickets for us with his own money as soon as he found out—paid an absolute fortune for them, I imagine. Says all he wants in return is an invite to the wedding."

Ray springs up from the floor, suddenly grasping at Teddy's head with two hands and planting a joyous kiss to his forehead. "Oh my god, I love you!"

Teddy wipes aggressively at the spot he kissed as Ray pulls him into a tight hug.

"Yeah, yeah." He pats Ray's back, slightly awkward from the show of affection. "Now come on, let's go get your man."

— 11:30 PM —

The taxi they'd grabbed from the airport takes them into town, the journey relatively speedy at first and then coming to a complete stop. The taxi driver curses.

"What is it?" Teddy asks.

"Sorry, gentleman. Seems the town center is blocked off for New Year's. You'll have to walk th—"

Ray is already scrambling out of the car and taking off in a sprint while Teddy hurriedly throws some cash at the driver. He hopes it's enough to cover their journey, but he doesn't have time to check. Unlike Ray, Teddy has no idea where they're going—he can't afford to lose sight of this lovesick man.

Teddy is exhausted as he runs after Ray. It's not the actual chasing that has him tired, but the fact he's had to play therapist ever since he knocked on Ray's apartment door this afternoon. He'd hoped that Ray's meltdown at the airport would be the last of it, but the whirlwind of tears and pleas and panic had continued throughout the flight, the man waxing poetic about Jamie every few minutes. Honestly, all this lovey-dovey stuff is making Teddy cringe, but he'll bear it. He'll keep pushing through for the sake of ~~meeting that cutie~~ his friend's happiness.

Trailing behind, Teddy watches as Ray deftly dodges the crowds, weaving through throngs of people mulling about. He's moving with more precision and purpose than Teddy has ever seen, the man usually a clumsy mess, and it has Teddy thinking that maybe he's tailing the wrong man until he hears Ray's voice.

"Apple!"

...*What?*

"Apple! Apple!" Ray shouts, wriggling past another group of people, jumping up and down as if he can hop straight over them if he keeps trying.

Shit... Teddy thinks to himself. *He's finally lost it, hasn't he? "Apple"? What's next—banana?*

But... *Oh.* Apple appears to be a person—who turns around at Ray's shouts. Ray pulls her into a quick hug, then grabs at her shoulders, shaking her a bit.

By the time Teddy catches up, the pair's conversation is pretty much over. Teddy only hears the woman saying, "Go get him!" as she hands Ray a set of what appear to be house keys. Ray takes off again the second they're in his hand, and the race is back on.

— 11:43 PM —

Ray unlocks the door of the bookstore, falling through it as soon as it's open, running to the back of the store without switching any lights on. Teddy dutifully follows, narrowly avoiding the door slamming him in the face and squinting through the darkness. Thankfully, Ray manages to turn on the light for the staircase and they pound up the stairs.

"You stay here." Ray points to a couch in the darkened living room as he throws off his coat and kicks off his shoes, skidding across the hardwood floors towards another set of stairs. Unable to do much else, Teddy complies. He feels a little lost now—without a madly-in-love man to follow as he strolls over to the couch and sits. He gets out his phone.

4% battery.

Shit. It's going to be a long night.

— 11:44 PM —

It's only when Ray is outside Jamie's bedroom door, out of breath and sweating profusely, that he thinks maybe this isn't such a good idea after all. He promised Jamie that he'd stay away. He *left him...*

Can he really just show up at his door like this?

Maybe he should leave, go back to New York and pretend like this hadn't happened, that this was just a little blip—an error of judgment?

No.

He thinks of the gift Jamie had given him—the book, the photo, the words on the back... Ray didn't come all this way just to chicken out again.

And so, Ray takes one big breath, a strong inhale followed by a shaky exhale, and knocks on the door.

There is a long moment of silence, and Ray is ready to knock again, to maybe call his name, but then there's the sound of footsteps. He hears the pattering approach, and then the door swings open.

Win scowls the second he sees Ray.

"What do you want?" Win asks, blocking the doorway with his small body. It doesn't make any difference—Ray can still see Jamie, right there, curled up in bed. And *god*, he looks tired, so heartbreakingly exhausted. And it's all Ray's fault.

Gulping, Ray wills his voice not to break as he responds, "I want to talk to Nh... To Jamie."

"Not a chance!" Win scoffs and goes to close the door.

"Wait! Wait, wait, wait, please!" Flailing, Ray begs for a moment more of Win's time. Maybe, if he can just explain the situation to him, it'll be okay. He just needs Win to listen.

Win checks that Jamie is still asleep before narrowing his eyes at Ray and stepping out into the hallway. His lips and cheeks are contorted into an angry pout, judgment and annoyance radiating off of him as he crosses his arms.

"I thought you went back to New York."

"I-I-I did," Ray stutters. "I got back there a-and I realized I made the wrong choice. I came back. I want to make things right."

The humorless chuckle that leaves Win's lips makes Ray's blood run cold. "Make things right?" Win smirks. "You want to *make things right*, do you?"

Ray nods.

"It's too fucking late for that!" Win roars, getting right into Ray's face, the words landing like a hard punch and making Ray stagger backwards.

Win seems to catch himself, lowering his voice but still pouring the same disgust into each word as he continues, "How dare you! Do you have any idea what you've done to him?" The hurt is obvious in Win's tone, eyes filling with rageful tears when he gestures towards Jamie's bedroom door. "That boy in there *loves you* and you hurt him, Ray. You broke his fucking heart."

The outburst seems to take a toll on Win, the boy deflating once he's done, wincing and rubbing his forehead. It seems that the stress of the last two days has affected everyone in Ray and Jamie's vicinity. Win's voice is weary when he next speaks, though the edge of anger is still there: "Ray, you shouldn't be here. Just go."

"Please." Ray doesn't know what else to say. All he can do is beg. "Please, let me try to fix this. Let me talk to him. If I can just—"

"Hia?"

Both Ray and Win snap their heads around at the sound, finding a pale-looking Jamie standing in the doorway.

"Nhu..." Relief floods Ray's veins. He's here and he's talking to him and he's not slamming the door and maybe there's hope and—

"I already told you, Ray." Win throws himself in front of Jamie, trying to break whatever trance Ray seems to be in. "Leave."

"NO!" both Ray and Jamie object, voices laced with desperation.

Win whips around to Jamie in shock.

"Give us a minute, okay?" Jamie pleads.

Win sighs. He doesn't budge from his spot, maintaining eye contact with Jamie like they're having a whole telepathic conversation.

"Please?" Jamie adds after several moments.

That seems to be the ticket. Win huffs out another sigh before begrudgingly heading off in the direction of the staircase, throwing one more dirty look in Ray's direction on his way.

Now it's just Ray and Jamie. Just the two of them, standing in the hallway. The last time Ray was here, he'd listened to Jamie's cries through the door as he tried to hold back his own sobs. He hopes today will not end in the same way.

All the things Ray had been wanting to say—the explanations, the excuses, the apologies—disappear. The sight of Jamie, the man he loves, looking so frail... it's too much to bear. But it's also a blessing to see him at all. And there are only three words Ray can form to summarize how he feels:

"I love you."

Jamie's chin starts to wobble, eyes brimming with tears in an instant. "H— Hia..." There is a request hidden in his broken words, a plea of, "Please, don't say those words, not now." But Ray ignores it.

"I love you, Jamie." He's not going to run away from this again. It's terrifying; to be so open and honest. But he'll do it. He'll do anything at all if there's even a chance he can have Jamie by his side. "Please, Nhu..."

Shaking his head, Jamie looks away. He's crying freely now, making no effort to hold back the tears as they escape down his cheeks. Maybe he just doesn't have the energy to hold them in anymore. Ray feels exactly the same, his broken heart splitting impossibly further as Jamie hiccups out another "H— Hia," before diving forward into Ray's arms.

His hands ball into fists at Ray's shoulders, grasping and ungrasping the fabric of his jacket, pulling and pushing at it as sobs rack his body. Ray cries, too, Jamie's pain amplifying his own, gently embracing the broken man as he sobs into his chest.

"You"—Jamie pulls in a harsh breath—"You left me." His knees give out and Ray is right there, holding him, gently lowering them both down to the floor.

"I was an idiot, Nhu," Ray chokes between tears, "I never should have left." He pulls the boy closer, squeezes him tight. "I never should have left *you.*"

Jamie sobs harder. He raises a fist, then pounds it against Ray's chest. It doesn't really hurt, and Ray says nothing as

Jamie repeats the motion, hitting him again and again until all his anger is burnt out, until all that's left is a young man crumbling against person who broke his heart. And all Ray says is a croaky, "I'm sorry. I love you." There's nothing else that needs to be said right now.

The way Jamie is curled up, looking so small, reminds Ray of that time he fell asleep on the couch. Without thinking, he goes to stroke Jamie's hair in the same way. He's surprised when Jamie allows it—neither discouraging or encouraging the action as he merely continues to sniff and shudder. Jamie's voice is so quiet, barely more than a whisper, when he speaks:

"I love you, too."

Ray gasps in a breath.

He still loves me, Ray's heart sings. He still has a chance.

"Then please, Nhu. Let me fix things. Be with me."

Jamie goes silent and Ray doesn't know what that means. He still won't look at Ray, burying his head in Ray's neck instead.

"I don't want to be without you," Ray admits. "I'll figure out some way that we can be together, if you still want me..."

Jamie's arms wrap tighter around Ray's waist. "I'll always want you, Ray."

"Then we'll make it work."

Jamie's apprehension is clear when he sits up enough for Ray to look at him, staying silent in his embrace, jaw working through words he has yet to verbalize.

"Nhu, do you trust me?" The words are an echo of a previous conversation, albeit one much less serious, at the skating rink. Ray had put his faith in Jamie then, and everything had worked out perfectly. Well, they'd fallen over on the ice, and Ray had been a bit of an idiot, but Jamie had stayed. Jamie had liked him, *loved him,* regardless of his flaws.

"Despite"—Jamie gulps—"everything..."—and probably against his better judgment—"yes."

"Then I promise, I'll find a way for us to be together." No matter what Ray has to do, he intends to keep his word. Whatever it takes.

Jamie seems to think for a moment before raising one hand in front of Ray, nervously peering up at him from under his bangs. "Pinky promise?"

Ray's chuckles mix with his sniffles as he interlocks his finger with Jamie's. "Mhm. Pinky promise." This one thing, this caress, this pledge, is so much bigger than the childish ritual suggests. It is an oath—a vow to each other and to themselves to be in love.

Bringing their joined hands to his lips, Jamie presses a soft kiss to Ray's knuckles. Not everything between them is fixed, but the events of this evening feel like a step in the right direction.

"Happy New Year, Hia."

Distantly, Ray realizes he can hear fireworks going off. It must be midnight. He's not going to go to a window to check, though. He's already got the most beautiful sight ever right in front of him.

"Happy New Year, Nhu."

- · * · -

Win waits, halfway down the staircase, and listens to the conversation unfold. After the stunt Ray pulled the last time Jamie was alone with him, there's no way Win's going to leave until he can be sure Ray won't do any more damage. He nearly storms back up the stairs when he hears his best friend crying, but Jamie quiets quickly and Ray utters another "I love you." Win's intuition tells him that there's no way Ray will run away to New York this time—not without working things out with Jamie first. Whether that means they end up staying together or they choose to go their separate ways, Win can't be sure. But, no matter how things turn out, at least Jamie won't be left in the dark about it this time. Win is sure

Jamie has opened the door to Ray's heart, he can hear it in the way—

"Ugh!"

Did that noise... come from downstairs?

Win tiptoes down the stairs, careful to avoid the parts that creak. He pokes his head around the corner into the living room, already taking a large inhale to scream at the intruder.

So, when his eyes land on the recent subject of his dirty dreams, it's fair to say he's a little shocked.

He gasps.

The man turns his head in the direction of the sound, a smirk slowly forming when he spots the wide-eyed boy looking at him from the foot of the staircase.

"Oh, hey."

Win takes a cautious step forwards, eyes drifting down over the man's neck, down to his collarbone, tracing the long line of his arms where they're resting on the back of the couch. The man is still speaking, though the sound is muffled to Win over the voice of his own brain screaming, *MUSCLES! MUSCLES! MUSCLES!*

"You must be Win. I'm—"

"Teddy Supasawat." Win actually remembers his name, and it's so satisfying to see Teddy's chest puff out at being known, the fabric of his shirt pulled taut across his pecs.

"Do you..." Teddy's eyes trail down Win's body, taking in every plane and curve. "Do you wanna get out of here?"

Well... Jamie isn't going to need Win to cuddle with now that Ray's here, so... "My place is twenty minutes away."

Teddy nods, already standing from the couch and heading towards the stairs, Win trots after him, not caring that he's in his pajamas as he pulls on his shoes and coat, the two men making their way down the stairs and out the door hurriedly. It's *New Year's Eve*. It doesn't matter if Win looks like a fool, Teddy is here, and Win *wants* him.

Sunday, January 1st

The sight of famous actor Ray Rawat Amarin asleep on the couch shouldn't be such a familiar sight to Apple. As it is, the woman merely chuckles, making her way over to him. She'd known he was here when she'd gotten back last night—had heard him talking to Jamie in his room—but hadn't spoken to him other than the few words they exchanged when he bounded up to her in the town square. It's a relief to see that he's still here. And, judging by the fact that it's Jamie's favorite blanket tucked around him, it seems that things are going to be much better today than yesterday.

Apple had stayed awake for at least an hour once they all got home, not exactly listening in on Jamie and Ray's conversation, but just... keeping an ear out for them. She had to make sure her baby wasn't about to get hurt any more than he already had been. But, as she had suspected from the moment Ray returned, she needn't have worried.

"Ray... Ray, Dear..."

- · ★ · -

Grumbling, Ray squeezes his eyelids shut. He'd been having such a lovely dream; that he was back in Ammersfield, that he'd gone to see Jamie, that he'd started to fix things. It had felt so real—still feels real—even down to the smell of Jamie's perfume, which somehow lingers.

"Ray, shall I make you some coffee?"

Is that... Apple's voice?

Ray opens his eyes and he's still here, in the Suwans' living room, curled up on their couch. "Mmhn?" It wasn't just a dream. It's all coming back to him now—talking for hours, sniffling through apologies and promises, until Jamie had started to yawn. And as much as Ray had wanted to crawl into bed with him and fall asleep with his arms full of the man he loves, he knew it was too soon. They both needed some time to process things. On their own. Not that Ray went far— asking if he could sleep on the couch so he wouldn't have to disturb his parents at three A.M.

"I'll take that as a yes." Apple ruffles Ray's hair briefly as she moves past him, and he hears her chuckle when he leans into the touch. He can't help but feel comfortable around her, especially when he's too sleepy to think much about conducting himself properly.

Ray is still blinking sluggishly, not having moved an inch, when Apple returns from the kitchen carrying a tray of coffees. "Would you like to take Jamie his morning cup of coffee, or shall I?"

"I'll do it!" So excited at the thought of seeing Jamie again, Ray flops off the couch and onto the floor in a mess of blankets and limbs.

"Okay, Dear." Apple titters, turning towards the staircase, and Ray dutifully follows after righting himself, flattening down his surely messy bedhead as best he can without a mirror.

When they reach Jamie's door, Ray knocks, Apple standing by his side.

No reply comes and Ray is unsure what to do. Does he knock again? Does he let himself in? Is that not an invasion of privacy? He's pretty positive they're dating again, but they haven't really spoken about specifics yet, too caught up in feelings of pain and relief and *home* to work out logistics. And even then, does that give him permission to...

- · ✳ · -

Ray is so hopelessly in love with her son. She can see it clearly in his nervousness, in how he stands outside Jamie's bedroom door, feet tapping back and forth against the floor like he can't quite make up his mind whether to knock again or not.

"Just go in, Ray." Apple sends a soft smile his way.

"Are... Are you sure?" Ray doesn't look convinced.

"He's waiting for you, Ray. Even when he's asleep, I'm sure he's waiting for you."

Something in Ray's expression shifts and he nods. He knocks on the door once more, saying a quiet, "I'm coming in," before opening it. Apple points out the correct mugs to him when he turns to her—Jamie's covered in cartoon cats, the one she'd chosen for Ray featuring a similar design with dogs. Only the cutest for her boys.

"Thank you," Ray murmurs with a smile, taking the mugs before entering the room. "Nhu... It's time to wake up now. I brought you some coffee."

Apple chuckles at Ray's adorably awkward nature as she pulls the door shut behind him. Those boys are going to be just fine.

- · ★ · -

It's when they're both sitting on Jamie's bed an hour later, mugs empty and bellies full of Apple's glorious cooking from the breakfast she'd brought them not long ago, that they start to discuss how to actually make this work. It makes Ray almost regret eating breakfast—only almost—as an anxious nausea claws at him. What if being together just isn't possible?

Ray offers to give up his work entirely. It's not like he needs the money anyway. And perhaps he could get a job here in his hometown if his savings ran out—maybe even help out at a certain bookstore if they needed an extra pair of hands. Jamie vetoes the idea immediately, frustrated at Ray's all-or-nothing approach.

"Hia! If we're going to do this, we're going to do it *together*."

He makes Ray call Karl, the manager giggling down the phone excitedly when Jamie introduces himself. Once Karl's excitement settles down a bit, they start to discuss logistics; which parts of Ray's schedule could be moved, when Jamie could come visit New York or Ray could come here, how to keep Jamie safe from the press until he's ready. Though it seems like they're moving too fast, like they're committing to this too quickly, this is *Ray and Jamie*; if they're going to do this, they're going to give it everything they've got. Now. No more waiting or holding back.

It's a lot, and Ray feels so very out of his depth. But when Jamie meets his eye, he knows he must feel the same. Somehow, that soothes him, knowing they're both a little scared. Ray takes hold of Jamie's hand, rubbing his thumb over his knuckles, a reassurance of, "I'm right here."

- · ✳ · -

When Jamie and Ray make their way down to the living room that afternoon, hand in hand and beaming from ear to ear, Apple, Banlue, and Tommy let out a collective sigh of relief. Jamie is okay. And better yet, Ray is still here.

"Mama..." Jamie's sweet tone—too sweet—makes Apple want to narrow her eyes. That particular voice always means he wants something.

"Hm?" Apple hums, feigning nonchalance.

"How would you feel if I..." Jamie glances at Ray out of the corner of his eye, gathering his courage. "How would you feel if I went to New York for a couple of days?"

A smile spreads over Apple's features. She'd been hoping he would say that. Apple had already dug out Jamie's suitcase that morning.

"I'll be back before classes start, I promise!" he's quick to add. "And you don't need to give me any money for flights or anything—I have my savings. Besides, you don't really need me at the shop for the next few days, right? I mean, Tommy doesn't have any plans so he could always—"

"Baby," Apple interrupts, holding up a hand to stop her son's rambling, "of course you can go. So long as that's what you want to do."

A bubbly giggle leaves Jamie's lips as he rushes forward, pulling his mom into a bone-crushing hug. "Thank you, Mama."

Glancing over Jamie's shoulder, Apple makes eye contact with Ray. He looks happy. A little scared, but excited, too. She holds his gaze, hoping that her message gets across.

Don't ever break his heart again, okay?

- · ★ · -

As they're packing Jamie's bags that evening, Ray can't help but think about the uncertainty of what lies ahead. Jamie's life is still here—his studies, his home, his family. But maybe a small part of Jamie could exist in New York, too, could bring color to Ray's monochrome apartment on weekend getaways. At least until Ray can leave that place and finally come home.

Their future is still largely unwritten, currently little more than a note on a pink, cat-shaped post-it, or a confession neatly penned on the back of a photograph. It could develop into something beautiful—a love story that spans the rest of their lives—if they're brave enough to take the risk.

"I, um,..." Ray starts, grabbing Jamie's attention, big doe eyes turning to him. "I really am sorry. For everything. The things I did to you..." Ray shakes his head, memories of Jamie's cries echoing in his ear. "I'm so sor—"

And then Jamie kisses him.

- · ☆ · -

Jamie pulls Ray into a kiss, the first kiss they've shared since Ray has been back. It's chaste and fleeting and so achingly perfect in every way. Then he shoots Ray a smile, that man's attention focused only on him, eyes sparkling with tears. "I don't want to hear any more apologies from you, okay?"

All day, Ray's been whispering apologies and fawning over him, even going so far as to pull his chair out for him at dinner (an action Tommy scoffed at while Apple and Banlue cooed). Jamie doesn't need the words to be repeated any more than they already have been. It's clear that Ray is sorry, practically droopy-eared like a remorseful puppy in how he's been trailing after him. Jamie just wants to move on—to embrace this new beginning.

Ray might not be ready to forgive himself yet, but... "I forgive you."

- · ★ · -

Ray nods, throat tight with emotion. Jamie's hand goes to the back of Ray's head, playing with the hairs at the nape of his neck, watching as Ray tries to accept the words.

Gently, Ray reaches out, caressing Jamie's cheek with his fingertips. He never thought he'd get to do this again—to have Jamie this close, looking at him *like that*. But they're here, together, and this is happening. And Ray is so happy. So ridiculously, unbelievably over the moon.

"Nhu... I love you," Ray breathes into the small space between their lips.

Jamie responds, voice quiet but clear, "I love you too, Hia."

Ray leans in and they're kissing again and it's everything he'll ever need. He knows he's crying, but it's okay, because Jamie is crying as well. So long as they're happy tears, Ray doesn't mind.

Resting their foreheads together, he brushes the tears from Jamie's cheeks, shushing him as he sniffles.

"It's okay, Nhu," Ray soothes. "I'm here."

Jamie gives Ray a watery smile and they both know they can do this; be in love, be *them*. No matter what life throws their way, or how hard things might get when they have to be apart, they'll find a way to make it through. Together.

"You know, Nhu…"
THE FOLLOWING CHRISTMAS

Friday, December 22nd

Jamie looks at his bedroom wall—at the couple dozen photos now stuck to it. They've spread out from the spot just above his desk, now trailing up and around the window. Most of them are of him and Ray, smiling or making funny faces at the camera, but there are a fair few of his family—both families—as well. There are a couple photos of August scattered in there, too, which Jamie is particularly proud of. It hadn't been easy to sneak up on the grumpy feline.

Sighing dreamily, he once again finds himself looking more closely at the photos of him and Ray from around this time last year. He'd ended up printing more than just the one photo from Christmas Eve, adding the picture from his mom's birthday party and one of the sneaky (and very blurry) selfies Ray had taken with him on the night of his first dinner with the Amarins, when Jamie had been given his new favorite hat. They're all fond memories, if a little tinged with the sadness that followed.

Since then, they've made lots of new, happy memories together, both in Ammersfield and in New York.

Jamie's first journey to New York with Ray, seeing the place Ray calls home for the majority of the year, had been... enlightening.

*

"Did you just move here?" Jamie had asked, wheeling his suitcase into Ray's apartment and surveying the space. The couch didn't look like anyone had ever sat on it, and when Jamie went to rest on it, he understood why. It was the worst couch Jamie had ever had the displeasure of sitting on.

"No," Ray answered, throwing his coat over the back of an equally uncomfortable looking chair, "I've been here for about... four years now?"

Trying to be polite, Jamie nodded, forcing a smile when he really wanted to gawk.

Four years? Sitting on a couch THIS bad?

He had tried to relax, forcing himself to sit back like he might at home. It didn't help.

"The couch is awful, isn't it?"

Jamie breathed a sigh of relief. At least he wasn't the only one who thought that. But he still tried to be respectful with his reply: "It's not the most comfortable, no."

Ray had chuckled, walking over to Jamie and offering a hand to pull him up from the offending piece of furniture. "Come on. I promise my bed is comfier."

Stopping halfway up from the couch, Jamie met Ray's eye with a raised eyebrow.

"Are you trying to take me to bed, Mr. Amarin?"

Jamie had never seen Ray blush so much. "N-no, I mean... Well, yes, but... I—"

It was true though. His bed was more comfortable. Especially when Ray was in it with him, holding him close.

"Jem? Baby?" Apple knocks on his bedroom door before cracking it open. "Isn't it time to head to the airport?"

Jamie checks his phone. "Ah! Yes!" He jumps up from his chair, picks up his handbag, and he's off. He's got to go meet his *boyfriend.*

- · ★ · -

Ten weeks and five days. That's how long they've been apart—the longest they've ever gone without seeing each other since Ray came home for Christmas last year and their relationship began. And now Ray is resisting the urge to skip and giggle through the airport like a schoolgirl, so excited that Jamie is coming to pick him up.

They've spent most of this year traveling back and forth; Ray using every excuse under the sun to disappear back to Ammersfield whenever he isn't needed in New York, Jamie coming to the city for weekend getaways when he can. In the summer, they'd managed to spend a whole three weeks together in Ammersfield for Jamie's birthday and to celebrate his graduation, Ray enjoying both the company and the break from the stifling city air that was always worse in the heat of summer.

They had spent every day together, either in Honeybun Bookstore or wandering around town—taking turns showing each other their favorite places, going out on dates while trying to keep it lowkey, not daring to do more than hold hands under the table at dinner. They hadn't made anything official yet, at this point. Not to anyone outside of their families (plus Win and Teddy, of course).

It was during one of these dates towards the end of Ray's stay, the pair having a picnic in the park, that Jamie leaned in to kiss him—the first time they would have kissed out in the open.

They had almost kissed in public, had gotten this close, last Christmas Eve. But Jamie had said he wasn't ready. Of course, the town had speculated about their connection to each other since then, but there still hadn't been any solid *proof.*

At the picnic, Ray stopped him at the last moment with a hand on his chest, whispering into the space between their lips, "Are you sure?"

Jamie had smiled, not taking his eyes off Ray for a second. "Yes."

They kissed and it felt like they'd both been set free. Particularly because nothing happened afterwards—no gossip articles popping up online, no photos of them circulating... Nothing. The townspeople paid them no more mind than they had before.

When they then first kissed in a public space in New York, in a restaurant on Ray's birthday a couple of months later, it felt equally as freeing. But, unlike that kiss in Ammersfield, this kiss led to an influx of journalists and talk show hosts asking to speak with Ray, no doubt having questions about their relationship and Ray's sexuality.

Ray had declined to speak with most of them, only choosing a few who he and Karl really trusted. And even then, his responses had left a lot of interviewers wanting; not saying much about Jamie, just saying that there was someone special in his life, that this person happened to be a man, and that they cared about each other deeply.

He wasn't sure whether it was a blessing or a curse that both he and Jamie had gotten busy with work around that time—Ray facing the press alone, but Jamie mercifully out of the spotlight—unable to visit each other again until now.

As Ray collects his luggage, he contemplates the aftermath of that birthday kiss. Despite his recent work-related interviews finally having a focus on his career again, questions about this mystery man he's dating still come up. But Ray won't say anything more. He and Jamie both agree—the world doesn't need to know more than that they are in love.

But there are still things Ray wants *Jamie* to know. There are things he wants to tell him, questions he wants to ask him... Spending ten weeks (*and five days*) without him has given Ray time to think, to really consider their relationship.

When Jamie had said he would come to pick him up from the airport, Ray knew this would be the perfect time to discuss their future. It might be one of the *only* times the pair will be alone together during this trip. So, dragging his suitcase towards the exit, Ray pulls the note from his hoodie pocket, going through his plan and script again:

- See Nhu
- Hug Nhu
- Kiss Nhu

Jamie, until I met you, I never dared to dream that

"Wawa!"

Ray's gaze snaps up from the paper to see Praew waving a glittery sign with his name on it, with Dan, his sisters, Jamie, and Jamie's family next to her.

Nhu...

Jamie looks like he wants to run to him, but he hesitates, and that just won't do. Ray shoves the note back into his pocket and quickens his pace until he's racing towards him, until Jamie starts bounding towards him, too. They meet in the middle; Ray letting go of his suitcase in time to catch Jamie as he jumps into his arms, twirling the shorter man and peppering his face with kisses as he giggles at Ray's over-enthusiastic display of affection.

Only once Jamie's feet are firmly back on the ground does Ray acknowledge the rest of the people who have come to see him—Praew getting extra cuddles to make up for him not greeting her first.

"I can't believe you're all here!" Ray can hear the slight hysteria in his own voice. He'd only been expecting *Jamie*. And... "What about the bookstore?"

Apple waves at him dismissively. "Banlue and I decided to close early for Christmas this year. Spending time with our favorite boys is more important, Dear." She pinches Ray's cheek and Ray can't help but feel shy.

As they split off into groups to head back to town, Ray going with the Suwans since he'll be staying with them, he feels a little deflated. He's happy to be home, happy to have Jamie by his side—the man currently looking both hot and cute behind the steering wheel, a North Star earring glinting at Ray from this angle—but he'd had *a plan*. And, with Apple, Banlue, and Tommy currently squeezed into the back of the car, asking him plenty of questions about his journey and what has kept him so busy in New York lately, Ray has to admit defeat. For now.

Hopefully, he'll get to talk to Jamie alone soon. Maybe he'll even get a chance when they reach Honeybun Bookstore.

- • ☆ • -

Jamie immediately excuses Ray and himself when they get home, practically bullying him up the stairs under the pretense of them needing to unpack Ray's bags. Really, Jamie wants to talk to Ray. Alone.

Something had seemed a little off about Ray at the airport. As soon as Jamie had spotted him, he'd been able to sense a nervous energy around him—clear in his clenched jaw and stiff, raised shoulders. Something was definitely up.

"Don't forget that you're meant to head to the Amarins' in about an hour, boys," Apple shouts up to them as Jamie reaches the top step. Ray had confessed he felt a little bad about choosing to stay with Jamie, so he had called his mom and promised that they'd come over for dinner on the first night to celebrate being back in town again. And Jamie, listening to the call by Ray's side, had promised her that they would come over on Christmas afternoon, too, wanting to split their time between the two families as fairly as possible.

"Okay, Mama."

When they reach Jamie's room, they really do start unpacking, falling into their typical routine. Ray unzips his suitcase and the pair start to pull items from it, hanging shirts up on spare hangers that Jamie leaves in his closet for this exact purpose.

Ray truly just... fits. He fits into Jamie's life like he's always been there, like the empty space in Jamie's closet was always his to fill, like the right side of Jamie's bed was made for him to fall into.

And fall *out of* on one memorable occasion—Ray forgetting where he was the first time he slept over and managing to roll onto the floor with a loud thud. The way he'd blinked up at Jamie, dazed with utter confusion as Jamie peered over the edge of the bed at him, was absolutely priceless. Ray still maintains that he hadn't been embarrassed and *definitely* hadn't blushed when Jamie laughed at him—that it was just the color of his bedside lamp that painted his cheeks so pink—but Jamie has his doubts.

With the amount of stuff Ray leaves here now, it doesn't take long to unpack the one suitcase he brought with him. But when Jamie goes to open his carry-on, readying himself to ask Ray what was wrong earlier...

"I'll do that!" Ray urges, almost screeches, hurrying to Jamie's side.

Huh?

"W-why don't you, um..." The way Ray's eyes scans the room, it's clear he's trying to come up with an excuse.

Well, if it's a moment to himself that he needs, Jamie can give him that.

"I'll go get you something to drink, Ilia. What would you like?"

Something like relief floods Ray's features. "Just some water would be great, thank you."

Jamie nods and turns to leave, but Ray pulls him into a hug, his chest against Jamie's back. Ray lets out a deep sigh and he seems to melt, the tension leaving his body as he wraps himself around Jamie, resting his chin on his shoulder. "I've missed you, Nhu," he mumbles against his ear before pressing a chaste kiss to his neck.

Maybe there's nothing going on. Maybe Ray's just missed him. After all, they've never been apart for this long before.

Jamie places his hands over Ray's where they're wrapped around his stomach, holding him tight. "I missed you, too."

He waits for Ray to loosen his grip and turns around in his arms. Jamie cups Ray's jaw in his hand, stroking his cheek with his thumb, admiring the man he loves. Ray definitely looks less on-edge than he had earlier, his eyes slipping shut under the affection. But...

Jamie's eyes go to Ray's still-packed carry-on, wondering what's inside. It's probably just his Christmas present, right? Maybe Ray hasn't wrapped it yet. What else would he be hiding in there? He takes a moment to consider it, but truly, nothing else comes to mind.

He probably wants whatever my gift is to be a surprise.

With that thought, Jamie clears his throat. "I'll go get you that glass of water."

- · ★ · -

Jamie shuts the door behind him and Ray listens as he makes his way down the stairs, waiting until he knows he must be in the kitchen before he lets himself groan. He buries his head in his hands, rubbing his face, and is suddenly very glad he hadn't put on any makeup today. It would have been a mess by now, otherwise.

That had been his chance. They'd been alone and he could have done it, could have told him, could have asked him...

But no. He'd seen Jamie approach his bag and he just panicked. With how tumultuous the start of their relationship had been, Ray is set on doing *this* right. He wants to prove how much he's changed, how much he's grown, this past year. There are some things you shouldn't just blurt out to your partner, and this is definitely one of them. Or that's Ray's opinion on the matter, at least.

He'll just have to wait until tomorrow. There's a reason he's booked a table at Fay's, the fanciest restaurant Ammersfield has to offer.

Walking with Jamie, swinging their joined hands between them, has got to be one of Ray's favorite things in the whole world. He can't stop smiling as they stroll to his parents' place, squeezing the smaller hand in his, a phantom feeling of warmth seeping through their gloves.

"—ia?"

"Hm?" Ray brings his attention to his boyfriend, who is eyeing him with concern.

"Are you alright, Hia? You looked a little..." Jamie's face contorts like he's trying to find the right words. "You looked a bit shaky at the airport. Like something was wrong. Is everything okay?"

Despite being an actor, Ray knows he's not good at lying. Not to people who know him. So he's immensely relieved that Jamie asks him *those* questions, and not something like, "What was that piece of paper you were looking at?"—because Ray's pretty sure he saw that—or "What are you thinking about?"

"Nothing is wrong, Nhu," Ray replies honestly. "Just a lot on my mind. But nothing bad, I promise. I'm okay."

Jamie nods, not looking entirely convinced. "Mmkay. Well, you know you can talk to me, okay?"

I want to. I desperately want to.

I want to ask if you—

They reach his parents' house and Ray has to shake the thoughts from his head. Now is not the time.

"I know, Nhu. Thank you."

Pat answers the door, pulling Ray and then Jamie in for hugs, and the conversation is forgotten.

*

Ray lies awake next to a sleeping Jamie. They'd gone to bed well over an hour ago, maybe closer to two, and Ray is still wide awake.

He'd started to drift off earlier, the edges of sleep creeping in, breaths softening, and then it had hit him...

He's going to talk to Jamie *tomorrow*.

In less than twenty-four hours, he will have his answer. Well, unless something goes wrong.

Letting out a shaky breath, Ray tries to calm himself. He tries to think about the script that's still in his hoodie pocket (which he should probably move before Jamie finds it—that man having a penchant for stealing his hoodies—now that he's thinking about it) and finds that he can't remember a single word he's written.

Calm down. It's okay.

Ray swallows against his suddenly too-dry throat and he knows he's panicking.

He also knows, logically, that there's no point in worrying about it right now—that he can look at it in the morning and memorize it again. He's an actor, memorizing scripts is his *job*.

But still...

I don't want to mess this up.

It takes Ray a couple hours more to fall asleep.

Saturday, December 23rd

"Are we still on for ice skating today, Dearies?" Apple asks everyone as she carries a mountain of pancakes into the dining room for breakfast.

"Um..." Jamie hesitates and looks at Ray. He looks tired—dark circles under his eyes, his hair slightly disheveled despite taking ages to style it in the bathroom. Jamie had woken up in the middle of the night to find Ray just staring at the ceiling, lips moving as if reciting lines from a script, still awake when Jamie nodded back off. There's no way Ray's had enough sleep. He should rest. "Actually, can we go another day?"

He knows his mom probably saw the way he just looked at Ray, probably understands the reason why he's suggesting this, but still adds, "I've got the concert tomorrow and, now that I know how clumsy *he* is on the ice," Jamie points his forkful of pancake accusingly at Ray, "I don't want to risk an injury this close to the performance."

Ray squawks out an affronted "Hey!" as Apple and Tommy struggle to hold back their laughter, even Banhie smiling. The whole family has seen the video Jamie took of Ray attempting to skate last year. Tommy had described Ray's skating style as "a cat trying not to fall into a bathtub," and Jamie hadn't been able to get the visual out of his head ever since.

"What? It's true!" Jamie laughs at Ray's pouty expression. "Now come on and eat your pancakes!"

Only once Ray is digging in, no longer looking sulky, does Tommy pipe up, "Then how about we decorate the tree today?"

Typically, the Suwans decorate their Christmas tree together, as a family, at least two weeks before Christmas. But, this year, Apple had said it didn't feel right to do it without Ray there. Jamie had blushed at the implication that Ray was now part of their family, though he couldn't help but agree. Ray is... Saying he's his boyfriend doesn't feel like enough. He's more than that, somehow.

"Sounds fun!" Ray agrees, his eyes lighting up. "Don't you think, Nhu?"

Jamie would rather they really took it easy today, just lie on the couch or in bed so Ray could sleep a bit more, but...

Despite Ray's obvious exhaustion, his smile is blinding.

"Yeah! Let's do it!"

- · ★ · -

Decorating the tree really takes Ray's mind off of everything. He gets lost in the stories Jamie's family tells about each ornament they hang on the tree: "Grandpa Gumpa sent this one from LA," "This one is from Jamie's first Christmas," "Tommy had cried in the store until I bought it."

Ray absorbs all of the information thrown his way, laughing along with them as they reminisce. He asks about each decoration before helping to hang it, his height becoming particularly useful when there's one that belongs slightly higher up the tree than any of the Suwans can reach.

"How's that?" Ray asks, holding a tiny needle-felted version of Jamie's cat, August, near a branch. When Ray found the decoration, looking curiously at its missing ear, Tommy had informed him that the feline was *not* a fan of his felted counterpart. Therefore, it has to be placed high up.

"Looking good, Dear." Apple gives a thumbs up before rooting through the decoration box for the one she wants to hang up next. Banlue aids her in her mission by rifling through another box on the floor, the two quietly bickering about who had packed the ornaments away last year.

It might be his first Christmas as Jamie's boyfriend (officially), and only his second Christmas even knowing the Suwans, but it doesn't feel that way. He feels like he's part of this family. He feels like he belongs.

- ˙ ☆ ˙ -

It seems Ray is feeling a bit better after they're done with the tree, smiling dopily at Jamie as he leads him to his bedroom for a nap after lunch.

Apple had suggested that they could walk around town, maybe pick up an ornament of their own—something to represent them as a couple—to put on the tree. And, as nice as that sounded, Ray looked like he was going to fall asleep into his bowl of soup, so Jamie said he was feeling a little tired and that he and Ray might go rest for a bit.

They make it to Jamie's room and Ray's lips are on his in an instant, Jamie making a noise of surprise when Ray kicks the door shut behind them.

"Hia!" Ray kisses him again. "Hia, when I said"—one to his left cheek—"we were going to nap"—one to his right—"I really meant it."

A hand to Ray's chest stops him from going in for another, his intentions clear with how his gaze is focused on Jamie's lips as the younger speaks again.

"You're tired. Sleep."

Ray pouts and Jamie has to remind himself, yet again, that this buffoon is apparently the internationally recognized heartthrob, self-proclaimed "cool" guy, Ray Rawat Amarin.

He presses a kiss to Ray's lips, just lingering long enough to make him smile again.

"Bedtime." Jamie marches him to the bed, climbing on top of the sheets with Ray and pulling a spare blanket over them both. "Goodnight, Hia."

Ray wraps his arms around Jamie and grumbles, something about not actually being tired that is too slurred by exhaustion to actually make sense, before he kisses Jamie's hair, wishing him pleasant dreams.

Within minutes, Ray is fast asleep.

Jamie doesn't intend to doze off. But something about Ray's quiet snores, about the warmth from the blanket and Ray's body wrapped around his own, soon has Jamie falling asleep beside him.

- · ✱ · -

Not long after they're both sound asleep, the door clicks open, August sauntering in. They probably they didn't quite shut the door properly.

August is not a friendly cat. He *withstands* humans. That's the limit of his affections.

He jumps up onto the bed and makes his way to Ray, plopping himself down behind Ray's head on the pillow.

He'll remain there until Ray tries to turn over in his sleep an hour later, sending August yowling and Ray bolting upright in shock, Jamie swiftly following.

- · ★ · -

When Ray had booked this fancy dinner, he'd planned for a lot of things.

He'd planned three different outfits, each complete with accessories, that he could wear.

Whatever it takes to match Jamie.

He'd planned at least a dozen different ways to bring up the thing he wants to talk about, all suitable for different times throughout their meal.

Whenever it most suits Jamie.

Heck, he'd even written a new script while Jamie had been in the shower this morning in case the one he'd been preparing for weeks wasn't good enough.

Only the best for Jamie.

But he hadn't prepared for this...

He lets his loving gaze, focused on his boyfriend, drift to the guy sitting *beside* his boyfriend. His eyes narrow.

"Did you really climb up the Eiffel Tower, Winnie? Even with your fear of heights?" Jamie asks him, eyes gleaming.

Jamie had asked Ray, when they were almost ready to leave the house, whether Win and Teddy could join them for dinner. According to Jamie, Win had been out of town for a couple of weeks to go on a vacation with Teddy, only making it back into town last night, and it was imperative that Jamie see him as soon as possible to find out about their trip. Of course, looking into Jamie's big, pleading eyes, Ray had agreed that their romantic date could become a *double* date. Plans be damned.

Anything for Jamie.

But now, feeling more like a third (or, in this case, fourth) wheel, he's slightly regretting saying yes.

"Mhm," Win replies, then reaches a hand across the table to hold Teddy's. "With my big, strong Teddy there, how could I be scared?"

Ray has not seen much of Teddy and Win together because of their busy schedules. And sure, he's noticed Teddy's tone getting a little sweeter each time he's seen him at work or gone drinking with him... but *this*? Seeing him with Win?

"You know you can always hug your Teddy Bear when you get scared, Babe," the man who is apparently Ray's friend, the man who used to be allergic to feelings, coos across the table.

Ray is struggling to comprehend that this "Teddy Bear" is the Teddy he's known for almost a decade.

But then Jamie is beaming at Ray from across the table, eyes lit up with joy, and Ray forgets that there's anyone else with them.

If only they really were alone.

He pats the inside pocket of his suit jacket as inconspicuously as he can, feeling for what he'd hidden there just before Jamie bounded into the bedroom asking if Win and Teddy could come to dinner with them.

If they were alone, Ray would recite the words from his script and ask...

Sunday, December 24th

"I'm not hungry," Jamie says, pushing his plate away at breakfast, and Ray knows that something is very, very wrong.

Since waking up that morning, Jamie's nerves for tonight's concert have begun to make themselves known. First, Jamie had told Ray he had a nightmare about the performance going wrong, then he'd cried and couldn't explain why, and now he's turning down *food*?

"Okay, Baby." Apple reaches across the table to hold Jamie's hand. She meets Ray's eye.

Ray can't be sure what that look means, but it feels like she's trying to soothe him—trying to convince them both that everything will be fine. He clearly isn't doing a good job of hiding his panicked expression.

Jamie goes upstairs with his mom soon after, saying he wants to double-check he's happy with his outfit for the concert, and Tommy disappears to go... do whatever Tommy does, probably play video games in his room. It leaves Ray and Banlue to do the dishes, Banlue washing them and Ray on drying duty, just to make himself feel a little less useless.

"He always gets like this," Banlue admits after a few minutes of silence. "Before a big performance, he doubts himself."

Ray nods, processing his words. It makes him feel relieved, in a way, that Jamie has been through this before, has *gotten through* these kinds of struggles before. But it still sucks. "Is there anything I can do? To make him feel a bit better?"

Pursing his lips, Banlue exhales loudly through his nose, eyes fixed to the tiles above the sink when he speaks. "Just be there. I think... I think that's all any of us can do. Just be there and support him. Tell him he can do it."

He holds out a plate to Ray and Ray tries to take it, but Banlue doesn't let it go. Ray looks to him in confusion and finds Banlue's gaze firmly on his.

"He's a strong man, Ray. He just needs reminding sometimes." The way Banlue continues to stare at Ray, raising one eyebrow almost imperceptibly, implies an "Understood?" at the end of his words. *Ray* needs to support Jamie. His family can do it, have done it, for years. But Banlue seems to know how important Ray is to Jamie—how much Ray's opinion matters to him.

"Okay, Sir— UH— Ba-Ban..." Ray takes a breath. "Yes, Banlue, Sir."

Banlue chuckles as Ray turns red, choosing to distract himself with drying the plate once Banlue lets go of it.

Ray isn't great with words, but... he can do that. He'll make sure Jamie knows he can do anything he sets his mind to. He'll tell him every day for the rest of his life if he has to.

Usually, Ray would just let himself into Jamie's bedroom. But, with Jamie as emotional as he is, Ray is also on-edge. So, he knocks. "Nhu... Can I come in?"

Silence.

"Are you okay, Nhu?"

Still nothing.

Without thinking, Ray rests his head against the door and suddenly he's back where he was a year ago, almost to the day—forehead pressed against Jamie's bedroom door while Jamie sobs on the other side of it, both heartbroken. He can still hear it, that gut-wrenching sound that was all his faul—

He jerks away from the door, shaking his head to rid himself of the painful memory.

Nhu forgave me.

Ray knows he fucked up back then, and how lucky he is that Jamie gave him a second chance. He's not going to let him regret it. They've worked through their issues and they're okay now. And Ray is never going to break Jamie's heart like that again. In fact, he wants to do something that feels like the opposite, he wants to ask Jamie to—

"Hia? What are you doing?"

So in his own head, he hadn't noticed Jamie come out of the bathroom. Now, Jamie looms over him, Ray having slid down to the floor at some point during his bout of introspection. He feels a little silly to have been found like this.

"N-nothing. Just came to check on you." As he stands back up, he notices Jamie's makeup. When they'd first met, Jamie hadn't really worn much makeup, if any, but he'd gradually started experimenting with it more after Ray taught him the basics. It enhances his natural beauty in a way that always makes Ray's heart skip a beat.

"You look... beautiful." He takes in the hint of eyeshadow, the tinted lip balm making his already kissable lips even more irresistible.

Focus, Ray. "Are you okay?"

Jamie smiles at him and it almost reaches his eyes.

"Mhm."

He pushes past Ray into his room, eyeing up his three handbags to pick which one to use today. "Which one do you think, Hia? I think the one you got me for my birthday will bring me luck, right?"

Come on, Rawat. Words. Say good words. You got this.

"Yeah."

Nailed it.

He watches as Jamie shuffles about his room, grabbing things to put in his bag; his lip balm, a packet of tissues, his phone. As Jamie grabs something from his desk, his gaze shifts to Ray's suit jacket still hanging over the back of his chair, making to grab it and— *The pocket! The thing! Ah!*

"LET'S GO OUT," Ray suddenly shouts.

Jamie turns to him, blinking a few times in rapid succession.

"We've, um... We've still got a few hours until we need to go to the town hall so let's just... go out. We can go look for our first Christmas tree ornament as a couple." It is both a nice save and something Ray was genuinely considering asking Jamie to do anyway, so... two birds, one stone!

His boyfriend seems a little unsure at first, no doubt caught off guard by how panicked Ray had sounded, but then his cheeks turn a pretty pink. "Okay, Hia."

- • ☆ • -

Jamie isn't sure what he and Ray are really looking for as their first ornament, whether Ray has a specific thing in mind—a certain color, shape, style... All Jamie knows is that it feels like a bit of a big deal. It *means something* to him. It shows that Ray is a part of his story, of his life, that their two worlds are intertwined. He doesn't want to represent that with something tacky. It needs to be... tasteful... classy... but also feel like *them*.

He looks over at Ray to see that he's currently eyeing up an ornament of a corgi in a Santa hat.

Don't. Even. Think about it.

As if feeling Jamie's stare, Ray turns to him. "See anything you like?"

Jamie shakes his head. This gift shop's options leave a lot to be desired.

Ray offers him his hand and they stroll along until they reach another store that looks like it might have something—a thrift store boasting a collection of "antique" ornaments. But nope. Nothing they have to offer feels quite right.

They go into a third store that sells nicknacks, Jamie already beginning to feel like it's all pointless and they're never going to find anything, when Ray gasps.

"Nhu!" He pulls Jamie through the narrow aisle of the shop, around a table covered in a selection of gloves and hats, to an ornament display. And there, right at his eye level, is a gleaming North Star. It's a beautiful golden color with embossed swirls, reflecting light in a way that makes it look like it shines.

Jamie raises his hand to one of his earrings, tracing the familiar outline of the star as he takes in the one in front of him. These earrings were his first gift from Ray, purchased after their first official date. It's how they started. Sure, there had been that *little blip* afterwards where things had gotten bad—Ray being an idiot and both of them being heartbroken—but the earrings had been there through it all. These stars are a sign of their resilience and strength as a couple.

"It's perfect."

There's just over an hour to go until Jamie's performance and he feels like he maybe, actually, *can't* do this.

They're sitting in the town hall, watching the local school's Nativity, and Jamie can't focus. He can't think of anything except that *he's* meant to be on that stage soon. His leg starts bouncing and Ray is quick to rest his hand on his knee, trying to calm him.

As far as he can tell, there aren't any reporters or paparazzi in the room—Jamie's gotten quite good at spotting them when they're in New York—but he still feels like there's more pressure on him than ever before. This year, he's not just some guy from the bookstore, he's *Ray Rawat Amarin's boyfriend*. He wants to make him proud.

But then Malai grabs his shoulder from her seat behind him, whisper-shouting, "Praew's part is coming up," and Jamie has to let it go. He's got his little princess to keep an eye on! His worrying can wait.

- · ★ · -

Much like last year, Jamie appeared to be okay once he saw Praew; cooing beside Ray at her ridiculously adorable innkeeper's outfit, giving her plenty of cuddles and praise after the performance. He'd been his usual, bubbly self around her, even lifting Praew up as if she hadn't gone through a growth spurt this year, carrying her outside to go and get food with everyone.

But, also much like last year, Jamie goes quiet when the choir starts heading back into the townhall to get ready.

"Hey." Ray pulls him in close by a hand on his waist. "You okay?"

It looks like he wants to shake his head, maybe cry. Instead, he asks, "Can you kiss me?"

It's not the response Ray expects, but—*if that's what Jamie needs*—who is he to say no?

He goes in for Jamie's lips...

"Can I kiss you? On the cheek. You know, for luck."

That's what Ray had said last year. He hadn't known what else to do to support him, to prove to him that he was there for him, that he cared.

He redirects and kisses Jamie's cheek, a brief touch of lips to his soft skin. "For luck," Ray repeats the words from the memory, hoping the familiarity will bring Jamie some comfort.

A smile plays at the corner of Jamie's lips as he looks up at him and Ray's breath catches in his throat. *He's just so...*

"All choir members, please head backstage within the next five minutes!" someone shouts, and Jamie's eyes dart down. Ray hears him gulp. But still, Jamie doesn't step away.

"Come with me," he pleads, nose brushing Ray's.

"What— Can I— Is that... allowed?" Ray stammers.

Jamie shushes him with a finger to his lips. "Just come backstage with me for a minute."

Ray nods and follows, Jamie barely stopping for any last hugs from their relatives apart from a one-armed hug with

Praew, his other arm busy holding onto Ray. Distantly, Ray is aware how this must look; his boyfriend dragging him from a public space into a decidedly *less* public space, a hand wrapped around his wrist, a blush on Ray's cheeks... But, in Ray's defense, he's only blushing this much because Jamie is *really fucking pretty* up close.

- · ☆ · -

Jamie just needs a minute, just a moment, where only they exist. He pulls Ray to the backstage area, then in the opposite direction of where the rest of the choir are gathering, turning down a corridor so they're out of sight.

If this were a movie, Jamie might have chosen to take him to a janitor's closet or a bathroom stall. He might have slammed the door shut behind them and kissed him; pressed his lips to Ray's until there was not a single other thought in his brain.

But it's not a movie. And Jamie doesn't necessarily want to be kissed senseless right now—he knows the choir will start looking for him soon.

For now, though...

"Hold me?" Jamie asks, stepping close enough to Ray that his nose brushes the fabric of his coat.

"Of course."

Ray's arms wrap around him and he can finally breathe again.

"I know you want your performance to be perfect, but..." Ray's voice is so soft and quiet, his words just for the two of them, "However it goes, I'll love it—love *you*—just the same."

He feels Ray nuzzling at his hair, no doubt leaving some sneaky kisses there.

"You can do this, Nhu."

Jamie squeezes Ray tight, hoping he knows how grateful he is. If he tries to voice his thanks, he'll start crying.

"You know, Nhu... I..." Jamie listens to Ray's shaky inhale. "I wanted to— to talk to you... I..."

Whatever Ray is thinking of saying, it's clearly making him nervous. And the last thing Jamie needs right now is *more* anxiety. He slaps Ray's back. "Less talking, more hugging."

"Oh, but..." Ray hesitates and Jamie squeezes him again. "Okay, okay." Ray finally gives in, chuckling as he pats Jamie's back.

- · ★ · -

Finding out just how frequently Jamie hums, tuneful notes pouring from his lips at any time, night or day, had been one of Ray's favorite discoveries in the year they've been together.

Jamie had been a little embarrassed about his habit at first, cheeks and ears turning red when Ray would stop whatever he was doing to listen, but how could Ray not? Even when he was just mumbling along to the lyrics of a song on the radio, he would get this aura around him that Ray couldn't describe, similar to the calm he'd seen on his face while skating. He looks... so confident, so at home in his own skin, when he sings.

Ray has told Jamie more times than he can count how much he adores his voice, how even his humming comforts him more than he ever thought possible. He's not been able to articulate it out loud in any more words than that. But he wants to. He wants to tell him that it makes him feel safe and soothed. He wants to tell him how very privileged he feels to be around him, to hear melodies spill from his lips like honey, sweet and smooth and warm.

It's breathtaking.

And hearing Jamie sing, backed up by the choir as he is now, is *even more breathtaking*. There's something different about him when he's on stage. He glows. Ray is sure it's not just the spotlight directed at him that lights him up, that it must come from within. There is no other explanation for it.

He's Ray's guiding light, his shining star, and... hopefully... someday soon—

Jamie meets his eye and Ray has to wipe the tears from his vision. He needs to see him clearly. He wants to remember this moment, this feeling, for the rest of his life.

- • ☆ • -

When Praew had asked Jamie to join her family in watching *The Muppet Christmas Carol* last year, Jamie hadn't been able to say yes. It would have meant becoming a part of her childhood Christmas traditions. It would have been a promise that he would be there not just for that one Christmas, but for all the ones after it. It would have been too much too soon. But this year...

Jamie swings Praew's hand, clasped in his, as Dan and Pim lead the way with Ray's parents. Ray holds Praew's other hand, looking over at Jamie with eyes still teary from Jamie's performance. He'd been a blubbering mess after the concert, dragging Jamie into a bone-crushing hug and littering his face with kisses as he praised him, obviously not caring one bit about the crowds around them. Jamie had pretended to be scandalized, shrieking out a "Hia!" and slapping his arm, but he understood. This is probably how Ray had wanted to act after the concert last year, too—to be open with his affections, to use his actions to convey everything he was feeling—and now he finally could.

"Who do you think is going to fall asleep first?" Pim asks over her shoulder.

"Uncle Wawa!" Praew answers immediately, Ray's gaze whipping down to her in an instant.

"Uh, no, Princess. I'm pretty sure it'll be you," Ray argues back like he, too, is eight years old.

"No, you!" Praew says, pulling on Ray's arm.

"No, *you*!" Ray sticks his tongue out at her, like that somehow means he's won the argument, and Jamie laughs.

*

As Praew predicted, Ray is the first to fall asleep, his head coming to rest on Jamie's shoulder where the pair are squished together on a beanbag, Praew draped across them both like a lounging cat. It's a close call, though, with Praew nodding off shortly after, grumbling as she turns over in Jamie's lap, away from the television, and clutches at his sweater. Jamie is content to stay there, playing with Praew's hair, for the rest of the movie.

"Come on, Mr. Sleepy Pants," Jamie groans as he pulls a drowsy Ray up from the beanbag, much to an equally drowsy Praew's amusement.

"Are you sure you can't stay for a sleepover?" Praew asks, holding onto her mom as she follows Jamie and Ray to the front door. She keeps making puppy eyes at Jamie and he's close to giving in, but...

Let's take it one Christmas at a time. Movie this year, maybe a sleepover next year.

"Not this time, Princess." Jamie smiles at her. He'd give her a hug, too, but he's currently got his arms full of a still half-asleep Ray, the man leaning heavily against him.

Praew nods. She lets go of Pim to hug Jamie and Ray instead, stretching her arms as far as she can around the both of them.

- · ★ · -

Ray becomes more alert as they walk back to Honeybun Bookstore, the cold night air against his face making him feel wide awake. He can't help but think about last Christmas Eve.

This time last year, they'd been doing exactly this; walking back to the bookstore, Ray's arm wrapped around Jamie's waist. It had been a little earlier in the evening, music still playing in the town square, Jamie humming along to it, and they'd said goodbye at the door.

This year, Jamie unlocks the front door and they go inside together.

This year, they kiss as they stumble through the bookstore, giggling as they find each other in the dark.

This year, they fall into bed in a tangle of limbs, Ray pulling away from Jamie's lips just long enough to say one thing, one word that encompasses everything about Jamie—his personality, his looks, his voice—"Beautiful."

Monday, December 25th

Waking up next to Jamie is always a blessing. But, as Ray is now learning, waking up next to him on *Christmas Day* is even more special. There's that thrum of excitement in the air that only Christmas can bring, and it feels as though everything is at peace. It's like they are the only two people who exist, that there is nothing beyond Jamie's bed. There's just Jamie gazing into Ray's eyes like he's the only thing that matters. Ray knows he's looking back at him the same way.

Before meeting Jamie, Ray had dated a couple of people, but he'd never had a relationship like this; one so loving that it makes his heart feel full. Something about being with Jamie, being loved by him, is different. It's like his entire perspective on life has shifted. Not that Jamie forced it to, more that it just... happened. Ray's whole world tipped off its axis the second he walked into Honeybun Bookstore a year and a half ago, the moment he looked up and saw him for the first time.

"Good morning, Hia," Jamie whispers, smiling shyly and hiding his face against his pillow. He always gets like this in the morning and Ray finds it so unbearably endearing.

Ray hums, a smile spreading on his own lips, and fumbles for Jamie's waist under the comforter to pull him closer. "Morning, Nhu."

Jamie burrows into Ray's chest, wiggling into his arms for cuddles. This is another thing that changed when Ray met

Jamie: Ray likes cuddles now. Having a partner who loves to hug and snuggle so much isn't something Ray thought he'd want, but now he can't picture a life without the affection, without *Jamie's* affection.

"What time is it?" Ray asks, letting his eyelids slip closed. He doesn't really want to know, because that will likely mean needing to actually get out of bed, and Ray would rather not right now. He's comfortable here. So very comfortable. But also... they've got plans today. And Ray also has his own *secret* plans. Today, he's going to do it. He's going to talk to Jamie about what he's been trying to talk to him about ever since he got back to Ammersfield.

"Just past eight," his boyfriend replies, voice muffled against Ray's chest. Jamie throws a leg over his waist, plastering himself to Ray. "We should get up."

"Mm," Ray hums fondly. "In a minute."

They lie there for far longer than a minute, both content, wrapped in each other's arms. It's peaceful. And, actually, maybe a perfect time to...

"Nhu?" Ray says softly, making sure he's still awake.

A "Hmmm?" drifts up from where Jamie is still buried against his chest.

"I was actually... hoping to ask if—"

There's a knock on the door, followed by Apple's cheerful voice. "Good morning, boys! Breakfast will be ready soon."

Ray suppresses a groan. He really thought for a second that he'd be able to talk to Jamie, at last, but no. Apparently not. Jamie is already bouncing out of bed, Ray's arms suddenly empty, at the mention of food.

Still, Ray can't be too upset. The love of his life looks extra lovely when he's this happy, doing a joyful little wiggle as he slides his slippers on after getting dressed.

"I love you," Ray says, just because he can.

Jamie looks at him over his shoulder, smiling from ear to ear. "I love you too, Hia."

And, just like that, Ray's heart feels like it's going to burst.

- · ☆ · -

Jamie had told Ray not to get him anything much for Christmas this year, that he didn't need a gift at all, really. To Jamie, being with Ray was enough. He didn't need anything more. Plus, he knew that whatever he could get for Ray this year wouldn't mean as much as the book last year. Getting the guy you like a signed copy of his favorite childhood book is a tough act to follow, especially with Jamie's dwindling funds after a year of flying back and forth to see him. Not that Ray hadn't tried to help with that—offering to pay for his flights every time Jamie came to visit. Jamie always said no. He was determined to be independent; to pay for things on his own, to make his own way in life. He didn't want Ray's money, he just wanted Ray.

But, at Ray's insistence, he'd agreed they could maybe exchange small presents. *Only* small ones!

So, when the whole family is busy opening presents and Ray mysteriously excuses himself, Jamie guesses he must be going to grab his gift from his still-packed carry-on. And, when he returns, hiding the gift behind his back with a wide grin on his face, Jamie is not at all surprised.

Well... He's not surprised. And then, when Ray reveals a small jewelry box, he is. It *is* small. So, technically, it fits the criteria. But Jamie already has a sneaking suspicion that it costs more than what he got for Ray.

He raises an eyebrow at his boyfriend, planning to scold him with eye contact alone, but then it hits him.

Ray has been acting weird since he got back—more nervous than Jamie has seen him since before they started dating. He's been trying to talk to Jamie about... About something, but never seems to get the words out. And now, he's standing in front of him, holding a small jewelry box that's wrapped only with a pretty pink bow.

Is it...? Is he going to ask me to....?

"Surprise!" Ray says, eyes sparkling with the reflection of the lights from the tree, and Jamie can't speak. His eyes dart to his parents and brother, finding them all looking as intrigued and startled as he feels.

With shaky hands, he reaches out to take the box, his stomach doing somersaults. Then his fingers brush against Ray's as he picks it up, and it's like he can feel the tension between them, the sizzle of electricity at the contact.

Nothing else exists in this moment. It's just him, Ray, and the box—his family, still in the room, forgotten. He takes in one last deep breath before he stops breathing altogether, looking up at Ray one more time before he opens the box to reveal—

"A necklace?"

Well, now Jamie just feels foolish.

Ray hums, his larger hands carefully plucking the pink, heart-shaped pendant from the box. "I thought it would go with those heart earrings you like to wear—the first ones I ever saw you in."

Jamie blinks rapidly, swallowing down a torrent of emotions. He's happy. He's so very happy. It's such a thoughtful gift, and he tells Ray as much as he brings him in for a hug before letting Ray put it on for him. But...

It's not a ring?

The future is something they tend not to speak about— never really discussing more than a vague idea that they'd both like to settle down eventually, a faraway-feeling dream of someday having a home that's theirs, but nothing more. And yet, in that moment, Jamie had really thought...

"Do you like it?" Ray murmurs into his ear before pulling away.

"I love it, Ray," he answers sincerely, despite feeling a little shaken.

After that, Jamie feels downright embarrassed about what he got for Ray, walking over to grab his gift from under the tree and then handing it to him. "Here."

He fiddles with the necklace as Ray opens it, now nervous of how Ray will take such a gag gift.

But then Ray gets a good look, unfolding the pajamas Jamie picked for him, the words "COOL DUDE" repeated all over the pants, and all his worries vanish. There truly is nothing funnier than watching Ray's brow furrow as he reads the text, then hearing him huff in mock annoyance as Tommy starts cackling. Jamie pulls out his phone to take a picture, unable to contain his own laughter as Ray looks right into the lens, a smile playing at his lips.

What Ray doesn't know is that Jamie has another gift for Ray, one that he'll give him later. He'd spotted a photo album in a store a few weeks ago, on a day he just so happened to be missing Ray a lot (like most days) and had to buy it. Jamie has a bedroom wall full of photos of the two of them—it's only fair that he gives Ray something similar to admire whenever they have to be apart.

But, for now, he instead watches his family exchange their gifts; Apple giving Ray a pair of slippers like the ones the rest of the Suwans receive—a true sign that he's been accepted as part of the family—and Ray giving out the presents he and Jamie bought for everyone. There's a sweater for Apple, a new glasses chain for Banlue because Apple had been complaining about the sticky tape holding his old one together, and some gaming controller *thing* for Tommy that he'd specifically asked for.

- · ★ · -

Ray is just putting on his new slippers, testing out how comfortable they are, when Jamie gasps, "Hia! We're late!"

"Huh? Really?" Ray knows they probably lost track of time a little, but it still surprises him.

"Yes, 'really'!" Jamie squawks, already heading up the stairs, probably going to grab the gifts Ray brought for his family.

By the time Ray takes off the slippers and thanks Apple for them again, Jamie is pounding back down the stairs, two large gift bags in his hands.

"Come on, Hia! Shoes on, let's go." Jamie shepherds him towards the door, stopping by the tree to grab his own set of gifts for the Amarins.

"Nhu, it's okay if we're not on time. Ma just said two-*ish*," Ray tries.

Jamie shakes his head. Ray knows how much he hates being late. But he also knows his mom really won't mind—that she only told Ray and his sisters to arrive at two because Malai is chronically late to everything. "Nuh-uh. Move it, Hotstuff."

Giving in, Ray puts one shoe on, and then he starts thinking...

There's still something in his suit jacket, now hanging in Jamie's closet. Maybe, on the way to his parents' house, or on the walk back later, he could...

"I'm just going to grab something from upstairs real quick, Nhu."

"What is it?"

Ray tries to think of something he could say. "It's, uh... I think there's still a gift upstairs." Not exactly a lie.

"Where is it?"

"In my suitcase." It's the first thing that popped into his head.

"I already checked," Jamie says, already putting his coat on, zipping it up.

"Oh... Well... I..."

Jamie just looks at him, waiting.

Think of something, anything at all.

"You must have grabbed it, then."

It'll have to wait a little longer.

Their afternoon at the Amarins' passes in a blur of food and gifts—the latter mostly for Praew, apart from the books Jamie bought for each of Ray's family members. Ray knew how self-conscious Jamie had been about "only" buying books for them; explaining to him that it was likely a coping mechanism, that he could pretend he was selecting books for customers instead of his boyfriend's family. He'd told Jamie not to worry, that they'd surely love whatever he gave them, and today he was proven correct.

"Let's head off, it's getting late," Ray murmurs to Jamie, sitting next to him on the couch, knowing that they'll likely both fall asleep here if they don't leave soon. Jamie, in particular, seems worn out—no doubt not used to being around an excitable child on Christmas Day. Praew is now sluggishly blinking as she flips through one of the books Jamie got for her, pretending to read despite her tiredness. Her earlier adrenaline has definitely worn off, now quite a bit more cranky than usual. And, of course, she's refusing to go to sleep.

Jamie whines, flopping into Ray's lap like he's suggesting they go to the dentist. "Don't wanna."

"See, Princess, Jamie doesn't want to go to bed either." Chuckling, Ray gently sits Jamie up and then tries to get him to look at him. "But he's going to be good and go to bed, isn't he?"

Catching Ray's drift, Jamie dials back his pout a little, though he still sounds sulky when he agrees. "Yeah."

Always a sucker for her *Uncle Jemmie*, Praew is tottering to her feet moments later, hugging both her uncles tiredly before finally allowing Pim and Dan to put her to bed upstairs without a tantrum.

"Goodnight, Princess!" Jamie calls after her as the family make their way up the stairs.

"Mhm," the little girl murmurs back, too tired for any other words.

Ray and Jamie say goodbye to Malai and Ray's parents, Jamie thanking Pat and Hathai over and over for letting him join them, and then they head back to Honeybun Bookstore. They walk slowly, Ray setting an ambling pace, wanting to enjoy a moment of peace after their hectic day. It's been good, definitely, but it's been a lot. And now it's just the two of them, at last, walking silently beneath a clear sky.

He wishes he had grabbed that thing from his jacket. Now would have been a perfect moment to...

*

Jamie, once again, looks like he's on the verge of falling asleep as he puts on his pajamas, stepping into the wrong leg of the pants at first. Ray laughs before offering him a hand.

He expects Jamie to crawl into bed as soon as he's in his pajamas, to burrow down under the covers immediately, just a whisper of "'Night, Hia" before he falls unconscious. But, instead, he grabs Ray's hand.

"I've got something for Hia," he mumbles, almost to himself, as he pulls Ray towards the closet. Ray panics for a moment that maybe he's seen what's in his suit jacket pocket, but instead he grabs a gift from underneath some bags.

Rather than give it to Ray, Jamie keeps hold of it, now pulling Ray to the bed. They both climb in, Jamie's eyes barely open when he finally passes the gift to him.

"For me?" Ray asks. He thought Jamie had already given him his present (those silly pajamas that he's now wearing).

Jamie nods, a gentle smile on his lips, and Ray starts to slowly remove the wrapping paper.

"Nhu..." Tears well up in Ray's eyes as soon as he works out what it is. How does Jamie keep doing this to him? He seems to be able to reach inside his mind, find the things that would mean the most to him, and then make them real.

He flips through the pages of the photo album quickly at first, feeling like his life is quite literally flashing before his eyes. And that's what this is, really. It's his life. His and Jamie's life, together.

Going back to the start, he looks again, now taking his time to appreciate each image. It has every photo of them from last Christmas up until the last time they'd been together, a couple of months ago in New York.

It's still so new for Ray—seeing himself like this. People take photos of him, and with him, all the time in his line of work. They crowd into his space to ask him for selfies, press photographers hollering at him to "Look over here! Ray! Over here!" He should be used to seeing photos of himself. But the way Jamie takes pictures of him is different. These are not photos of the famous actor Ray Rawat Amarin. These are just... Ray. Just Ray and Jamie. It's everything he's ever wanted.

"Nhu, I..." Ray steels himself. There will never be a better moment than this. "There's something I've been meaning to ask you. I was wondering, please, if you would do me the honor of—"

Of course, when Ray turns to look at Jamie, to look him in the eye as he finally asks... he finds him fast asleep.

Ray chuckles to himself, brushing the tears from his eyes before closing the photo album. He gets up, putting it on Jamie's desk for safe keeping, and looks at the photos on Jamie's wall. There's more of them here than in the book—photos of Jamie's family and cat interspersed with pictures of the two of them. It seems that everything that's important to Jamie ends up on this wall, and Ray feels privileged to be a part of it.

He turns off the light and climbs into bed, Jamie shuffling closer once he's settled so Ray can wrap his arms around him.

"Goodnight, Nhu," he mumbles, pressing a kiss to the top of Jamie's head. "I love you."

Tuesday, December 26th

Today has been another long but pleasant day, celebrating Apple's birthday in much the same way as last year; her extended family descending on the house early in the morning and not leaving until late in the evening. Ray had felt slightly more comfortable at the party this time around, now knowing the family a little bit better (though he still mentally patted himself on the back each time he remembered a relative's name). The guests had also seemed more relaxed in Ray's presence this time, not as starstruck since they'd gotten to know him as a person, and no longer having to worry about cropping Ray from any pictures they took. Yes, the ban on sharing photos of Ray had definitely been lifted. He didn't care how many pictures he was in the background of, or even the foreground of, with these people. In fact, he wanted to be in their photos. He wanted to make memories with them, to embrace being a part of their lives.

Jamie's great aunt, Suzie, had been particularly keen to catch up with Ray. Apparently, she'd had no idea who Ray was until after Apple's last birthday party—not until one of her grandchildren took her to the movie theater and she kept squinting at the leading man, thinking he looked oddly familiar. The realization that the suave detective on the screen was the same man she'd heard stutter through some small-talk about the weather had, reportedly, made her gasp loudly enough to get shushed by the rest of the movie-goers.

Something else Ray had taken particular pleasure in today was seeing Teddy be the new guy—watching him try to find his feet among Apple's relatives in much the same way he had done the previous year. Honestly, Ray was initially surprised to find out that Teddy had even been invited. But, given how close Win is to Jamie, it kind of made sense. All of Jamie's family clearly treated Win like he was one of their own. Relatives so distantly and complexly related that Ray couldn't quite remember their exact connection coming up to greet Win upon his arrival, chatting and then drinking with him as the day wore on, rejoicing with him that he finally had a steady boyfriend.

Ray lies down on Jamie's bed, looking through all the photos the family have been sending each other in the group chat (which Ray is now a very proud member of) while Jamie finishes up in the bathroom. It's the first day of this trip that Ray has truly relaxed. Up until today, he'd been stressing himself out over trying to find just the right moment to talk to Jamie. Today, that conversation has barely crossed his mind. Well, it has, in the sense that Ray is always thinking about Jamie and how much he loves him—how much he wants to spend the rest of his life with him. But he hadn't thought about asking him *that question* today. It was Apple's birthday, and Ray didn't want to distract from that.

Getting up, Ray goes to the closet, to his suit jacket hanging in there. He reaches inside the pocket, pulling out the ring box and opening it.

He looks at the ring. He'd spent several weeks hunting for one that was just right—one that felt elegant and romantic, and could also capture some of Jamie's sparkle. Of course, it had to have a diamond in it. Ray was hoping he'd get to see it on Jamie's finger on Christmas Eve, shining under the spotlight while he sang. He was hoping it would be on his hand today, not to try and steal the attention from Apple's birthday, but just so Ray could watch him blush and show it off to his relatives, or maybe even try to hide it if he was feeling particularly shy.

Now, he realizes he's been going about this all wrong, almost repeating his mistake from when he'd arrived in Ammersfield last December. He'd put so much pressure on himself to apologize to *The Boy* about knocking over some books, to do it as soon as he could, that he'd lost his cool. Offering the guy he liked hush money is not something he's particularly proud of.

Ray exhales a laugh, lip ticking up at the memory. It seems he'll never learn. Or maybe, really, he's changed more than he gives himself credit for. He feels more calm, more sure of himself, these days. It's been slow progress, and sometimes he still has periods where he gets too in his head (like the past few days), but he's trying. He only needs to relax. There's no deadline for him to ask this question, no day he's set to leave and maybe never return.

His eyes shift to Jamie's bedroom wall, to the photos that cover it. Looking at them soothes him. Every picture is proof that Jamie is a part of Ray's life and Ray is a part of his, and he can't see that changing. Not any time soon, not ever.

The right moment will come along. He knows it will. He just needs to be patient. And he can be—he has the time to be.

He looks at the diamond ring once more, tilting it to catch the light.

Yes, Ray tells himself, *we have all the time in the world.*

"Hia, have you seen my—"

Ray whips his head around to see Jamie standing in the doorway, a towel wrapped around his waist. The clothes tucked under Jamie's arm fall to the floor when he sees the item in Ray's hand, his breath catching, his mouth hanging open with the unfinished sentence.

Well...

Ray takes a deep, calming breath.

It seems now is the time.

ACKNOWLEDGEMENTS

I never would have been able to do this without the support and guidance of my beta-reader-turned-editor-turned-internet-mom, Amy. This book simply wouldn't exist without her tutelage. I will forever be grateful that she chose to take on this project with me (after some *gentle* persuasion).

A massive thank you goes out to Selicia for beta-reading this. After looking at this story for so long, I was really struggling to know how to move forward. Her endless comments of "this feels unfinished?" and "briiittiishhh" have been incredibly valuable, even if I did sometimes wish to reach through the screen and shake her until she elaborated.

I would also like to thank everyone who has supported me along the way—Amber, Chai, Jen, and all of my readers. Whether it's been the emotional support of someone to cry to when things go wrong, or someone to double-check a piece of punctuation when I'm not sure, I feel very lucky to have such amazing people on my side.

Last but certainly not least, thank you to my mom. I'm sure that the fact I started writing came as a bit of a surprise to her, but she's been nothing but supportive. Even on the numerous occasions when I've been grouchy from editing all day on barely any sleep!

ABOUT THE AUTHOR

Maeve Hudson is a self-proclaimed internet gremlin who spends their time writing queer romance stories, as well as working as an animator and illustrator.

They can be found on X
@huddersmaeve

Printed in Great Britain
by Amazon